GREGORY HALL

MORTAL REMAINS

HarperCollins*Publishers*

HarperCollins*Publishers*
77–85 Fulham Palace Road,
Hammersmith, London W6 8JB

The HarperCollins website address is:
www.fireandwater.com

This paperback edition 1999

1 3 5 7 9 8 6 4 2

First published in Great Britain by
HarperCollins*Publishers* 1999

ISBN 0 00 651134 1

Set in Plantin light by
Rowland Phototypesetting Ltd,
Bury St Edmunds, Suffolk

Printed and bound in Great Britain by
Clays Ltd, St Ives plc

For Berna

And what the dead had no speech for, when living,
They can tell you, being dead: the communication
Of the dead is tongued with fire beyond the language of
  the living.

T.S. Eliot: *Little Gidding*

I

The phone call from Jack telling me of the dreadful thing he'd dug up came as Carrie Bloxham, a plump and stolid Mark Antony, was burying Julius Caesar.

'"The evil that men do lives after them,
    The good is oft interred with their bones;"' she yelled in her broad Oxfordshire vowels above the noise of the class, an enthusiastic Roman crowd, as the door opened to reveal Mrs Linda Rice, the headteacher of Waterbury Comprehensive School.

Her formidable presence immediately permeated the room, even to the furry-lipped adolescent boys at the back, and a hush fell. This was one of the black arts of teaching in which she was supreme. Big Linda to the pupils, she was known in the staffroom as the Third Rice.

She beckoned me to her, her mouth a thin line of official disapproval – personal calls were forbidden during class contact hours – but her eyes were bright with curiosity.

'Your brother, Miss Armitage. He's holding for you on the office telephone.' Her voice dropped even lower. 'An emergency. Perhaps your mother . . .'

I felt a momentary bolt of anxiety, quickly suppressed. Linda was all agog to see my reaction – that's why she had brought the message herself. I disobliged her, coolly replying, 'Thank you, Mrs Rice. Please stay with the class for a minute or two.'

But I didn't feel in the least cool. It couldn't be Mother, I reassured myself as I hurried along the wide corridor, the highly polished vinyl tiles squeaking under the soles of my trainers. Mrs Hargreaves, her nurse from the village, was with her. Jack was at the dig – at least that was where he was supposed to be.

'Damn him!' I cursed, banging angrily through the double fire doors into the admin. suite. What sort of mess had he got himself into now? Emergency, my foot. He'd probably run out of money again. This would be one more thing for the Third Rice to note on my file. First Mother, now Jack. 'Her domestic commitments have on occasions interfered with her professional duties . . .' I flung into the office. Sally, the school secretary, handed me the phone with a languid arm, then tactfully returned to clicking at her keyboard. I jabbed down the recall button. 'I was teaching, as you must have known. What on earth do you want?'

'Bugger your class. You've got to come here right now.'

'Stop shouting at me for Christ's sake. I can't just walk out without a reason. What is this about, for heaven's sake?'

He started to cough, the percussive sounds echoing tinnily in the receiver. Then I heard his breath inhaled in great gulps. After a few seconds, I realised with a shock that he was not coughing, he was sobbing.

I glanced at Sally, trying to keep the note of alarm out of my voice. 'Jack, tell me. What is it?'

'I can't explain on the phone. Please, for God's sake, Liz.'

'Jack! Have you had an accident? Are you in Crowcester?'

Again, there was the sound of crying, the more frightening because I hadn't heard him like that for years, not since . . .

'No accident. Yes. At the dig. Please come. I need you. Please. I've found something, something terrible.'

The excavation had from the beginning aroused in me a strange fear. I am not superstitious, but the image of long undisturbed ground being opened up was one which haunted me quite, as I thought, without rational basis. That fear came back to me on that bright June morning as I hurriedly got into the car.

Jack had found something, something terrible. But quite how terrible would be that thing he had wrested from the silent earth, I had then no inkling. Only later would I know the danger into which it would plunge us both.

The morning traffic in Waterbury was in its usual state of anarchy. I queued for ages at the lights in the centre of town then shunted at a snail's pace along the Oxford Road. The frustration caused by the jam made me even more tense.

Accompanying and not entirely displacing the anger that had first struck me was the visceral anxiety I experienced when Jack was in trouble. I had always felt responsible for him, even when we were children. This feeling had persisted even through those awful bouts of jealousy when I fantasised his being dead, and my then getting the favourable treatment that was always given to him. To Mother, Jack was the son, the valued one, who would go out into the world and achieve things, and I was only the pretty daughter.

I hated that, and most of the time I thought I hated Jack, but I had nevertheless looked out for him. Being Jack I don't suppose he ever noticed, or was grateful if he did. Although I was two years the younger, it was always I who made up his excuses, got him out of innumerable scrapes and bandaged his wounds.

That pattern of taking care of an unappreciative brother had continued, I shuddered to recall, into early adulthood. Even now, I reflected, with more than a tinge of bitterness, I was again running after him. But I felt I had no choice. His evident distress and the desperate appeal in his voice had closed the gulf that the events of years before had opened up between us. Those deep feelings had been reawakened, and, once more, made me drop everything to rush to his aid.

But what was it this time? He'd said it had not been an accident. To be fair to him, it wasn't like Jack to get into that sort of state over nothing. He didn't scare easily. As a child, he'd been completely matter of fact about injuries which would have had others screaming their heads off. In the past – with one terrifying exception – he'd stayed cool in what even I would have regarded as some pretty frightening situations. But now? Something he'd found? Something terrible? What could he mean? Had his drinking got so bad as to start giving him the horrors at eleven o'clock in the morning? Or was it drugs? I'd never had the impression that he took them, but anything was possible, knowing Jack.

And who knew him better than his sister? I knew him well enough to have been aware right from the beginning that his coming back to The Hollies, our old family house in the nearby village of Crowcester, would almost certainly be a mistake. With Jack, disasters, minor and major, were always just round the corner. I'd already, in the past months, had reason to be reminded of that. It had been only a matter of time before something really awful happened. Maybe this was it. Why on earth then had I let myself be swayed by sentiment, imagining that he would have changed, imagining that the past was over and done with, imagining that we really could start afresh?

I had found his letter waiting for me amongst the pile of circulars and bills which Mrs Hargreaves had put on the hall table when I got home from school on a foully wet evening just before the February half-term. I always glanced at what was there, but it was my rule not to open it until after supper.

I suspected Mrs Hargreaves of scrutinising the envelopes for clues as to their contents as she collected them from the postman. She might well have been intrigued by the big black angular handwriting almost carved into the paper with a heavy fountain pen nib. The writing was like Jack himself. Distinctive. Assertive. And, I remember thinking, premonitory. Conveniently for household spies like Mrs Hargreaves, on the face of the envelope, in the American fashion which Jack must have picked up and not discarded when he returned to England, was a printed label with his name and address.

My first instinct had been to toss it out. But, I reminded

myself, Mrs Hargreaves would remember my brother all too well. His antics as a young man were still an occasional subject of village gossip. She might have chatted about him to Mother. It would be just my luck if Mother were going through one of her more lucid periods and became anxious to be told about the contents of the letter from her darling prodigal son. That thought had been enough to destroy my initial impulse, and allow my natural curiosity to take over.

I didn't open it straight away. I wasn't going to let Jack barge his way back into my life by altering the routine I'd established for myself so satisfactorily. So I hung my coat on its peg in the cloakroom, went through to the kitchen and put the casserole I had made at the weekend into the oven, and looked in on Mother in the quarters I had created for her out of the morning room.

She was sitting in an armchair before the fireplace in which a gas fire was burning. She had a thick rug round her knees, and she was staring fixedly at the oil-portrait of herself aged about twenty or so, wearing an off-the-shoulder magenta velvet evening dress, the rich colour of the material complementing her softly curling dark blonde hair and her wonderfully fair skin.

She had always loved this painting, and I had hung it here in the hope it would remind her of better times. I knew from experience, however, that, for most of her day, she saw neither the portrait nor anything else, if by seeing we mean that the mind is engaged in active examination of what the eyes present to it. Mother was not blind, but she seldom connected with the real world, or rather the world that she was absorbed in was far more real to her.

Mrs Hargreaves had put her into a clean dress. Her now white hair was fluffy with washing and neatly brushed. Around her neck she wore on its cord the alarm pendant with its central red button. Her hands were clasped in her lap.

I remembered those hands from childhood, beautiful hands, the fingers long but strong, the nails always well manicured. Those hands were not only ornamental. They could cook delicious meals and create wonderful cakes and pastries, and sew and knit and embroider and sketch and paint in water-colours, all of which I had never as a girl been able to get to grips with. Mother had always been rather contemptuous of my lack of such feminine accomplishments. She regarded my succession of almost embarrassingly laudatory school reports as indicative of an unladylike obsession with the male preserves of scholarship and intellect. Only with my prowess at games was she demonstrably pleased.

Now the flesh of those hands was sunk in on the bones, like the frail skeleton of a bird. The whirligig of time had brought in its revenges. I had now of necessity been forced to accommodate myself to the demands of housekeeping and its myriad of irritating and tedious tasks, matters which the self-assured young intellectual of thirty years before would have regarded as utterly beneath her.

How long was it since Mother had been like this? I realised with a start that it was almost ten years. Ten years of drudgery and disappointment.

She had said that morning that she was feeling 'not quite myself'. This was Mother-speak for being ill. Mother had never allowed herself to be ill. So this confession of mild weakness was more concerning than it would have been in someone less stoical. I had noticed small things from time to time. A dentist's appointment she had missed. Visitors who had arrived in response to an invitation for tea, who found Mother in her gardening gloves, deadheading the roses and oblivious of the occasion.

Now it was I who remembered to ring round and cancel the meeting of the Best Kept Village Committee which had been due to take place in the drawing room at four thirty. I asked her if I should stay at home to look after her. 'Don't be ridiculous, Elizabeth. Now off you go to your work.' When

I got home from the school that evening, I was surprised to find that she was still in bed, apparently asleep.

'Mother,' I called softly, 'are you all right?'

She came to with a start, her eyes wide and staring.

'I've just got back. You've been asleep. Did you have any lunch?'

She struggled upright, and tried to climb out of the bed, apparently terrified.

When I touched her, she screamed once, horribly, then huddled back into the bedclothes like a child who fears the dark.

Doctor Phillips who, as an old friend of the family, came round straight away when I phoned him at home, was uncharacteristically grave. Some combination of neurological and psychological disturbance, perhaps the long-delayed shock of the tragedy which had befallen our family, had irrevocably triggered the dementia from which she was now suffering. I had seen some of the emerging symptoms. Probably Mother's strong-willed refusal to acknowledge that anything was wrong had masked others.

I heard in my mind the clang as a heavy prison door closed on me. What I had feared for years as my eventual fate had now indubitably come to pass.

'Hello, Mother.'

For a long moment she seemed not to have registered my presence, then, turning her head, she mouthed rather than spoke the word. 'Elizabeth.'

'That's right, Mother. You must be feeling well today. Did you have a lovely bath?'

She stared at me uncomprehendingly for a moment, then resumed her contemplation of the picture. Most days were like this, then suddenly, like a curtain being twitched aside in a darkened room, her face was bright with animation. But it was a distant light. The years had run backwards. She would ask me how things had gone at school, whether I had been to my cookery lesson instead of bunking off to the

7

library, and whether I had played well in the hockey match.

I settled the rug around her, stood watching her silently for a moment, the mixture of dread and pity I felt pressing on my mind like a physical pain, then I softly closed the door behind me and went upstairs to change.

I had had the same bedroom since I was a child, in the old nursery wing at the back of the house. Since Mother had moved to the ground floor, I could have taken one of the huge rooms, each with its own dressing room and bathroom at the front of the house which had been hers and Daddy's, or had my pick of one of the other ten, not to mention the old servants' quarters in the attics. But this smallish square room with its pretty white marble fireplace and cast-iron grate still suited me.

I had redecorated it myself quite recently, in a wallpaper with a Moorish geometric pattern in blue and white, reminding me of the precious holiday I had taken the previous year in what the tourist board called the Real Spain, my first in years, achieved only after lengthy and costly negotiations with Mrs Hargreaves and her married daughter Ellen Norton regarding the care of Mother.

The mullion window faced south-east across the grass tennis court, where in the endless summers of my youth, I had played and won countless matches against the youth of the district, practising for my ultimate dream, Wimbledon, for which I had in fact, in the *annus mirabilis* that was my eighteenth year, only narrowly missed qualifying. I had played for years for Oxfordshire County Women and I was the best player they'd had for a generation. Then, in my mature prime, my tennis days had ended, abruptly. I still felt sick at the memory of how even that had been taken away from me. The old court was overgrown with weeds and scrub, the netting rotted away and the chain-link fencing rusted and collapsed.

I shuddered. Those remains should have been cleared up long ago. For years there had not been the money for

8

substantial work on The Hollies. The complicated roofs, pseudo-baronial turrets, and elaborate wood and stone carvings, the product of the High Victorian age, were gradually falling to pieces.

In 1865, Thomas Aston, my great-grandfather, had sold up the engineering and manufacturing business in Birmingham which his forebears had built up over generations. He was impatient, despite his wealth, of being regarded as nothing more than a tradesman. He turned his back on modernity and sought a new life as a member of the leisured class. He removed to the northern edge of the Cotswolds, and there built The Hollies, his monument to himself, in the self-consciously archaic Gothic style.

He had ensured that his only son Richard, my maternal grandfather, received an education which had entirely removed from him the taste for trade. He had been called to the Bar of Lincoln's Inn where he became fashionable and successful in the kinds of law suits which embroiled the aristocracy in pointless wrangles over diminishing inheritances. However, he didn't intend to remain only a Chancery barrister, but harboured political ambitions.

Thomas died in 1912, and my grandfather inherited the estate. By that time, he had become Member of Parliament for a Midlands constituency, which he hardly ever visited, except at elections. He spent most of the term time in London, either at the Bar, where he had taken silk, and become head of his chambers, or in Parliament.

His daughter Celia, my mother, was born in 1916. After Westonbirt, she worked in the library at the Victoria and Albert Museum. My grandfather, who did not believe in the higher education of women, had obtained the post for her to give her something to do before she met a suitably well-off young man and married. Instead, to her family's distress, she met my father, a clever but relatively penniless civil servant.

He had come originally from Wallsend, near Newcastle

upon Tyne. An only child, his father had been killed in a shipyard accident and his mother had died in the influenza epidemic which swept Europe after the Great War. He had been largely brought up by his grandmother, who had died when he was an undergraduate.

There was neither privilege nor wealth in his background, but real poverty, which he had relieved by his power of intellect and capacity for hard work.

To my childish eyes, he seemed brilliantly clever. No one was better at devising elaborate treasure hunts or charades. He could make up tales or verses effortlessly. He loved crosswords, puzzles and brain teasers of every kind. Like many men of a donnish cast of mind, he enjoyed detective stories and murder mysteries. The Sherlock Holmes stories he knew virtually by heart, and Wilkie Collins and Edgar Allan Poe, and also the moderns, Dorothy L. Sayers, Margery Allingham and Michael Innes.

He had won a scholarship to Balliol from his grammar school. After Oxford, he had been successful in the examination for the Civil Service, and was marked out as one of the high flyers.

He had met my mother in London the following year, at a party given by an old university acquaintance who had joined the staff of the V & A.

The young ambitious Robert Armitage had believed another war to be inevitable. He had joined the university naval cadet corps, then the RNVR. He resigned his post and was commissioned into the Royal Navy the day war was declared. He proved a heroic and resourceful commander. For his actions during the D-Day invasion, he was awarded the DSO.

He and my mother were married in 1940 – a serving naval officer being more acceptable to my grandfather than a mere pen-pusher, no matter how brilliant – and apart from periods of leave, saw little of each other for the duration. She joined the WRAF and spent the war at various obscure locations around the country, returning to the Air Ministry in London only towards the end of hostilities.

My father left the Navy and returned to his post at the Admiralty at the end of the war. My mother, as she had vowed, returned to The Hollies. Both Jack and I had been born there.

When my grandfather – by then Sir Richard – died in 1951, just in time to see his beloved Tory party returned to power, he settled the house on my mother for her life, her children to inherit in equal shares after her death. There was income from the trust to assist with educational expenses and my father had, by the standards of the day, a substantial salary.

He stayed up in town during most of the week, in a service flat, returning to Oxfordshire at the weekends. My mother loved The Hollies and the narrow lanes and gentle hills of Oxfordshire too much to wish to live in London again. She looked after her two children and kept house and garden with the help of a couple from the village. She served on the Parish and Rural District Councils, and was a leading light in the Church, the WI, the WVS and a host of other charitable activities.

In the summer of 1956, we were living comfortably in a way typical of the upper reaches of the professional middle class.

By the autumn of that year, our lives had been utterly changed. My father went out one Sunday evening at the end of October for his usual stroll and never came back. He had, quite without warning, deserted my mother for another woman.

So long ago it was, but the terrible pain of that precipitate abandonment persisted still.

I took off the navy suit and white silk blouse I wore for school. The Third Rice's dress code applied strictly to staff as well as pupils, and my only gesture of defiance was the white Nike trainers. I had absolutely refused to negotiate Waterbury's slippery miles of corridors and crumbling concrete steps in heels. I put on jeans and a sloppy sweater. I looked at myself in the slightly spotted mirror of the Edwardian mahogany double wardrobe.

I was tall and gratifyingly almost as slim as that young tennis player of thirty years before. I had turned to long-distance running when I'd had to give up tennis. At school I coached the girls' cross country team and I could show a clean pair of heels to all but the best of them. My blonde hair had no hint of grey, and my complexion had still much of its youthful radiance. My breasts and my bottom were firm. I had not, I smiled to myself, entirely lost the cool English allure that had, once, made me think there was nothing and no one I couldn't have if I wanted.

Not bad for a middle-aged schoolteacher. It amused me that I still got looks not only from male members of staff but from some of the boys. Perhaps I figured in their fantasies. There was a time when my school nickname of Iceberg had irked me – what the hell did they know? – but now I took a kind of pleasure in it. Only the much desired was stigmatised as unobtainable.

I smiled as I put on jeans and sweater, a smile tinged with bitterness. I had to blank out, as always, the shadow which accompanied such self-congratulation. If only, in my youth, I had acted more wisely. *Si jeunesse savait . . .*

I had eaten the chicken from the casserole, and drunk about half the bottle of Crozes-Hermitage before I took a deep breath, slit open the envelope with the cheese knife, and unfolded Jack's letter.

My Dearest old Lizard (I read)

So you have opened it. You would have had every right to have dumped it straight in the bin when you recognised the script. I wanted you to have that opportunity. I did think of typing the envelope, but no, that would have ducked out of the essential test.

12

So I've not been chucked. Well, then, at least part of you must have wondered why I was writing, if only to find out what the hell <u>does</u> that utter shit want after all these years?

I put the first sheet down and tipped more wine into my glass.

I picked up the second page of thick handmade cream notepaper – still nothing but the best for our Jack.

Well what I want first of all, (it continued) is to say what an utterly unfeeling and contemptible sod I was to you. I blamed myself for what happened and I hated you for saving me. I wanted to be a martyr and you pulled me out of the flames. I was too cowardly to stop you. One day I want us to talk about it properly, but even now I'm still afraid. I have bad dreams, terrible dreams. Please try to understand. And I left you to cope with Mother. I can't ever adequately apologise for any of it. I can only abjectly beg your forgiveness.

I was weeping despite myself. Oh Jack, why leave it this late? Twenty years of misery. You can't put that right with one letter. The heavy handwriting blurred with my tears. I refilled my glass.

I wiped my eyes, picked up the next page and read on.

Now, darling Liz, I want you to take a deep breath, pour yourself a drink if you haven't already. What I'm going to say will be a dreadful shock. Here goes. Because my life is in the most awful mess for all kinds of reasons, I want to come home. For an extended visit, not just for a few days.

Do say that you'll let me. Please, please, Liz, don't go all stone-faced and say over my dead body and try to stop me. I really haven't anywhere else to turn to. We can't ever forget the past, but let's agree that it is the past and that we can start afresh. And the old place is certainly big enough for us not to be falling over one another. You'll hardly know I'm there. And I'll pay my whack of the housekeeping. It won't be forever. Only until I get myself sorted out. Please.

The tears dried on my face. I tossed the sheet back on to the table. So that was it. Typical of my darling brother. Eat the humble pie, then turn on the pleading little boy charm. I've been so nasty, now I want to come home. To sort myself out. I let out a long and scornful laugh at this last. When had Jack ever sorted himself out?

He'd had so many advantages. He was clever and, to begin with, he had the quality most admired by Napoleon: he was lucky. He'd taken a brilliant first in Greats at Oxford and could have stayed to become a Fellow of his College, or even of All Souls. Instead, he'd followed the bent he'd had since he was a schoolboy and gone as a field archaeologist to hunt Roman remains in the Middle East.

Caught up in the Six Day War of 1967, when his dig in the Sinai was overrun by the Israelis, he had tagged along with their advancing army all the way to the Suez Canal. Interviewed on his experiences by assorted TV journalists, his relaxed and confident screen appearance had stuck in the mind of one of the producers at the BBC. A few years later, when he was back in Oxford, at the Institute of Archaeology, he was approached by the same woman – of course, it had to be a woman – to become the presenter of a new popular archaeology and history programme.

Tempus ran for several years, collecting awards. I saw a good deal of him in this period. He would spend long summer weekends at The Hollies with Mother and me, and we would play tennis on the old grass court by the shrubbery, and go for long walks in the Cotswolds as we had when we were children, except that the old issues between us seemed to be miraculously resolved in a new spirit of harmony. They were the happiest days of my adult life. I took joy in my brother's pleasure in his life and for the first time in a long while, I began to think of how I might restore mine to the way I wanted it.

One weekend Jack announced he was bringing a girl home with him. Mother and I were surprised to hear this. From his schooldays Jack had had an active and notorious sex-life. To my mother's annoyance, he had chosen his girlfriends mainly from what she snobbishly referred to as the lower classes. Jack's taste, even at Oxford, was for young and pretty shop assistants, hairdressers, nurses and secretaries. These affairs didn't last and he had never once suggested that he might introduce any of these women to his family. This one, Mother and I surmised, must be special.

Indeed she was. Fiona Campbell was dark and beautiful, a Scottish grandee's daughter, and thoroughly a match for Jack's wayward but considerable intellectual brilliance. Fresh from Cambridge, she was working at Macmillan's, the publishers, as an editorial assistant, and was clearly destined for higher things. Fiona was delightful, and more importantly seemed to know how to handle Jack. I began to think that she might be the saving of him.

For it had become impossible even for me to ignore, desperate as I was to maintain my illusions, that Jack needed to be taken in hand. He was not in good shape. He had become famous with that bewildering swiftness conferred by television upon those it loves. He relished the fame, but couldn't handle it. He'd always been arrogant, but endearingly so, a small boy's self-importance. He was becoming merely insufferable. He was drinking far more heavily than usual. He had started to brow-beat publicly on his programme rival academic archaeologists with whose views he did not agree, and in a manner which suggested he was more than a little under the weather. His wayward brilliance seemed mere perversity, and his eccentricity self-destructiveness. There was,

15

according to the papers, murmuring in Shepherd's Bush about his future. His luck was about to run out. More than ever, he needed the strength that Fiona could provide.

Not of course that Jack let such things worry him. He lived as if things would last for ever. We saw them nearly every weekend. It made Mother happier than she had been for years, to see Jack behaving in a way that she thought that young men of his age and class should behave.

Even now I can hardly bear to think of how the wonderful promise of that summer, the prospect of a kind of rebirth for Jack, the end for me of the depression and guilt in which I had been enveloped since I left university, ended so suddenly and so tragically one Sunday evening on the road from Chipping Norton.

After that, nothing was the same. Jack said he never wanted to see me again. For years afterwards, I felt I was sleepwalking through life. When I finally came to, I realised that I would never be anything other than a provincial schoolmistress, living with her ageing mother in a house, which as it decayed, reminded me of the ruin of my hopes.

As for Jack, he never went back to the BBC. I read in *The Times* that his contract had been terminated 'by mutual agreement'. A month or so later he phoned Mother and told her he was off to America to take up a post at a college in New York state. He refused to talk to me.

Over the years which followed, he would write occasionally to Mother. I wouldn't read his letters, but she told me he had married. A few years later, I heard that the marriage had ended, that he'd had some disagreement with the chairman of his department and was back in England. Somehow he'd wangled a job at the Farebrother Museum in London.

When Mother had become ill and unable to reply, the letters had ceased. Even though he was back in the country, he never made any attempt to make contact, or to find out how things were with me. After so much rejection and humiliation, I never felt able to make the first move. I was overwhelmed by my responsibility for Mother. In the years which followed, I heard nothing from him.

I snatched up the final page of his letter, expecting it to aggravate my hurt and anger, yet as I read it, all I felt was a sense of recognition, and despite everything, of pity.

> The thing is, I'm out of the Farebrother. Shot at dawn. Early retirement on health grounds they call it. Don't you believe it. I'm fit as a flea. Hardly drinking at all. I'll give you the gory details when I see you. I've only a minuscule pension so I've had to let the house. Nice gay couple. One's an actor in some soap on the telly. Plenty of the readies. That's why I need a base pro tem. Think about what to do for the rest of my life. Might even get down to some more writing.

I liked the 'more'. A well-received but short study of the Romans in Palestine, adapted from his doctoral thesis, published in the very early part of his career had been, as far as I was aware, the sum total of his *œuvre*. Jack had been, it seemed, ignominiously kicked out. For doing God knew what.

Poor, dear Jack had messed up his life for the last time. All he had left, as in the old days, was Liz to pick up the pieces. I scribbled a reply and ran out with it to the post box in the lane. 'Come for lunch at one o'clock on Saturday' was all I had allowed myself to say. He would know what I really meant.

A little to my surprise, Jack, who'd never been one for punctuality, had arrived the following Saturday, at the time stipulated.

I was in the kitchen, at the back of the house, still arranging the freshly washed leaves of a lettuce I'd picked from the garden that morning in the embossed creamware bowl, a wedding present from my father's fellow naval officers, when

I heard tyres churning through the shingle of the drive with the sound of a breaking wave.

I hastily wiped my hands, flicked back a few stray hairs from my face, and went through into the long wide hall. The elaborate original Victorian encaustic tiles, more and more of which had worked loose, made a clicking sound like the keys of a computer keyboard as I approached the front door.

I took a deep breath, twisted back the knob of the Yale lock and pulled open the heavy oak panel, the bottom of which as usual snagged on the brass threshold – once lovingly polished, now green with verdigris.

'Hello, Jack.'

He stood there, his untidy hair, once dark as a raven's wing, now peppered with grey, and with streaks of silver at the temples.

'Liz.' He enveloped me in a great bear hug. He was a head taller, and my face was pressed against the thick wool of the shoulder of his jumper. I could smell the mustiness of old sweat.

I struggled free from his embrace, but he held on to my upper arms, gazing down on me, with a slight stoop.

For a moment, there was silence. Then he said, 'I ought to say something like it's been a long time. But it really doesn't seem that way. You look the same as ever, little sister.'

I pushed away his hands. 'Jack. I'm forty-eight, remember? Spare me the cliché of my unchanging youth.'

He shrugged as if disappointed at my refusal of his banter. What the hell had he expected?

'Come and have a drink.'

I led the way into the old servants' passageway, holding open for him the swinging green baize-covered door under the curve of the staircase.

I followed him into the kitchen.

'I practically live in here these days.'

He glanced round. 'Not changed a bit. Oh dear, I've said

it again! But it's still true. Those old biscuit tins on top of the dresser. And the Aga, of course.' He frowned and gave a theatrical shiver. 'Not on, though.'

'I can't afford to run it. Solid fuel's the price of gold-dust these days. Besides, it drove me mad having to stoke it. Drink? I've only got G & T.'

He nodded and I plonked two tumblers and the bottles on the scrubbed top of the kitchen table. I sloshed out a couple of generous measures and unscrewed the cap of the plastic bottle of tonic water. 'Help yourself.'

He added a minimal dilution and drank it down in a couple of swallows.

I gave him another. This time he added more tonic, took a small sip and put the glass down again.

We looked at each other in silence. Spring sunshine fell on the table making it gleam as white as bone. I could hear the birds chirruping in the garden through the half-open sash. From the hall came the dull tick of the long case clock.

Jack prodded at the base of his drink with his little finger, gazing intently down at the pale brown raised grain of the pine. Then he looked up at me. 'I said it in the letter, now I can say it to your face. I'm sorry.'

'For what in particular? For going away? For being an all-round shit? For coming back? It's a very convenient kind of sorrow that coincides with when you need something from me again.' I gulped at my gin to hide the catch in my voice and the incipient tears pricking at my eyelids.

'Lizzie, please.' The reproach in his voice was mild. I'd half expected, half hoped he'd fling out of the house in a rage. Jump in his car, go right back to London. The old Jack would have done. Had done. Perhaps he had changed.

'You can't imagine what it was like for me after you went off. What I did, I did for you. And you threw it back in my face. Then being on my own, coping with Mother. And this house. Work. Money. Christ, Jack. What kind of life do you think I've had? How did you expect me to feel? What did you expect me to say?'

He winced. 'How is Mother?'

'Thanks for your interest. How she has been for years. Some days she's better than others, little windows of sense amid the babble or the silence. Physically, she's quite weak now – she can barely hobble to the loo by herself. She can't be left alone in the house. Mrs Hargreaves comes every day, except weekends. They're my responsibility. It restricts one's social life.'

'Did she take in that I was coming back?'

'It's hard to say. It seemed to register. Then again, perhaps it didn't.'

'She should be in a home. We ought to sell this place, great barn that it is.'

'It's already such a relief having you here, Jack. Your incisive masculine brain. The way it cuts through to the nub of my problems. Put Mother in a home. Of course. Why didn't I think of that? I'm just a silly old spinster schoolmistress. Not a famous archaeologist. After all she's not a person. Just a piece of furniture. Occupying valuable real estate. Move her to a home. Much more efficient. So efficient it would kill her. You know that she'd never leave here willingly. That really would solve the problem, wouldn't it? Except that I'm not into taking that kind of decision, Jack. As for selling the house, it can't be done. It's not ours to sell. We're bound by Grandfather's trust. It's Mother's for life. Williamson takes his role as a trustee very seriously, as you'd expect with a lawyer. He would never agree to doing anything that he thought Mother wouldn't agree with.'

I fought back the tears. This was how it was going to be. Then Jack would swan off again, leaving me with the endless hassles.

He raised his hands in a gesture of surrender. 'I'm sorry, yet again. It was tactless. Obviously you've thought through the possible solutions. I know you wouldn't want to be a martyr, Liz. But how about directing some of your caring to me? After all, I've had quite a shock. Quite a fall.'

'"From morn to noon he fell, from noon to dewy eve a summer's day." And landed with a bump. You should be used to being expelled from heaven by now, Jack. So what happened?'

'After lunch. I'm hungry. Don't you eat anything? Just gin is it these days?'

'It's quiche and salad. But I did make a bread and butter pudding for afters.'

His face lit up like a greedy schoolboy's. 'Liz, whatever you say you do love me.'

He'd had two helpings of the pudding, and afterwards, in the English fashion, we finished up the wine with slabs of Stilton and Wensleydale. I'd remembered that Jack couldn't stand foreign soft cheeses.

After lunch, I made coffee and took it into the drawing room. We sat opposite each other in the faded plum velvet armchairs in the huge stone-mullioned window which looked out over the lawn to the spinney where the beeches my great-grandfather had planted stood grey and gaunt, the wisps and whorls of green bursting from their long brown papery buds invisible at this distance.

I put down my coffee cup on the walnut occasional table at my elbow. 'If you're not ill, Jack, and you certainly don't look it, what did happen at the Farebrother?'

He grimaced. 'It's a horror story.'

'I expected nothing less. Come on, spit it out.'

'It started with Clarissa's appointment as Director. Clarissa Hetherington-Browne, that is.'

'Oh yes. I remember reading about that in the paper. I wondered how you'd get on with a woman boss, Jack. Not very well, clearly.'

He was indignant. 'That didn't bother me at all, actually. I've lived in the US, remember? I'm very politically correct. Mind you, it was total culture shock to my colleagues. They'd

21

be happy on Mount Athos. I remember Ben Chalke of Printed Books and Manuscripts was almost out of his tiny mind. He burst into my office when the news of her appointment came out. "It is an outrage, Jack. An insult. A woman would be bad enough. But an impostor into the bargain. By all accounts, she is not a scholar, never even been near a museum, never mind run one. Who is she? A civil servant. A bloody pen-pusher."'

I laughed at Jack's mimicry of a plummy voice attempting unsuccessfully to conceal its origin in the Welsh Valleys. It conjured up his colleague in all his splenetic pomposity. 'Very good, Jack. But she was hardly a mere pen-pusher. The thing I read in *The Times* indicated she was a special assistant on the think tank they had in the eighties, then involved in the Funding Council they set up to bash the universities. High-powered stuff.'

'Oh yes, Ben was jealous. He'd put in for it himself, silly bugger. Didn't have a snowball's. No more than I would have. Clarissa was nothing if not high-powered, as we soon found out. And she was Greville's woman.'

'Greville?' Although I'd prepared for it, I nevertheless had difficulty in hiding the catch in my voice, and in keeping it even and casual as if I had indeed heard the name for the first time.

Jack was, however, far too intent on the sound of his own eloquence to notice any suspicious emotion in my tone, though he was scornful of my apparent ignorance.

'The Right Honourable the Lord Greville, Chairman of the Trustees. You must have heard of him, surely? Used to be one of the local MPs: his constituency was the Cowley division of Oxford, wasn't it? In Heath's cabinet for a bit and then lost his seat in '74. Sent upstairs to the Lords. Went back into business and made a mint. Newspapers, distribution, road transport, what have you. He's been in the Chair for ages.'

I nodded. 'Yes, I think I have seen the name in the newspaper, now you mention it.'

'Anyway, when Scarsdale, the previous Director who'd been there since the year dot, dropped dead suddenly, Greville took the opportunity to put his own man or rather woman in place. Clarissa showed her colours at her first meeting with the Keepers. She called it for eight thirty. A.m. Breakfast time. She wasted no time in putting in the boot. She said,' Jack's voice rose an octave or two, ' "Gentlemen, as we all of us know, a reputation can be like one of those super-tankers which continues on its course for several miles despite the fact that the engines have stopped. The name of the physical law which describes this phenomenon is as I'm sure I don't need to remind you inertia. The Farebrother is with rare exceptions an institution which is driven by inertia. It trades on its past glories. It sits back on its fat arse and it does fuck-all." '

I choked into my coffee. 'She said that? She must be some woman.'

'She is. We sat there stunned. Chalke went as white as his name. I thought Earnshaw had had a coronary and died. The rest of them gazed down on their blotters, in silent outrage and embarrassment like a Bateman cartoon. It was as if someone had asked the Queen whether she gave good head.'

I burst out laughing, something I hadn't done for ages. I had forgotten how amusing a raconteur Jack could be.

Encouraged by my response, he continued. 'Well, Clarissa merely glanced with magnificent disdain at these scattered corpses resulting from the fateful lightning of her terrible swift sword, and continued to tramp out her wrathful vintage. Her truth went marching on. Annual visitor numbers not merely declining but plunging. Scholarly enquiries static. Publications ditto. The guide-book had not been redesigned or fully revised since 1958. Library subscriptions and usage at an all time low. The Museum shop in deficit. The café a culinary and aesthetic disaster. The loos an unhygienic shambles. The roofs of the galleries leaked in fifty different places, the buckets catching the drips having become museum pieces themselves. Most of the display cases were dusty, the objects ill lit and poorly conserved. Many of the warders were so old or so mentally deficient that they hardly knew their own names, never mind the nature of what they were attending.'

'Was all that true?'

He made a face. 'Pretty much. With honourable exceptions. Like the Roman and Dark Ages galleries, my patch.'

'So, you ought to have come out of this Inquisition quite well?'

'Alas. We come to the painful part of this narrative.' He gazed mournfully around. 'Have you any brandy? I need a drink to steady my nerves.'

'Brandy in the afternoon, Jack? I think there is a bottle of some Spanish stuff in the Boulle cabinet.'

He brought it over with a couple of glasses. 'Join me on the journey to oblivion. Ugh, it tastes like liquid toffee.'

I sipped at my brimming glass. 'Now you're lubricated, finish the story.'

'You've no idea of the shambles she produced. Management consultants appeared. God, the time we had to spend answering their stupid questions. They were all about twelve years old. Then marketing consultants. All right, so the shop, the café and the publications needed to be sorted out. I'm not against making money in the right way, but not by selling bloody tea-towels and oven gloves covered in Egyptian hieroglyphs. Their report went on about how we had to "build the Farebrother as a major brand name in the National Heritage industry". A brand name, for Christ's sake. But it was the ad campaign on the Tube after the café had been done up at vast expense that really pissed me off. "A cool place to lunch, no bones about it." "Swords and saucery." "Tea and history." And the absolute pits, a glass display case full of Danish pastries and sandwiches: "Serve yourself to some of our exhibits."'

I shook my head sadly. This was beginning to sound

horribly familiar. 'Where did you make these views known, Jack? Presumably not just privately amongst colleagues?'

'No, unfortunately not. You know me too well, Liz. There was a reception for bigwigs in commerce, the City and industry to persuade them to sponsor Clarissa's new development plan. It was a really mega occasion. Presentations, speeches, the lot. I did my bit, pretty well, I thought, and then they wheeled out the booze. Champagne – the real stuff, not Australian pop. God, I must have been insane. First, I made a pass at some woman who turned out to be the wife of the head man at Hazenbach's, the merchant bank, who were very much in the frame for a substantial wad. That was bad enough. Then I spotted Greville in a huddle with some very expensive suits. I was feeling particularly steamed up with him because Clarissa had told me only that day that the Trustees – i.e. Greville – had refused to publish my monograph on the Museum's collection of Roman silver.'

'Your monograph, Jack? You mean you actually wrote it yourself?'

'Of course I did. It took me ages. It was the first proper piece of research I'd managed to complete in years. I was rather proud of it, as a matter of fact.'

'And so you should be, Jack. An original Armitage. A great rarity.'

'I don't know why you have to take that tone. What have you ever written? Whatever became of that great book you were going to write?'

'I've made notes,' I said defensively.

'You and Dr Casaubon,' he retorted, with some justification, although still woundingly.

'So, what was the problem with publication?'

He gulped down the brandy and poured another. 'Money, for one thing – though how they could claim that when they were lashing it out on Clarissa's reforms. But worse was what she told me was Greville's personal comment.'

'Which was?'

'Armitage has no reputation as a scholar. We cannot put such stuff out under the Museum's imprimatur. If unsound, it would make the Museum a laughing-stock.'

'Oh, Jack! How cruel. How unnecessarily cruel. I'm surprised that . . .'

Just in time, I stopped myself from blurting out something injudicious. But Jack hadn't noticed, being locked in the memory.

'It was not unsound. I'd gone out of my way to check every reference, verify every statement. Of course, the conclusion about the unity of the Lothbury Treasure may have been a little controversial but . . .'

'Lothbury Treasure? What's that?'

'One of the Museum's star items. A set of Roman silver table ware, of extraordinary quality and state of preservation. Not as well known as it should be, but that's the Farebrother for you.'

'You said your conclusion about it was controversial? I recollect that's a scholarly word for bloody outrageous?'

'Not at all. I'd been the first person to examine the Treasure scrupulously since its acquisition in the fifties. It wouldn't be surprising if I'd reached different conclusions. Besides, I only expressed the view that the Treasure may have been assembled from two different hoards. It happened all the time in the nineteenth century, when people bought on the Continent from unscrupulous dealers. It wasn't as if I'd said it wasn't genuine. It certainly is that.'

Jack had dropped his usual languid drawl and spoke with unusual passion on this arcane subject. I saw in him something of the fierce brilliance he had used on *Tempus* to terrify his colleagues. I had a sick foreboding of what had occurred at this ill-fated soiree.

'Oh dear, Jack, so with all this to unload, not to mention the champagne, you didn't I suppose confine your observations to the weather?'

'On the nail again, dear heart. I weighed in and told him,

26

and by extension the rest of the conclave, exactly what I thought of the attempt to sell what was still a great Museum like a package holiday to Torremolinos. I said that genuine scholarship was being ditched in favour of gimmickry and tackiness. I went on at some length, until it penetrated even my fuddled mind that the Chairman was looking, to put it mildly, a little strained. He did his best to shut me up, but I was too far gone, and when he put his arm round my shoulder and tried to usher me over to the window – "Feeling a little unwell, Armitage, old man? I think you need some fresh air" – I . . .'

He lapsed into silence as he poured yet more brandy.

I stared at him in horror, already sick with the inevitability of the answer as I demanded, 'What did you do, Jack?'

'I didn't mean to hit him, but I must have sort of pushed him away harder than I'd intended and he slipped on the shiny marble floor and fell back and fortunately one of the suits caught him before he . . .'

'Oh Jack.'

'Yes, you're right. I was an utter bloody fool. Anyway they hustled me out and hushed it up. They let me resign and packaged my departure for public consumption, but everyone in the Museum down to the bog cleaners knew that I'd been summarily sacked and why. The worst thing was the look I got from Clarissa. She didn't say anything. She didn't have to.'

I went over to his chair, bent down and held him tightly. 'I'm so sorry, Jack.'

He answered my hug and we clung together for a moment as we had as children. 'So what are you going to do now?'

'I said in my letter. Maybe I'll do some writing. Who knows? Something may turn up.'

I took a deep breath. 'Well, if you are going to stay here for a little while there are a number of things we have to get straight. About Mother, for a start. There are certain things that you can help with.'

27

I saw a shadow of distaste flit across his face. Squeamishness, no doubt. Men were so bloody transparent sometimes, that is when they weren't being devious. 'Don't worry. Nothing intimate. Mrs Hargreaves and I will do anything of that kind. You can read to her, talk to her. There are long stretches when it doesn't seem to have any effect, but every now and again she says something which indicates she's been listening. Then there's handyman stuff. Gardening. That kind of thing.'

He seemed relieved, almost eager.

'Yes. I can do that. Whatever you say, boss.'

His compliant mood made me more relaxed than I had been since I had received his letter. I realised that he had seriously entertained the possibility of rejection, and that would, in spite of his natural insouciance, have hurt him. Whether it would last was another matter. There would undeniably be certain advantages while it did.

Jack could do the things I couldn't or wouldn't do. He certainly used to be a practical fellow, needing strength and resourcefulness in his fieldwork. He could attend to the constant problems with plugs, drains, tap washers, fuses, locks, hinges, leaks. Things I had to pay the earth to have fixed to smirking oafish cheaply cologned young men.

Maybe it wouldn't be so bad, I had thought to myself.

In some ways, it hadn't been. Jack had done everything I had asked him and more around the house. He read to Mother, and often sat with her talking to her of the old days. These occasions were oddly touching.

One day, she asked me, 'That man who comes to see me. Who is he?'

I smiled, I hoped with the sweet patience of the carer. 'It's Jack, Mother. Your son Jack. Don't you remember I told you he was staying with us?'

'Jack? No, dear, Jack isn't a big man like that. Only a boy. I have a little daughter as well. She is called Elizabeth and she is very pretty. Why do they never come to see me any more?'

In many ways, it had been like old times, as for instance, when he had asked me for money three weeks after his return.

'Bit of a delay with the rent for the flat. And I had a hell of a bill on the car the other day after that contretemps with the oik in the Cavalier. You remember I had to take it back to Malvern Link.'

'I thought you said your tenants were reliable.'

'They are but their work isn't. Neil's character in *Victoria Square* has been rested for a few episodes, apparently. It was in the papers.'

'Not the one I read. I suppose being temporarily embarrassed for cash struck a sympathetic chord with you?'

He gave that quick, disarmingly frank grin that had fluttered hearts ever since he had sung *Panis Angelicus* as a nine-year-old choirboy in the parish church at the Crowcester Festival.

'I suppose it did. It takes one to know one. Come on, Liz. A measly hundred for a week at the outside.'

'I don't know why you don't get rid of that car. A Morgan, for God's sake. Why don't you grow up and drive a Ford like everyone else?'

He gave me the kind of look he would have given if I'd suggested we drank Ribena with our evening meal. 'Please, Liz. I had this kind of hassle when I was married. It's one of the many reasons I'm not any more. And I'm a big boy now. I don't need advice from my little sister.'

'No, only her money.' I rummaged in my handbag for my wallet. 'Here's fifty. I'll give you the rest when I've been to the bank tomorrow.'

He kissed the sheaf of notes theatrically and stuffed them away in his pocket.

He hadn't paid me back, of course.

A week or so later, I was woken up by a call in the small hours. It wasn't a heavy breather, but the police station in Oxford. I recalled sleepily that Jack had gone there for some kind of college reunion and had not returned by the time I went to bed. It must have been a good party because he had been found sleeping soundly on the pavement of St Aldates opposite Christ Church. The Oxford constabulary were well used to drunken toffs and they were proposing to send him home in a cab, rather than keep him overnight in a cell which might be needed for a genuine member of the criminal classes. As Jack appeared to have no cash on him, would I, etc.?

I did so, naturally. And I had to drive him back into Oxford the following day to recover the Morgan, which, as I'd expected, had been parked on a double yellow and been towed away to the pound.

After that, there had been some kind of scene in the Trout in Crowcester and he'd been thrown out. I'd warned him about chatting up Ellen Norton, and he must as usual have taken no notice. Jack had not a clue about the delicacies necessary in village society, and I could hardly walk down to the village without people he'd insulted or nearly run over coming up to me to bend my ear.

I could have said that he was nothing to do with me, but that wouldn't have gone down too well in a place like Crowcester, where the inhabitants of The Hollies had been part of the social fabric for three generations. I was my brother's keeper, whether I wanted to be or not. I relied too much on the goodwill of my neighbours to risk a breakdown of relations over Jack. As I am not naturally a diplomatic or emollient personality, this constant negotiation was wearing and increased my irritation with the author of it.

These matters, however, were, in the larger scheme of our relationship, minor annoyances, and very much what I had expected. Their impact was also cushioned at the beginning by my belief that Jack, whatever his protestations to the contrary, would not stay long at The Hollies. A month or so of dull provincial life would have been enough for him. He would return to London and we could re-establish our relationship on a weekend basis, which was what had always worked so well in the past.

It soon became disturbingly clear that this would not happen. Jack, quite by chance, immediately on his return, came upon a project which would, if it materialised, keep him in Crowcester for months.

He had decided on what seemed to me very slight evidence that a Roman villa lay beneath the site of the old Crowcester Brewery. He also convinced himself that this was his long-delayed *magnum opus*. He threw himself into planning its excavation with the kind of manic energy which was always lurking beneath his indolent, careless façade. I had, frankly, gone along with it as far as I had only in the certain expectation that he would fail in his crazy attempts to raise finance for his cockeyed scheme.

His success in finding the money, therefore, came as an unpleasant surprise, the more so as I had done my best to persuade the owner of the site to have nothing to do with Jack's scheme. Jack suddenly became not an amusing temporary visitor, whose foibles were tempered by the thought of his imminent departure, but a long-term problem. His activities were beginning to affect me in ways which I had never imagined.

It had, by malign fortune, brought Jack into close, maybe even intimate, contact with the one person in Crowcester whom I had wanted him to avoid. The thought of someone very dear to me being subject to Jack's attentions filled me with anguish.

That fresh summer morning, as I drove down the narrow lane which led to Crowcester, fearful of what I would find there, I sincerely wished that my brother had never returned to dig up the past.

I slowed down, signalling left for the turn into Crowcester village. Over the single-arched bridge spanning the little River Crow, I took another left along a narrow track, the asphalt surface of which was broken at the crown by invasive grass and weeds. Through the decrepit post-and-rail fence which ran on the right, I could see beyond the overgrown meadow the squat grey tower of All Saints, the parish church of Crowcester.

The track ended at a metal five-barred gate, beyond which was a concrete yard surrounded by a range of brick and stone buildings. A board announced in peeling, faded lettering:

Crowcester Brewery
Home of Old Crow Ale

To my amazement, slewed across the yard behind the gate was a white Transit van with POLICE stencilled on the side. Flanking it were two white saloons with blue lights on top and red side-flashes which the kids at school called jam sandwiches. A collapsible metal-frame white on blue sign read:

CRIME SCENE
DO NOT ENTER

Run on to the verge of the lane on my side of the gate was a dark blue Mondeo, with the unmistakable air of another official conveyance, CID presumably.

Having no alternative but to stop, I pulled on to the verge behind it. I sat in the car for a few moments wondering why the Thames Valley Police had turned out in such force and feeling sick at the prospect that Jack was the cause of such attention.

As I got out, a uniformed policeman in a flat cap materialised in the lane.

'Excuse me, madam, you can't . . .' he began, then he saw who it was. We knew each other. He gave me an embarrassed half-salute. 'Morning, Miss Armitage.'

'Good morning, Constable Enstone,' I said in my best lady-of-the-manor tones. Gary Enstone had been a pupil not so long ago at Waterbury. That acned adolescent, it was hard to credit, was now what was officially known as the

Crowcester Community Liaison Officer, which meant he drove through the village once in the morning and if we were lucky, once in the afternoon. The locals called him the sleeping policeman.

This was obviously a special day. 'My brother asked me to come here. Have you seen him?'

Poor Gary looked even more embarrassed at the mention of Jack. It began to look worse and worse. 'I think you'd better speak to DCI Green, Miss. He's with the . . . I mean . . .'

I was saved from further inarticulate floundering by the appearance of Jack himself.

'Liz, thank God you're here.' He was terribly pale and his eyes were so bright they almost glittered. He staggered towards me.

Enstone, tactfully, moved slightly to one side.

'Jack, for Christ's sake. No more mysterious hints. Please tell me what's going on here. Why the police? You said you found something. What on earth is it?'

'We've found him. But just bones. And a few scraps of clothing . . .' He clutched me close to him and I could feel his big frame racked with sobs.

I admit in my relief to see him I scarcely listened. I caught only the one word and my anger flared up, freed from the restraint of my anxiety. I struggled out of his embrace. 'Damn you, Jack. Bones? Is that all? Is that why you've dragged me back here in the middle of my working day? You find bones all the time in your business. What the hell's that to do with me?'

He raised his hands to his brow and held them there. When he looked at me again, his eyes were even more sunken into their dark hollows, his face paler and his hair even more disordered. 'Liz, you don't understand. Why do you think the police are here? The bones we found, they're not ancient, they're only forty years old. His skull had been bashed in. He'd been murdered.' He started to cry, again bending his head in an attempt to rest it on my shoulder.

I started from him in alarm, concern flooding back into my heart. Had he gone mad? 'Jack, what do you mean, with him, his skull, he'd been murdered. You're talking as if it's someone you knew. Jack!'

He lifted his head slowly, the dark eyes boring into mine. 'I knew him,' he said in a voice which sounded as if to use it was a cause of infinite weariness. 'And so did you, Liz.'

II

The morning I found him, I had been in the site office, making preliminary assessment notes on the latest finds – items from the backfilled spoil of the original dig which had been missed by the excavators – when I heard Bob Farmington yelling from the Glebe. He'd got in unusually early – perhaps he hadn't been to bed at all – and none of the others had yet shown up. He had immediately set to work on the task I had allotted to him the previous evening, the completion of the re-excavation of the known part of the old aqueduct.

I was surprised and alarmed that Bob was shouting in such a frantic manner. Surely he wouldn't make this fuss over finding a bit of rubbish? A coin, maybe? Or had he hurt himself? I put down my pen, hurried into the brewery yard, through the gap in the wall carved by the JCB the day before and over to where I could see him leaning on his spade. As I drew close, I smelt the sour stench of vomit.

He was still retching as I took him by the arm.

'Christ, Bob. Hello would have been enough. Too much booze last night?'

He breathed deeply, shaking his head. Then he pointed down to the sector where he'd been digging.

I knew as soon as I saw the bones that they couldn't be ancient. Not even the amateurs of the 1956 excavation would have missed a human skeleton, and it was evident that until Bob had happened on them they hadn't been disturbed since they had been put there. And when the hell was that? This could hardly have been an official burial so far away from the consecrated ground of the churchyard.

I jumped down into the culvert, and gently swept the lumps of soil away from the skull. Around the vertebrae of the neck were wound the blackened fragments of a piece of cloth. A neck-tie. There were more cloth fragments around the collapsed rib cage. I sat back on my heels, baffled and disturbed. Bob had quietened down now. He had handed the responsibility to me. He was only a kid, after all. He peered over cautiously, wiping the mess from around his mouth with a filthy handkerchief.

I looked up at him. 'This isn't a job for an archaeologist, but a forensic scientist. If you're feeling up to it, Bob, you'd better ring the police. Use my car-phone. Stay by the gate and wait until the coppers come. And don't let on to anyone about this, OK? Tell anyone else who turns up that the site is closed today.'

He nodded, and trotted away, grateful no doubt to be released.

I looked down once more at the half uncovered bones. The sun chose that moment to come from behind a cloud and I felt its warmth on the back of my neck. In my nostrils, there was the familiar scent of damp earth and, perhaps only in my memory, something else: the fetid odour of death. For a moment, I was back in the desert, the tumbled corpses of the Egyptian soldiers in their burned-out tank being gleefully pointed out to me by the Israelis, as I caught on the hot breeze the sickly stench of decay.

It was at that moment that I saw in a shaft of sunlight the glint of gold. I knew that I should not disturb anything, but gold is a lure that no treasure hunter can resist. I felt in my pocket for the soft paintbrush and delicately flicked at the soil with its bristles.

The face of a man's gold wristwatch emerged. A Rolex.

I picked it up carefully. It was as if it were electrified. It seemed to twist in my hand. A wave of nausea swept through

36

me. I stared at it in disbelief. It could not be. It must be a similar model. But something told me that it was not. The memory of the ten-year-old boy who was always begging to handle it or to wind it was unimpeachable. With hands that shook, I turned the watch over. The engraving banished incredulity.

As I stared at that inscription, trembling with the horror of it, it was as if I were a dying man whose life flashed through his mind in the seconds before his extinction. I experienced the combination of circumstances which had brought me to this intersection of time and place not as a disconnected series of events, but as an inevitable sequence.

The Romans would have been familiar with that epiphany, of course. They were unashamedly teleological. A god had prompted me to go for the stroll after lunch on the day of my return to The Hollies. A god with an inscrutable purpose. A god who knew me well.

I'd walked along the paved path by what was once a herbaceous border into the old kitchen garden, the enclosing red-brick walls of which were crumbling at their tops and bowed under immense cloaks of thick dark-green ivy. Along the south-facing wall were the remains of a glass-house, the wooden frame rotted and green with mildew, the panes cracked or missing altogether. To one side was a wooden door, once painted blue. I had the heavy old key in my pocket. I'd taken it from the board in the kitchen where it had always hung. Liz said she often used it when she wanted to walk into the village. The key turned easily in the lock. I pulled the door open and stepped into the lane beyond.

It was as if I had stepped through into the past. How many times hadn't I gone this way, following the curve of the road, under the beeches which still arched overhead, their smooth grey branches delicately stippled with the light green of new leaves? On the right was Well House, where I'd often been to tea with the Westoby boys, and played till sunset in their tree house, until they moved away and the new childless owners had the ramshackle wooden structure demolished.

Below the high stone wall, I could see the gully where the tiny brook formed by the spring which gave the house its name emerged and flowed in a channel at the roadside down to the Crow by the Trout Inn. That day, the stream bed was dry, and filled with dead leaves.

I followed the curve of the wall towards the village. Rounding the corner, I saw that the paddock where the Westobys had kept their pony had been developed, apparently fairly recently, into a small estate of houses, the kind advertised as executive homes. They were built of imitation Cotswold stone and dominated by huge detached double garages plonked at the end of purple brick-paved driveways. A blond-haired man in a padded bodywarmer was polishing an already immaculate BMW in front of the house nearest the lane. I called out a greeting. He replied with a suspicious nod, as if making a mental note to alert his chums in Neighbourhood Watch. Welcome to the country, mate.

I should hardly be surprised. These kinds of changes were happening everywhere. Besides, an archaeologist had to have a different concept of time. The present would in an archaeological instant become the distant past and be obliterated under layers of subsequent occupations. One man's rubble was another man's foundation. It was comforting that Garage Man and all his tacky works would be only a few centimetres of a settlement of what might become known to its Chinese excavators as the late Imperialist Christian Era.

The lane ended at a T-junction with the main street of Crowcester. It straggled downhill flanked by terraces of small cottages, interspersed with the occasional more substantial dwelling set back from the pavement and guarded by walls or iron railings. At the bottom of the hill, there was what passed for the village centre: the one remaining shop, the post office, the Trout Inn, and, behind a stand of yew trees, All Saints, the parish church.

When I was a boy, there were several stores: a baker, a butcher, a grocer, a greengrocer, a cobbler and, my own favourite, an ironmonger's and blacksmith's where bicycles and farm machinery were repaired and horses shod, the sort of set-up you would find in Europe today, if at all, only in somewhere like Bulgaria.

I went into the Mini-Market. The island shelves were crammed with tins and packets but the drinks and tobacco were kept behind the till, away from thieving hands. The young woman at the counter looked up at the sound of the doorbell and put down the fat paperback with the lurid cover she'd been reading. She was, I guessed, in her mid-twenties, blonde from a bottle, but pretty enough and with breasts which strained interestingly against the white nylon overall she wore.

I asked for a pack of Marlboro. As she reached behind for the cigarettes, I caught a glimpse of well-shaped leg and thigh as the overall rode up. When she turned back, she stared at me, colouring slightly as she did so.

'You're Mr Armitage, aren't you? I've seen photos of you at The Hollies and Miss Armitage told my mum her brother was coming to stay. I'm Ellen Norton. Hargreaves as was.'

'I'm very pleased to meet you, Ellen.' I smiled broadly, and held out my hand. She gave it a brief touch of acknowledgement.

I thrust my change into my trouser pocket, feeling the stirring of interest down there, what my house-master used to refer to as the stiffening of resolve. Crowcester might have its fun side after all.

'Mum said you used to be on the telly, years ago. I don't remember. I was too little. Something to do with history?'

'Archaeology. Digging up the past.'

She nodded. 'Are you going to do some digging here then? Brian, my uncle, said that there were Roman remains found here, years and years ago. Before I was born.'

I smiled. In her mind, anything beyond her life-span was

probably as remote as Julius Caesar. 'I'm just here for . . . a break. From my job in London. Your uncle was right, though. There was undoubtedly a Roman settlement here, although probably not a military camp, despite the name.'

She looked blank.

'Oh, sorry. The "cester" ending is usually taken to be the Latin *castra*, which means fortified encampment. Actually, it comes from the Anglo-Saxon version of that word. In my opinion, they applied it to wherever there was any kind of Roman settlement.'

'I see. Well, I'm not much of a scholar, I'm afraid. Failed my GCSEs, which meant I couldn't do proper nursing. Only child-minding, and the shop – and I see to Mrs Armitage on occasions. In our family, it's only my cousin Fran who's really got the brains. Miss Armitage helped her to get into Oxford. She's doing ever so well.'

Unfortunately, just as it was moving up a notch or two in intimacy, our little colloquium was interrupted by the sound of the doorbell. As a stern looking elderly woman plonked her wicker basket on the counter, I picked up my cigarettes and left.

I sat on a bench in the churchyard and smoked. Strange how pretty little Ellen had mentioned the dig which had taken place here, what, forty years ago?

Gervase Tuddenham, the vicar, had been looking through the church maintenance records kept by one of his nineteenth-century predecessors and had seen mention of tiles and stone-work being uncovered when the foundations for a new wall in the churchyard were being dug. He managed to identify the area concerned, which was on the southern boundary. He mentioned this to Sir George Shotover of Crowcester Hall, who, he knew, was a bit of an antiquarian. Sir George told his pals in the Waterbury and District Archaeological Society, and in the summer of 1956, a preliminary investigation was undertaken, labour being provided by sturdy village lads, including myself.

I owed my involvement, the childhood hobby it inspired, and the career which grew out of that, to Gervase. He had suggested to his ten-year-old choirboy that he might like to take an interest in the excavations.

I'd not thought of him for years. He'd not stayed in the parish long, but moved onward and upward. I recalled that eventually he'd become a bishop. He must be retired, by now. Presumably even bishops retired these days.

Despite the overwhelming misery of the following autumn, which had forever clouded my childhood, I still remembered that summer fondly. Not that what we found in our amateurish way was all that fascinating to me. I was still young enough to long to discover buried treasure. There was, of course, nothing of that kind, but I did learn enough to realise that treasure hunting is only a part of the work of the archaeologist. The painstaking sifting of earth, the recording of levels, the observation of the topography of the site are all part of the gradual process by which knowledge is gained. And even the amateurs were clear that what we were seeking was knowledge.

I remember Shotover telling me, 'We have to get the history right, my boy. History tells us who we are now. Never forget that.' In my grave ten-year-old way, I had replied, 'I won't, sir.' And I never had.

As far as could be ascertained, we had discovered a rank of outhouses belonging to what was probably a villa. Unfortunately, it was clear from what we had found that the site of the main dwelling lay away from the church, outside the boundary of the open field known locally as the Glebe. On that side was the high brick wall enclosing the yard and buildings belonging to the flourishing Crowcester Brewery, the village's main employer. If there were a Roman villa, it was effectively and immutably buried beneath tons of brick and concrete.

I strolled through the burial ground and leaned on the wall to look over this formative location. It was exactly as I

41

remembered it. Three acres or so, full of bumps and hollows, covered with coarse grass and clumps of bramble. It was at present home to a small flock of Jacob sheep, no doubt the property of some hobby farmer. In the silence, the tearing sound as they grazed was audible even from several yards away.

Over the wall on the far side, I could see the roofs of the brewery buildings. Or rather, I saw with a quickening of interest, the shattered remains of the roofs. Large areas had been stripped of slates. Daylight showed through ragged holes. Poking over the top of the wall was the raised yellow back hoe of a mechanical digger. It seemed that demolition was in progress.

I stubbed out my cigarette on the coping of the churchyard wall, scrambled over it and set off across the field to investigate, the sheep fanning out before me and bleating in surprise at this intrusion.

An hour later, I was back at The Hollies. Liz was in the drawing room, a pile of dog-eared blue-covered exercise books on the carpet in front of her chair. She looked up from the one she had on her lap, red pencil in hand.

'Good walk? You look hot, as if you've been running.'

'I have,' I panted, my heart pounding and my lungs still on fire with this unaccustomed exercise. I sank down on the sofa.

'You never went in for cross-country even at school, I remember. More the effortless stroke with the willow type, you were.'

'Don't be arch, Liz. I'm in too good a mood. I wasn't jogging. I ran home because I was bursting to tell you of my discovery. You know how it was always you I wanted to tell first.'

'Except when it wasn't. So what's new on the Rialto?'

'The old brewery site has been sold for development. They're knocking it down.'

'Jack, a five-minute trot round the village hardly gives you

42

an exclusive insight into the last umpteen years of local history. I do live here, you know. The closure of the brewery was front-page news in the *Waterbury Advertiser* for weeks. It was taken over by one of those national chains. Old Crow Ale, "The ploughman's choice", is now made in a stainless steel factory near Reading. You can see it from the M4.'

'I don't give a shit about the beer,' I replied impatiently. 'It's the brewery site. I want it. I want to excavate it.'

She stared at me. 'Why on earth do you want to do that?'

'Because I've got a hunch that underneath is a Roman villa, a big one judging from the size of the outbuildings that we found during the dig that Gervase Tuddenham and old Shotover got going when I was still at prep school. In '56. Funny that Ellen in the shop mentioned it. Don't you remember, Liz?'

'How could I forget 1956? But I don't remember the dig. I was eight at the time. More interested in ponies than Roman remains. So you're going to return to the scene of your earliest triumph. Complete your life's work. Is that it?'

'I have to do something with my life. As soon as I saw that the demo men had moved in, it reawakened those memories. Nothing wrong with that, is there?'

'You need money for an excavation. You haven't got any.'

'Of course. I'll have to raise it.'

'Who's going to give you that kind of money on the basis of this hunch of yours, Jack?'

'Leave that to me. I'm persuasive. Very persuasive indeed.'

'I know you are, Jack. That's always been your problem. Charm by the bucketful. And by the way, if you're minded to start persuading Ellen Norton, then think again. I should stay away from her. Barry Norton is half your age and very muscular. A scaffolder, I believe.'

'I had no thoughts in that direction, and it's none of your damn business anyway. Now you can be helpful if you want and tell me what you know about Crowvale Properties. It's

43

their board up on the site. Acquired for a superior residential development, it says.'

'What are you going to do?'

'Speak to them, today, if possible. Sound them out. Sponsorship even.'

She'd been smiling up to this point as if she'd thought I wasn't entirely serious. Suddenly, she seemed to realise that I was in earnest.

'Jack, I'm not sure this is really a good idea. If you start this thing, it would mean that you'd be staying around here for at least the rest of the summer, wouldn't it?'

'Naturally.'

'I don't know whether I could handle that. There are things about my . . . , about village life that you just don't . . .'

She hesitated, her eyes awkwardly downcast.

The way she was behaving immediately reminded me of all those times when she'd refused to tell me things. Liz could be very secretive when she wanted to be.

'Liz, please. Give me a break. I need something to occupy myself. I promise I won't intrude on you more than absolutely necessary. You know everything that goes on here. I really need your help.'

She shrugged. 'All right, Jack. I only hope I don't live to regret it.'

How could she not regret it now? I had disinterred, from the darkness of our souls where we had concealed it, the hurt and anguish of our childhood.

But how long ago the seeds of fate had been planted. I would never have taken that fateful stroll had I not returned for my own selfish reasons to The Hollies.

I had been a bit drunk that evening in February, as I sat alone in the sitting room of my house in Barnsbury Street. I was feeling more than a little sorry for myself. I was disappointed in my profession. I had the prospect of being virtually penniless. These things had concentrated my mind.

I had had heaped in front of me on the coffee table a mess of bills, cheque stubs, credit card receipts, bank statements and figures scribbled on scraps of paper. However I totted them up, they gave the same message. Even with the fairly substantial rent Geoffrey Lamplighter, doyen of Islington estate agents and an old drinking buddy from the King's Head in Upper Street, had got for the house, financially I would be in a hole.

It was my own fault of course. The Farebrother Museum had been a cushy berth and, as I'd done before, I'd gone and ruined it. If only I hadn't . . . But I had, as per usual. God, what wouldn't I have given to have shoved the arrow of time back, so that I could have rerun just a few minutes of my life.

But no Mephistopheles appeared in the darkness of my book-lined room to offer me a Faustian bargain.

I dulled the ache with whisky. It wasn't as if I was really bad. Reckless, thoughtless, insensitive, perhaps. But not bad. Though I had done bad things, that was true. Almost twenty years before, I had done a dreadful thing and I suffered for it yet. I always would.

I still woke up night after night from the same nightmare: blinding headlights, jarring thuds as the car ran off the road out of control, the wrenching impact as it hit the tree, the screams dying away into utter silence, and Fiona's face a mask of blood.

I'd killed Fiona and maimed my sister. Poor Liz. Her arm was smashed so badly in the accident, she never played again the competitive tennis which had been so important to her. Despite that, she'd saved me. I had hated her for it. I hadn't wanted to be saved, and yet I was too much of a coward to resist. I had been vile to her.

As I twisted these thoughts in my mind, the idea of making my peace with her, of atonement, of craving her forgiveness for that part of my life seemed inordinately appealing. Compelling, even. I staggered over to the roll-top desk and rummaged out a few sheets of writing paper, foreign stuff left behind by Chantal, a French beautician I'd picked up in Harvey Nicks, my brief affair with whom had ended a couple of months back.

It was only then that it came to me that not only was my sister a means by which I could redeem some of my past, but the key to how I might save my own future. Although I was in the middle of the dark wood, I was not entirely lost. There was a light among the trees, the faint radiance of the place where I had grown up, which long ago had enshrined all that was most precious. I who was lost should return whence I came. Back at The Hollies, I would be able to make something of my life, to fulfil the promise that I had once believed I had. I'd also save the money I would have had to spend on rent.

Borne along by this alcoholic tide of nostalgia polluted by self-interest, I finished the letter and, late as it was, hastened to the post office in Upper Street and with hope surging in my breast, thrust it into the mailbox.

As I awaited her reply, I was nervous of receiving it. Another rejection would go hard with me. And yet what could I expect? Twenty years was a long estrangement. Twenty years. It seemed incredible that I had let so much precious time elapse. My relationship with Liz had for years been the most valued and the most stable thing in my life. Out of pride and grief, I had rejected it. Perhaps I had destroyed it for ever.

When I got Liz's letter, it was a profound relief, a deliverance. The hand I had held out was not being spurned, even though the note itself was in its brevity little more than a curt acknowledgement. I knew my sister well enough to know that if she was going to persist in our estrangement she would have held out no false hopes. I would have done the same. Liz and I had always been direct in our dealings with each other.

In fact it was that lack of dissimulation which had ruled the manner of our parting. She had acted in what she thought

46

were my best interests, and I had told her that what she had done had disgusted me. So it had, though later I realised that the disgust was more for myself and my own weakness than for poor Liz. Having said what I had said, it seemed a doubling of weakness to go back on it. I couldn't, in my immaturity, admit to her that I was in the wrong. It would have been an admission that the balance of our childhood relationship was wrong also.

Liz had always been jealous of me, and had made me aware of it time after time. This was not simply the usual rivalry of a younger child close in age to the elder, nor solely because my sister had a temperament that was, at the best of times, prickly and difficult. She was envious because she was aware from infancy that, by any reasonable theory of upbringing, she was treated with quite shocking unfairness. In a way that is probably inconceivable now, my mother and father always regarded her as inferior to me. At the time, of course, with the casual brutality of the child, I was entirely unyielding in my satisfaction that I was getting what was my due as the elder, and being male, self-evidently the better. This attitude drove Liz to frustrated distraction. As a result, the feeling that she had started out under a handicap dominated her early life.

When I went away to board at Summerfields in Oxford, she was sent to a crummy private day school in Waterbury. When I followed my grandfather by winning a foundation scholarship to Charterhouse, Liz had to make do with the local grammar school. Despite her furious protests, there was never any question of her going to public school. It was not merely that there was no money in my grandfather's trust to pay for us both. Even if there had been, my mother, in her old-fashioned English upper-middle-class way, was opposed to the expensive and, as she saw it, pointless education of young women, whose main role in life was to marry well, produce a family, dress with taste, possess womanly skills, attend the Church of England, and do good works.

47

Liz who was, in truth, just as clever if not cleverer than I was, saw her future quite differently. She had set her heart upon an academic career and she was utterly determined to go to university. In that aim, she at last had some luck. Although she initially despised the idea of Waterbury Girls' Grammar, and although it was hardly in the same league as Charterhouse, it was actually a good school, certainly for the pupil of exceptional promise. In those days there were still a few dedicated schoolmistresses, frustrated scholars them-selves, no doubt, who believed in teaching real subjects – classics, modern languages, literature, maths, science. They were delighted to spend the extra time and effort a vora-ciously intelligent girl like Liz required of them.

Liz repaid them with the quality of her achievements. She worked and played with an Amazonian fury that appalled my mother. She won every prize there was to win, captained every team there was to captain. She was a quite exceptional tennis player. I played a bit myself, though I was nothing like as good, and in the summer vacs it would be twilight before we came off the grass court at The Hollies.

Mother had become reconciled to the fact that Liz would sail through Oxford Schools and go up to St Hilda's, where I, then at Christ Church, could keep an eye on her, and she could return home from college every weekend. She held still, however, to a modified version of her original world-view – she could not give it up entirely, as that would have meant the collapse of Christian civilisation – by assuming that once at Oxford, Liz would meet a young man, of eminent suit-ability and inordinate means, who would make her forget her blue-stocking ways, and return her to the true womanly faith.

However, Liz had already decided that she had no inten-tion of following in my footsteps as merely my sister, or even more of fulfilling the romantic fantasies of her parent. When it came to her university entrance, she scandalised Mother by making University College, London – the godless insti-tution in Gower Street – her first choice. She compounded

48

this by taking a year off to study in the south of France, financing this entirely herself by fixing up a place as an au pair and working through the summer vac. as a temp in Oxford.

When she came home at the end of that year, she was tanned, more beautiful than ever – even her brother had to admit she was what we called in the slang of the day, which now seemed as antique as the English of Chaucer, 'really stupendous' – and about to embark on what no one doubted would be her conquest of the capital.

But I was quite wrong. Liz's university career, which had begun brilliantly, ended in failure.

It wasn't an unfamiliar story. She got herself pregnant. I don't know whether the man proved to be a shit and refused to have anything to do with her or whether Liz was too proud to ask him. She never told me. In fact, she never even said who he was. She perhaps thought I would have given him a bloody good hiding. I would have, too.

Being Liz, she probably blamed herself. She had indefinite leave of absence to sort herself out. I was digging up Roman graves in Syria at this time, so I don't know the full story. She had decided to have the child, despite my mother's urging her to get rid of it. She was living at home and keeping up with her course work, intending to return, somehow, to the academic life she had set her heart on, after the birth.

However, the gods set their own agenda. The abortion that Liz refused to have happened naturally. There was a lot of blood and mess, apparently, and she nearly died. When she recovered, the quacks told her she would be unlikely to carry a child to full term, and that it would be dangerous if she tried. To some women, this might have been a relief, but Liz took it immensely hard. She insisted on taking her finals but, disastrously, got only a pass degree.

After that, she stayed at The Hollies to recuperate. When she was better, she went to see the headmistress of her old school – its ghastly fate as a comprehensive had not yet overtaken it – and got a post in the English department. There she had remained. I had effectively abandoned her. It was no wonder she resented me. At times, I still felt it radiating from her. I knew she hadn't wanted me to stay long in Crowcester, still less to become involved in a long-term project. But I had been determined to back my hunch.

I had, for quite some time, no premonitions of the trouble to come. Difficulties melted away in the weeks which followed my arrival. Liz, despite her misgivings, helped me a great deal. I felt exhilarated in a way I hadn't been for years. Of course, I hadn't done a dig from scratch since my twenties, since my days in the Middle East. In fact, I didn't know too much at first hand about the latest techniques. But the Farebrother was a good name to bandy around.

The Archaeological Society were got on board fairly easily. Liz knew the old buffer who had succeeded old Shotover, who had popped his clogs years before. We had sherry in his charming seventeenth-century house, all mellow Hornton stone and old-fashioned roses in the prettiest part of Crowcester. He wasn't actually such an old buffer, but a retired solicitor and one of those gifted amateurs of whom the archaeological world is full. Fortunately, I remembered reading a couple of his papers in *Britannia*. I lavished praise on his description of the excavation of one of the pottery factories in North Oxford, a model of its kind and all that.

Liz also knew Martin Rice, the chap who ran Crowvale Properties, as he was the husband of the headmistress of Waterbury Comprehensive. She got us asked over for drinks one evening. We had whiskies and sodas in the sitting room of their rather posh house.

He clearly set out to appear the kind of super-smooth estate agent type you'd find in the country branch office of one of those up-market Knightsbridge or Mayfair firms. But I could tell he wasn't kosher. Beneath the Savile Row tailoring, there was a barrow-boy. But that didn't concern me a bit.

The most important result of the meeting was that it established he was quite relaxed about the idea of a dig. He hadn't intended to start the development of the site until the following spring. The demolition work could be phased in accordance with my requirements and I could use one of the buildings on the site as an office.

He was very tickled by the idea that he would be able to use a Roman theme as part of the sales pitch on the new estate. He was shrewd enough to know that the great British public are potty about 'heritage'. He even agreed to fund a JCB and driver for the initial ground-work.

His wife was not at all as welcoming. I got the impression that she and Liz were not on the best of terms. There was that kind of over-scrupulous politeness between them. Linda was not unattractive in her way, being tall, blonde and full figured – Brünnhilde to the life – but she and I did not hit it off. I made the mistake of remarking how lucky she was to have such a great educational opportunity on her doorstep. She gave me in return a lecture on how modern education could not be obsessed by the past, and had to be 'relevant' and 'vocationally oriented' and other such piffle.

Rice said he would put me in touch with his pals on the County and District Councils and in the Waterbury Chamber of Commerce, and he was as good as his word. After a considerable charm offensive on my part, I had got together the bare funding for one season's basic excavation.

While waiting for the good weather, I had set to work to remedy some of the holes in my knowledge of the practical side of archaeological excavation and to refresh my memory by mugging up on everything I could find about the Roman settlements in Oxfordshire.

I became somewhat of a local celebrity. A few days before the dig was due to start, I was interviewed for the *Waterbury Advertiser* by a delightful little cubette reporter, to whom I would have been keen to reveal myself more intimately if I had not been fully stretched one way or another. I contented

51

myself on this occasion with having only my vanity stroked.

The reason for this unusual restraint was that I had finally managed to fulfil the other expectation aroused on the day of my arrival. After weeks of whispered conversations in the shop, lengthy phone calls and, finally, a clandestine lunch at a pub in Stow-on-the-Wold, I had persuaded Ellen Norton to allow me to visit her the next time her husband Barry was away doing his scaffolding.

I was congratulating myself on the successful outcome of these negotiations and looking forward to an early consummation when I dropped into the Trout in the evening for a night-cap.

The Trout was a hostelry of the old-fashioned kind. Everything about it was genuinely old from the deep yellow colour of the ceiling and walls, stained by generations of tobacco smoke, to the worn-down flags of the stone floor. The landlord was a miserable sod, who didn't give you the time of day, never mind wish you had a nice one. Only with born and bred villagers was he at all conversational.

The Trout was for locals to drink in, that had been clear the first time I'd opened the heavy ledge and brace door. There had been a turning of heads from the bar and the pool table where the youth congregated, and a lull in the conversation, then, after a moment or two, someone had muttered, 'Jack Armitage, ain't he?' and there had been confirmatory grunts. After that, I had been more or less accepted. I even got a nod of welcome from time to time from the landlord when I was served.

On that particular evening, I bought and paid for my usual double whisky, and sat in a creaky Windsor chair by the smoky coal fire which was kept burning whatever the weather or the season.

I noticed as I scanned the room that there was a new face among the lads around the pool table, a pale, sharp-looking youth with longish, lank blond hair. He wore a black leather jacket with a hand-painted skull and crossbones on the back. He seemed to be a mate of Barry Norton, who, I was displeased to note, was in there as well, as he frequently was when at home. Norton, as you would expect from his chosen trade, was a heavily muscled fellow, with a small head, scantily covered with bristly crew-cut dark hair. He and I usually, and reassuringly for me, hardly gave each other a second glance.

That night, though, Barry seemed to be looking in my direction more frequently than usual, and the looks were accompanied by nudges and whispered conversations with his unfamiliar companion. The other village boys seemed rather in awe of this type. I noticed he didn't ever go up to the bar for a round, but seemed to be treated.

I had just decided that I'd had enough of being stared at in this faintly hostile way and was drinking up before leaving, when I saw a very large hand appear in front of my face. It swept towards me very fast, and it was only an equally fast and totally instinctive drawing back of the head on my part that avoided my glass being smashed into my nose and chin. As it was, it was knocked out of my hand and shattered on the floor. The hand thumped into my shoulder, I lost balance and the chair and I in our turn toppled to the ground.

There was silence for a moment from the company, then the sharp-faced youth said, 'Nice one, Bazza.' I was getting to my feet, when Norton's foot kicked me hard in the ribs, throwing me back on to the floor. Winded, I crawled quickly out of range, and staggered upright.

I felt a hand on my shoulder. It was the landlord's. 'I think you'd better go home, squire. And not come back.'

'Yeah, you must be pissed, falling off your chair like that.'

There was a chorus of laughter at this, from the youths gathered around the stranger, and cries of 'You tell him, Del.'

Norton was cradling his right fist in his open palm. 'Folks here know about you, and what you are, mister,' he slurred.

'You been seen chatting up my missus. You leave her alone, or what you've got now'll be just a taster, see?'

I picked my jacket off the fallen chair. 'You've got me all wrong, Barry. But no hard feelings, eh?'

As I went out, the hubbub rose again and I noticed that several customers who turned to watch me go had the grace to look rather ashamed.

I decided to avoid the Trout in future. It had been a narrow squeak. Either Barry or one of his mates must have observed me talking once too often to Ellen in the shop. That and my reputation from years ago was enough. I winced as I thought what he might have done if he had known how things really stood with Ellen and me.

I gathered from Liz that the incident was the talk of the village, so I made a point of not going into the shop either. Barry was working locally, so a rendezvous with Ellen was off the agenda pro tem. I thought he would cool down and forget about me.

But I was wrong.

On the first day of the dig, the omens were auspicious. The weather was dry and bright. The first trench we cut was in exactly the right place. Everything was as it should be and hardly ever is.

Over the next few days, we made good progress. I found that my little team worked well together, despite the mix of ages and their lack of experience. Apart from myself, only Miss Masterton, one of the stalwarts of the Archaeological Society, a retired librarian at the Bodleian, elderly but inde-fatigable, who was the meticulous draughtsman, plan maker and recorder of the finds, had any experience of excavation.

There were a half-dozen adolescents – two boys and four girls – from Waterbury Comp's sixth form, who, having finished their exams, had time on their hands and had answered the recruiting poster I'd given Liz to stick on the school notice board. There was Hamish, whom I'd got from the labour exchange or whatever fancy name it went under these days on some Government make-work scheme. He was an enormous red-haired and red-bearded young man who spoke little and understood less, but who had a prodigious capacity for the shifting of earth. And there was Bob Farmington. He claimed to be a student at some university in the Midlands. He was an amiable sort of chap, quite bright and hard-working when he wasn't pissed or stoned.

In terms of modern professional archaeology, with its electronic gewgaws and legions of Ph.D.s, we must have seemed a shambolic bunch, but it had been the best I could do in the time and with the money available.

As for being untrained amateurs, many of archaeology's great finds, such as the Mildenhall Treasure, or Fishbourne Palace, have been made by accident by ploughmen or workmen, or their dogs. At least in me, we had someone who knew what he was looking for.

The more I looked at the site, the more I was convinced that I was on to something extraordinary. The only regret I had was that I had spent so much of my life away from field archaeology, my first love. I had hearkened after the gods of fame and fortune, and look where their fickleness had landed me. If only I'd had the sense to see what lay on my doorstep.

When Fran walked on to the site and into my life, I was full of hope that I might also have found, after so many years, someone to fill the void in my life, someone with whom I could recover the love I had recklessly lost.

On that wonderful second day, we uncovered the first part of the old watercourse.

It had been the memory of this that had convinced me that the Crowcester villa might be something special. Water was an essential element of the Roman way of life. In the villas, water was channelled and piped from springs and streams sometimes considerable distances away by smaller equivalents of the vast aqueducts which supplied the daily needs of millions in the great cities of the Empire.

The original excavation had uncovered a portion of a stone-faced culvert about two feet square. It no longer carried flowing water, only the run-off from the field which soaked down into it. It had been surmised in the Archaeological Society's published report that the source of the water had been a spring in the rising ground on the other side of the modern road beyond the Glebe.

There were still springs there, as I had seen myself. I thought it was very likely that the construction of the turnpike in the eighteenth century on higher ground north of the old cart track through the water meadows, which had in turn been widened and asphalted to serve as the main road through the village, had cut through the channel of the Roman watercourse or maybe the drainage of the land for agriculture on the upper slopes of the valley had caused the spring to dry up. According to local legend, the monks of Crowcester Priory had built a brewery here. If that were true, the reason they had chosen this site might well have been the presence of a clean and fresh supply of water, courtesy of the Romans of a thousand years before.

As I examined what Hamish had uncovered, I was more than ever convinced that only a very substantial establishment would have needed such a solid piece of civil engineering.

I gathered round the rest of the team to examine it. I must admit I got rather a kick out of showing off my expertise, leaping into the trench to point out the careful dressing of the stones and the precise fit of those coping slabs which still remained.

But the really exciting thing was that in tracing the channel across the Glebe, we could gain a better idea of the layout of the site and hence of the buildings which lay beneath the brick and concrete of the modern brewery. I spent the rest of the afternoon pegging out the probable alignment and dividing up new blocks for excavation. We would shortly progress from the old workings to completely undisturbed ground, where I expected the real discoveries to be made.

That afternoon, when I handed out the tasks for the next day, I asked Bob Farmington to continue re-excavating the watercourse the next morning. I thought the original excavators might have missed a few items, so I'd asked him to proceed cautiously. Never in my wildest nightmares would I have imagined what he would discover.

In fact, if what happened later that evening had gone as it was clearly intended, I would not have lived to see it.

I worked late that night in the office. This room was in the former Brewery admin. block, a single-storey construction of plate glass and wood panels. I had begged and borrowed a few items of furniture – trestle tables and stacking chairs – from one of Rice's connections.

I had just finished sorting through the pro forma record sheets I had prepared and photocopied at Rice's office that afternoon, assisted by his very pretty blonde secretary, and had decided to pack it in for the day. It was getting late, and beyond the flickering light from a single dusty fluorescent tube suspended above my head, the room was in shadow.

At that moment, I thought I heard a noise in the corridor outside. I strained my ears to hear, but there was nothing. There was the hoot of an owl. It had probably been that or some other nocturnal creature stirring. I picked up the heavy-duty rubber torch I needed to find my way around, as the power to the site had been cut, with the exception of that to this room. As it was quite cool, I had slipped on, but not buttoned up, my thick black double-breasted leather overcoat – my Gestapo coat, as Liz unkindly referred to it. It was a bit old and worn and not very fashionable, but I was fond of it. I still am fond of it. It saved my life.

I turned off the switch, and opened the door. There were no working lights in the passage. Using the torch to find my way, I was halfway along when I heard a sound close behind. This time I knew it was no night creature. It was the squeak of rubber soles on the vinyl tiles. I stopped and as I was about to turn, I felt something thump into the back of my coat where it hung loose.

I pulled away and whirled round in time to see a dark figure lunging forward in another blow. The torch beam gleamed for an instant on the blade in his hand. Without thinking, I lashed out with the torch and by pure chance connected with the weapon. There was a ringing sound as the knife fell to the floor. Its wielder muttered a curse and obligingly dropped to his haunches to grope for it in the darkness. I clouted him hard on the head, using the heavy torch as a club, following up with a kick to where I thought his balls were. This was a mistake as, even as he reeled and swore viciously with the pain of the blow, he grabbed my foot, and twisted it.

I would have fallen if I hadn't managed to hop back against the wall, dragging him with me. I struggled to free my foot from his grasp, lashing at him wildly, but he held on, and I felt myself sliding down, my other leg buckling. I made myself relax my trapped leg, then gave one more terrific heave which sent him toppling backwards, holding my shoe in his hands.

I ran like hell down the corridor, yanked open the plate-glass door and legged it across the yard to where I had parked the Morgan. I hoped that my attacker would have wasted valuable seconds retrieving his knife. Liz is always on at me for not only not locking my car but leaving the keys in the ignition but on this occasion I blessed my carelessness. The engine fired first time, and I burned rubber through the gates and along the bumpy track to the main road.

When I got back to The Hollies, I sat for several minutes in the driving seat, shivering violently all over. Having recovered sufficiently, I opened the front door quietly. There was a light under the green baize door at the end of the hall, showing that Liz was in the kitchen, so I stepped in quietly and went straight up to my room.

I had already decided to say nothing about the incident. I couldn't prove it was Barry and an unsuccessful accusation would have unpleasant consequences for my life in the village. Even if Barry were prosecuted, I wasn't sure Ellen would take all that kindly to her husband's going to gaol. Or, even worse, his absence might make her entertain foolish notions of making our affair more permanent. Whatever happened, there would be publicity of the worst kind for the dig. The last thing that I wanted the worthies I had conned into sponsoring me to know was that I was a philanderer with a taste for young uneducated women. Not at all good for the professional image.

I hoped that after the shock of tonight, young Norton might reflect on how near he had come to being saddled with a serious assault charge and cease behaving as if this was Sicily rather than staid old Oxfordshire and decide to call it quits.

However, when I took off the coat to examine it, I realised that I had underestimated the danger I had been in. The sturdy material had been sliced through from armpit to pocket as cleanly as if it had been paper. The blade must have been razor sharp and have come within millimetres of my back. A knife like that wielded in that manner could have had only one intended result. Barry Norton had not just been trying to hurt me. He had done his best to kill me.

As I stared at the ripped coat, I almost changed my mind about going to the cops. I had never dreamed that he would go so far. He must be a nut-case. Was Ellen worth it? Christ, was any woman worth that? I sat on the bed with my head in my hands, trembling.

That night, however, strange to say, I slept soundly, the first decent sleep I'd had for years. The next morning was so glorious, I was on site at six. The incident of the previous night might not have occurred, were it not for my shoe in the corridor where I had left it.

The memory of it was, in any event, obliterated by Bob Farmington's discovery later that morning.

★ ★ ★

I came out of my reverie. The present moment was incontestable reality, no hallucination, no flash-back from some of the stuff I'd dabbled with in my youth.

I still held the wafer of thin gold in my hands. Its floridly engraved inscription still read:

To my darling Robert, from your Celia
15th January 1940

The date was my parents' wedding day. The watch was my mother's handsome wedding gift to my father.

I sprang out of the culvert, grabbed the spade which lay near by and began desperately to free his lower limbs from their prison of earth.

When Bob came back with the police, I was crouching, shivering and crying, in the aqueduct, the watch gripped tightly in my hand, gazing at my father's remains.

III

'Those damned barbarians are at the gate already.'

Jack slammed the kitchen door, making the china on the dresser tinkle in protest.

I handed him my copy of *The Times*. 'Feast your eyes on that.'

He stared angrily at the front page headline. 'CROWCESTER SKELETON MAY BE COLD WAR SPY SUSPECT. What a bloody cheek! To drag up that business again. It's a pity you can't libel the dead. I'd sue.'

'No, you wouldn't, Jack. Litigation would bore you to tears. I suppose we'll have to get used to it for a while longer. We're not just a one-day wonder, we're a continuing news item. Famous for rather more than fifteen minutes.'

I could see Jack wasn't listening, but continuing to read. When he condescended to look up from the page, I was surprised to see he was grinning with an air of self-satisfaction. 'Did you see this? "Dr Jack Armitage (50) was well known in the seventies as presenter of the TV history programme *Tempus*. He recently retired from the post of Keeper of Roman and Dark Ages Antiquities at London's Farebrother Museum. The dig being undertaken in Crowcester was started as a result of his enthusiastic advocacy and had been extremely promising, according to Miss Elsie Masterton (62), a member of the Committee of the Waterbury Archaeological Society. The former Oxford University librarian said yesterday that all the excavation team had been devastated by the discovery and were full of sympathy for Dr Armitage, his sister and his mother." Good old Elsie. She has a soft spot for me, you know.'

I snorted. 'Of course she has, Jack. Not even the most confirmed spinster in North Oxfordshire is immune to your charm. She certainly seems to have cheered you up.'

'Who was it who said there was no such thing as bad publicity? "Enthusiastic advocacy", "extremely promising". I'd have spoken to those reporters myself if I thought I was going to get something as good as that out of it.'

'If you had, you wouldn't, Jack. Don't even think of it, otherwise we'll never get rid of them. I've got a life to get on with, even if you haven't.'

'You don't seem to realise, Liz, how important the Glebe site is for me. I'm convinced I'm on the track of something big. It could be the saving of me, you know.'

'I do understand that, Jack. But don't you feel differently about it now?'

'No, why should I? I want to go on with it, of course, once the police have finished their poking about.'

I shook my head in wonderment. 'Honestly, Jack. After the way you were, I thought you'd never want to see that field again.'

'I was really all over the place, wasn't I? No stiff upper lip in evidence at all.'

'You can be forgiven for that, Jack. It was an utterly horrible thing to have happened.'

'What about you, Liz? You didn't seem upset at the time. You don't seem upset now. It didn't seem to affect you at all.'

'Of course it affected me, Jack. It still does. But not in the same way as it did you. I wasn't on the spot and besides I was mentally prepared for something by the time I arrived. Though not that, admittedly. Anyway, I think I'm still working through my reaction. Look at you. You've got over yours. You're thinking about opening up the dig again already.'

'It doesn't mean I'm not still upset, Liz,' he protested, his

62

face open with the appeal he had had since he was in rompers. 'I don't think the two things are contradictory, given the circumstances. I grieve for my father, remembering him how he was. I grieve for the missing years. I grieve for the fact that, for forty years, we've misjudged him in some manner, but I'm not in mourning for him. You can't mourn someone who hasn't been part of your life for that length of time. Besides, logic would have dictated, if I'd thought about it, that he would in all probability have died by now.'

Jack's logic had the impeccable result, which he shared with many men I had known, that it justified him in doing what he wanted to do.

I watched him as he ate his egg and his toast with gusto, as he did so scanning the other pages of my newspaper which, as usual, he had appropriated without asking whether I'd finished with it. I felt oddly moved at this spectacle, remembering how he had been only the day before. It was good to see him more or less back to normal.

Later, as I tidied up the kitchen and put away the dishes which Jack had washed, I wondered exactly what it was I did feel about what had happened. Perhaps it was too soon for analysis. The events themselves had crowded into my mind.

He had clung to me in the yard of the brewery for what seemed a long time. Then he had gently disengaged. Just as when we were children, the act of sharing had made the nasty thing bearable.

I allowed him to lead me through the old brewery, and out by the gap torn through the brick wall into the Glebe field. In the middle of the excavations, a bright blue plastic tent had been erected, as if by early-season campers. Standing outside was a youngish man with very short fair hair, wearing a flashily cut blue suit.

He came towards us, and offered me his hand. 'Miss Armitage? Detective Chief Inspector Green. I'm very sorry that . . .'

'How do you do, Chief Inspector? May I see my father's body now?'

'Oh, yes, of course, ma'am, but Mr Arm . . . your brother will have explained that it was a . . . I mean there are only . . .'

'It's all right. I'm not expecting him to be lying in a silk-lined coffin. You were trying to say that it was a skeleton, yes?'

He nodded and held open the flap of the tent. Inside a man in a leather jacket and jeans was crouched down pointing a large and professional-looking camera at the trench across the centre of the enclosure. There was a click and a flash which brilliantly illuminated for a fraction of a second the thing which lay in the gloom at his feet.

The photographer glanced up at us as he fiddled with the mechanism. 'Last one, Guv,' he said to Green. 'Off now. Got another over on the M40. RTA. More messy than this, I dare say.'

Green went close to him, bent down and spoke briefly and fiercely. The other man looked at Jack and me again. 'Right. Sorry if I . . .' He grabbed his shiny ribbed aluminium equipment case and scuttled out.

I stared down into the pit, shining the torch which Green had slipped into my hand. There was a damp chill and the strong mushroom scent of newly dug earth. The eye sockets of the skull stared up at me. He lay there, as neatly articulated as an anatomist's demonstration. I heard Jack's voice. He was standing by my right elbow. He seemed once more on the edge of hysteria, describing how he'd completed the excavation. 'I've had lots of practice at that. Those Roman cemeteries. Almost as if I was training for it.'

I took his arm. 'Come on, little Jacko, let's leave the police to do what they have to. Where's the flask of tea I made for you this morning? The cup that cheers but not inebriates, as Mrs Pritchard used to say.'

Outside, Green motioned me aside. 'I would like to ask a few questions now, please, ma'am, so as to get clear some of the facts right from the beginning. But if your brother isn't able to . . .'

'He'll be all right in a moment, Chief Inspector. We're both as anxious as you are to find out why our father is lying out here, believe me.'

He asked us his 'few questions' in a ground-floor room in one of the old brewery buildings, which the excavation team had commandeered for a site office. We sat on filthy grey polythene stacking chairs around the laminate-topped trestle table. Jack and I faced one another at each end, and Green sat between us.

He pushed a hand over his crew-cut. It was so short that pink scalp showed through. I thought of Eliot's lines about the skull beneath the skin.

'Must be a great shock to you both, this.'

I stared at the dirt-encrusted window giving on the yard.

Jack said, his voice still sounding high-pitched with nerves, 'Of course it is. One is hardly mentally prepared to dig up one's father's grave. So can we get this over with? I really would like to go home. I've had quite enough of this place for the time being.'

'Home being The Hollies, like Miss Armitage?'

'I'm staying there temporarily.'

'I believe the deceased's widow Mrs Armitage lives there as well. I assume you'll break the news to her, but if you'd rather someone came with you . . .'

I turned back from my scrutiny of the window. 'I'll do it, not probably that there'll be much point. My mother is eighty years old. She suffers from senile dementia. Most of the time she doesn't know who I am or indeed who she is. Besides, even before her illness, she never spoke of my father to me or to anyone else. Consequently, the fact that he's now dead would hardly be of great concern to her if she possessed all her faculties.'

'I see. I'm sorry.' The policeman paused, as if uncertain

65

how to begin. Then he said, 'I gather from what Mr Armitage said earlier that your late father was last seen alive in 1956. Perhaps you could enlarge on the circumstances of his disappearance.'

I looked at Jack. He seemed dazed, his head slumped forward on to his chest, staring at the grimy top of the table in front of him.

'The point is, Chief Inspector, that he didn't disappear, as you put it. The reality was more mundane and more sordid. My father went out for his usual Sunday evening walk over the Glebe to the Trout Inn for a night-cap. He never came back. He had left his wife and family for another woman. As I said, my mother was devastated at this betrayal. We were forbidden as children even to mention his name.'

Jack's head came up sharply, his dark eyes burning in his white face. Then he burst out, 'But Liz, that isn't now the point! That didn't happen. He couldn't have run away to Paris with Teresa. He was murdered virtually on his own doorstep. All that stuff in the papers about his having been a spy, how he'd been a traitor. He couldn't have gone over to the Russians. He was already dead. It was all a misunderstanding, a ghastly mistake.'

'What are you saying? He wrote to Mother. A letter from Paris. She told us, don't you remember?'

'Of course I remember. I can't explain that. But don't you see that what's happened today has changed all that we've ever believed? We were completely wrong. I know that now. I found his body. That tells us everything.'

I wanted suddenly to kick him under the table, but he was out of reach. Father's favourite location for interrogating us about childish misdemeanours was at the breakfast table. Jack was always ready to blurt out the truth on these occasions if not given a physical reminder to keep quiet.

The policeman was looking in turns at both of us. His professional lack of expression was no doubt concealing his bafflement.

'Hold on, can we please go back to the beginning, please, sir? That student type, Bob Farmington he said his name was, who found the remains told me that you were an archaeologist in charge of an excavation. What were you looking for here?'

'The remains of a substantial Roman building, probably a villa, which I believe lies beneath the site. As a preliminary, I was re-excavating the limited dig in the Glebe which took place in 1956.'

I saw Green's pale blue eyes brighten at this. There were no flies on the Chief Inspector, that was clear. I could see him as he might have been in the classroom twenty years ago, a bright kid from a council estate, determined to get on.

'1956? When precisely did your father leave home?'

'At the end of October, only a matter of days after the excavation was completed. It's the kind of thing you remember.'

The policeman steepled his hands under his chin. 'So, may I summarise the position? Your father, Robert Armitage, apparently walks out on his wife and children at the end of October 1956. He's never seen again. Forty years later his bones are discovered by chance by his son. He is buried in the field where, before his disappearance, there had been an archaeological dig in progress, and where he was accustomed to take a stroll. The preliminary conclusion we might reach is that he was attacked on the Glebe and his body was buried in a spot where, conveniently, the earth had been already disturbed, and where further disturbance in the immediate future was highly unlikely.'

'You're forgetting the letter from Paris, Chief Inspector.'

'Ah yes, Miss Armitage. That clearly is a problem. If it was written contemporaneously by your father, then it cannot be his body which has been found. If the body is your father's, then the letter might be considered a device to convince all who knew him that he was still alive. A very successful device, it would appear. Until today.'

67

Jack said, 'So it must have been my father's murderer, or someone in league with them, who sent the letter?'

'I believe so, sir. The murderer would certainly have a strong reason to make it appear that Mr Armitage was still alive.'

'Hang on a minute, Chief Inspector,' I said, conscious that my voice was rising in pitch as it does when I'm agitated. 'All this is pure speculation, isn't it? Aren't we in danger of making a very basic and quite possibly wrong assumption? You said yourself that if the body were my father's, etc. It's very unscientific, if you don't mind my saying so. We know that there are human remains in that trench, but how do we know that they're my father's? One skeleton looks pretty much like another to me. I dare say that even your superior experience of these matters doesn't enable you to be any more definite. We don't know whether it's that of a man or a woman, or how long it's been there, except that 1956 is probably the *terminus a quo*.'

'I beg your pardon, Miss, what's that about a terminus?'

Jack, even when grief-stricken, was alert to a challenge to his learning. He jumped in before I could reply. 'Honestly, Liz. You can leave the Latin tags to me. I'm the classicist. What my sister means is that 1956 is the starting point. He couldn't have been buried before then because of the excavation. Which is obvious anyway as he wasn't dead before then. Why are you trying to baffle us with science, Liz, and undermine what's completely certain? I found his watch.'

The urge to kick him returned. 'You may think you're the classicist, Jack – not that your Latin A-level grade was any better than mine – but it seems I'm the logician. All right, so you found his watch. But that in itself is not conclusive evidence of identification of the body it was found with. It could have been someone to whom he gave or sold the watch or more likely someone who stole it from him.'

I stared at the policeman and he stared back at me.

Jack had been wriggling in his seat as I spoke. 'Lizzie, that's

68

ridiculous! If Father's watch had been stolen, don't you think we would have heard about it? And of course the idea that he would have given it away or sold it is preposterous. And anyway, I know it's Father. I felt it when I . . .'

'Be quiet, Jack. I haven't finished. OK, so even if it is him, we're still a long way from knowing how he died. There appears to be massive damage to the skull, but that might have been done after death, by agricultural work, or by an animal, a badger, say. I'm right about all this aren't I, Chief Inspector?'

He shrugged. 'I can't quarrel with any of what you say, in principle. The evidence is circumstantial at present. There can be no absolute certainty without forensic examination being carried out. But that may well take some time. I have to begin the investigation by making what appear to be reasonable assumptions. The most useful assumption, in my opinion, is that the remains are those of your father, and that his death was not due to natural causes, distressing as that may be for his family. A natural death would not surely have been concealed in so calculated a manner. At the very least, we're talking about homicide in some form.' He turned his gaze directly on me. 'I regret that it will be necessary to interview your mother in the next day or so. Perhaps you could suggest a time when that would be convenient?'

'That's quite out of the question, Chief Inspector. I told you her mental state.'

'I'd like to form my own view of that.'

To my relief, Jack finally stirred himself to think of some-one other than himself. 'That's absolutely not on. Liz is right. Mother is in no fit state for anything of that sort. It would confuse and upset her. She wouldn't have to answer any questions if she were well, never mind the way she is at present. We can provide all the information you need.'

Green shrugged. 'Maybe so. I won't press the point at this time.' He looked at his watch. 'That's all for now, I think. Thank you so much for your assistance at this distressing time.' He looked at me closely as he said this but there was no discernible irony in his voice. 'Obviously, sir, your activities on the site will have to be suspended for the time being until my colleagues have finished here. Perhaps you could inform everyone concerned. In the meantime, I'd be very grateful if you would both arrange to attend the police station in Waterbury to make formal statements confirming what you've said today.'

He stood up. Class dismissed. 'By the way, Miss Armitage, the letter your mother received from Paris is clearly very material to the investigation. I should be obliged if you would make a thorough search for it in your mother's papers.'

I nodded. 'Of course, Chief Inspector. As I said, I am most anxious to find out how my father died.'

'I kept a scrapbook, you know.'

I'd got out the gin when we had returned to The Hollies. We sat in the drawing room, the warm afternoon sun forcing slabs of yellow light through the great mullion window like cheese through the wires of a cutter. Jack was on the Knole sofa, his head thrown back and his long legs stretched before him. He'd adopted this pose as an undergraduate, having copied it from a don at his college aged enough to have had some connection with Bloomsbury.

'A scrapbook?'

'About Daddy. I made it after he . . . disappeared.'

'Did you really? I never knew. You never showed it me.'

'No. I never showed anyone. It was my special book.' I paused, seeing myself at the age of eight, at the desk in my bedroom, with tongue protruding between my teeth, as I worked on my labour of love. I said with a deliberate casualness spoiled by the tremor in my voice, 'Would you like to see it? I've got it in my room.'

He'd sat upright as I spoke. 'Very much.'

I glanced into Mother's quarters before I went upstairs. I'd sent a surprised Mrs Hargreaves home. I gave her no explanation, but no doubt the village bush telegraph, in which she was a vital link, would have already started to broadcast news of the events at the Glebe.

Mother was asleep in her easy chair, her mouth fallen open, gently snoring. A reassuring sound as it meant she was still alive. Her pale hands, the fingers bent in a curl, lay on her lap, outside the rug which covered her knees. I went over and tucked them beneath it.

I handed Jack the black leatherette-bound volume, an old-fashioned photograph album. He took it gingerly. I sat beside him as he opened it.

On the stiff black card of the first page I'd written Daddy in big curvy letters with a white crayon. I'd decorated the corners with scrolls and flowers in yellow because I hadn't had the gold I should have preferred. He turned the page. Next was a black and white portrait photograph which almost filled the space. I'd fixed it with black passepartout corners: our father in the uniform of a lieutenant commander in the Royal Navy. It had been taken, according to the note on the back, in Portsmouth in June 1944. It must have been just before his destroyer sailed for Normandy as part of the escort for the D-Day invasion force.

The picture had stood on Mother's dressing table until the day he'd left. She had thrown it into the dustbin from where I had retrieved it, gently releasing it from the smashed glass and splintered lacquered wood of its frame.

Jack slowly turned the pages. There were other photos, snapshots of the family together in the garden: teas on the lawn, wild games of rounders, him and me with my spaniel Goldilocks, who'd lived until 1962 and been buried with all due ceremony in the pets' cemetery in the shrubbery, Daddy pushing Jack on his first bicycle, Daddy and Mother standing awkwardly side by side on the terrace, posing for me and my new Kodak Brownie 127.

There was a letter from him to me:

71

My darling Lizzie,
A terribly boring office thing means I won't be able to be home to see you ride in the gymkhana on Saturday, as I'd hoped. I'm so sorry. Best of luck.
Your very loving Daddy.

There were the cards he'd sent me at birthdays and Christmas. There was a postcard of a Gloucester Old Spot sow and piglets he'd bought me in Stow-on-the-Wold when we stopped for tea after a Cotswold ramble one summer Sunday afternoon.

I stood up to pour myself another drink. With my back to him I said, 'It's the sort of thing little girls do. The last part's the worst. The newspaper cuttings. I don't think I quite realised what they were about. All I knew was they were about Daddy. That was the most important thing.'

Once again, I saw that eight-year-old at her desk, carefully snipping out the slim printed columns from *The Times*, the house's daily newspaper in those days.

I sat down beside him again and turned over the page myself.

In those days *The Times* didn't go in for banner headlines. It didn't even have news on its front page, only closely printed columns of small ads. But the discreet story inside remained as hard-hitting to me as the giant typeface of a modern tabloid.

SENIOR CIVIL SERVANT MISSING

It is reported from Whitehall that Mr Robert Armitage DSO, deputy secretary of the Board of Admiralty, has not returned to his post following weekend leave. It is understood that Mr Armitage, who is 41, and was formerly on active service in the Royal Navy with the rank of

Lieutenant Commander, has not been in communication with the department to explain his absence, nor have officials been able to contact him at his home in Oxfordshire. Mr Armitage has not apparently been unwell. He has not been suspended, and disciplinary action is not contemplated at this time.

A few days later, there had been another brief report.

QUESTION IN HOUSE CONCERNING MR ARMITAGE

Mr Addison (Kingston-upon-Hull, South, Lab.): Is the Prime Minister able to substantiate reports that Mr Robert Armitage, deputy secretary of the Board of Admiralty, has been observed entering the Soviet Embassy in Paris?
Prime Minister: I am aware of these reports, but the honourable member will know that I am unable to comment on matters relating to national security.

I knew from what I had heard much later that the Soviet Embassy story had been splashed over the newspapers for several days. 1956 was a year of horrors for what was then, however misguidedly, still referred to as the British Empire. The Cold War was becoming entrenched in the popular psyche. The country was still reeling from the defections only a few years earlier of the Foreign Office officials Burgess and Maclean, and journalists were all too eager, then as now, to exploit their readers' credulity.

But there were no more such items for my scrapbook.

Mother had cancelled *The Times* and I was forbidden to listen to the Home Service news on the wireless.

Jack looked up from the final page in astonishment. 'I never knew you had collected this stuff.'

I shrugged. 'I felt I had to. Mother wouldn't talk. After she got the letter, she stayed in her room, crying, for days. You weren't here, remember. You were sent back to school.'

'It was bad enough there. I didn't tell you about it. But the prefects made my life a misery. They called him a traitor. "How does it feel to be a traitor's son, Armitage?" I got yelled at in the quad. "What's the news from Moscow, Armitage?" What could I say? That my father wasn't a traitor, he'd merely run off with another woman? I hated him so much, you know. The awful humiliation, the weakness of it. And now . . .'

'And now, everything is changed. I keep thinking of how he died. Beaten to death and buried in a ditch.'

'So you think it is him buried there?'

I stared at him. 'Why do you say that?'

'Come off it, Liz! You gave the copper the third degree. Just play-acting was it?'

I didn't reply, but carefully folded the album and set it on the table in front of us.

'They can prove it, you know. Lots of ways. Teeth. DNA. Soon there won't be any doubt. The forensic boys will be crawling all over the site for evidence. There was really no need to try to confuse the issue. It merely draws attention to what you were attempting to conceal.'

'And what was that?'

'Don't go all wide-eyed innocent, Liz. It doesn't work. Not with me. And not with that copper either. He may look like a twerp, but he's sharp enough. He reminds me of one of the nastier specimens of warder at the Farebrother who mugged up bits of Roman history, and then asked me questions about it, trying to trip me up, the pillock.'

'So what is it that he's going to catch me out on? I'm

not being innocent, Jack. I really don't know what you mean.'

He laughed, shaking his head until a stray lock of hair flopped down over his forehead. He pushed it back, his gaze suddenly serious.

'This isn't a game, Liz. Not one of your plays. I remember how good an actress you were. You might have been able to fool one of the old-style forelock-touching Oxford plods, but not these new types. Green isn't one generation from the plough. He's an urban prole. Dragged himself out of some shit housing estate like Blackbird Leys. Passed his exams, knows all the answers. One of the things he knows is that most murders in this country are domestic. He won't easily be shifted from his view that Father's isn't any exception. Then he can write his report, close his file, move on to something a bit higher profile, more likely to get him the super's job he's desperate for. Drugs or armed robbery.'

'And you think we should let him do that? Do you want Mother plastered over every tabloid in the country? You can see the headlines: Is she a murderer? Did sweet old lady bash in husband's skull in jealous rage? There won't be a damned thing we can do about it. I have to live in this village, Jack. How do you think life's going to be when that gets out? Will Mrs Hargreaves want to go on nursing Mother if she's virtually accused of murder? Who else is going to take her place?'

'They'll be queuing up for the opportunity. To them it'll be like something out of *Psycho*. Brighten up their boring lives.'

'Now who's treating it like a game? You can waltz off, Jack, having caused all this devastation, just as you always did. I get the pieces to pick up.'

'I don't think that any of that will happen. Neither Green nor his Chief Constable will want the publicity. They won't want to be seen to be pointing the finger, with no evidence, at the helpless widow. They'll bury the matter in a file once

75

they've gone through the motions. Everybody's a politician these days. Looking to their image, and the size of their dollop when the gravy train calls. But whatever you do, you won't be able to stop him personally drawing what are, after all, the obvious conclusions.'

'What are you saying, Jack? That Mother murdered Father? How can you even think such a thing?'

'I don't want to think it. Christ Almighty, of course I don't. But there isn't anyone else. No one else had a motive. You have to think back forty years, Liz. Mother wasn't then a weak, crazed old woman. She was formidable. She'd been brought up with a sense of her position in the world. She wouldn't want to be thrown over for another woman. Particularly a foreigner. She'd fight back.'

'Precisely, Jack. Why should Mother kill the person one would have expected her to want to hold on to? To murder Father would have brought her the worst of everything – as indeed it did. She lost out in a big way. In those days, people weren't so forgiving of the kind of scandal that blew up. The whole idea is ludicrous. Mother was a sane member of the English middle class, not a . . .'

Agitated by my train of thought, I got up out of my chair, and went over to the drawing room window. It looked south-west over the lawn which Jack had so painstakingly begun to recreate. On the far edge was the shrubbery. The laurel and cotoneasters, fire-thorn, sumach, viburnum and potentilla planted in Grandfather's day were massively overgrown, the winding paths between the clumps where we had played as children, even in those days impassable to adults, had now vanished completely. It was a jungle for foxes, and home to a colonising tribe of semi-feral cats composed of throw-outs from the neighbouring council housing estate. Over it towered the hundred foot or so of the Wellingtonia, old even in Grandfather's day.

I heard Jack getting out of his seat. Then I felt his hands on my shoulders.

'What is it, Liz? You're trembling. What was it you were about to say?'

'It's obvious, isn't it? Mother couldn't have murdered him. But someone else could. She went through the war. You remember those hints. I bet what she didn't know about killing wasn't worth knowing.'

'Christ, you mean Teresa.'

'Of course. Maybe he said he wasn't going to go away with her after all. Maybe they had an argument. She could have done it – and she could have sent the letter from Paris afterwards. She would have known about how to obtain forged papers. A letter in Father's handwriting would have been child's play compared with documents intended to fool the Nazis.'

There was genuine anguish in Jack's voice as he burst out, 'Not Teresa. She would never have done that. I don't believe she could have been capable of such a thing. Not someone she must have loved. In the war, she might have, but not afterwards.'

'You're very tender hearted all of a sudden, considering you've just made it clear you could imagine your own mother as a murderer.'

'For Christ's sake, Liz. I don't know what to think. I don't know anything any more. Don't you feel as if everything you think you've known for the past forty years has sort of dissolved? Suddenly we're talking about the guilt or innocence of the people we knew and loved. I keep thinking that it's a betrayal of them to think like that. But then there's Father lying rotting in the cold earth of that field for all that time. I have a duty to him as well. I hated him for ruining my childhood. But that hatred was completely mistaken. Perhaps he never meant to abandon us. He might have stayed and everything would have been all right.'

The last words were sobbed out and once more we hugged each other. I shut my eyes tightly with the fierceness of a child shutting out the terrors of the enfolding night.

★ ★ ★

Later, after a supper of cold leftovers, we strolled around the old orchard in the gathering dusk.

There was a chill in the air. I wore a heavy wool sweater and my waxed jacket, Jack, his awful leather coat which he'd just had back from the menders, after he had with typical carelessness ripped it on a tree branch.

He had picked up a stick and swished at the long grass, the sweet dewy smell of it heady with the memory of summers long ago.

We came to the wooden five-barred gate which looked out over the paddock, now empty, where the New Forest pony we both rode as small children had been kept. Neither of us had been keen on riding, and the animal had been sold. I usually let the field for grass-keep in the summer, but this year there had been no takers.

Jack leaned on the top-rail and said, 'When I came back here, I was amazed by how big it still seemed, how much land there is. You expect places you've known as a child to seem small in comparison to how they appeared to you then.'

'I used to think of it as an island, like the Neverland, in Peter Pan. I'd lie awake at night, listening to the wind in the trees. I pretended that the waves were beating on the shore, that on the other side of a bay, a pirate ship was riding at anchor. I would plan the adventures we would have when you came home from school in the holidays. I missed you in those days, Jack.'

'I know. I hated prep school. I wanted to be at home, like William and the Outlaws. I wanted to climb trees, to camp out at night, to light fires and stay up late. I looked forward so much to the holidays. To being here with you and Mother and Father. I never realised then how much things could change.'

'We were playing in the woods, that summer – the summer before Father . . . went away. Do you remember? That's how we met Teresa.'

'Of course I remember. For years afterwards, I thought it was all my fault. If I hadn't . . .'

'You couldn't have known. We just didn't know in those days that that kind of thing could happen. Not with parents.'

'And now I've dug up all that buried past again, Liz. Like some terrible beast in a fairy story. I've woken it up again. This is only the beginning.'

The shadowed vista of grass and trees blurred with my tears as the memories flooded back. I wept for all that had been and all that could now never be. Jack put his arm around my shoulders and we walked back silently to the house, the path we trod flanked by swathes of narcissi. In the spring they had gleamed like fallen stars. Now the stems were leaning, the flowers dead and shrivelled.

I collected the album from the drawing room before I went up. Jack was sitting with a bottle of whisky, the room lit only by the television screen, on which was the face of the presenter of the late news programme.

When he saw what I was doing, he said, 'I've been thinking. To do that,' he pointed at the volume under my arm. 'It's as if you'd believed you'd never see him again.'

'That's the difference between us. You were angry with him, hating him, hating even to hear his name mentioned. I never was. I wanted to remember the good times.'

'But that's what I mean. It's not just a scrapbook. It's like a memorial. It's as if, even as a child, you thought he was dead.'

That night I lay awake for a long time, watching the events of forty years before, as if they were projected, like a home-movie, on to my bedroom wall.

There was I, eight years old, dressed in what I fondly imagined to be a likeness of Tiger Lily, in a old brown curtain from the tin steamer trunk in the playroom where the dressing-up stuff lived, a crow feather stuck in a cardboard band around my forehead. Jack had but recently returned home from school for the summer holidays, but discarded with a vengeance was the capped, blazered and short-trousered apparition which had emerged amid puffs of steam from the grimy maroon carriage on to the down platform of Waterbury railway station.

He wore an ancient pair of Father's bags, cut down and held up with knotted twine, voluminous enough to suggest a cowboy's chaps, an equally ancient Viyella check shirt, and a black felt Stetson which Father had bought him at Hamleys of Regent Street. In his hand, he brandished an alarmingly realistic shiny chrome toy pistol he'd bought himself at Woolworths in Oxford.

He chased me through the shrubbery into the spinney beyond, whooping wildly and firing off caps. I ran dodging overhanging branches and ensnaring undergrowth. I was laughing and shrieking, so excited by the chase that before I knew it, I had charged through a gap between two young beeches, over the rotten timbers of the boundary fence and was out of the wood and into the lane beyond.

I was too late to stop myself from cannoning into the person who was walking along the grass verge. Startled, we disengaged and stood back to look at each other. She was a tall woman, with long black hair spread over the collar of her wide-shouldered grey trench-coat.

'Sorry,' I panted. 'Didn't see you. Jack – he's my brother, he was chasing me, you see and . . .'

'Do not worry, it is quite all right. An accident.'

Even to my childish ears, her accent sounded odd. Not local, not even English. Foreign.

From the wood came the crack of a cap being fired. My new acquaintance flinched and a shadow of fear crossed her very pale high-cheek-boned face. I was about to explain what it was when to a shout of 'Where are you, Lizard?' Jack crashed out of the trees, his face flushed and his eyes flashing. I saw her stiffen in shock, as she beheld the shiny thing in his hand.

Jack saw it too, and with the casual cruelty of the small boy, he took advantage of it. He pointed the gun at her. 'You're on my land, stranger,' he rasped in an imitation of the voices we heard in the B movie Westerns we had watched at matinees in the Majestic cinema in Waterbury. 'Hands up! You're my prisoner, come right along and no tricks!'

The woman's apparent alarm was now under control once more. She raised her hands, at the same time brushing back a tress which had fallen forward over her face. She smiled a radiant smile, which reached beyond her full-lipped mouth and into her fine wide-apart dark eyes. I suddenly realised that she was extraordinarily beautiful. 'Where to, please?' she asked in that richly suggestive and mysterious foreign voice.

Under its spell, Jack ceased to be the aggressive urchin and became the embarrassed prep-school pupil. He stuffed the revolver away in his pocket. 'Sorry, I was being silly. Lizard always says I get sort of carried away.' His downcast face brightened and in recollection of the social graces they were no doubt attempting to din into him at school, he asked shyly, by way of making amends, 'I should like it awfully if you came to tea.'

Our mother was amazed to see us marching up to the front door with our companion. When she heard the story of our meeting, she was fulsome in her apologies. 'I don't know what I've done to deserve two such dreadful children. Jack, your father will have to speak to you very sternly when he gets back. We can't have you careering round the countryside acting like a highwayman. Now you really must stay to tea, Miss . . . That is if we haven't convinced you that we are a pack of savages.'

She held out her hand to Mother. 'My name is Teresa Korzeniowska. I am from Poland. I am very pleased to make your acquaintance, Mrs Armitage. And I beg you do not cause my friend Jack to be punished on my account. He is a most charming young man. And I would never have known that the ambush is not an English custom.'

A little later my father came home.

Was it then that it had happened? Had the spark between them been ignited over the tea-tray – the gold-rimmed Spode teapot filled with the strong Indian tea which Father bought at Jacksons of Piccadilly?

Why not? Jack and I had each fallen in love with her that day, as we confessed to each other in the lamp-lit darkness of the playroom later that evening. Even Mother, at first, coolly polite in the English way – 'Do have some more fruit-cake, Miss Korzeniowska' – succumbed to her lambent beauty and her husky-voiced charm.

Teresa came to Sunday afternoon tea on several occasions in the weeks which followed. She was living in Waterbury, and working in a factory making potted meats. She clearly disliked this menial work – in her own country, she told us, she had been well-educated, and, but for the war, would have gone to the university in Krakow, to study law, like her father.

The war had changed everything. She had been sent out of Poland before the German invasion, to relatives in Paris. Her parents had stayed behind, despite the inevitability of defeat. The fall of France had made her flee once more, and she had managed to get out to North Africa, and from there to Portugal and finally to London. In London she had contacted the Polish Government in exile, and as she was young and fit, spoke both French and German fluently, and was desperate to pay back the Nazis for what they had done to her country, she had manoeuvred herself into the Free Polish Forces and from there into SOE, the British organisation which sent agents into Occupied Europe to co-ordinate resistance to the invaders, to supply weapons and commit acts of sabotage.

She was reluctant to enlarge on this, to us, almost impossibly thrilling aspect of her life. She hinted at having seen and done things, in the cause of freedom, which now horrified her. In that reticence, she resembled my father, who rarely opened up to us on his exploits in the Navy, saying that to him it was not appropriate to turn a conflict in which so many of his friends were dead or maimed into an exciting story for children.

Despite my father's warnings, Jack and I both regretted that we had been born too late. In Jack's *Lion* comic, the war was portrayed as a kind of bloodless cricket match played by clean-cut Englishmen against bumbling foreigners, with unthreatening, childish nicknames like Hun or Jerry, forever crying out 'Achtung Englander!' We had grown up on this heady mixture of nostalgia and propaganda, intended to maintain the high of victory, and to conceal what the price of that victory had been.

Teresa changed all that. She had brought to me an indelible sense of the horror and of the destructiveness of war, the equal bitterness of winning and losing.

For Teresa, an inhabitant of the country on whose behalf the war had ostensibly begun, and who had been on the victorious side, had lost everything. Her family was dead. She hated the Russians as much as the Germans, and could not return to Poland while they were in control. As a foreigner amidst the petty prejudice of England, she was condemned to do work below her true capability. But still she radiated health and confidence and beauty.

In those few weeks, she had influenced me greatly, endowing me, I believed, with some of her indomitable spirit.

Forty years later, I still could not hate her, could not believe she was responsible for my father's death, even though she might have been capable of it. Why would she, of all people, have killed him? What had happened that night? Had she waited long dark hours for a lover who never arrived? Had she, wherever she was, spent the intervening years wondering? Had she read of the discovery in the Glebe, and did she too weep for her loss? Or had she died and never known the truth?

If my father's bones could speak, what would they tell us?

At whom would his skeletal finger point? And what name would emerge from his lipless mouth?

The reporters had laid siege to The Hollies. There were half a dozen or so in a kind of encampment on the little green at the end of the driveway. There they lay in wait, drinking beer, or made occasional forays into the shrubbery and the copse to snitch photographs of the house and garden.

Linda had reluctantly given me leave of absence until the fuss had died down. Then, at last, one morning, we awoke to find the encampment deserted. It was all over. The moving fingers had writ, and having writ had moved on. The caravan had departed, leaving only empty beer cans and sandwich wrappings to mark its passing. The Crowcester mystery, while still as mysterious, was no longer news.

We too had to progress. Daddy's remains were still undergoing forensic examination, so there was to be no funeral yet. In the absence of that more usual catharsis, the disappearance of both the media circus and the police presence on the Glebe, together with my return to school on the following Monday, provided the necessary occasion for a feast to celebrate the departed. That Saturday evening, Jack and I went out to dinner together in Oxford.

I booked us a table for eight thirty. I allowed forty-five minutes for the drive and parking, so by a quarter to eight I was waiting in the hall with coat on, having settled Mrs Hargreaves in front of the television. Of Jack, ominously, there was no sign.

I'd seen him through the drawing room window earlier that afternoon, as I sat there marking Year 10 essays on 'The character of Brutus' which Helen Sanderson, my deputy in the English department, had brought round on her way in that morning. He was heading out through the walled garden. He hadn't stayed long in the village, because the front door had slammed about an hour later and I heard his heavy tread on the stairs.

Since then there had been silence. Had he forgotten? Or had he been drinking himself blotto in his room? Irritated, I ran up and knocked loudly on his door.

'Jack? Are you ready? We have to be there by half past.'

No answer.

I tried the door but it was locked. This time I really hammered on the panel. 'Jack, for crying out loud!'

There was a stirring and a scuffling from within the room, then a drowsy voice, 'That you, Liz? What do you want?'

'Jack, open the door!'

I heard the key turn, and he pulled the door open, supporting himself on the jamb with one hand whilst the other rubbed sleep out of his eyes. He looked a mess, his face white and puffy, his grizzled hair standing on end, barefoot and clad only in a T-shirt and boxer shorts.

'Do you know what the time is, Jack? We're going out together, remember?'

'Oh yes. I was taking a nap. What's the matter? Plenty of time. Not catching a plane, are we?'

'They may not hold the table and . . .'

'Christ, this is like being married. Stop worrying about the blasted restaurant, Liz. Go down, have a drink, and I'll be with you.'

'I can't drink. We agreed I'd drive.'

'All right, mark a few more essays, then.'

He closed the door in my face, and I was reduced to watching some stupid soap with Mrs Hargreaves for fifteen minutes until he bounced down the stairs, and appeared at the drawing room door, his hair damp and darkly glistening from the shower, in a dark blue suit.

'Hello, Mrs H. Come on, Liz, no time for you to watch that till the end. You can catch up tomorrow, eh?'

Despite Jack's insouciance, the restaurant was actually very full, mainly of university types, judging from the snatches of conversation about research grants and fellowships I over-heard as we were shown to our table.

Jack settled himself in with a bottle of claret. I stuck to mineral water.

The atmosphere in the car had been chilly. Now that we were here, I felt a little more relaxed. But not totally.

'Anything to say to me, Jack?'

'Me? It was you who were in a huff.'

'You were late. I can't bear to be late. You know that – or at any rate you used to know it.'

'One forgets.'

'You forget, Jack.'

'You're right, I do. Some things. But not others. Like you. You've remembered lots of little things, but today you forgot one big thing. I wasn't going to remind you, not today when we're up to our necks in memories. But I shall remind you. What's one more memory?'

'What are you talking about, Jack?'

He poured another glass of wine. 'I'm talking about 30 June 1976.'

'Oh my God. Twenty years ago today. I'm sorry, Jack.' I reached out and took his hand. 'I really had forgotten.'

'I wish I could forget the day I killed the woman I loved. Dear God, I've tried often enough.'

His voice was quiet, but even in the noise and bustle of the restaurant it seemed that everyone would hear him. 'Jack, I'm really very sorry. That's why, this afternoon you were . . .'

'I wasn't pissed. I'd taken a couple of pills. Nothing too heavy, but they knock me out for a bit. Before that I'd gone to the church. I sat in a pew and mumbled a few words. I know there's no one there, but somehow the saying it helps. Every year, I do the same. Wherever I happen to be. That's the good thing about churches, isn't it? Always one handy, like petrol stations. I say the same thing. To Fiona. Forgive me. Forgive me for robbing you of life.'

'Oh Jack.'

'The worst thing was that Fiona was pregnant. Did you know? It showed up on the post-mortem. So I killed both of them because I was too pissed to drive and too bloody arrogant to admit it. Perhaps I should have taken a few more pills this afternoon. Solved things, wouldn't it?'

'I don't think so.'

'Maybe not. But ever since then, I've sometimes felt as if my life hasn't really belonged to me. I've gone through the motions, but it's been like watching a film. As if I'd died in that car wreck, as I should have done. At the very least, I should have been punished. You should have let me go to gaol, Liz.'

'For God's sake, keep your voice down. What good is it to go through it all again, reproaching yourself? It won't bring her back. And what good would it have been to destroy your own life as well as hers? I did what I did because I thought it was best. Do you think I didn't for years have nightmares about it too? It's on my conscience as well. I had to make a choice, and I chose to save you, Jack. And, by God, I'd do it again. I'd kill for you if I had to.'

He stared at me, as if taken aback by my fierceness. 'I believe you would, Liz. I know you did what you thought was best. I went along with it. I should never have gone on blaming you.'

'If you've really forgiven me, then maybe you could forgive yourself.'

'Maybe.'

The arrival of the food brought a temporary end to the conversation. By the time it resumed, after we had taken our first appreciative mouthfuls, the mood had altered.

Jack looked at once brighter. He waved a cheerful arm to order another bottle.

I said, 'So what are we going to do now?'

'Do? About what?' Jack paused in the act of raising his glass to his lips.

87

'About Daddy's murder of course.'

He looked surprised. 'There's nothing we can do. We should leave it to the police to deal with.'

'What about what you were saying the other day about your duty to him?'

He pressed his hand to his forehead and closed his eyes. The black mood seemed about to return. But when he withdrew his hand, he was smiling, albeit wanly.

'I've thought about that over the last few days while we've been cooped up in The Hollies. Father's death on the Glebe means that he couldn't have sent a letter from Paris. If Mother didn't receive such a letter, then why did she tell us she had? If she lied about that because she had some hand in his death, then, frankly, Liz, I don't want to know. If she really did receive the letter, then only Teresa could have sent it. That surely implicates her. They must at least have been having an affair: if not, then why did she never reappear, if only to offer sympathy? All that spy stuff was all over the papers. Even if she'd moved away, she would have seen it. The fact that she stayed away surely indicates that something was going on. But what? Even if the police can trace Teresa, she's not going to answer any questions. After all this time, there's no proof without a confession. There's nothing to be done, Liz. We can't resurrect our childhood. Mother is too far gone to know or care. Teresa must be in her seventies, even assuming she's still alive. Father might well have died by now of natural causes. For forty years, he's been out of our lives. There's no reason to change all that. Time itself has worked its own justice.'

'It sounds very neat and logical, Jack. But do you really not want to know the truth? Your father's character is blackened, unjustly. He's murdered and thrown into a ditch. Doesn't that make you want to find out why and make sure whoever did it is punished?'

'Frankly I'd be more intellectually engaged if I'd discovered a Roman burial.'

I almost slapped his face as he sat there, his hand reaching for yet another slurp of wine. 'Jack! How can you sit there getting pissed and say that sort of thing. Your own father.'

'What am I supposed to say, "I with wings as swift as meditation or the thoughts of love may sweep to my revenge"? Come off it, Liz. This is England, not Elsinore. Father's dead, nothing can undo that.'

'So you're not going to help me, Jack?'

'To dig around the circumstances of Father's death? No, I'm not. And if you have any sense, neither will you.'

'You want the police to close the file with the conclusion that Mother killed Daddy? That's what's going to happen.'

'I already told you. They would have no proof. They couldn't ever say so publicly. Who really cares?'

'That's not how you feel about Fiona, is it? There you're determined to punish yourself for ever. Twenty years. Why can't time work its own justice there?'

He sighed. 'As I was trying to say, my relationship with my father doesn't have the same intensity. I'm not Hamlet. Rightly or wrongly, my emotions are no longer engaged. When I found his skeleton, and particularly the watch, I had a sudden outrush of feelings. You saw what they did to me. But they haven't been sustained. Like a flood, they've washed everything away. But with Fiona, the emotion is altogether different. It isn't a residual sense of loss. It's a burning pain. It's the sense of might have been which makes it so. I've never found happiness with another woman. God knows there have been plenty of them. My career is in ruins. If I died there would be nothing. Nothing I could leave behind to show that I had existed. No child, no posterity. Even the humblest has that.'

I stared into the flame of the candle burning in its glass prison, my mind caught like a moth by what he had said. 'Posterity. We don't have much luck with that, do we? The last of the Armitages.' I pretended to sneeze, then scrabbled around in my handbag for a hanky. I blew hard, then bent down to return the bag to the floor.

I felt a light touch on the hand which remained on the table top, and when I sat straight again in my chair, I saw that Jack's big paw was resting on mine.

He smiled his crooked smile and said, 'I know what that was about.'

'Do you, Jack?'

'Yes, I do. You're just as good at punishing yourself as I am, aren't you?'

'What do you mean?'

'You know. No one except you wants you to stay with Mother in that ghastly old prison of a house. It's your choice, Liz. It's your penance. But don't you think it's gone on far too long? Give it up, Liz, before it's too late to enjoy the time you've got. None of us know how long that will be.'

'We had this conversation the day you came back. You know I could never move Mother out of her home. It would kill her.'

'Maybe it would, maybe it wouldn't. In any case, if all you have to live for is a crummy room in The Hollies, it's not much of a life. And you don't know any longer whether that is what she does want. But to have both of you incarcerated in that charnel house is dreadful.'

'It's our family home, Jack. We were happy there.'

'Were we? I was sent off to school when I was eight. After that I was only there in the holidays. Yes, there were good times. But mostly I remember Mother on those nights before I had to go back to school telling me to grow up and be a man when all I wanted was to be hugged and cry my eyes out like a little boy.'

'It was hard for her. She had to be a mother and a father.'

'It was hard for us. It was made hard for us. That's why you jumped into bed with the first man who said he loved you.'

'No, you're wrong there. He wasn't the first. And he never

mentioned love.' I couldn't hold back the tears any longer. 'The miscarriage was my fault, Jack. I killed my child through my own stupid ignorance, selfishness and carelessness. I didn't know about looking after myself. I thought I could go on doing everything, succeeding at everything. I didn't realise a human life is so vulnerable, so easily lost.' I had never talked to him or anyone else like this, and the weight on my heart felt as if it were a boat lifting with an incoming tide.

He moved close and put his arm around me. 'Let it go, Liz. It's all over. Let it all go.'

'I don't know, Jack. I don't know whether I can.'

'Nor do I.'

We didn't speak as I drove us home that evening. Jack stared out of the passenger window as the fields, copses and hedgerows of the peaceful Oxfordshire countryside glided past, blanched by the moonlight, quiet under the summer stars. Was he, as I was, reliving that car journey of twenty years before beneath the same clear sky?

That Sunday, Jack, Fiona and I had walked all day on the Cotswold hills around Chipping Campden. It was during that ramble that I had a long talk with Fiona. She told me that Jack had asked her to marry him. She hadn't given him a definite answer. She loved him, but she needed to be sure. And there was something else, she said, after a little hesitation. Something she had not told a soul, not even Jack. I could perhaps guess what it was? I nodded, the familiar feelings mounting within me, much as I tried to force them down. She had been certain for only a couple of days. But it was Jack's child, she assured me. There was no doubt of that whatever. She was going to tell him before she accepted his proposal. She had been looking for the right moment the whole weekend.

Jack had seen us talking and guessed the subject, part of it. He insisted that instead of going home, we had dinner together to, as he put it, celebrate their unofficial engagement. We did celebrate, in Jack's usual lavish style, in the Lygon Arms at Broadway, one of England's finest restaurants.

I'd made a point of holding back on the booze, so Jack and Fiona had between them drunk most of the four bottles of wine and champagne we had ordered, as well as several gins and tonics in the bar before dinner. In the car park, I demanded the keys of the Bentley Continental he drove in those days.

He refused, saying he wouldn't let anyone else touch his car. He said he was perfectly capable, and if we didn't like it, we could go home in a cab. We argued but he was adamant. Fiona, who was herself fairly smashed, said she wasn't going to hang around waiting for a cab to arrive. It was hardly Piccadilly Circus, was it? She plonked herself firmly in the front seat.

Many times since, I'd tormented myself with what I could have done. Forced Jack to hand over the keys? Dragged Fiona out of the car? Remembered to make her do up her seat belt? What I did do was to climb into the back.

For several miles, Jack drove in his usual fast but competent way. He and Fiona chatted and I began to relax. Then, after Chipping Norton, he started to complain about being dazzled by oncoming cars. I suddenly felt sick and tense again. I asked him to stop and take a breather or let me drive. He told me to fuck off.

Jack always insisted to me that it was the lorry which was over the centre line of the road, and that, blinded by its headlights, he had had to swerve. I remember only a flaring whiteness filling the car and Fiona screaming. There was a splintering crash as we smashed through a post-and-rail fence bordering the road, a horrible jolting as we careered across a field, then the final devastating impact as we hit a tree in the spinney beyond. I was thrown forward heavily against the driver's seat and on to the floor – the car had no rear seat belts. I must have blacked out for a moment.

I came to and struggled out, dimly conscious of pain and dizziness in my head, and a numb stiffness in my right shoulder and arm. The moon, shining through the black branches of the tree, dappled the grasses of the woodland floor with silver. The dreadful stillness was broken only intermittently by the sounds of vehicles travelling at speed on the road a hundred yards away, oblivious of the accident.

One of the car headlights was still working. In its light, made ghastly by the steam rising from the smashed radiator, I could see that Jack was pushing to open the driver's door. I yanked at it with my left hand and together we got it open. He was cut about the face, but otherwise unhurt, as far as I could gather. He had been wearing his seat belt. I screamed at him that we had to get Fiona out. The car might catch fire. His look told me everything.

I clambered in behind the wheel. She had been thrown forward against the dashboard. I reached across and touched her neck but could feel no pulse. I put my arm around her and pulled her gently back into the seat, but her head lolled to one side. Her exposed cheek and neck shone blinding white under the moon, and dark blood had trickled from a place on her forehead thankfully hidden by a fallen curtain of black hair.

I remember shouting at him. Selfish, stupid bastard! Why the hell hadn't he made sure she had done up her seat belt? But I could have asked myself the same question. Jack was beyond words. As when we were children, I had to do the thinking for him. And all I could think of was that somehow something had to be saved from this mess.

Then I knew what had to be done. I turned to him. 'Get her into the driving seat. Now, before someone comes.'

He started to protest, but I yelled at him. 'She's dead. You've killed her! Do you want to go to prison? Because that's where you'll go.'

It was a hard and sickening tussle to drag her limp body

across the transmission tunnel and seat her in front of the steering wheel. As I helped him with my left arm, the pain began to throb and pulsate in my right. Finally we had managed it. Then together we staggered back to the road and flagged down a car.

I had worried that Jack would not be able to stick to our story, but some deep instinct of self-preservation must have operated. Although the police clearly did not believe us – Fiona's injuries were not entirely consistent with her having been the driver – there was nothing they could do about it, as no witnesses came forward to contradict us.

I had saved Jack, but he had despised me for it. In return, I had hated him, because I also had loved Fiona. Until now, I had blocked the memory of that night from my conscious mind, reliving it only as an occasional shapeless sweating terror waiting in the vast ocean of sleep to grasp at me from the depths.

As I negotiated the potholed drive of The Hollies, and its great obscure bulk, relieved only by the yellow chinks of light around the drawing room curtains where Mrs Hargreaves waited upon our return, reared up against the starry sky, for a moment I wished passionately, so passionately that it was almost a prayer, that my brother had never returned to reopen these wounds long sutured by passing time.

In the days when my mother had been the leading light of every charitable and voluntary activity in North Oxfordshire, she had used the dressing room adjoining the big front bedroom – which was always known semi-facetiously as her boudoir – as her base of operations. If, as I doubted, she had kept the letter purporting to be from my father in Paris, it would be in here.

The room had been left virtually as it had been on the first day of her illness, the last day of her normal life. At the beginning I or Mrs Hargreaves had gone in from time to time to open the window, and give it a dusting. But that had been a long time ago, when there was still hope – however illusory – that Mother would recover. Since then it had been neglected, apart from occasional visits of inspection, like the outpost of a crumbling empire. Other than to find and remove such things as her cheque-books and building society account books when it became clear that she was never going to manage her own affairs again, I had refrained until now from investigating this last sanctuary of Mother as she had once been. The ghost of Mother's intensely private personality had kept it guarded. Until now. But now more inexorable forces than ghosts were in motion.

I opened the door of the room. I had to push it hard as it was stuck in the frame. Inside, it felt chilly despite the mild day outside and sunlight which slanted through the tall sash window. There was a musty smell of damp, and I glanced up to see tell-tale patches on the ceiling and stains on the chimney breast where the roof had leaked.

There, still in an old mahogany bookcase, were old-fashioned box files containing her voluminous correspondence relating to the Mothers Union, the WVS, the Red Cross, the Haig Fund, the Parish Council, and dozens of others. At the massive bureau, she had sat writing in her stately copperplate. As a very small child I had sometimes played there at her feet, tracing with my finger the faded figures in the ancient Persian rug.

Mother always locked the top of the desk and the four drawers. I had followed her example ten years ago, the last occasion I had had access to it, replacing the key under a Staffordshire dog figurine on the right of the small marble mantelpiece, the survivor of a pair which had once been installed in the drawing room, the other having been pur-loined and broken by Jack with a catapult, the incident having confined him to his room for a whole day of the precious summer holidays.

I lifted the heavy porcelain, took the small, slightly rusted steel key and turned it stiffly in the lock. I pulled down the heavy wooden flap, lined with green leather, much worn and cracked. Out wafted the pungent scent of camphor wood and old paper. There were the usual rows of pigeon holes, filled with folded bundles. Cheque-book stubs, bank statements, counterfoils from share dividends. Hundreds of old bills from long defunct tradesmen. I unfolded one at random. In the apologetic tone of a deferential age, Messrs A. Jones & Sons, Purveyors of Quality Groceries, of The High Street, Crowcester enquired as to whether they might be permitted to present their account to Mrs Armitage for the month of August 1951. There were piles of similar stuff. Electricity. Coal. Rates. Of interest only to someone in Jack's line of business. When some cataclysm of history had buried them in dust and ashes, they would be unearthed to cast their unreliable light on the everyday life of a mid-twentieth-century middle-class household.

I unlocked the drawers one by one. There were piles of personal letters from friends and relations. To the names of some of the correspondents, I could fit a faint memory of a face or an occasion. Others, I recalled only as weddings or funerals. There were Christmas and birthday cards, kept for the messages they contained. There were the letters which Jack, no doubt under compulsion, had written every week from prep school. I laughed as I read the childish scrawl. 'I hurt my leg at rugger yesterday it has got a plaster but I am alright. Matron said I was v. brave.'

There too were the infrequent missives he had despatched as an adult, from Oxford. And a pile of picture postcards from his days of fieldwork and travel. A feast of ruins. Rome. Palmyra. Leptis Magna. Pompeii.

And then there were my letters. From Girl Guide camp, from my pre-university stay in Aix-en-Provence. I hurried over this embarrassingly adolescent philosophising – 'Art is what gives meaning to Life' – had I really believed that, capital letters and all?

Then there were the ones I had written from the university,

full of my petty triumphs, the alpha double pluses for my essays, the plaudits for my acting in the Drama Society's 'The White Devil' cut from the student newspaper – 'Liz Armitage's Vittoria Corombona, an astonishingly mature performance of unrepentant sexuality, drags Webster out of the library and into Hollywood.'

That was when I thought the world lay at my feet. Too bad my mind had been so full of art and literature it had no space for biology. My hands flew involuntarily to my middle, and I groaned with the memory of pain and loss. I remembered my mother's face, white and strained, tight-lipped, vengeful as a Fury. 'Who is this man, Elizabeth? Tell me and I shall force him to do the decent thing by you.'

When I refused, she decided that he must be already married and that I was protecting him out of a misplaced sense of loyalty. Her anger was turned on me. 'If you can't or won't get married, then you must get rid of it. There's a new law now. It can be arranged. I'll talk to Dr Phillips today.' When I had refused that also, she had spun on her heel and slammed out of my room, and we had scarcely spoken for weeks.

It was only after I woke up, festooned with tubes, in the Radcliffe where I had been rushed after collapsing that morning in the bathroom, to see my mother weeping at my bedside, abandoned to her emotion in a way I had scarcely seen her before, that the rift was healed. She laid her cold hand on mine. 'Dear Elizabeth. I thought I had lost you. They said that left any longer, you would have bled to . . .'

I smiled weakly. 'You always told me I came from tough stock.'

She nodded tearfully. 'That's true. You take after me. The Astons. We're survivors. Whatever fate throws our way.' Suddenly her eyes were distant, as if she were no longer thinking of me. 'However we are misled and betrayed, we have to keep going. That is the English way, you know.'

I shook myself out of reminiscence and dried my tears.

The last drawer, the bottom, stuck as I tried to pull it out. It was crammed with thick brown manila envelopes. Maybe here there would be some trace of the man she had been married to. But there was nothing of his. She must have destroyed all their correspondence in the days after he had left, the way she had torn his photographs from the family albums, only the ones I had kept or retrieved myself had escaped the inferno.

Instead there were only more wads of old papers, going back to Grandfather's time, when Mother had taken over the running of the house and its affairs, and the old man had spent his time pottering in the conservatory, and pondering the writing of his memoirs, which, however, had not progressed to burden posterity. There were solicitors' letters relating to land deals and easements, the installation of new electric wiring, a new gas main, the letting of the houses which the family had owned in Birmingham, most of which had been flattened by bombing in the war or pulled down as slums after it. The Astons never threw anything away. In the attic, there were tin trunks full of the family papers going back to the year dot. One day when I had nothing else to do, I would send the whole lot to a university or research institute which might be interested in such stuff.

I was about to put everything back, annoyed at the futility of the search – the letter from Paris would almost certainly have been the first thing that Mother would have thrown out – but at least satisfied that I would be able to tell the Chief Inspector that I had done as I had been advised, when I noticed at the very back of the drawer a small packet of letters pinched together with a rubber band. They were in square blue Basildon Bond envelopes. I did not recognise the neat, precise handwriting on the top envelope. It was simply addressed to Mrs Celia Armitage, by hand.

Intrigued, I slipped off the band. The envelope had been slit open by a paper knife, a habitual practice with my mother.

She thought the ripping open of correspondence was unseemly and a sign of ill-breeding. I pulled out the single sheet within.

I read the brief contents with astonishment.

Crowcester, 2nd May 1956

My dearest Celia,

Believe me that what happened this afternoon had nothing sinful in it. A God of love will not frown on the true union of hearts and minds. Where that has been lacking there is no true marriage and therefore no adultery. I have always loved you from a distance since our first meeting. I felt constrained by our respective positions from expressing anything other than admiration, fearful that I would be rebuffed. What joy it was to find that you would grant my deepest desires. How I long to see you again.

With all my love, G.

The letter fluttered to the carpet as I sat on my heels in the chilly room, barely warmed by a shaft of pale sunshine. I had never in my wildest dreams imagined that, despite the tensions of her marriage to my father, of which, even as a small child, I was dimly aware, my mother could have taken a lover. Yet in all respects she had been an attractive woman, who took care and pleasure in her appearance and her dress. But even in the long empty years after Daddy disappeared, there had never been to my knowledge the least hint that she was remotely drawn to anyone else. The thought of an affair while he was still alive – as the date indicated – was utterly preposterous. Yet here in the somewhat congested lover's prose was proof of something, everything. What else could the coy reference to the events of the afternoon mean if not a sexual encounter?

But who was this man who went on so authoritatively

about sin and adultery? Certainly someone who was already close to my mother to know the cast of her mind in these matters. G? Who was G?

I picked up the next letter.

16th May 1956

My darling Celia,
You are a saint among women to bring the joys of heaven to earth in such a manner. When we are together, there is nothing but rapture. Please hasten the next time that we can enjoy the fruits of our love.

Your faithful servant, G.

There followed several further notes in similar vein. Clearly he was the sort of lover who followed up his visits with a kind of reassuring note. I could imagine Mother as racked with guilt, as I knew how deeply she respected the institution of marriage. There must be something powerful about this G to make her break her vows.

The next letter confirmed this, returning to the self-justifying tone of the first.

Crowcester, 7th August 1956

My darling,
You say that we are sinners. Indeed we are, but no more or less than is everyone on this earth. But, my darling, what is proper in our hearts can never be improper in the sight of heaven. All men, whatever their calling, must acknowledge the body as well as the soul. Your unhappiness in your marriage was not to be borne. To seek consolation is no sin. I pray every night for us. Pray for me.

With deepest love, G.

As I stared at the tiny writing on the pale blue paper, I realised what it was about the tone and content of these letters that seemed familiar, why Mother's piously ardent lover wrote of God and prayer. He was, of course, a clergyman.

In fact, he was the clergyman Jack had referred to, the instigator of the first excavation of the Glebe, Gervase Tuddenham. Mother and he had indeed been closely linked through her involvement in all the activities of the church. That must have been how they had become lovers. One day his pastoral concern for his parishioner had crossed the shadow line into intimacy. No wonder Mother felt guilty.

I felt an instinctive revulsion for this man, for how he must have exploited and abused his position of trust, gaining her confidence, before seducing her. The cheesy hypocrite. I tried to remember him. I had a vague impression of a small neat man, fair haired, a little boyish, certainly younger than my mother by several years. Had he made a practice of consoling attractive women of a certain age whose husbands were frequently absent?

The next letter was the last.

Crowcester, 28th October 1956

My dear Celia,
The joy that we have shared will be one of my most precious memories. I think, however, it is best for both of us that we do not attempt to prolong a love which, like the fairest flowers, is all the more fair for having its due season.

I hope you will understand. Pray for me as I shall pray for you, my love. G.

I sat back on my heels, stiff and shivering in the chill of the darkening room, the envelopes and their contents scattered on the carpet. I felt as if another grave had been opened.

I read again sadly that last, dismissive, curt and hurtful

note. Then I noticed the date. Could it be? I ran out of the room and back downstairs to the library. Daddy used to buy *Whitaker's Almanac* every year, a practice my mother had discontinued. The last volume on the top shelf of the case between the windows was dated 1956. I flicked anxiously to the calendar for October. I was right. Oh my prophetic soul! The 28th was a Sunday. It might just have been a coincidence, but that was the same day my father had met his destiny on the Glebe.

I found Gervase Tuddenham quite easily through *Crockford*. He was living in Wells, having apparently, some years before, retired as Bishop of Ilminster.

The little city of Wells is chocolate-box England, in spades. The ancient cathedral, its west front described as the finest medieval sculpture gallery in Europe, arises from a wondrous garden, its towers and buttresses reflected in the crystal pool into which bubble the springs which give the place its name. On the moat of the Bishop's Palace where the water-weed ripples like the long tresses of a drowned maiden, swans glide and politely ring a bell at the drawbridge of the gate-house at feeding time. In the cobbled High Street there are old inns groaning with dark beams, and tea shops preserve the afternoon rituals of the Edwardian age.

It was exactly the kind of place where you would expect a Church of England clergyman to have retired, a sort of waiting room for Paradise. After Wells, though, even heaven might seem rather imperfect.

His house was a gem of late Georgian architecture. A meticulously swept stone-paved path led through borders of lavender and rue to the ornate wrought-iron porch, around which grew stately hollyhocks. It had the comfortable unostentatious air which in England means a certain kind of upper-middle-class prosperity.

I rapped gently on the shiny panelled door with the polished brass ring-in-hand knocker. There was the sound of steps within and then a big grey-haired woman in a flowered apron stood on the threshold. I could see at a glance she was not a wife. So the old fellow had a housekeeper.

She looked me up and down. 'Yes?'

I was wearing black, with no make-up. I gave her my most charmingly diffident smile and said, 'I was hoping that Bishop Tuddenham could spare me a minute or two. You see, many years ago, before he became a bishop, he married my late husband and me. Luke died recently.' I took out a handkerchief and wiped the corners of my eyes. 'He remembered him in his will – a small sum of money to be donated to a charity nominated by him. I know I should have made an appointment . . .'

The old bat's face softened. Nothing like a posh accent and the feeblest of sob stories to melt even the stoniest female plebeian heart.

'If you'd care to wait just a moment, Madam. I'll see if he's engaged. And the name was . . .'

'Mrs Emma Johnson.'

She ushered me inside and bustled away down the stone-flagged hallway. I heard a murmur of conversation from the room at the end, then she reappeared.

'Bishop Tuddenham will see you now. This way please, Madam.'

He was writing with a fountain pen at his handsome mahogany desk, the tooled-leather top spread with sheets of manuscript and piled with thick volumes in which paper bookmarks were liberally interleaved.

Without raising his head, he said, 'You'll forgive me for finishing this whilst it's in my mind. My regular piece for the *Church Times*. Please do sit down.' He waved a long delicate hand at the armchair facing the desk.

He finished writing, read over the page and made a few small amendments. Still absorbed in his work, he said, 'Mrs Johnson, you told Mrs Forsyth. I don't remember you I'm afraid.'

'You wouldn't. I'm not called Johnson.' This made his head snap up and he looked at me for the first time. I noticed that his hand was straying to the bell push on the desk which presumably summoned the formidable-looking Mrs Forsyth, so I spoke quickly. 'My name is Elizabeth Armitage.'

At the mention of my name, a spasm of pain or alarm turned down the corners of his mouth. I thought for a horrible moment that he was going to have some kind of attack, but he rallied. The hand came away from the bell push and with forced casualness loosened the tie about his turkey neck.

'Armitage,' he croaked, finally. 'What do you want?'

'I want to talk to you about my mother.'

He moistened his withered lips. The face that I vaguely remembered as full and rosy with good health now showed all too clearly the skull beneath, the skin stretched tight over the cheek-bones, with yellowish brown blotches of disease or age, if the two could be distinguished. To what base uses we may return, Horatio.

To my surprise, when he spoke he seemed suddenly more relaxed.

'So you're little Lizzie. Well, well, I would hardly have recognised you. Now I look at you closely, though, I can still see the girl in you. You wish to discuss your mother? I have not heard from her now for many years. How is she? Or has she died? How sad. You're collecting items for some kind of memoir? You should have said.'

'She's not dead. She suffers from senile dementia. I am interested in your memories of her, however. Particularly the fact that forty years ago, when parish priest of Crowcester, you had an affair with her.'

It was as if he had not heard. 'I remember Mrs Armitage so well, of course. An indefatigable worker for the parish and the Church.'

'I repeat. You and she were lovers.'

His gaze was cold and hard. 'I had the honour to be one of her admirers, though not at all in the sense you mention.

104

In fact, I strongly refute the base suggestion that there was anything improper in the relationship. A calumny, given that I was her priest.'

'I found your letters to her.'

'I don't recall a correspondence, but no doubt if there is such it contains some friendly sentiments which you have clearly and shamefully misconstrued. I'm sure if your mother were in health she would set your mind at rest. Now, Miss Armitage, I have many pressing matters to attend to . . .'

'Please listen. You may be aware that a matter of days ago, my father's remains were found buried in the Glebe in Crowcester. They had evidently been there since he disappeared in 1956. He had not merely left home, he had been murdered. Yesterday I discovered that you and my mother had been having an affair at the same time.'

His assurance leaked away as I spoke. His face had turned ashen and his hands clutched and unclutched convulsively on the desk top. Again I feared that he was having some kind of attack. 'I don't know what you are talking about, Miss Armitage. I know nothing of this unfortunate discovery you mention, as I no longer read the secular press or listen to broadcast news. I hardly knew your father. He spent a great deal of time away in London, as I recall.'

'You broke off the affair the very day my father went away. Why did you choose that day? What do you know about his death?'

He was struggling to his feet, his hands flat on the desk, forcing him upright, his voice trembling. 'Get out of here, Miss Armitage. Get out of here, before I summon the police to throw you out. I am a man of God. What you are suggesting is quite monstrous, monstrous.'

'Please, Mr Tuddenham. Sit down. I'm not accusing you of anything. I merely want to know the truth about my father's death. As my mother cannot tell me, I came to you. I want to know whether at any time you suspected she might have had any part in it. Did she ever suggest such a thing to you?'

He sank back in the chair. 'No, never, never. How can you think such a thing of your own mother? She had no part in your father's death. I swear before God.' He closed his eyes and I saw his lips moving.

When he opened them, his face was stricken. 'I cannot help you, Miss Armitage. Please leave me alone. I am unwell.'

There was nothing more to be gained at this time. I let myself out of his perfect house, my face stiff, a choking pain in my throat. I ran heedless across the road into the cathedral close and into the great building. There in a chair, hidden in the shadow of one of the piers of the almost deserted nave, I wept with relief.

Tuddenham's ringing affirmation of my mother's innocence had the authentically moving note of truth, and I thanked the God in whom I had never believed for it.

When the storm had passed and I had dried my eyes, I could reflect on the other things which I had learned from the visit.

It was understandable that he had lied about the affair, believing that I could not prove it, or that even if I could, I had every reason not to make it public. But he clearly knew something about my father. The very mention of my name had caused him palpitations: it was only when I mentioned that it was my mother I was concerned with that he had recovered. And again, he showed the same distress when he thought that I was accusing him of being in some way involved in my father's death. He had convinced me that my mother was not involved, but I was far from convinced about his own role.

For he had lied about being ignorant of the discovery of the body. He certainly took a newspaper. I had seen a bundle of old copies of the *Daily Telegraph* by the door, awaiting collection. The matter had been front-page news for days.

It was inconceivable that he could have missed something affecting his old parish and a family with whom he had been so intimately connected.

It was clear to me now from what had just occurred that the reason Tuddenham had broken off the affair with my mother so abruptly and brutally in 1956 was that he must have known that my father was dead. To write to her on the very same day as his disappearance was no coincidence: it indicated an instinctive sense of self-preservation. He was desperately dissociating himself from her. The affair if continued would have given him a motive for murder. That was why he was so willing to admit to me that she was not involved. In his mind, if I were convinced of that, I would cease to suspect him.

He had succeeded: I didn't think he was capable of the deed itself. But the way that he had acted showed that, by some means I couldn't even guess at, he knew or suspected who was.

It would be no easy task to persuade him to speak. He had revealed himself to be not only a man with an uneasy conscience, but, more than that, one who was in mortal fear.

Jimmy Philpott, the sole occupant of the staffroom, glanced up from his copy of the *Daily Telegraph* as I came in. He saw my expression and removed the briar from his mouth. 'Had a hard time with the Third Rice?'

'What do you think?'

Jimmy was the titular head of maths. Bald-headed, bespectacled and tweed-jacketed, he epitomised the old style of schoolmaster. He'd already been ages at the Boys' Grammar when I'd joined the Girls' twenty-five years ago. He'd got in his forty years, and could retire on full pension whenever he felt like it. He spent most of his time with the top sets, leaving the tougher classes to the young and still idealistic members of his department. He had a great many free periods.

I went over to the sink unit in the corner of the large, untidy room, filled the plastic jug kettle, and banged it savagely back on the worktop. I picked up my mug – All Saints, Crowcester Organ Restoration Appeal 1993 – from amongst the others carelessly upended on the draining board, and chucked in a spoonful of instant coffee from the catering-sized drum. While I had my back to Jimmy I wiped my eyes with a paper towel.

'You do push your luck with her don't you, Liz?'

I shrugged. 'I'm not very good at grovelling.'

'Is it grovelling to be co-operative? Me, I don't rock the boat. She doesn't care whether I sit in here all day. She knows that young Barnes is really running things.'

'She also knows that you're a brilliant teacher.'

'So are you, Liz. And the plays. The school's Shakespeare is always one of the highlights of the Waterbury Spring Festival.'

'Was. There won't be one next year.'

'Why not?'

'That's what I was seeing Linda about. She wanted me to put on some dreadful piece of youth theatre by one of her pals from Birmingham. She said it was more "relevant" than "yet another production of the world's most dreary and unconvincing so-called love story". Her description of *Romeo and Juliet*. And it's set for GCSE next year. When I refused, she said she'd get Barton to do her thing, and he will, the ambitious little prat. She's determined to kill off the classics. She thinks they're elitist.'

'I suppose she has a sort of point there. The Festival doesn't pack them in from the council estates.'

'Only because it's been made elitist by the market forces she worships. Actually she didn't only want to stop the play. She wants to get rid of me, too. Thought I might make it a resignation issue.'

'Well, you are on the top of your scale. She could save quite a bit if she replaced you with someone younger. Sorry, I mean less experienced.'

'You were right the first time, Jimmy. If I didn't need the money, I shouldn't care.'

'You would. You care too much, Liz. You wouldn't put in all those extra hours if you didn't. You should be more like me. Stop fighting her and she'd leave you alone. Waterbury Girls' Grammar School is dead and buried. They're not ever going to bring it back, not in this town, and certainly not while Linda's around. Most of the Governors think the sun shines out of her bottom.'

'That isn't the point, Jimmy. I believed in the comprehensive ideal as much as anyone. I didn't think the grammar school was perfect, far from it. But Frank Bartleby knew that there were features of it that were worth keeping. Learning for its own sake, for one thing. It's all about getting and spending, these days. Having to find someone to pay for the result, and then to make sure it's the one they'll like.'

'You miss Frank, don't you? I know I do. No age to go, was it? Only fifty-five. But it's not all change and decay. We still get students who are real stars, genuine scholars. Francesca Rollright, for example.'

The mention of her name startled me. The coffee slopped around in my mug as my hand jerked. I hurriedly set it down on the table.

I spoke with deliberate casualness. 'Oh, her. Yes, she was quite good.'

He nodded, poking at his pipe with a dead match, and scraping the dottle into an ashtray. I noticed his hand trembled as he did this. He really was getting on. 'You're being modest, Liz. You really helped that girl. Four A star grades at A-level. St Hilda's grabbed her straight away. She'll get a Congratulatory First. Now, Derek, her younger brother, was quite a contrast, wasn't he? There was some intelligence there, but it was perverted.'

'He seemed no different from some of the others,' I said, and picked up the staffroom copy of the *Times Ed.*, hoping he would drop the subject of the Rollrights.

But Jimmy ploughed on obliviously. 'He'd only just left here when he robbed the little supermarket in River Street.

109

Of course, he did take a few quid from the till. It was what he did to the owner, though. He terrorised her. If he hadn't been interrupted by a late customer, he might have raped or killed her. The poor woman was so shattered, she gave up the business. That wasn't just a bit of nastiness. I'd describe it as evil. And what did he get? Youth custody, I ask you.'

I didn't reply. I had heard all there was to hear about Derek Rollright from a more reliable source than the *Waterbury Advertiser*.

'He must be out by now. I wonder what he's up to?'

I shrugged, in what I hoped was a dismissive manner.

'Yes, funny those two are so unlike. But it does happen, eh? Cain and Abel. Romulus and Remus.'

I was saved from any more of the Rollright saga by the ringing of the bell.

I swallowed the rest of the coffee hastily. 'Got to go. Year 10 and the tide in the affairs of men.'

I was in the walled garden that evening, weeding the patch I still managed to maintain for salad vegetables amidst the overgrown wilderness when I heard a car in the drive. It didn't have the ferocious growl of the Morgan's exhaust, and besides Jack had gone off somewhere for the evening, and probably most of the night – I didn't ask and he didn't tell. I took off my gardening gloves, called out, 'Shan't be a sec!' and hurried round to the front of the house. Waiting in the porch was the by now familiar figure of DCI Green.

'Ah, an inspector calls. Working late? Though I suppose when constabulary duty's to be done . . .'

'I was on my way home, as a matter of fact. As I pass through Crowcester and as you're out at work all day, I thought this might be the best time to catch you. Perhaps you could spare a moment to run through one or two things with me, Miss Armitage?'

I showed him into the drawing room. He sat in the armchair I indicated. I hovered in front of the mantelpiece.

'Drink?' I nodded over at the baroque collection of bottles Jack had assembled on a silver tray.

He shook his head. 'Wouldn't do for me to get stopped driving, would it?'

'Indeed not. I'm going to have one if you don't mind.'

I poured myself a gin and tonic and sat opposite him. I smiled encouragingly. 'Well, now?'

'One what you might call development is that nothing has developed.'

'I see. Like the curious incident of the dog in the night?'

'Pardon?'

'Sherlock Holmes? The dog did nothing in the night, that was the curious incident?'

He went on looking blank. 'Sorry, Chief Inspector. Obscure literary reference – one of the perils of being an English teacher.'

'I see. As I was saying. The fact is, Miss Armitage, that as far as this Miss Korzeniowska is concerned, we've made no progress at all. I told you I didn't think there'd be any problem tracing her. Well I was wrong. The Home Office has no records of anyone of that name and description entering or leaving the country around that time. We've approached every other official department and authority we could think of. Nothing. We've checked all the firms and factories, hotels, pubs and boarding houses in Waterbury and the surrounding area which would have been operating in the fifties, and people who used to run such businesses and we've not turned anything up. Despite a mass of enquiries, we haven't found anyone, apart, of course, from yourself and your brother, either in Crowcester or Waterbury who remembers a Polish woman resembling her.'

'It was a very long time ago, Chief Inspector.'

'In my experience people have long memories about such things. Foreigners, particularly strikingly attractive foreigners, weren't that common in the provinces at that time, I don't imagine.' He hesitated, then looked directly at me.

111

'The fact remains that the only people who can say anything about this person are yourself and your brother.'

'You think we invented her?'

He seemed somewhat taken aback by my candour, as if he'd been expecting to have to dig around a bit before getting to that point. From the expression on his face, I could see that that or something similar was exactly what he had been thinking.

'But why on earth would we do that, Chief Inspector?'

He didn't reply, but rummaged in his briefcase and produced a slim manila file. He removed a sheet of paper and laid it on the table top in front of me. 'There is this as well. Did you know about this?'

It was a photocopy of a newspaper article. At the top was typed the date and source. The *Waterbury Advertiser*, Monday, 22nd October 1956.

> Police were late last Saturday night called to an incident at the home of Mr and Mrs Robert Armitage in Crowcester. It is understood that a man was arrested and interviewed at Crowcester Police Station, but that no charges are to be brought.

I raised my eyes to meet his, controlling my emotions. 'Even as a child, I could hardly avoid knowing that my parents had their differences. He would not have left her for another woman, otherwise.'

'A little bit more than a difference, Miss Armitage. I checked the arrest book for the old Crowcester station. Your father was arrested for assault. The charge being considered was ABH. Then your mother said that she was not prepared to make a statement and the matter was dropped.'

'This is ancient history, Chief Inspector.'

'It's an ancient crime. The date, Miss Armitage. About a week before he disappeared.'

'So, they had a row before he walked out. It sounds a bad row, but I don't remember it at the time.'

'Weren't you here?'

'I was eight, Chief Inspector. Children of that age sleep soundly. This is a large house. I slept well away from Mother and Father's room.'

'Did your parents frequently have violent arguments?'

'I already said. They had their differences. Yes, they shouted at one another. But they weren't usually violent in a physical sense so far as I know.'

'So the cutting I've just shown you came as a surprise? You didn't seem surprised.'

'I wasn't. I implied as much. My mother told me about it. She told us that she and Daddy had had a bit of a spat. He'd pushed her, she'd fallen, got into a temper and phoned the police. Then she realised how silly she'd been and told them to forget about it. She told me that after she'd had the letter from him in Paris. When she told us he wouldn't ever be coming back.'

'Ah yes. The letter. Have you come across it by any chance?'

'No. I haven't. Although I did look for it as you suggested. You don't believe that my father ran away with Teresa, do you, Chief Inspector?'

'Evidence is what I'm after, Miss Armitage. So far, I have a set of human remains, of a man provisionally identified as Robert John Armitage, a homicide victim, who, the forensic evidence suggests, was killed by being battered with some kind of heavy bladed implement, probably a spade, then buried in a field in Crowcester. That is evidence. I have also a story told to me by his son and daughter forty years later that he is supposed to have run away to Paris with his exotic foreign mistress. This story is uncorroborated by any independent witness. Moreover, a letter which might have supported it cannot be found. That is not evidence. Your father's

113

Civil Service file indicates that he failed to return from week-end leave. There is no trace of any communication either from Mr Armitage or from his wife informing the Admiralty of the reason for his unauthorised absence.'

'Mother would have been far too humiliated to do that. You must see that.'

'She preferred to let her husband be branded a traitor? I've read the newspaper reports of the time. Your father was for weeks a topic of considerable interest. As far as one can see, at no time did Mrs Armitage attempt to defend his reputation with what you say she believed to be the truth.'

'But can't you see how that would have been for her? To tell the press, and particularly that part of the press she despised, that her husband wasn't a traitor but an adulterer. There wasn't the frankness then about that sort of thing that there is now. And perhaps, in any event, part of her wanted to . . .'

I hesitated, but Green was quite well aware of what I was going to say. He was quick, there was no doubt about it. Beta double plus at least.

'Punish him? Is that what you're saying, Miss Armitage?'

'Yes. There's no doubt my mother was devastated. Hurt and very angry. Jack and I were forbidden to talk of our father. He ceased to exist.'

'And now, forty years later, perhaps you think she should be spared further hurt? You both knew who would be the first suspect in a case of this nature. You knew that, and that's why you might take certain steps to confuse the issue. Understandable, but not at all advisable. If you came out with this story at the inquest and I showed that not only was it false, but that you knew it to be false, then you could be charged with perjury and conspiracy to pervert the course of justice. Of course, if this Miss Korzeniowska were even at this stage to come forward, that would clearly aid the investigation . . .'

'You really think my mother murdered my father, don't you?'

'I've already said. She must be a suspect.'

114

'And even if she had killed him, which she didn't, you could never prosecute. She's unfit to plead. This is just for your bloody clear-up rate isn't it? A confidential report to the Chief Constable. All neat and tidy. A pat on the back. Won't do your promotion prospects any harm. Well, I won't let you get kudos from libelling my mother. You're completely wrong, Chief Inspector. I know you're wrong.'

He seemed taken aback by my vehemence. 'I'm very sorry, Miss Armitage. It is obviously very distressing for you, this whole episode. It can't be easy having to think of one's parents like this. It's not something I like doing, delving into people's private lives. But where there has been a serious crime, even a very old one, I have no choice.'

'I repeat, I know Mother did not kill Daddy.'

'Do you mean you have real evidence?'

I hesitated. There was no way that Tuddenham would talk to the police. I had only got so far with him because I had caught him off guard. Now he was forewarned. But I had no choice. He was the only lead. I had no belief that I would succeed in finding Teresa when the police had failed. She might even be dead herself.

'I can get it.'

He stared at me, his manner radiating disbelief. Then he shrugged and stood up. 'I wish you'd be more frank with me, Miss Armitage. If you are concealing something, then there are, as I have said, potentially serious penalties.'

'I thought the police were the experts at such things nowadays, if one is to believe the newspapers.'

'If I were to match your offensiveness, Miss Armitage, I might say that certain allegations have been made to me since I began this investigation about a certain fatal road traffic accident some years ago involving your brother, yourself and a third party.'

'How fortunate then that you are concerned only with evidence and not baseless slander, Chief Inspector.'

★ ★ ★

115

The next morning, as I sat alone in the kitchen, Jack not having surfaced from his night on the tiles, I decided to phone in sick and go back to Wells. I was thinking about the best way to tackle Tuddenham, at the same time flicking through *The Times* when to my horror and amazement, my eye tripped over a name in the obituary columns. I read:

> The Right Rev. Gervase Tuddenham, former Bishop of Ilminster and Assistant Bishop of Bath and Wells, who has died tragically aged 75, was one of the most prominent and articulate members of the Anglo-Catholic party of the Church of England. Author of many works of devotion and theology, he was latterly a prolific writer of articles and pamphlets on the subject of the ordination of women, of which he was a formidably intellectual opponent.

It went on for several more paragraphs, but by then I had stopped reading. I felt shocked, even guilty. Had my visit in some way hastened his death? But, surely, on reflection, the death by stroke or heart attack – the kinds of illnesses I might have unwittingly exacerbated – of such an elderly man would hardly have merited the use of the word 'tragically'. The writer must know that something other than natural causes was involved?

Whatever the reason, the fact of his death destroyed the entire hope I had of solving the riddle of my father's death.

Later that morning, still sick with anxiety, I called the newspaper's obituaries editor, and asked, as a former parishioner of his, what the old man had died of.

The young man I spoke to searched the computer file and had the answer in a moment. 'The story came through on the wire. We didn't run it in the main paper, just the obit. Not really news, I'm afraid, any longer, an old man, even an ex-Bish, killed in a road accident. Hit and run on a pedestrian crossing, driver failed to stop, no proper description of the vehicle, etc, etc. I expect the local paper in, where was it? Wells has more details. I could give you the number?'

I thanked him and mechanically took it down. I was absolved from any responsibility for old Tuddenham's sudden demise. A hit and run in Wells of all places.

The disappointment crushed my spirits for the rest of the day, no matter how hard I tried to reason that I would never have persuaded him to tell me what it was he knew. And indeed, perhaps I had imagined the cause of his unease, allowed myself to construct a fantasy more comfortable to bear than the unacceptable facts which clamoured for my attention.

Then another thought chilled me to the core of my being. Tuddenham had been afraid, and perhaps not only of the authorities. Had what he had feared come to pass? Was his death so soon after my visit a coincidence, or was it a deliberate act to prevent him talking of what he knew?

IV

'Jack. Are you awake?'

Of course I was. I lay on my side, staring out into the room, shadowed beyond the pool of pink light shed by the bedside lamp. The floral wallpaper and the cream long-pile carpet were decently obscured. Only the white Formica fitted wardrobes along the opposite wall were a ghostly presence.

The flimsy double divan creaked and shuddered as I turned over.

She was half-sitting up, the duvet drawn up to her chin. I slid my hand under the quilt, found the soft, warm convexity of her stomach, then moved it further down to the swelling mound between her thighs, her pubic hair deliciously wiry and abundant, and still damp.

She wriggled away and out of the bed before I could grab her. There was a fleeting glimpse of her beautiful back and wonderfully rounded buttocks before she wrapped herself in a long shiny pink satin negligee.

'No, Jack. It's nearly time you were going. Charlie opposite's on the early shift. I don't want you running into him.'

I made no move to get up. 'Must I, Ellen, darling? "It is not yet near day; it was the nightingale, and not the lark, that pierced the fearful hollow of thine ear; nightly she sings on yon pomegranate tree: believe me, love, it was the night-ingale."'

'What are you going on about, Jack? Nightingales and pomegranate trees? In Crowcester, I ask you. All I know is

118

you've got to be out of here pdq or my nosy neighbours will see you.'

'OK, OK.' I sighed, swung my legs over the side of the bed, bent over and fished about on the carpet for my shorts.

She came over to watch me as I dressed, the gown loosely gathered and belted, her magnificent breasts half exposed. 'It isn't that I really want you to go,' she said softly, a touching note of anxiety in her voice. 'You know that, don't you?'

I reached out a hand and drew her to me, seating her on my lap, with some difficulty owing to the mounting interest this manoeuvre caused me. As I did so the gown slipped apart over her thighs, and I rested my hand in the warm hollow between them. 'I know that, Ellen, darling. Of course I know that.'

'I worried about you. Mum told me about what was happening at The Hollies. Barry followed it all in the *Sun*. Really enjoyed it he did. He made me that mad and I couldn't say anything. It must have been so horrible, Jack. Finding that . . . your father, like that. I've had nightmares about it. We used to play on the Glebe when we were kids. Everyone used the path across it as a short cut. Were you cross with me for calling you?'

I slid my hand further into the comforting crevice between her thighs. 'Of course I wasn't cross with you. I missed you so much when we were cooped up in the house with those reporters. They'd have been bound to follow me if I tried to sneak out. That wouldn't have been a good idea if we'd ended up on the front page of the *Sun*, would it?'

She laughed. 'I suppose it wouldn't. But it seemed a long time and you hadn't called me.'

'I made up for it tonight, didn't I?'

I felt her shudder with pleasure at the memory. 'I've never felt like you make me feel with anyone before, you know? Like I'm kind of special. And the champagne, that was special too.'

'You are special, Ellen. Must I keep reassuring you?'

'You say that, but I'm not like you, though, am I? Like just now, half the things you say, I don't understand. Quotations. The first time I saw you, you were on about Romans.'

'So I was.'

'I left school at sixteen. I work in a shop. I know you can't see much in me.'

'I see a great deal in you, darling Ellen.'

She kissed me, pressing herself against me. 'I know you can't think of me like, well like that other girl you told me about, the one who was . . .'

'No, I can't think of anyone as I did of her,' I cut in, not succeeding in suppressing the painful anger that flared at the thought of her. I saw Ellen's face flinch as if from a blow. 'Not even you.'

'But you do like me a bit, now, don't you, Jack? Better than anyone else apart from her?'

I was about to shrug away this questioning, when I realised from the sudden tremor in her voice and the intensity of her gaze that she was not speaking in general terms.

'There is no one else, Ellen, honestly.'

'Really, cross your heart.'

'And hope to die.'

'What about my cousin Fran then?'

This was something I hadn't anticipated. 'What about her? She's a student volunteer at the dig, that's all.'

'You like her, don't you, Jack?' She stared up at me, her blue eyes searching mine, clutching the dressing gown around her, in the process thrusting my hand out of its nest.

'Yes, I do. She's a lovely girl.'

'She is, isn't she? Brains and beauty. Got into Oxford. Destined for higher things than living in this dump and serving in a shop and minding nutty old ladies, if you'll excuse the expression. More your type altogether. I heard two of those schoolgirls who worked at the dig in the shop yesterday. They were saying how dead handsome you were, for quite an old bloke, and how you were always making sheep's eyes at Fran. "Real keen on her he is," they were saying.' She turned away and began to fold and refold the nylon satin of her belt.

'She's only a kid. I'm old enough to be her father.'

'She isn't that much younger than me. It didn't stop you in my case, did it?'

I drew her back against me. 'Listen to me, Ellen. Forget the village gossip. There is absolutely nothing between Fran and me. Not in that way. Honestly. I like her. Of course I do. I think she's clever and capable and attractive. But I don't have the same feelings for her as I do for you. Cross my heart.'

'And hope to die? Really and truly?'

She eyed me nervously like a child who's spoken out and fears the consequences, then turned away as she spoke. 'Jack, are you mad at me for thinking that about you and Fran? It was only because I thought you wouldn't fancy me any more once you saw her regularly.'

'I told you, there's nothing like that at all.'

'Please don't snap at me like that. I believe you. I know you wouldn't lie to me. I oughtn't to be jealous of Fran. She's done all right for herself in the end. Unlike that brother of hers. Miss Armitage helped her a lot, of course. But she had a rotten start.'

I paused in the midst of tying my shoelaces, trying to make my interest sound only casual. 'Rotten start?'

'Yes. Her father's a layabout, either out of a job or inside. He finished his last stretch in Gloucester jail only last week. Her mother ran off when Fran was only a toddler. No one knew where she went. Just walked out one day, without a word, by all accounts.'

'Poor kid. Didn't she ever try to keep in touch?' Fran's abandonment mirrored mine and resonated so strongly with me, I could hardly keep its timbre out of my voice.

'No. Left her, and her brother hardly more than a baby. No one ever saw her again.'

121

'Christ. Poor Fran. I never knew that.'

'Even the famous Dr Armitage can't know everything.'

'I know some things.' I ran a hand through her hair, then gently pulled her lips down to mine, at the same time cupping my hand over her breast to feel a rapidly hardening nipple through the thin material of her gown.

She was murmuring with the beginnings of desire, then struggled off my knee, pushing my hand away.

'Jack! No. We can't risk it. I don't want Barry to hear about us from the neighbours.'

'So you think he really might have another go at me?'

'You mean like that time in the pub? I told you, he'd had a few and his mates were going on at him. He wouldn't ever admit it, but he was a bit ashamed about what he done. He's not a bad bloke at heart. He believed what I told him. That's why I don't want him to find out like that.'

I avoided her gaze by searching on the carpet for my pants. 'You ought to know I felt I took quite a risk for you when I came here tonight. I don't think you realise what Barry might be capable of, Ellen.'

'He's really got you going hasn't he? I'm not saying that he mightn't get fired up with booze and take a bit of a poke at you again like he did, but that'd be all. He don't want no proper trouble. All you have to do is stay out of his way, and out of the Trout. Don't be scared, darling.' She gave my cheek a pinch in a way I found annoyingly patronising.

'Well I was scared,' I burst out with real anger. 'I have stayed out of his way. It didn't stop him trying to kill me over at the old Brewery. He jumped me in the dark. With a knife. If I hadn't been wearing a heavy coat he would have ripped me open from shoulder to hip.'

She whirled round and almost sprang at me, her blue eyes wide, flaring out her bright hair with her fingers, so that it seemed to crackle with static. She pushed her face close to mine. 'Have you gone raving mad, Jack Armitage? Barry try to knife you? That's ridiculous.'

'Ridiculous or not, it happened.'

She turned away, wrapping the gown tightly about her with exasperation. 'Are you serious, Jack? It's not one of your little jokes? Because I could say a lot of things about Barry Norton, but never that he would sneak up on anyone, and particularly not with a knife. That just isn't my Barry. In your face with his fists, that's him. Not a knife, never. Knives are no way his style. I'd swear that on oath. Whoever attacked you it wasn't Barry.'

I shook my head, somewhat stunned by her vehemence, and bemused by the collapse of the tidy explanation of the business. 'All right, I believe you. But why should anyone else do that? He didn't try to rob me. I hadn't disturbed him on the premises. He was after me, I'm sure. Only Barry had a motive for that. But if it wasn't Barry, then who the hell was it?'

She didn't reply, but was pale and rather distant, as if offended by what I had said, as I pulled on the rest of my clothes. I reflected on the passing strangeness of human relationships. Ellen would deceive Barry with me, but would still defend him fiercely against calumny.

She opened the door a crack and peered out. There was a whitish glimmer of dawn in the sky. 'Coast's clear. Off you go.'

I kissed her cold lips in the darkened hall and slipped out.

As I opened the garden gate into the back alley, and turned my coat collar up over my face, I reflected that I was getting a bit old for this hole-and-corner stuff. Scuttling back in the grey mist of morning from the Grange estate was too much like the behaviour of a middle-aged sad-hat, only a few points up from kerb-crawling. Moreover, I now had the nasty feeling that someone else had it in for me, for some unknown reason. Someone, compared to whom, if Ellen were to be believed, the lumpen Barry was a mere pussy cat.

The long case clock in the hall was striking six as I opened the front door. The house was silent. I mounted the stairs as quietly as I could, but the threadbare carpet and the creaking boards made a mockery of my efforts. I lay on the bed in my room and tried to read an article in French on Gaulish villas my chum at the Bodleian had photocopied and sent to me. I couldn't concentrate.

First there appeared Ellen's well-fleshed nakedness, thighs invitingly apart, her vulva pinkly ripe and luscious as a peach, then floating before me like an angel was Fran's pale and lovely della Robbia face with its grey-blue intelligent eyes.

Eros and Agape.

I remembered the first time I saw her. I was in the office late one afternoon. The dig had only just started. I had been absorbed in tagging and bagging various bits and bobs, tile fragments and potsherds and suchlike, mostly sifted from the earth of the previous excavation, when I heard a discreet clearing of the throat. I looked up from the trestle table to find a slim, dark-haired, very attractive girl of about nineteen or so standing before me with a quizzical expression on her face.

'Excuse me. Dr Armitage?'

I grinned, pleased at this interruption, and stood up. 'Yes. I'm Jack Armitage.' I wiped my grimy hand on a cloth and held it out. 'How do you do, Miss . . .'

Her long fingers briefly brushed mine. 'I'm Fran Rollright. I read about the excavation in the paper. How you were looking for helpers. I'd like to volunteer.'

'Splendid,' I said with quite genuine enthusiasm. They hadn't actually been flocking in, and none of them was like this girl. 'Done any digging before?'

'No, never. I thought it might be something a bit different for me. I'm helping a College Fellow with some research – she's found a cache of fifteenth-century MS, Oxfordshire's answer to the Paston letters she claims – and I'm waitressing evenings at the motel at Kidlington, but it would be nice to do something outdoors in the morning.'

124

'You're an undergrad?'

'St Hilda's, reading English. I used to be at Waterbury Comp. Your sister taught me. I wouldn't have got to Oxford without her. Liz is great. I admire her a lot.'

I smiled at the use of my sister's Christian name: Waterbury's own Miss Jean Brodie. 'You're right to. She is admirable. Now, as to the dig. Don't get your hopes too high of finding buried treasure. It's not like on the telly. They only show the interesting bits. We haven't got all that fancy electronic equipment for a start. There's lots of hard graft.'

'I don't mind that.'

I ran through some practical details with her. Her eyes showed a quick understanding, her full mouth a readiness to smile.

'Not put you off? Start tomorrow, about nine, then?'

She nodded.

Through the grimy metal-framed window, I watched her tall, upright figure as she strode across the yard and out of the gate. I felt a tremor as I did so, not only at the firm breasts swelling at the scoop-neck of her sweat-shirt, not only at her slim hips and athletic bottom in the tight blue jeans, but at the youthful energy she radiated, like a glowing light. A quotation floated into my mind. 'O! she doth teach the torches to burn bright.' I was old and full of sin, and she had Oxford and all life before her.

The following day, she turned up, bright and early, as promised. I introduced her to the others.

At our mid-morning tea break, I sauntered over, coffee-mug in hand, to where my new recruit was leaning back in the sunshine against a mound of earth. Her damp shirt clung pleasingly to her figure, revealing that she wore no bra, nor needed one.

I sat down beside her. 'How's it going?'

'I think it's fun. It'll keep me fit at any rate. I got quite a kick out of finding that bit of tile. How do you know it was genuine?'

I stretched a little in the warmth, the great archaeologist preparing to lecture the adoring young acolyte. 'There are many indications, but principally, it's a question of level. The trench where you were working was a little outside the original excavation, a probe as it were to see if the buildings we've already found extend in the direction I think they do. We've gone down to the depth of the Roman level we've found elsewhere. Consequently, if the soil is undisturbed, which it is, then anything we find there can only be an ancient artefact. But even without that there are indications – texture, workmanship, markings. When you've seen as many of these things as I have you get a feel for them.'

'So you've done a lot of these digs?'

'A fair few, though latterly, I was Keeper of Roman Antiquities in a museum. We didn't do excavations. There was no need. We had drawers full of stuff that had hardly seen the light of day since the early nineteenth century. All needing to be re-examined and reclassified according to the light of current knowledge.'

'I see. Sounds a bit boring, endless bits of old pot, if you don't mind my saying so. I mean, finding it is one thing, but there must be a limit to what you can find out from rubble.'

I did mind her saying so. 'Actually, I don't agree. That bit of tile may well have become dislodged from the roof of a building we haven't found yet. Even rubble as you call it has its message. When did it become rubble? Was it burnt or did it fall into disrepair? Why was it not rebuilt? All important historical questions. If, that is, you think history is important in the first place.'

Now it was her turn to be nettled. 'Yes, of course history is important.'

'Good,' I said, mollified by this response, and remembering that despite her body, she was still only a kid, really.

'So what is it you're actually looking for here?'

I hesitated. I'd been fairly circumspect up to now with the Archaeological Society, in case they began to think that I was

126

either hopelessly wrong, and therefore not to be let loose on the site, or that I was right, in which case they would insist that I handed the project over to someone far more up to date and experienced in excavation technique. But with this girl, I couldn't resist the temptation to boast a little. 'Something extraordinary. On a scale that hasn't been found in England for thirty years. Not since Fishbourne.'

'What's Fishbourne?'

'A Roman palace. A huge building near Chichester, which nobody suspected was there for over fifteen hundred years. In that case, a workman was digging a trench for a water pipe, when bingo! he digs into something solid which turns out to be a Roman pavement. Which then turns out to be part of one of the most splendid Roman buildings yet found in England. That's the exciting thing about excavation. You don't know what you're going to find in the most unpromising soil.'

'And you think you're on to something like that. Why?'

'The scale of what's been found already. If what was uncovered in the fifties was only the outbuildings, then the main structure is correspondingly enormous. It can't be an ordinary villa. What's more, it may have survived fairly intact. As far as I have been able to discover, the Glebe has never been ploughed, a sure sign that it was thought unsuitable for growing crops. That often happens when there are substantial structures under the soil. The brewery buildings are, most of them, nineteenth century, but they were probably built on medieval foundations – there's a local legend that the brewery was originally started by the monks of Waterbury Abbey. It may be that when they dug the original footings, what they thought was firm subsoil was Roman brick and mortar.'

She looked suitably impressed, even excited. 'So you think there may be things like those mosaic floors. I remember going to the Museum at Cirencester on a school trip.'

'The correct term is tessellated pavement. But you're right to mention Cirencester. As Corinium, we believe it was the centre of a school of artisans who designed and made such pavements over south-west England. There are several with motifs such as Orpheus in common. Another Orpheus pavement would be a wonderful find.'

Feeling I had caught her attention, I was reluctant to let it go. I felt in my jacket pocket. 'Look, this is a plan of the site drawn up by Miss Masterton, superimposed on a blow-up of the large scale Ordnance Survey map. And there in pencil I've sketched how I think the layout of the site may have been.' I felt her move closer, her warm breath on my cheek, as she leaned to examine the drawing. 'You see, there are the outbuildings, and that may well have been a central court-yard for farm vehicles, with a possible entrance here.'

She was silent for a few moments, then she said, laying her long index finger on the paper, its nail unvarnished and even slightly bitten, 'Hey, look how that lane there seems to point right at the entrance you've drawn, even though it's a good long way away.'

I stared, jolted by a bolt of electricity that this time was intellectual and not sexual. 'Christ, you're absolutely right. They align. Of course, it could be a coincidence, but on the other hand . . .' I squinted at the tiny lettering on the map. South Street. 'Maybe South Street is built on a vestige of the Roman approach road.' I stared at her in genuine admiration. 'Well done. I must have stared at that map a hundred times and never put it together. I'll make sure you get your very own footnote. "I owe this suggestion to my assistant Miss Fran Rollright." What about a drink tonight to celebrate. Anywhere but the Trout,' I added hastily.

She shook her head. 'Sorry, I'm on bar duty tonight. And the rest of the week.'

'What about Sunday lunchtime, then.'

'Sorry again. I've got some friends from college coming over.'

I shrugged. To persist was humiliating.

Since that occasion I had stuck to small talk and dig

technicalities. Sometimes, I would stand for minutes at a time just watching her lithe body and her graceful movements. I fondly imagined that my little lectures to the team would particularly impress her, and when she smiled at one of my jokes, it made me feel warm and happy. I hadn't felt like that since . . . since the day Fiona died.

As I finally gave up on Gaulish villas and ran a tepid bath, I was forced to admit to myself what I had been trying to ignore for days: that I was missing her like hell.

The Rollrights lived in West End, the incongruously named down-market end of the High Street. The tiny terraced stone cottages had doors which opened directly on to the pavement. One or two appeared, from the Laura Ashley curtains and the stripped wood doors, to have been bought by weekenders from town.

Number twenty-five was clearly inhabited by an old-style village resident. The reeded glass front door was obscured by a grubby nylon net, as were the small windows. The paint of the wood work was blistered and the joints cracked open. I walked past it once, feeling almost as awkward as I had when I was about thirteen or so, when I, the nervous Romeo, had first done this kind of thing.

Enough of this nonsense. I turned on my heel, retraced my steps and banged confidently on the glass panel. Silence. She was out. I was about to go when a female voice called from inside, 'Who is it?'

I glanced up and down the street, but it was empty. 'It's Jack. Jack Armitage.'

'Jack? Hang on a minute.' There was a rustling from behind the door, then a hand appeared between the glass and the curtain feeling for the latch. She opened it a fraction. 'Jack? What do you want?'

'I was just passing. I've got some news. Can I come in?'

'I'm not dressed.'

'I'm very broad-minded.'

She laughed and opened the door. Disappointingly, she wore a long faded pink brushed cotton nightie, buttoned up to the neck, the kind a twelve-year-old might have found a bit staid.

'I'll go and put some clothes on. Sit down and make yourself at home.'

She ducked through a plank door beside the big stone fireplace and up the old-fashioned spiral staircase which lay beyond. I had a glimpse of her small naked feet on the bare wooden treads.

I sat down on the hideous green imitation leather sofa. The slippery cushion wheezed and squeaked as I did so. The sunny day outside hardly penetrated the low, net-curtained window, but could itself be glimpsed tantalisingly, like the brightness at the mouth of a dark cave.

I stared around the small stuffy room. The fitted carpet was, even in the gloom, a headachy concoction of yellow and orange swirls. Against the opposite wall, half folded, was an imitation wood laminate gate-leg dining table and two chairs, alongside a flush-panel sliding door, presumably leading to the kitchen. There were a couple of armchairs in a worn green tweedy fabric. Between the sofa and the hearth was a teak coffee table on which were a half-empty mug of cold coffee, a packet of Benson & Hedges, and a paperback copy of Karl Popper's *The Poverty of Historicism*, marked about halfway through with a Blackwell's bookmark.

There was a pounding on the stairwell and she reappeared in jeans and white T-shirt, her feet still bare but in sandals.

'Do you want some coffee?'

'Thanks.' I replied without enthusiasm, feeling more and more like a complete twerp.

She slid back the kitchen door and stepped into the narrow lean-to beyond. I got up from the sofa and watched her fill a tin whistling kettle with water at the enamel sink unit and set it on one of the rings of the small gas stove. She slopped out and rinsed cursorily a couple of mugs from the collection of dirty crockery on the drainer, then dashed in each a spoon-ful of instant coffee from a jar bearing a brand name I'd never heard of. Then she turned back to face me, leaning back against the sink unit, a pose which caused her breasts to swell against her shirt.

'What's new on the Rialto, then?'

Any answer was precluded by the whistling of the kettle on the hob. She swivelled back to the stove, picked up the kettle with a filthy oven glove and tipped water into the mugs. 'Milk?'

I nodded. She splashed some in from an open and rather crusty-looking bottle left out on the counter and handed me mine.

I was finding it hard to conceal my air of distaste at these preparations and at the Rollright home generally. I'd never been into the squalor thing as a student and I certainly wasn't now. Ellen's house was naff, but it was very clean.

She gave me a look and said, in an exaggeratedly posh voice, 'Sorry, it's not quite like you're used to, is it?'

'How do you mean?'

'Oh, come on now. The Hollies. I've been there.'

I shrugged, then moved out of the doorway, back into the sitting room.

She followed, sitting down in one of the easy chairs, while I subsided gingerly back on to the sofa. 'Go on then.'

She sipped her coffee, staring at me with her cool grey-blue eyes. I felt once more uncomfortably adolescent.

'I'm reopening the dig next Monday. I thought I'd let you know.'

'You came round specially to tell me?'

'Well I was in the village and . . .'

'Jack, I'm not sure I want to come back to the dig. It was fun, and we had a few laughs, but . . .'

Even though I was partly prepared, I still felt the shock of it like a physical pain shooting through my chest. I covered my alarm as best I could by making light of it. 'I say, you

131

don't mean you're put off by finding the ... my father's body?'

'That's nothing to do with why I'm not coming back.'

My disappointment turned to irritation. 'You're bored with archaeology? Been there, done that? Is that it? Or is it the rock festival season starting?'

'I'm not into that kind of thing.'

'So what is it?'

For the first time since I had known her, she suddenly seemed very young. Her assurance seemed to have deserted her. She gazed down on her slender hands twisting together in her lap. With her eyes still lowered she spoke softly.

'I could say that I've found it too much, what with the research work for Professor Hutton, and my reading for next term, as well as working in the motel. While that might be partly true, it's not really the reason. The real reason is you, Jack.'

'Me? Whatever do you mean?'

She raised her head and stared straight at me. Her voice had a harsh edge I'd never heard before. 'Don't put on that act with me. You know exactly what I mean.' Her tone softened again. 'I don't want to hurt your feelings, Jack. And I might even be wrong. But I think you want me to be at the dig not because you think I should be interested in the Romans, but because you think I should be interested in you. And ...'

'And you're not?'

'No, not in that way. I think you're clever and knowledgeable and charming and witty. But ...'

'But too old, too much the slippered pantaloon. Eh?'

'No, it isn't the age thing. I feel fond of you, Jack. It's fun being with you. And you are of course a very attractive man, to other people. But I'm not attracted to you in that way. I'm sorry.'

'And that's for all time is it?'

'Yes. I'd very much like us to be friends, but I'm not sure whether that would be helpful to you. It might keep your hopes up.'

'And there really isn't any hope?'

'No.'

I felt all at once sick and old. My legs shook as I levered myself to my feet out of the clammy embrace of the sofa. 'Thank you for the coffee.'

I hadn't done more than sip the vile stuff. Yet one more sign of the gap between us. God what a fool I had been. But being rejected had never hurt this much.

I had opened the front door and was on my way out when I saw it.

On the wall in the chimney alcove hung a depressing set of cheap pine knick-knack shelves, crowded with a number of gimcrack ornaments: a couple of Capodimonte figurines, a shiny glazed plate, a souvenir of Clovelly, a cut-glass flower vase, a pair of miniature brass candlesticks and various other worthless trinkets.

The sun pouring in sparkled with a pure radiance on something hidden in the shadows on the top shelf. I can't explain what it was that drew me to investigate, maybe the old treasure hunter's instinct, but it was compelling.

In amazement I stared at the intricately moulded curve of silver.

Curious at my behaviour, she moved beside me. I could feel her breath on my face as she spoke.

'Couldn't resist examining the Rollright heirlooms? Rubbish, aren't they?'

I pointed at the metal fragment. 'That isn't rubbish.'

'Isn't it? I wouldn't know. It's Dad's. He won't let Derek or me touch it. He says it's silver. Says he found it. Pinched it more like.'

'It's not only silver, it's Roman silver.'

'You're joking.'

'No joke. I'll show you.' I was reaching up when a shout

133

came from behind. I took my hand away, and turned to come face to face with a man.

He was short, heavily built, run to fat and unhealthily pale. He wore a dirty white T-shirt, and his belly bulged over the waistband of his corduroy jeans. Even from several feet away the sweetish stench of drink on his breath was overpowering.

We eyed each other like hostile animals.

He spoke first. 'Get your hands off of that, mister! Who the fuck are you?'

Fran stepped between us. 'Dad. This is Dr Armitage. He's a-doing the dig on the Glebe. I told you about it when you got out of . . . came back.'

I noticed that her voice changed when she spoke to this fellow, the local accent and idiom more evident. It also shook with what I was infuriated to realise was fear.

'Armitage? Like Lady Muck at The Hollies?'

'He's Liz Armitage's brother. He's an archaeologist.'

He snorted like a buffalo, almost pawing the ground. 'I recognise him now. You don't need to tell me about him. I know all about Mr Jack fucking Armitage. The whole village does. Used to think he were Lord of the bleeding Manor. Anything he fancied he helped himself to. Times has changed, mister. You're not wanted round here. You should fuck off back to London. By all accounts, Barry Norton had the right idea about how to sort you out.'

'Dad! Honestly. I'm sorry, Jack, really.'

'That's all right, Fran. I was just on my way actually, Mr Rollright, when you came in.'

He moved away from the open door. 'Get the fuck out of here then. And don't you come back bothering my daughter again or it'll be the worse for you.'

'I think that's a matter for Fran.'

'Don't you tell me who it's a matter for, mister. I told you to fuck off.' He shot out his thick hairy arm and shoved me out into the street. I regained my balance and was swinging my arm back to give him a thump in his tub of guts when

134

Fran shouted, 'No, Jack. Please. Just go away. Please!'

I saw her anguished face in the darkness of the doorway behind the sack-like figure of her father. Her clear pallor had a glow of blood in it, making it almost luminous.

Rollright's face bore a contemptuous grin.

I took a deep breath and dropped my arm. I said quietly, 'Don't you ever touch me again, you fat bastard.'

I strode off down the street, aware that our little contretemps had attracted quite an audience from passers-by and neighbours. I could imagine what they were whispering. That Jack Armitage up to his old tricks again.

Rollright must have found his bit of silver on the Glebe. I vaguely resolved to ask Fran to find out exactly where. But then, unfortunately, subsequent events drove it out of my mind.

I drove the Morgan up the lane to the metal gates of the brewery yard, climbed out and swung them open. I loved this time of the morning, so cool and fresh before the sun was strong enough to burn off the dew which sparkled on every blade of grass with a gemlike fire.

I strolled across the yard, a patchwork of concrete, tarmac and old cobblestones, the latter a reminder of the days when Old Crow had been delivered by horse-drawn dray. It was good to be back in business.

I was cheerfully and tunelessly singing Papageno's song from *The Magic Flute*: '*Ein Vogelfänger bin ich ja!*' I fumbled in my pocket for the keys to the building.

When I came up to the doors, however, I saw that the keys would be unnecessary. They hung wide open, the safety glass panels crazed and grotesquely bulging where the inner layer of wire netting had held together against the impact.

I stepped gingerly over the dozens of glittering fragments into the corridor. Sprayed on the cream painted walls were obscene words and drawings, interspersed with the hieroglyphics that those who do this kind of thing call their tags.

135

The door to the room we used was nothing but matchwood. Inside, the tables had been overthrown and smashed, papers thrown around and torn up. From somewhere, a tin of black bitumen paint had been found to splash around on the floor in sticky half-dried pools; the chemical stench of it made me gag. The lock of the tool cupboard had been forced, and the wooden handles of the picks and shovels had been broken, presumably after being used to further the work of destruction. In the centre of the room, a large blob of human excrement reposed with derision on an unbroken plate taken from the sink unit in the corner of the room.

Worst of all, the boxes and bags of clay and pottery fragments and other artefacts had been emptied and strewn everywhere, their contents stamped on so hard they had been crushed to powder.

Fortunately, I had removed the few more significant items we had found – coins, and some bronze pins – for safekeeping to The Hollies. I saw now that I should have taken everything. But I had never in my nightmares imagined wanton and malicious destruction on this scale.

I had been naive, of course. Out of touch with the tenor of the times. Everywhere else in England, the barbarian hordes had taken over city centres, and left their marks of brutality and ignorance. Why not in Crowcester? I suddenly felt faint and old. Why the fuck had I bothered? Weeks of work destroyed, not to mention the effect it would have on the morale of the team.

No doubt nobody had heard a thing. The brewery was well away from any houses. The cops would suck their teeth, poke the toes of their boots at the mess, and lament the passing of the respectable villain who might nick things but never made a mess, the same comments which had been made when my house in London had been burgled fairly untidily a couple of years ago. They wouldn't ever catch the ones responsible, and it wouldn't help me if they did.

I bent down to pick up a sheaf of notes which I saw had

escaped being ripped to shreds. They were smeared with paint, but otherwise intact. Maybe it wasn't as bad as it looked. I could get in some people to clear it up. Perhaps Mrs Hargreaves would help. Or even Ellen. Didn't village communities pull together when this sort of thing happened?

I was comforting myself with these glimmerings of hope, when from somewhere outside, I heard a brain-numbing scream, an appalling ululation that seemed to last for ever.

There was something so primitive and elemental about that howl that I almost cringed before it, the hairs on my neck literally bristling.

The dreadful sound was repeated, and I realised it came from the Glebe. I threw down the papers in my hand and tore out of the building. I ran at full tilt across the yard and through the hole in the wall into the field beyond.

I could see there was a small knot of figures by the first line of trenches, staring at the white thing on the wooden pole stuck in the ground beside them.

As I drew near, I saw that it was the blood-stained body of a dead sheep which rose from the ground like some hideous totem of a savage tribe.

It was one of the Jacobs from the fenced-off section of the Glebe. Its throat had been cut and it had been partially disembowelled, the red tatters of its entrails dangling from a slash in its white belly. Its straggly brown-patched wool fluttered in the breeze, with a chilling simulacrum of life. The long fencing post on which it had been erected had been driven through its anus, and burst through the top of its skull like the stump of a third horn. Its dark lips were drawn back revealing the yellow chunks of teeth in a rictus of death. Around the dark congealing wounds black flies were beginning to buzz.

I have seen some fairly terrible things in my time, but this appalling image in the midst of the sweet scents, melodious sounds and soft colours of an English summer meadow made my flesh crawl and my gorge rise.

Sarah, one of the schoolgirl volunteers, had been the one who had screamed. Her white face was blotched red and wet with tears. Her shoulders heaved convulsively as she sobbed. She was being comforted by a couple of the other girls.

I put a consoling arm around her shoulders. She was still shivering but the sobs had subsided. 'Better now?'

She nodded.

'She was a bit ahead of us coming through the churchyard,' contributed Emma, one of the comforters. 'We ran like hell when we heard her yelling her head off.'

It was time I got out of the state of shock I was subsiding into and took charge of these youngsters. 'OK. Now we've had nasty visitors in the office, too. So I don't want anyone going in there. Emma and Nicola, would you please take Sarah home, then go home yourselves.' I turned to one of the youths. 'Pete, you get down to the end of the lane and stop anyone who turns up. Say I said the site's closed because of vandalism.'

After they had gone, I nodded grimly to Hamish and then to the sheep.

'Help me pull this thing out of the ground, then get some sacks to cover it up.'

The police came round later in the shape of PC Enstone. I was sitting smoking a cigarette outside the office building in front of the smashed doors when the panda car rolled into the yard. He got out and adjusted his flat cap, strolling over to me, nonchalantly.

'Good morning, Dr Armitage.' He gazed at the doors and shook his head. 'What a shambles.'

'Wait till you see the rest.'

We toured the ravaged building, then I marched him over to the Glebe. I lifted the corner of one of plastic sacks we had laid over the body of the sheep. I heard his sharp intake of breath. 'Very nasty, that. I don't think I've ever seen

138

anything this bad, sir. It's usually just a bit of graffiti or a smashed window, even in Waterbury on a Saturday night. This looks more . . .' He paused, flummoxed by the absence of the appropriate official vocabulary.

'Calculated?' I suggested.

He stared at me, digesting the significance of the word. 'Calculated to do what, sir?'

I let the cover drop. There was a buzzing from underneath it and a warm stink of corruption. 'Terrify. It frightened me, and I've seen plenty of horrors. Ever read *Lord of the Flies*, Constable?'

'Oh yes, sir, at school, with Miss Armitage, I mean your sister.' Then the reason for the question sank in. 'I see what you mean. Looks like someone else read the same book. This site is not providing the happiest of experiences for you, is it, Dr Armitage?'

'No, it isn't.'

'You don't think there's any connection between this and the other matter, sir?'

I paused, asking myself the question I'd rather avoided earlier. 'I don't see how there could be,' I said slowly. 'No, Constable, I think what happened here is aimed at me. I had very personal reasons for wanting the excavation to succeed. It seems to me that whoever did this knew that.'

'You don't have any theories then about who this might have been, sir? Anyone with a grudge against you?'

I smiled wryly. 'Not now.'

He gave me a keen look. He might have been just a kid, but he wasn't stupid. 'Now, sir? You mean at one time there might have been?'

I nodded warily.

I suppose it was the training that made policemen suspicious. He said, 'Have there been any other incidents of this kind then, sir?'

I hesitated, then decided it was best to own up, partially anyway. 'There was one. I didn't report it because I thought

139

I knew what it was about, then I . . . heard something which changed my mind. Now I don't know.'

'Do you want to make a statement about that, sir?'

'I'll think about it.'

Again, he gave me a shrewdly appraising look. 'There was talk in the village of some trouble in the pub. I had a quiet word with the landlord, but I didn't take any other action because no formal complaint had been made. Of course, this matter changes things considerably. Would there be any connection, sir?'

'No, Constable.' I spoke as emphatically as I could. 'That was a misunderstanding, now completely resolved. This is altogether different.'

'I see, so the person allegedly concerned in that incident hasn't given you any further cause for complaint?'

'Absolutely not, Constable.'

That seemed to end the matter. He took out his radio and I heard him arranging for a photographer and a fingerprint officer to be sent. We walked back to the yard. He opened the door of the panda car and was about to get in, when he said, 'The individual in the Trout, sir, did you notice whether he was with anyone in particular?'

Suddenly I had a clear mental picture of the pale youth in the black leather jacket. 'I did, now you mention it.' I gave him a description and he nodded. 'Do you know this character?'

'Oh yes, sir. I know him very well indeed. I can't say I was very happy when I heard he was around again. I had heard he'd got himself a job somewhere out of the county. In Gloucestershire, I believe. When I heard he was around again, I dropped a heavy hint that I'd be keeping a very close eye on him. A very nasty piece of work, sir, just like his father.'

'Who is he?'

'Anyone in the village could tell you his name, sir. You wouldn't need to have heard it from me. Ask your sister about him. His name's Derek Rollright. You know his sister Fran, I understand. No comparison, there.'

I watched as the white car bumped its way over the broken surface of the yard. I thought back to that night in the Trout, seeing the scenario quite differently.

It was clear it had been Derek Rollright who had egged on Barry Norton to attack me publicly. The later knife attack on me at the brewery, quite out of character for Barry, was the work of Derek himself. If the attack had succeeded, plenty of people would have pointed the finger at Barry, no matter how much his loyal little wife had protested. Derek would have been in the clear, having no particular motive. And that was precisely the point.

Why had he done it? I didn't know him. What had Derek Rollright got against me?

When Liz came home late that afternoon, she had already heard about the incident.

'Jack, I stopped by the shop on the way. The whole place is humming with the new horror over at the Glebe. Nicola Gale's mother buttonholed me and said her daughter would be going back to that place over her dead body.'

'Very appropriately, in the circumstances. Have a drink.' I poured myself another stiff whisky.

'No thanks. Haven't you got any better response than to get pissed?'

'It seems an excellent response to me. I recommend it heartily. Dr Armitage's remedy for the slings and arrows of outrageous fortune. Actually, as usual, you misjudge me, little sister, it's the first I've had all day.'

'I had a bad feeling from the beginning of this business, Jack. It seems to get worse and worse. What are you going to do?'

'I thought about packing it in, but then that would be giving in, wouldn't it? Running away as you've always said I do when the going gets tough. Well this time, I'm sticking with it. I've already got the council to clear the dead sheep away. I've spoken to Mrs Hargreaves about helping with cleaning up the mess in the office. I've been on the phone to most of the kids' parents to reassure them. Mrs Gale is next on the list as a matter of fact. First thing tomorrow, we go in there and kick ass.'

'I can be home by four tomorrow afternoon, Jack, ready and willing to help in any way you want.'

I leapt up and gave her an enormous bear hug, lifting her clear off the ground. 'Of course, you can, old Lizard. Join the team.'

'Put me down for God's sake, Jack. I can't breathe. I must be mad to get involved in your crazy scheme. You'd better give me that drink now.'

That evening, I had a call from Fran. 'Jack,' she said in her quiet voice, 'I heard what happened. I'll be there to help clear up first thing in the morning.'

I put the phone down with exultation in my heart.

By the end of the week, thanks to the enormous efforts everyone, not excluding me, had made, the mess had been cleared, and the site left tidy. Everything was in place for a start the following week.

At my urging, Liz and I had made Sunday breakfasts an occasion for us to be together. We took the meal in the dining room, which was otherwise hardly ever used and lingered over our coffee and newspapers. Usually Liz was relaxed and cheerful. That morning, however, I could sense from her manner that a storm was brewing.

She lowered her copy of *The Sunday Times* and addressed me in the peremptory tone she had had since we were children and which she had picked up from Mother. She used it to correct what she believed to be deficiencies in my conduct or character. There would have been hell to pay, of course, if I'd ever adopted the same manner with her. 'Jack. I couldn't avoid noticing the way you were with Francesca Rollright at the dig. I know from what people are saying in the village that I'm not the only one.'

I was furious to find that, like the schoolboy, I still started guiltily. 'What on earth do you mean?'

She sighed in that way she'd also copied from Mother. 'Jack. Let's pretend we're grown-ups. You know as well as I do how a middle-aged man looks at a very attractive much younger woman, and what that look means.'

'So what?' I shrugged defiantly. 'It isn't any of your business.'

'It is very much my business, Jack. Francesca was one of my best students. She went up to St Hilda's last year. She's brilliant. She's capable of a First. Provided that she doesn't do anything silly.'

'Silly? What are you getting at?'

'It's no good looking at me like that, Jack. I know it used to work on Mother when you went all ugly about the mouth. "Don't provoke your brother," she'd say. Well she isn't here to say it now. And I'm not going to take any notice.'

'I'm glad that you display such concern for her moral welfare. I suppose you're afraid she'll follow your own example.'

She flushed. 'You're a bastard, aren't you, Jack? You haven't changed a bit. Yes, I am concerned for her welfare. She and I worked damned hard to get her where she is. Yes, I do remember what happened to me. Is it any wonder? You know nothing about her. If you did, you might tread more carefully.'

'I know more than you think. I know her mother walked out on the family. I know about her bastard of a father and her delinquent brother. I've seen the squalid hovel she calls home.'

She shook her head in the patronising way women never have to learn from their mothers. 'Jack, you know nothing. Stick to Roman remains. Leave women alone. You're no good for them. All you've ever thought about in connection with them is sex. Fran's no different. She's just a target for your fading virility.' Her tone changed to its most icy. 'Leave

143

her alone, Jack. She deserves better than to get mixed up with you. Act your age for once in your life.'

The mention of age swept away any apologetic tone. That and the bloody unfairness of the accusation. All that from Ellen and now Liz and I hadn't even laid a finger on the girl. 'My age, Liz? Sometimes you talk as if you're twice yours. You're getting like the old biddies who've got nothing better to do in this hicksville than gossip. Why is it everyone is on at me to leave this girl alone? She volunteered to work on the site.'

'I don't know who this everyone is who's on at you, Jack.' She paused, then I saw the penny drop and once again cursed my loose tongue. 'Oh yes, I do. You and little Ellen. Don't say I didn't warn you, Jack. Barry Norton has a temper, as you already know.'

I said nothing, angry beyond words at how I'd mishandled the matter.

She carried on, obviously amused by my humiliation, but her words were hard and serious.

'Christ, Jack, you'd think your ageing libido would be satisfied with one woman. You'd think ruining Ellen's life would be enough for you. But if you continue to see or attempt to see Fran, you will no longer be welcome in this house. I shall insist that you leave.'

I sat back in my chair, gazing at the portrait of Grandfather which hung over the mantel opposite. His long ascetic features and pale eyes seemed to regard me with distaste, as if I were one of the great unwashed whom he had spent his whole political life struggling to keep down.

Then I stared back at Liz. 'You've a pretty low opinion of me, don't you? Maybe you're right to. Not that I concede that you've any right to monitor my sex-life. But, for your information in this instance, you're way off, sister. Not in the same state, never mind ball-park.'

'So you're not sleeping with her?'

'I haven't even kissed her.'

144

I saw a surge of relief on her face, then a gleam of triumph. 'Oh, dear, brother. You don't mean to say that on her side, age differences did matter. How upsetting for you, Jack, to be turned down.'

This was too much. 'Fuck off, Liz. Give your prurient mind a rest. I'm no angel, but at least I get my kicks directly, not from fantasising about what other people get up to. You obviously have problems, dear sister. What used to go through your mind when you asked Fran round for coffee?' I put on a quavering falsetto, '"I need to discuss your latest essay, my dear." Was she the latest in a line of lovely, brainy girls you gave tuition to? Be honest with yourself, Liz. It's not me who wants to fuck Fran Rollright, it's you.'

Liz said not a word. Her face spoke for her. She picked up her mug and flung its contents in my face. Then she ran out of the room. I heard her feet pounding on the stairs, then the door of her room slam.

I wiped my face and shirt front with a napkin. Fortunately the mug had been half empty and the coffee only lukewarm.

I went up to my room, washed and put on a clean shirt. There was silence from Liz's room. I'd leave her for the moment. I had wished straight away, just like all the other times, that I hadn't said what I'd said. It was equally hurtful whether or not it was true.

Half an hour later, I banged on Liz's bedroom door. 'I'm desperately sorry about what I said, Lizard. Fran told me how you helped her. I shouldn't have said what I said. Things have got too pressured here. I'm going back to London for a while.'

Her muffled tearful voice came from within. 'What do you mean, going back? You've nowhere to go to. Or had you forgotten that detail?'

'I had a letter a couple of weeks ago. From my tenants. Neil has got a part in a Hollywood movie. I released them from the tenancy, generous sod that I am. They left for the coast last week, so the house is empty. Lamplighter hasn't

145

found anyone yet. So a break in town is altogether possible, as well as desirable. The site reopening will have to wait.'

There was silence for a moment, then her voice was clearer, as if she had raised her head from her pillow. 'You are coming back, though, aren't you? Jack, please, I'm sorry. If it were anyone else but Fran . . . I don't want you to go off in a huff again. Please.'

I was touched by her change of tone. Liz was like that. So was I for that matter. 'Yes, of course, I'm coming back. I've given up running away. Promise.'

It was good being back in my own place again, after the memory-ridden mausoleum of The Hollies. The boys had left it far cleaner and tidier than I ever had. On the pine table in the basement kitchen was a bottle of Margaux and a note.

Dear Jack,
You've been such a super, understanding landlord. Here's something to wish us luck with. We're so excited about LA. We're crossing everything we've got – and we do mean everything – that it all works out.
   Love,
   Neil and Andy.

I opened the wine and raised my glass, in a silent toast. Tomorrow, I had to see Geoffrey Lamplighter. He had some prospective tenants lined up.

I contemplated the evening ahead. A solitary meal looked in prospect. I didn't feel like going far so I ran my finger down the list of restaurants and phone numbers pinned up on the bulletin board. What about Italian? A nice big plate of spaghetti alla vongole, followed by saltimbocca was just the ticket. I was about to pick up the phone to call Due Franco, one of my favourite Islington places, when it rang.

I hesitated. It was almost certainly one of Neil and Andy's

146

luvvie pals, not yet up to date with their change of fortune. It would be mean not to answer as I had their US address and phone number in front of me. I picked it up.

'Jack?'

It was a woman's voice, but so faint I hardly recognised it at first. Then I did. For fuck's sake! A ghost from the past like Caesar haunting Brutus on the eve of Philippi. Not so much ghost as Nemesis.

With elaborate calm, I said, 'Hello, Clarissa,' then waited.

When she spoke again, there was, unusually for her, tentativeness in her words. 'You must wonder why I'm calling you. I know I'm the last person in the world who should ask you this, but I'd like you to help me. Something of the greatest seriousness has come up. It would be a very great kindness to me, Jack, if you would meet me to discuss it.'

'I don't understand. What can you and I possibly have to talk about? Can you give me some idea?'

'No, not on the phone. It's too complicated. Look, I quite understand if you don't want to . . .'

'Hang on, I didn't say I wouldn't.'

'You will, then?'

'Yes.'

'Thank you, Jack. I'm taking my son to the Round Pond in Kensington Gardens tomorrow afternoon. Can you be there at three?'

I saw Clarissa before she saw me. She is small, scarcely more than five feet two or three, with curly, slightly unruly dark hair and precisely chiselled features, which I might, in another woman, have called elfin. I guessed that she was in no more than her late thirties.

She was accompanied by a small boy, presumably the issue of her short-lived marriage to one Julian Hetherington-Browne of the F.C.O. He held in his arms with the possessive joy of the ten-year-old a large model sailing yacht. I dropped my eyes back to my newspaper, of which I hadn't read so much as a single paragraph, and waited for them to spot me.

Then I felt her hand on my arm. 'Jack, hello.'

I scrambled to my feet, wondering, stupidly, for a second whether I should embrace her but then I saw that she was holding out her small hand and I touched its cold bones briefly. She indicated the boy. 'My son, James.' Then she put her arm round him and drew him forward. 'This is Dr Armitage. He used to work with me at the Museum.'

The child shuffled the boat around to free up his right hand, shaking mine with the politeness which is dinned unmercifully into the prep-school pupil. 'How do you do, sir?'

'How do you do, James? You can call me Jack, by the way. That's a fine-looking craft you have there.'

'Grandpa gave it to me for my birthday.' He cast an anxious glance over to the pond, clearly impatient at this detention.

His mother smiled. 'Off you go, James. But be careful.'

'Thanks, Mum.' He dashed off.

Clarissa stared after him fondly for a moment, then turned back to me, her wide-apart brown eyes scrutinising me. Now she was up close, I noticed that her hair was more tightly curled and shorter than it had been when I'd last seen her. Her pale face had lost none of its air of strained intensity. I had never before seen her in casual gear. At the Museum she had worn power suits, white blouses and black tights. On that day, she wore white slacks and a pale yellow cotton top, buttoned up to the throat with a Nehru collar. Her shoulders were thin and she had no bosom to speak of. She wore the man's steel Breitling watch which had so amused the older women staff at the Farebrother, but no other jewellery, not even a wedding ring.

She sat down beside me on the bench as I shoved aside the sections of the *Observer*. 'Jack, I read about . . . your father in *The Times*. It must have been terrible.'

'Yes. It was.'

'Have the police made any progress?'

'No. None at all. Not that you'd expect them to, in the circumstances. They're not so hot on crimes committed last week, never mind forty years ago.'

She smiled wanly. 'True. But it must be hard on you. According to the paper it was you found the . . . your . . .'

I stepped in to help her over this difficult bit. 'My father's remains. I'm over the worst of the shock now. Actually, in the end, it makes things better not worse that I know he's dead. At least one has certainty.'

She nodded, and I could sense the relief that she could move on to safer ground. 'I gathered you were doing an excavation.'

'Yes. A rescue dig on a housing development site. I think there's a villa there. A big villa.'

'Sounds interesting. So have you . . .'

'Yes and no. The forensic guys finished quite quickly, but there were some more problems on the site. They come not single spies but in battalions. Vandalism, actually, this time. It was fairly nasty. I've closed it down for the moment. I'm not sure some of the younger volunteers will come back. I had to sort out the let of my London house, so I've taken a break.'

There was another pause, the atmosphere between us charged with the events of our last encounter, like a divorcing couple meeting for the first time after the final definitive row.

I kept silent. It was her move. I sensed that she felt if not exactly nervous, then not entirely in control. I knew from experience that I was witnessing a relatively rare phenomenon. Clarissa at a temporary loss for words.

Then, abruptly, she spoke. 'To stoop to cliché, you must be wondering, Jack, why I asked you to meet me here.'

I shrugged. 'Not really. You heard I was in town. You thought why don't I dig out my friend Jack for a stroll in the Park? Cheer him up a bit. Talk over old times, the good old days.'

She gave me a look that could have punched a hole in concrete. 'Jack, please don't be childish. I'm not here to apologise for the events of last February. Although I have to say, as you will see, it is only because you no longer have any connection with the Museum that we are here. Believe me, Jack. You are the last person on earth I'd call upon if there were any alternative. You have no judgement and no discretion. You are an intelligent man adept at concealing his intelligence.'

I wondered for a moment whether to walk out after this encomium, but my curiosity, which had drawn me here in the first place, wouldn't let me. The questions were lining up like cabs in a rank. Did the fact that I wasn't at the Farebrother mean that the matter concerned its affairs? If so, why was this usually ice-cold superwoman thawing enough to ask for my advice when she had studiously ignored it when I had been in post? I was surprised at the vehemence of her utterance, and at something else: a hint of an accent more definite than the neutral educated tone I'd heard before. I wasn't any good at such things – was it Yorkshire or Lancashire? – somewhere north of Watford, anyway. For someone as smart and self-assured as Clarissa, to speak in such a manner and to leave such a verbal slip showing must mean that she was really quite rattled.

She had lapsed into silence, sitting with her head bowed, twisting her slender hands in her lap. Then she looked up.

I put out my hand and let it rest on hers for a moment. 'I'm sorry. I didn't mean to start acting the goat. It was only because I'm actually quite nervous. I don't have to spell out why, do I? So why did you ask me here? If there is a reason, other than the pleasure of my company, I wish you'd tell me what it is.'

She smiled ruefully, a slight glow of warmth in her drawn, chilled features. 'I'm sorry. I just wish I wasn't in this position. I never have been before.'

'Neither have I if it's any comfort.'

150

'Obviously what I'm going to tell you must remain totally confidential. I really mean that, Jack.'

'I'm only indiscreet about myself. Truly.'

I saw her shudder as she drew in her breath. Her voice when it came was hardly more than a whisper. 'I have reluctantly reached the conclusion that the Chairman of the Trustees is engaged in dishonest activities with regard to the Museum.'

I stared at her in absolute amazement, my numbed brain struggling to disentangle the meaning of the bureaucratic phrases. 'Christ Almighty. What are you saying in plain English? Dishonest activities? Do you mean stealing?'

'Stealing, theft, fraud. It amounts to the same thing. Yes, I am saying that.'

'Jesus! Of course, people do steal from museums. Loonies, burglars, bent security oiks, light-fingered conservation technicians. Even curatorial staff. Ben Chalke had an assistant a few years back who turned out to have a taste for the rarer incunabula. Police raided his flat. Got them all back. Barmy bugger said he'd only borrowed them. But the Chairman of Trustees, the Right Honourable the Lord Greville PC. Did you see him opening one of the glass cases or what?'

The momentarily healthy flush on Clarissa's face had vanished. 'I was kidding myself this wouldn't be a waste of time, Jack. You obviously don't believe me. Why should you, after all? I shouldn't have asked you here.'

'Clarissa, please.' I reached out and this time I got a good grip on her cold and fragile hand, tugging her gently round to face me.

She pulled out of my grasp. Her huge eyes were downcast, but I could see that they were brimming bright with moisture on the point of becoming tears.

'Not quite the image is it, this? I started out thinking I could handle it alone, but the pressure's built up so much, I sometimes feel my head's bursting with it. I had to get help. I had to tell someone. You were the only possible person. I had hoped you might listen seriously to me. But I was wrong.'

She reached down to her handbag on the bench beside her for a handkerchief, blew her nose and passed a hand over her forehead.

'I didn't say I didn't believe you. But it's hard to take in. Please tell me about it. I'm still stunned. But fascinated. Please. You can trust me.'

Her moment of vulnerability had passed. When she spoke it was with her usual cool control. 'I hope so, Jack. I very much hope so. My career hangs upon it. Now, I'd better go right back to when it started. Just after you left the Museum, I began to look into the Keepers' systems for recording and administering the artefacts, which the consultants had reported as being deficient.

'I was amazed to find how lax the whole thing was. There was a complete lack of what I would call basic stock control. In theory, as you know, the system is simple and effective. Every artefact is marked with a unique number consisting of the date of acquisition and a number reflecting the order in which it was acquired in that year. A full description of the item is entered against this number in the acquisition ledgers. All items not on display or loan or removed for conservation should be in their correctly numbered places in the basement store. Wherever I looked there were discrepancies. Consequently, I ordered a full inventory, something which hadn't been done, apparently, for years, if ever. It caused an outcry. The Keepers immediately went over my head to the Chairman. They complained of lack of staff time and resources, and produced every bureaucratic obstacle known to man.

'Instead of sending them away, Greville agreed with them. He suggested that I should give myself time as he put it to bed down in the job. I should concentrate on the public presentation side of the Museum. I felt let down.

'One evening before close of business, a very junior member of the Conservators slipped into my office. She was very nervous. She begged me to see her even though the

Head Conservator didn't know she had come. She had been working on the repair of the Melwood Virgin. It was after your time, Jack, an accident with a workman's ladder.'

I chuckled. 'I read about it. Some oiks who were more used to working on demo sites. Cheapest tender or something.'

'The circumstances are not relevant,' she continued huffily. 'The young woman told me that in her view the fragments of alabaster that she was working on bore traces of chemical treatment designed apparently artificially to age the material. In other words, it was a fake.'

I was absolutely astonished. 'What are you saying? The Virgin is one of the finest pieces of late medieval sculpture in Britain. It can't be a fake. It's been in the Museum since the Founder's day.'

'That's what I said to her. I suggested she should have the fragments checked by her superior. She told me she'd already done that, and been assured that her worries were groundless. She was so clearly upset by the business, and intelligent and conscientious, that I said I would look into it.'

'And did you?'

'Of course. I saw the Head Conservator. He told me the young woman was entirely wrong. When I asked to see her results file, he told me that she was on sick leave, and that her original test results could not be found. I was so annoyed by what I regarded as at best unhelpfulness and at worst deliberate obfuscation that I found the woman's phone number from personnel and called her in the evening from home. She seemed frightened and told me that she'd been completely mistaken. I said she'd been sure enough to come to me. Then she started crying and said she daren't talk to me any more and put the phone down. I rang again and got an answering machine.

'The next day, I demanded to see for myself the fragments of the sculpture she had been working on. I was informed that they had been reassembled, and that the whole sculpture was undergoing a long-term conservation procedure which could not be disturbed.

'I was so frustrated by these obstructions that I went round to the young woman's flat, at Archway. I was told by a girl she shared with that she'd left very suddenly that morning, saying she'd been offered a job abroad, but she hadn't given a forwarding address.'

'These things happen,' I said, trying to convince myself. 'Young people do move around these days.'

'That's what I told myself. But she wasn't, from what I saw of her, that kind of young woman. Very serious, a bit uptight.'

'Perhaps she reminded you of someone,' I hazarded.

Her mouth set in a hard line. 'Perhaps she did. And I wouldn't have done that. I think she was scared. I think someone had scared her.'

'But why Greville?'

'It was his reaction. I told him of the allegations about the Virgin. He said he had already been informed of something of the kind. When I suggested they should be reported to the next meeting of the Trustees, he was absolutely furious. He said quasi-public discussion of such sensitive matters would cast unnecessary doubt on the authenticity of the object, about which there was no doubt. He also adamantly forbade any independent expert's examination of the object for the same reason. He pontificated to me about the extent to which the Museum world is riddled with jealousy and backbiting. "We can't afford the loss of confidence it would imply about our expertise."'

'He had a point. The accusation was made by someone who'd skipped off, apparently.'

'Apparently and very conveniently. However, I had to acknowledge the situation. It was another matter entirely which made me suspicious of his motives.'

She picked up her handbag and took from it a folded wad of glossy paper. 'This.'

154

She handed it to me. It consisted of several pages torn from the magazine *Country Life*. I glanced at them, then back at her. 'What am I supposed to do?'

'Read it, of course,' she ordered.

I complied. It was one of its features on distinguished English country houses. They follow a pattern. An introduction to the house and its architectural history, then a description of its present-day state, and the principal items of furniture or art it contains. The extant proprietor is photographed amongst his treasures, and given a fulsome tribute, particularly, as in this case, if he is some nouveau type who's spent squillions on it.

The house concerned in this one was Windsoredge House, near Cirencester, Gloucestershire, and the latter-day nabob was Lord Greville.

I finished reading it, laid it on my knee and looked at her. 'So? He lives in the kind of place you'd expect. It looks in better nick than The Hollies. I must ask him who his builder is.'

'Did you look at the photographs?'

'Yes, of course. He's got some nice stuff.'

'You didn't notice anything particularly nice?'

The way she said it made me turn back to the article. There were half a dozen photographs, three of the exterior and grounds and three of the interior, two in black and white showing the magnificent hall and staircase, with ceiling paintings by Sir James Thornhill and the dining room with its oak panelling and Jacobean moulded plasterwork. The third, in colour, showed the library, with Lord Greville leaning against a chesterfield with the hint of a smile on his narrow, saturnine face.

I looked closely at all of them, then I said, 'It's not my period, but there are what look like some particularly good Greek pots. You can see them in the glass case there in the library, just beside his nibs.'

'Good, Jack. Very good. Now what would you say if I told

you that one of those vases came from the Farebrother?'

I stared at her. 'I'd say it was very hard to tell, even for an, well someone who . . .' I floundered to a halt at her flushed and angry expression.

'What you're trying to say, Jack, is how does an ignoramus like me claim to be able to identify a piece of Greek pottery? I know what you and your ex-colleagues said about me – especially that old pouf Benedict Chalke. Doesn't know the first thing about museums, etc, etc. Greville thought that too: he was too arrogantly sure of his opinion to check if he were right. Do you know, at my so-called interview in his office in Piccadilly, he didn't ask me a single question. He talked non-stop for half an hour about himself and the Farebrother, then offered me the job. Well you were all bloody wrong. I do know something about Greek art – not in a formal academic sense. My father was only a carpenter, but he was an autodidact and had a passion for everything Greek. In our house we must have had every book on Greece and Greek art published in English in the last hundred years or so. I caught the bug from him. Every year we spent our holidays in Greece. Every year, we came up to London two or three times to go round the museums, the Farebrother included. I do know what I'm talking about. The vase in the photograph formed part of the Harrington bequest. It shows a shoemaker at work in his shop.'

'Well, I don't see the problem. If the photo shows Greville in possession of a stolen vase, tell the police. They have a special unit for art theft nowadays.'

'That's the whole point, Jack. The vase hasn't been stolen. It's still on display.'

I stared at her in amazement. 'Well if it hasn't been stolen, Greville can't have it in his house.'

'Stop looking at me as if I were out of my mind, Jack. Think.'

'You can't be certain from that photograph whether the one Greville has is just similar.'

'That's a fair point. I saw the article in the magazine quite by chance as my secretary's father takes it and she thought I might be interested. Last weekend, I made an excuse to call at Windsoredge – said I was staying with friends near by for the weekend and had some urgent papers for him to sign. Of course, while I was there he couldn't resist the opportunity to show me round. The man is vain, as the article shows. I saw the collection and I'm convinced that it's identical to the one in the Museum.'

'Then it must be a copy.'

'No, I think the one in the Museum is the copy.'

'You can't know that.'

'Everything I know about Greville supports it. He would never be content with second best. He wouldn't display a copy at Windsoredge. It would be the only thing there that isn't absolutely genuine and first class of its type.'

'Then why take such a risk, invite in *Country Life*, show you around?'

'There was no risk with the magazine. No one would notice and if they did, they would think he had one very similar. It must have been sheer bravado that he let them photograph it. He got a kick out of showing off how clever he is. As for me, he thinks of me as you all did. I'm a boring civil servant, and a woman to boot. He doesn't believe I know one end of an artefact from another. He didn't want anyone in charge who knew anything. He wanted someone who would throw the furniture around, keep everyone preoccupied, not have time to spot what was going on.'

'Going on?'

'Yes. There's a pattern to what I've discovered. A deliberate, orchestrated carelessness about record-keeping. The implication that a famous Museum exhibit like the Virgin, whose authenticity has never been questioned, is claimed by someone who examined it closely to be a fake. The matter of the Greek vase. Do you not see what I'm getting at?'

'I think so. The best way to steal internationally known

157

works of art would be to conceal the fact that they had been stolen. You steal items from the reserve collection, then hide their disappearance in chaotic records. Other items, you replace with such high-quality fakes that their removal goes unnoticed.'

'Precisely.'

I gazed at the children launching their toy boats on to the gleaming water of the pond. Their cries seemed muted by the pounding blood in my skull.

'You really believe that's what's been happening?'

'Yes. I think the Greek vase was a vanity project – something for himself. But he's mainly in it for the money. Lots of it.'

'But why? Greville's rolling. He doesn't need money.'

'How do you know?'

'The newspapers, television. Hardly a day goes by without some high-profile deal being mentioned.'

'And you believe that? You wouldn't believe anything you read or heard about your own specialism, would you? What if the *Sun* said there had been a major discovery of Roman remains?'

I hesitated. 'I'd assume some bloke had found an old hat-pin on his allotment.'

'Precisely. I'm an economist. I did my own research on Greville's enterprises. I know a lot of people who will talk to me off the record. Old colleagues at the DTI and the Monopolies and Mergers Commission. The word is that Greville is in trouble. The companies he controls are skilfully presented but there's very little underneath the gloss. And he's had major setbacks. His motor trade division lost the franchise for one of the smaller Japanese car companies last year. That was covered up as part of a corporate reorganisation, but it was damaging. The haulage, dispatch and security companies have had to become less profitable because of competition. His investment in a Canadian mining consortium went belly up after a bad environmental assessment. All that affects his pocket directly. You see, his personal wealth, as so often with these types, is on paper. Shares in his own companies. Bank loans backed by those shares. Even his properties – Windsoredge House and a place in town – are mortgaged to the hilt as security for various deals. He needs the money all right.'

'Even Greville couldn't have done this by himself. Other Keepers would have to be involved. Are you seriously suggesting he's corrupted them all?'

'Why do you think I'm talking to you, Jack? Greville made no objection to your being asked to resign. In fact he was quite insistent you had to go. Not,' she added hastily, 'that I disagreed with that assessment. But if you had been in on the scam, there would surely have been pressure on me for you to keep your job. Therefore I can trust only you. I'm convinced that, with the possible exception of Benedict Chalke, the rest of them are involved in some manner. And whatever the problems of our relationship, Jack,' she continued drily, 'you don't have Chalke's pathological hatred and jealousy of me. That alone would make it impossible for us to work together. Besides, you're the only person I can offer a deal to.'

'What deal?'

'I want you to help me stop Greville's game, Jack. In return for which, you have my word that you will be found a place at the Museum of a similar status and remuneration to the one you had.'

'So what do I have to do to gain this munificent reward. You haven't said.'

'I want to get proof that the vase in the Farebrother is a fake. There's only one way to do that without alerting Greville's suspicions. I want you to steal it.'

V

'Good morning, Liz. Mr Armitage's out early, is he?'

I looked up from the newspaper. Mrs Hargreaves was standing at the front door of the kitchen, having let herself in at the front.

'Only I noticed that car of his weren't there.'

I had suggested in a fit of democracy several years before that Mrs Hargreaves and I, given that we found ourselves thrown together so much, should be on Christian name terms. Jack had never made this concession.

'Good morning, Sue. Jack's gone to London. He left yesterday morning.'

She helped herself to tea. 'Bit sudden, wasn't it? I mean there'll be people surprised that he's upped and offed. But that was always his way, I remember.'

I didn't want to get into discussing my brother or the future of his relationship with Ellen, to which she was obviously referring. I stood up and slipped *The Times* into my briefcase, saying coldly and firmly, as I put on my coat in the hall, 'He's gone to deal with the tenancy of his house, as a matter of fact.'

I had come out of my bedroom when I heard the slam of the front door. The roar of the Morgan down the drive had confirmed Jack's precipitate departure. I had expected after the horrible row we had had, and the nasty things he had said to me, to feel pleased to be on my own once more. Since then, however, the house had seemed gloomy and cavernous in a way it had not before he had arrived. I even missed the sound of his moving about the house in the early hours, plagued by his insomnia, which had infuriated me when it woke me at the beginning of his stay.

I felt all at once strangely alone and depressed. I had been looking forward to getting back to my old routine, without the intrusions of his presence, but now the week stretching before me felt empty and oppressive.

I felt a surge of anger as I turned the car round in front of the house, yanking the steering wheel with unnecessary force and jabbing my foot so hard on the gas that the front tyres spun, rattling the shingle in the wheel arches. Jack had felt free to dish out more shit and walk out on me again, as I had always thought he would. He'd promised to come back. Promises, as Mrs Pritchard used to say to us as children, were pie crust, made to be broken.

'Do sit down, Liz. I'll be with you in a moment.'

I sat obediently in the black leather chair, my hands demurely in my lap and waited for Linda Rice to finish making amendments to a typescript in her minute hand-writing.

Linda's office was a large room on the upper floor of the school. From the picture window she had a panoramic view of the paved internal quadrangle at the centre, which, like the forum of ancient Rome, was the main hub of activity. It was a school legend that she kept a pair of high-powered binoculars to scan the area for miscreants.

When Linda had taken over from Frank Bartleby, the big, sloppy liberal-to-a-fault Yorkshireman who had piloted the school from its start as a comprehensive formed from the town's two grammar schools, she had thrown out the battered leather-topped desk, decrepit bookcases, sagging chairs and threadbare carpet with which he had surrounded himself, rather like an old bear in a scruffy cave. To replace them had come a vast matt black table on anodised aluminium

161

legs, black leather chairs, and industrial-type white enamelled metal shelving. There were not one but two computer monitors on a white metal console.

She shuffled the papers together, screwed the cap back on her gold fountain pen and laid it on top. Then she raised her head and looked at me.

Linda was a few years younger than I, and in her prime. She was too tall and powerfully built to be conventionally attractive, but she had well-shaped regular features, perfect skin and an abundance of severely coiled and braided ash-blonde hair. She dressed expensively in well-tailored skirts and jackets. Today's was dark grey with a discreet chalk-stripe.

'Well, Liz. The reason I've asked you to see me. I have had a complaint.'

'Oh?' I said, with deliberately casual interest. 'From whom?'

'Mrs Ogilvie. Concerning her eldest daughter.'

'What about Emily?'

'A singularly delicate matter.' Linda was at her most orotund. 'Her mother alleges that you have formed an unhealthily close attachment to Emily.'

'The stupid bitch!'

'Is that your considered response?'

'No, on consideration, I'd add "ignorant".'

Her face flushed red. I'd managed to achieve the difficult feat of disturbing her massive sphinx-like calm.

'This is not a joke, Liz. I'd like your serious attention to this matter.'

'I was perfectly serious. Mrs Ogilvie is on the Social Services Committee of the County Council, God help us. She sees sexual abuse behind every bush. I don't say Emily doesn't have a crush on me. That's a normal developmental stage. I neither encourage nor discourage it.'

'You've apparently given her additional personal tuition at your home.'

162

'She needs it. She'll be first-class honours material, provided her mother's hysterical attitudes don't ruin her.'

'Do you give me your word that there is no substance in the accusation?'

'Of course.'

She sighed and looked away. 'Then I must believe you. I don't think you live in the real world, Liz. You're not sensitive to how things are. I want you to stop seeing pupils at home. It encourages inappropriate personal relationships.'

'I always thought education was supposed to be personal.'

She gave me one of her narrow-eyed stares, the sort that made grown men howl. 'I don't want to have this kind of conversation with you again, Liz. Is that clearly understood?'

I went straight into the female staff washroom and burst into tears. It was too much. First the plays and now this. So much for the hours of unpaid overtime I put in. Then, to impugn my sexuality, and imply I had corrupted my students into the bargain, the second time in days that that hurtful accusation had been made. The nasty cow.

If only she knew the truth about my sexuality. Well one day, I'd make sure she did.

I was finishing my supper that evening when the door bell rang. It was Chief Inspector Green.

I took him into the drawing room and gave him coffee. He sat on the chesterfield looking ill at ease.

'The forensic people are in some difficulty. Bones, particularly ones which have been in the earth as long as your father's, can be a problem.'

'How do you mean?'

'In terms of identification. There's no problem with a body. You have fingerprints, as well as features and characteristics. Eventually someone recognises them. Bones are not very helpful.'

I stared at him, my heart beginning to pound. 'You mean you're not sure it's my father's body?'

'I didn't say that. I'm sure as I can be that it is. I've been certain of that since that first day. All the evidence pointed to it. The circumstances, the watch. And the lab analysed the scraps of clothing which remained and they checked out for materials and period of manufacture. But as to direct evidence from the remains themselves, all they can say is that it was a male of approximately the same age and height as your father. When you're talking of an inquest on a homicide victim, we ought to be more precise.'

'I thought you could tell from the teeth?'

'Yes, they're the usual way. But in this case, despite extensive enquiries, we haven't been able to find any of Mr Armitage's dental records. We've checked all the local practices, including the successor of the one you told us you went to as a child, which have been in operation since the fifties, and they have no charts. Nor have the MOD been able to turn anything up from his service records.'

'What about DNA testing?'

'That's normally used the other way round in police investigations. You want to find a live body, not identify a dead one. You have a scene of crime tissue sample. Then you try and match its DNA to your suspect's. But in this particular case there's no tissue sample to match with the DNA in the bones.'

'What do you mean by a tissue sample?'

'Anything organic. Blood, skin, hair . . . What's the matter, Miss Armitage? You've gone terribly pale. Can I get you a glass of water or . . . ?'

I held up a hand. 'No, don't worry, I'm all right. I think I can solve your problem, if hair will do. I have some of my father's hair. In a locket. He . . . I asked him to give me some. The sort of thing little girls do. I'll get it for you.'

I handed him the tiny gold case on the thin gold chain. My hands were shaking so I left him to pop open the catch. Inside was a loop of dark hair.

'You're sure this is your father's?'

164

'Absolutely sure.'

'I'm no expert on these things, but this may be just what we need.'

He fished in his pocket for a plastic envelope and slipped the locket into it. 'I'll need a statement to that effect, if you could drop into the station in the next few days.'

I nodded. 'You'll let me have it back, won't you? I mean will they need it all?'

For once his official expression softened. 'I'm sure they can get everything they need from just a few hairs. I'll make sure you get your keepsake back, promise.'

'Going somewhere nice, Miss Armitage?' Ellen Norton hung her brown suede jacket on the hall stand and fluffed up her blonde hair which had been dampened down by the evening drizzle. She regarded herself critically in the glass. 'What a drowned rat. Should have brought my brolly. Miserable for the time of year, isn't it?'

'It's only a boring meeting with colleagues, I'm afraid, Ellen. Curriculum planning for next year.'

She nodded without interest, picking up her Marks and Spencer carrier bag from the top of which protruded the tops of a couple of glossy magazines.

'You know where everything is, of course. Help yourself to tea or coffee and there's some cake in the larder. I'm afraid the television's gone wrong, and I haven't had time to get someone to fix it.'

'It's all right. I've got these books. The latest ones. Borrowed them from the shop. Don't tell old grumble guts, will you?' She chuckled, her blue eyes sparkling with mischief at this description of her surly employer, and I smiled in return.

It didn't seem so long ago that Ellen Hargreaves, in a too-short skirt and a scarlet lip-gloss which magnified the sensual pout of her lips, had been one of the under-age sirens whose precocious sexuality had seriously disturbed the equilibrium of the GCSE English literature class. I'd always thought that beneath the candy-floss a more able and serious girl had been lurking, but had never succeeded in reaching it and now never would.

'Jack . . . I mean Mr Armitage still away?' she asked, apparently casually, as I picked up my mac and handbag and reached for the rim lock of the front door.

I'd been dreading her asking this. What made me know instinctively that Jack hadn't been in touch with her? But I was damned if I was going to lie for him. It was time Ellen knew the kind of man she was involved with, like the rest of the world.

'I really don't know how long he's staying up. Could be a couple of weeks.'

She'd gone pale. 'Weeks. He never said anything.'

I opened the door, not wanting to get any deeper into Jack's sordid little affair. 'Sorry, Ellen. 'Bye, back about midnight, OK?'

I arrived as the light was fading, following the red Jaguar which had been waiting for me as arranged in the lay-by outside Stow-on-the-Wold. We drove down a deserted deep lane, turned into a green tunnel by huge trees arching overhead. On my right I saw the tall honey-stone gate pillars, the wrought iron gates flung wide. We turned on to the weed-free shingle sweep.

It was a perfect eighteenth-century Cotswold stone manor house, the kind which features in one of those homes magazines. There were beautiful arched windows and a columned entrance porch with pink and white roses climbing over it. It was much smaller than The Hollies, more graceful and much more beautifully maintained.

He was fiddling with keys at the front door. 'Miss Armitage? Do come in.'

The hall was paved with worn paving slabs of the same honey-stone as the house. There was genuine linenfold wainscot panelling on either side.

'It's a lovely property, isn't it?'

'Everything you said it was. I'm longing to see over it.'

'OK. Let's start with the heart of the house. The kitchen.' He threw open a door. 'Feast your eyes on this.'

'God. This must have cost a fortune.'

'It did, Miss Armitage. All real old pine. Baltic yellow. Sailing ships were made of it. Proper wood, properly seasoned, not the stuff they force up like rhubarb and pump full of chemicals. And look at the equipment. The owner fancies himself as a chef.'

A stone arch led to the dining room beyond. Through leaded, mullion windows, I could glimpse a huge lawn, flanked by a stone-paved path, a herbaceous border and a high dry-stone wall, and backed by beech trees. The dying rays of the sun sparkled on the raindrops sprinkling the closely mown turf and gleamed on the wet surface of the stones. The mahogany dining table and the eight matching chairs looked like genuine Chippendale.

There was a big comfortable sitting room, thickly carpeted, filled with flowery chintz furniture, and the kind of multiple drape curtains, using yards and yards of material you only see in places where the interior designer has been given a blank cheque. A table groaned with piles of arty picture books. There were good pictures on the walls, and a cabinet full of early Wedgwood.

We glanced into a study, and what he called the music room. Then he led me up the cantilevered stone staircase.

'The master bedroom suite.'

Here there was a French Empire theme. Lots of gilt, lots of curves. A vast bed was covered with an elaborate scarlet satin and lace counterpane. A stunning carved gilt and mahogany looking glass, cherubs blowing trumpets, cheeks distended, hung over the white marble fireplace, reflecting the whole room.

The view from the window was even more beautiful than from the dining room. The wooded slopes of a small valley softly cradled the house and its garden. The sun was setting in a blaze of gold and scarlet. I opened the casement and leant out. There was a heady scent of jasmine and honeysuckle borne upwards on the moist warm air from the pergola-covered courtyard below.

Then I heard him close behind me.

'Do you like it?'

'It's beautiful.'

'It's not the only thing that's beautiful.'

'What do you mean?' I half turned to look at him, but the expression on his face was lost in shadow.

'I mean you. You're an extremely beautiful woman, Miss Armitage. You have a marvellous figure.'

I turned fully round, pressing myself back against the windowsill. He stood in front of me, a tall, dark athletic man, his hands on his hips, quite relaxed.

'I think it's time I went.'

I moved as if to get past. He put out his hand, and pushed me back gently but firmly.

'No, don't go. We were starting to have an interesting conversation. Don't look so frightened, I'm not going to hurt you. We were talking about your figure, if you remember.'

'I told you. I want to leave here now. Please let me go.'

'No, not yet, Miss Armitage. A schoolmistress, I believe. Lucky schoolboys, is what I say. Does it turn you on when you catch them looking up your skirt? I wonder if you get much extra-curricular activity? I bet you don't. I bet you have to make your own entertainment.'

'Please. I absolutely insist. Let me past. I swear if you do, I won't mention this to your boss.'

'Mention what? That we had a little conversation? You happened to mention how little excitement there was in your life. You shared one of your fantasies with me.'

'I can't believe I'm hearing this. You're mad. A pervert.'

He held up his hand and for a moment a quite different expression from his bland smile flashed across his face. 'No

168

nasty name-calling, please. Now, about that fantasy of yours. It was like this. You'd always wanted to take off your clothes in front of a complete stranger. And then have some fun with yourself, while he watched.'

'Oh, my God. No, I won't. You can't make me.'

'I don't have to make you. It's caught your imagination, you see. You want to. Look at you, you're trembling.'

'You bastard. You absolute bastard.'

'First, your jacket. Come on, no tears, get on with it. That's better, now your blouse. Unbutton it slowly, that's it. Now slip it off.'

I felt the chill of the room on my shoulders, as I stood there before him.

'God, you are so beautiful. What wonderful breasts. Let me see them. Reach up and unhook your bra, and ease out of it. Oh yes, superb. Now the skirt.'

Again I saw the same expression on his face, a hardening of the mouth and jaw and a hooding of the eyes. I unzipped my skirt and stepped out of it. 'All right, you've had your little joke. Please let's stop this now.'

'Stop? When we're getting to the interesting bit? Not on your life. Roll off your stockings. First one leg, then the other. Lovely. Now the *pièce de résistance*. Slide them down, all the way.'

I was shivering all over now. I pushed the lace-trimmed pants down over my hips and let them fall to the floor. I stood in front of him completely naked. 'I beg you, please, for God's sake, leave me alone.'

'Oh, a natural blonde. I do like a plentiful bush. I don't like them all shaved. Why are you getting stressed up? I'm not doing anything, am I? You're enjoying yourself, aren't you, really? I know you women always say no when you mean yes. Now, start to fondle your breasts with the palms of your hands. Round and round. Can you feel your nipples getting harder?'

'For pity's sake!'

He took a step towards me, and his voice had a rougher edge. 'Now, the real business. Just like you would on a quiet evening at home on the sofa, with something slow and sexy on the hi-fi.'

With one last mute expression of appeal, I shuddered, parted my thighs and slid my right hand between them.

'That's it, nice and slow. You see, you are enjoying it. I can see that. I knew you would. I can always tell. Now turn round. I want a back view. Bend over, but don't stop.'

I faced the window again. Behind me there was a scuffling sound, then he was leaning on me, pressing me against the sill.

I wriggled furiously but his weight jammed my legs against the wall beneath the window. He was hard against me and I felt his hands unbuckling his belt. 'You utter shit,' I sobbed.

'I won't hurt you. You're ready for me.'

'You'll never get away with this. I'm going to scream the place down.'

'We're a long way from the nearest house. Besides, you'll sound like a pheasant. Or a vixen.'

His knee forced itself between my naked thighs, spreading them. His hands were claws on my shoulders. I felt the heat of him as he entered me, and then my whole body seemed to expand and blossom, even as the red-gold disc of the sun dipped into the blanket of grey cloud which edged the horizon.

'How was it for you?' Martin Rice breathed softly into my ear.

I stretched drowsily under the duvet. 'All right.'

'What do you mean all right? It was spectacular. What did you think of the new wrinkle?'

'Typical male fantasy. What is it about men and schoolmistresses?'

'Cheeky bitch! What about you? You certainly entered into the spirit of the thing. You were turned on, admit it.'

170

'Maybe.'

'There's no maybe about it. I should know. Perhaps it was the ambience. I'll bet you were surprised when you realised where I was leading you.'

'I thought it was risky.'

'There aren't any neighbours. Linda's gone off to stay with her mother for the weekend. She said she hadn't seen her for ages.'

'Lucky old her. I still think it was taking a chance.'

'Life's all about risk, isn't it? If you hadn't liked a touch of danger, you'd never have gone along with these games in the first place. You're pretty cool, though, Liz. I wonder how you would have reacted if I'd been a real rapist? Would you still have enjoyed it?'

I shrugged. 'It would depend what the alternative was. What about you? You were authentically creepy at times. Perhaps you fancy yourself as a real villain? You even put on a touch of sarf London accent.' I paused, then added, 'Or did that come naturally?'

He shot me a look that was disturbingly similar to the one he had given me in our role-play. I realised that my remark had touched a raw nerve.

'What a sharp one you are, Elizabeth. You're right as a matter of fact. I grew up in a Lewisham council flat. I'm not ashamed of where I came from. It shows how far I've gone. I've done pretty well for myself, through my own efforts. As you can see from this house. Funnily enough, it will actually be on the market soon. There's something coming up I like even better. With a long carriage drive. I've always fancied that.'

'Estate agency is booming then?'

'Estate agency, property, leisure. Everything booms, my darling Liz, if you know what you're doing. You could be living the good life. No more penny pinching.'

'What do you mean? All I have is a teacher's salary. I can't run a Jag on that.'

171

'Come off it, Liz. Think about it. You may not have the income, but look at all that lovely capital. You're sitting on a whole pile of it. The Hollies. To the right buyer, it's worth a fortune. I've always thought so.'

'It's practically falling down.'

'No, it's not. It's basically a very solid house. A builder would sort it out in no time. Of course, a private buyer wouldn't want it, but it would be ideal as a nursing-cum-retirement home. It's a big business now, you know. All that land round the main house, you could get masses of sheltered housing units on it. Sun City comes to Oxfordshire. It's the future.'

'It's my mother's house, Martin, not mine.'

'Come off it, Liz. Your mother neither knows nor cares where she is any more. Your lawyer could easily get round any problems.'

He spoke with the casual confidence of a man used to circumventing the tiresome demands of legality.

'Think about it. You'd be crazy not to. Meanwhile, I'm going to have a little of the usual before we continue. You're sure you don't want to indulge?'

'You know I won't touch that filthy stuff, Martin.'

'You don't know what you're missing. The school ma'am in you's never far away, is she Liz? Even stark naked with your legs apart.'

I ignored this and deliberately looked away as he fumbled in the bedside cabinet.

I spat the semen discreetly into a tissue from the box on the bedside table. Martin was dead to the world, as he always was on these occasions, sprawled out on the rucked-up quilt, a contented grin over his tanned face, with its strong nose and well-moulded chin.

For a man of forty or so, he was in good shape. His chest, rising and falling with deep and contented breathing, was, beneath its mat of hair, solid with muscle. There was

172

no flab either on his hips, and his stomach was firm and flat.

His prick was gradually subsiding, collapsing in on itself, the head losing its stretched glossy smoothness, the foreskin shrivelling like a melting candle, retreating into the dark lair of pubic hair as if it were one of those animals which, having puffed itself into a terrifying show of aggression well beyond its actual physical capabilities, takes a well-earned breather.

The window was a black mirror. Night had long since fallen.

I ought to have been, as usual, exhilarated to have had sex with this desirable man who clearly found me desirable, a pleasure in itself and spiced moreover with the thought that Linda Rice would be more than considerably enraged to know not only that Martin was having an affair, but an affair with me.

But on that occasion, I sank back on the pillow and felt terrible.

I'd met him at this very house, at the lavish party Linda had held at the beginning of her reign at Waterbury. I'd been tempted into a game of tennis on the brand new court by an old school friend I hadn't seen in years. Despite my wonky arm, I'd managed to beat her convincingly.

Linda had showed me up to one of the guest rooms so I could shower. When I came out of the en suite bathroom, a towel around my waist, Martin Rice was sitting in an armchair.

'Hi, feeling better?'

'Do you normally come spying on your guests?'

He stood up. 'Only when I think I'll like what I see.'

I let the towel fall to the floor. 'And do you?'

He moved towards me. 'Oh yes,' he said. 'Very much.'

And that had been, as they say, that. We were discreet. Martin had the excuse of business trips away and in any case Linda was a workaholic, always buried in papers or out at meetings. We never met in public places. We never wasted time on preliminaries in bars or restaurants. From the very first time we had made love, we were fairly adventurous.

We had found the ideal way of putting into practice our mutual fantasies. Martin's firm had from time to time on its books properties which by a combination of their seclusion and the frequent absences of their owners were ideal for clandestine meetings. We both enjoyed the variety of games we played in these pilfered surroundings.

It was reassuring to me to be wanted fiercely and passionately by a good-looking man. It wasn't love, but I'd never expected to find that chimera. Martin and I in fact had rather more reason to despise each other.

I thought he was, in the manner of those Edwardian novels I had devoured in The Hollies library as a girl, a cad and a bounder, an impression gained from what I knew and heard around the town of his business ethics, and from what I saw for myself of his personal behaviour. I particularly loathed his cocaine habit. At least I hadn't come down to his level there. In that respect I retained some dignity.

As for Martin, I had supposed that I represented to him the upper-middle-class bitch he spent his professional life being polite to. In screwing me, he screwed a whole bag of psychological hang-ups.

Thus, we had nothing but sexual needs, and the urge to satisfy them, in common. It wasn't much but it was enough.

Now, as I lay on my side in the disordered bed, the sweat of our urgent embraces still cooling on my naked skin, even the limited integrity of that bond had revealed itself as an illusion. The penny had dropped. I knew why Martin Rice had singled me out from all the possible women in Oxfordshire and beyond. I had been stupidly naive to believe in my erotic appeal. No, in my case, the turn-on was not sex, but money.

The rat was after The Hollies. He'd been careful enough up to now not to breathe a word of it. But just now, he hadn't been able to resist dropping it into the conversation, as he'd no doubt been planning to when he had the right opportunity.

He was smooth and clever, but he'd made one slip. He said he'd always thought that The Hollies was worth a fortune. 'Always' meaning before he'd had the idea of having intimate relations with the occupier.

Of course, the house came first with a guy like Martin. He'd been around this part of the world for some time. He would have checked out all the angles on his territory as a matter of course. When he realised that I held the key to The Hollies, of course he'd been aroused. And when I was sufficiently softened up by the experience, it would no doubt transpire that the right buyer for it would, in some shape or form, be Martin Rice himself.

I roused myself from this bitter reverie, yawned, and glanced at my watch. It was time to get back. I picked up my scattered clothing, dressed carefully and brushed my hair. I didn't want to look rumpled. Ellen might twig that my meeting had been more exciting than I'd let on. Or perhaps not. As I was as old as her mother, she probably didn't regard sex as any longer on my agenda.

I leant over Martin and shook him. 'I have to go.'

He grunted sleepily. 'By the way, can't do next week. I'm away on business. Besides, it might be good to have a bit of a break and miss the week after too. Linda suspects I've been having a fling. With Dawn.'

'And you haven't of course?'

'Of course not. Cross my heart, miss.'

I was fairly sure that, despite his routine denial, Martin was screwing the new recruit to his firm. I'd seen her through the window of his office when I passed it a few days ago. Martin's type, like me, tall, blonde, athletic, good looking. Except she was twenty years younger.

It was the final straw. He was keeping me on the hook because of The Hollies, but the real sport was elsewhere. If I continued to refuse to play on the property side, there would, as he'd just hinted, be no more out-of-school entertainment for little Lizzie.

I descended the staircase. We had turned off the lights, but I had no problem in finding my way. Through the tall, round-headed landing window the moonlight streamed, bleaching the colour from the furniture of the hall. There was no sound from upstairs. Martin must have gone back to sleep.

I had my hand on the latch of the front door, and I was about to let myself out, when the hurt and anger caused by the indignity of my situation made me pause.

If my affair with Martin was going to be over soon, then why should I not put an end to the humiliation now? I had nothing to lose. And why should that shit get away with it? How about some indignity and humiliation for him. It was pay-back time for his bitch of a wife as well. It might not be her mud, but it would stick just the same.

I had noticed that there was a telephone in the room on the left of the front door when we had been doing the 'view'. It was set up as a study-cum-library in the male idiom, all dark wood bookcases and thick Persian rugs, Martin indulging himself in the kind of London club surroundings which, despite his wealth, he would never really measure up to.

I hesitated. Was this proper retribution or simply the jealous fury of a scorned woman? What the hell, I'd do it anyway. I'd ring the police, report anonymously that Martin Rice was in possession of an illegal drug at Ewescombe Manor, then clear off, leaving the front door ajar.

I turned the knob and went in. There was a fancy modern reading lamp on the desk. I switched it on. As I did so I knocked over with a clatter a large silver photograph frame which had stood there. I listened, alarmed in case the sound should have woken the sleeper upstairs, but there was nothing.

As I picked up the frame to replace it, I saw the colour photograph it contained.

It had been taken here. It had as a background the tree-clad

176

valley, and there was a glimpse of the house over a rolling lawn in the lower corner. It unashamedly evoked the great period of English portraiture. A modern version of Gainsborough's Mr and Mrs Andrews.

On a rustic garden bench were seated Mr and Mrs Rice. He, in tweed jacket and flannels, stared at the camera, tanned, square jawed and straight backed, the image of the country gentleman. Linda looked at her most winsome, in a flowery print dress, her usually severely braided blonde hair blowing free around her shoulders, her complexion, unblemished as a ripening peach, and her smile calm and sweetly assured.

This mendacious image would have served only to fuel my anger, were it not for the other persons in the foreground.

In the centre lay a curly-coated golden retriever, and on either side of the dog, like the tutelary nymphs of the locality, in the reclining posture suggestive of the drowsy ease of a summer afternoon, were two young girls, in the blonde perfection of maidenhood, with the looks of their mother, their long tresses seeming to wave in the gentle breeze that must have wafted over the scene. They wore frocks which covered discreetly their bare legs, leaving only a glimpse of calf and ankle beyond the drape of the hem. In the real world of teenagers in which I moved such dresses would have been as outlandish as crinolines or bustles.

Linda's daughters had never been near Waterbury Comprehensive, but attended a private boarding school near Warwick. Linda understandably kept very quiet about this. Consequently, I had never seen them before.

As I gazed at them, their radiant innocence illuminated my innermost being. *Et in arcadia ego*.

The tears started to my eyes. I had put my hand to the phone, but I withdrew it, my resolution gone. It had been a pleasant fantasy, but to do it in reality would have been despicable. I had known the damage a father's disgrace could wreak on a child. I could not inflict it myself on these delightful beings. All too soon, with a father like Martin Rice, they

177

would know the truth. But as long as ignorance was bliss, it would be worse than folly to make them wise.

I dried my eyes and was fumbling for the button on the lamp, when there was a subdued electronic beeping, then a whirring hum as of a machine starting up. Startled, I peered towards its source, seeing the glow of a tiny green light. A fax machine in receive mode.

The paper curled out of the slot and I detected on the still cool air of the room the warm chemical scent of it. I stared at it.

Who on earth would be sending messages to Martin Rice at this time of night? Perhaps someone from another time-zone, one of those mysterious international business partners that I'd heard him rather vaguely boasting about. So what exactly was this business? I had never admitted it to him, but I was curious.

The fax message lay there, invitingly available. To read it I had merely to pick it up. As a little girl I had been severely coached by my mother that it was impolite to read other people's correspondence. What better excuse could there be? I grabbed it from the machine.

The study door flew open, and the room was flooded with light. I whirled round to see Martin Rice, still naked, standing on the threshold, his hand on the switch.

For a moment we stared at one another speechless. Then he demanded in a voice much louder and rougher than his usual emollient tones, 'Liz. What the fucking hell are you doing in here?' I noticed that he dropped his aitches in his agitation.

'I was phoning home, of course. It's a bit later than I told Ellen to expect me. Did you think I was a burglar?'

He gave me a hard look which I returned defiantly. Then he seemed to relax. He conjured up a rueful grin and a faint shrug. 'I was startled. I thought you'd gone. I was coming down to get a drink when I saw the light under the door.'

He stood in the porch watching me as I crunched over the

shingle to the Escort and scrambled in. The engine started first time, and I was out of the entrance gates in a matter of seconds.

I drove home through the rainy night. Despite the heater's being on full blast, I was shivering. The swathe of road lit by the headlamps blurred with the tears I couldn't hold back. I certainly didn't love Martin. I didn't even respect him. But I grieved for what I thought we had had together, no matter how little. I had given him something of myself, and in return I had been deceived.

I didn't then recall, amid the flurry of emotions and events, that I had stuffed the shiny piece of fax paper into my coat pocket instinctively to avoid being caught reading it when he had burst into the study.

It took an effort to shake myself out of my upset when I arrived back at The Hollies. I apologised to Ellen for keeping her so late – these staff meetings did run on so – and offered to run her home by way of compensation. She also seemed deep in thought, and the short journey to her house on the estate on the other side of the village was a silent affair.

It was as I was returning down the hill past the church that I saw the light on the Glebe.

I stopped the car at the roadside and turned off the engine. There was a dry-stone wall on the boundary, and from inside the car, I could see nothing of what was going on within.

I sat in the darkness listening to the ticking sounds as the engine cooled. Thick clouds obscured the moon. The rain had stopped but a stiff wind was blowing. It moaned softly in the body work, occasionally making the car rock gently on its suspension. I was exhausted by the events of the evening and feeling utterly reluctant to leave the warm car, climb over the wall and find out what the wielder of the torch was up to, as I knew I ought for several reasons.

It was too late and too miserable a night for alfresco lovers or even the most dedicated of dog walkers. It might be kids fooling about. But it might also be the dedicated vandal who had wrought such havoc the previous week, havoc that I personally had helped to clear up. Jack had also on several occasions inveighed against treasure hunters with metal detectors and the damage they could do to a site. The publicity might have attracted some sicko looking for mortal rather than Roman remains.

I could phone the police if the call-box was working, but by the time they arrived the damage might have been done. The part of me which had been a schoolmistress for so long was also contributing its two penn'orth to the argument. I was used to enquiring of smirking boys and girls where they were going, what they were intending to do there and whether they had permission to do it.

Thus decided, I clicked open the door and slid quietly out. The wall was low enough for me to see over without climbing. I clasped the clammy upright stones of the coping and gazed into the pitch darkness. There was no sign of a light. I strained to hear, but there was nothing except the wind whistling through the gaps in the wall, and rustling the trees, whose fretted tops I could barely distinguish against the faint starry radiance of the sky.

Then, from across the field, there came the soft bleating of the Jacob sheep for which Mrs Evans at Well House won prizes at the Royal Show and the faint thud of their hooves as they moved uneasily about. Since the dig had started they had been temporarily penned into a narrow strip on the far side. Something or someone was bothering them now. I stared in their direction and, at that moment, in the middle of the Glebe, the light of a torch suddenly stabbed the darkness. Holding it was, I could faintly distinguish, the dark figure of a man.

Perhaps he'd heard the car, turned off the torch and kept quiet until the coast appeared to be clear. There was a row of cottages on the opposite side of the road, their windows unlit, and a number of the residents used to park on the verge alongside the wall. He may have thought I was one of them coming home late.

I watched him. He wasn't exercising his dog, that was for sure. The Jacobs would have been far more vocal in their objections if there had been a dog about, and the dog would hardly have refrained from barking in excitement.

As I stood gazing at the moving light, I became aware that there was a pattern to it. The beam was sweeping the ground from side to side, then the figure advanced and the sweeping motion started again. He was quite clearly searching for something.

Then all at once he stopped. I saw him bend down and place something on the ground, then the torch beam flashed around and pointed for a moment directly at me. I froze, hoping my profile blended with the jagged coping stones of the wall. When my eyes readjusted, I saw that he had come only a short distance in my direction. The light was once again directed at the ground, and shone upon a bulky, faintly familiar object standing there. In a moment, he half stooped to grasp it, and I heard his grunt of effort, as if it were heavy. Then I heard a faint mechanical squeaking and I realised what was happening: he was pushing a wheelbarrow. The beam of light wavered as he manoeuvred the barrow back in the direction from which he had come.

The light swept around once more. He must have placed a marker of some kind at the spot he had previously discovered. He stopped once again and there was the clink of metal, then the unmistakable scraping sound of a spade cutting into turf. My friend in the Glebe had started his own excavation.

What in hell's name was he up to? Was he a treasure hunter? What could he be expecting to find? I checked my watch, the luminous dots piercingly bright. Half past midnight. I'd been out of the house for half an hour. I ought not to leave Mother for much longer. Usually she went through the night, but occasionally she didn't, and she would be terribly upset if no one answered her call.

I shivered. This was a cold and pointless vigil. I had already seen enough to go home and phone the police.

The scraping sounds were joined by the intermittent thump of earth being thrown from the spade or shovel. I could hear, in the stillness of the night, the man panting with exertion. The steady scrape-thump rhythm of the digging continued, whilst I leaned there indecisively.

I had just made up my mind to go, and turned back to the car, when from the field there was a sharp clang of steel upon stone, then a muffled exclamation. Then a clatter as if the tool was flung down, followed by another clanging thud and a series of grunts of extreme exertion. Extraordinarily as it seemed, the man had found what he was looking for.

Even at that time I thought I was taking a risk. Looking back, I think I must have been crazy. But the habits of one's upbringing become ingrained. Crowcester was my village and I was used to knowing what was going on. I hadn't entirely lost that feeling of invulnerability with which the middle classes once confronted wrongdoers. That was why I scrambled over the wall and ran lightly over the thick grass, wet with dew, to the stooping, black clad figure.

'Hey, what do you think you're doing?'

In the pool of light cast by the heavy-duty hand lamp, which he'd hung with a loop of twine from the handle of a fork stuck in to the turf, I could see the dark square hole he had dug. He whirled round, still crouching, when he heard me. His face was obscured by a balaclava helmet, in which his eyes were gleaming points of light, his mouth a gaping void. In both hands he grasped a long crow-bar. The light gleamed on its slick black surface.

'I said what do you think you're doing?'

He made no reply, then to my horror, he raised the length of thick steel and swung it at my head.

I have fast reactions, but even so I almost didn't jump back quickly enough. I felt it graze my cheek and the pain as it caught a lock of hair and tugged it out.

At once I was sick with fear. If it had connected, the blow could have killed me.

Now he was coming after me, the crow-bar this time held forward like a lance.

I dodged as he feinted at me, desperately trying to evade the probing jab of the pointed end. I saw with alarm that he was moving between me and the direction of the road, with the intention of forcing me deeper into the field, to the temporary fence erected to pen the flock of sheep. Once he'd got me against the barbed wire, there was no escape. He'd cut me down before I could climb over.

I screamed for help, and the sound of it rose up and vanished into the vastness of the inky sky. Behind me, the sheep set up a disturbed bleating, but their sympathetic chorus succeeded only in drowning my own cries.

All the time, I was asking myself, why the hell is he doing this? What's at stake? Why kill me over a bit of illegal treasure hunting?

He was grunting and breathing heavily, like a man unfit, as if the effort of that first missed blow had somehow drained him, jerking his weapon towards me convulsively, as if building up to another massive swing which would finish me.

I retreated a further pace, then almost tripped as the backs of my knees connected with an iron rim. The wheelbarrow. My hands reached instinctively back, and closed on a chill, smooth cylinder, the handle of some kind of implement, a spade perhaps. I grabbed it gratefully, then, without conscious thought, in one smooth, almost effortless movement, as if I were playing a forehand smash, swung the wooden shaft at the hands that held the crow-bar.

I felt the blade bite with a jarring crunch into his right forearm. He screamed in agony at the dreadful blow and dropped his weapon. I threw down the spade and ran, sobbing and gasping, the bile rising in my throat, towards the road. I half-scrambled, half-vaulted over the wall, wrenched open the car door, slammed it to, and mashed down the stalk on the sill, hearing the satisfying slithering click as the central locking engaged. I roared the engine into life, and drove off, spinning the front wheels.

I remember nothing of the drive back to The Hollies. The next thing I was aware of was fumbling in my bag for the keys to the front door, virtually falling through it on to the cold tiles. On my knees, I banged the door shut. Using the hall stand, I dragged myself to my feet and lurched along the corridor into the kitchen. With a finger that shook convulsively I punched out 999.

'You've no idea who this man was, Madam?'

I shook my head, still feeling sick, even though over an hour had passed since the attack. I reached forward to pour another mug of tea from the pot that the policewoman had made for me. She gently set aside my trembling hand and filled the mug for me.

'Thanks. No. I told you. He was wearing a balaclava.'

'Did he give any sign that he knew who you were?'

'If he's local, it's very likely he would have recognised me. And that's what I couldn't, can't understand. Why did he attack me?'

'I deal with attacks on women all the time, I'm afraid. Nothing much surprises me any more.'

'Yes. I know there's that kind of attack. But it wasn't like that, I'm convinced of it. I approached him, stupidly as it turned out. And he didn't use the opportunity to assault or rob me. That first blow was aimed at my head. It would have almost certainly killed me. Look. It only just missed.' I pulled aside the curtain of hair over my right cheek to show her the graze of the crow-bar point. I winced as I did so. It wasn't deep, but it stung and my skin felt stiff and bruised around it. My hair was sticky where it had picked up the salve I had smeared hastily on the wound.

'We'll have to get that photographed. It's evidence of the assault.'

'What do you mean, evidence? I've just told you, he tried to kill me.'

'And you defended yourself successfully. With a spade. It's likely he was badly hurt himself. He might tell a different story.'

I was out of my chair, my hands on the table, glaring down at her pasty pudgy features. The wardress type. 'What the hell are you accusing me of? A different story? Do you think I'm in the habit of attacking men? I wanted to find out what the hell he was doing there. My concern was quite natural. My father's body's just been found there. My brother has put a great deal of effort into an excavation which was vandalised very recently. The man was digging at gone midnight. It's not a bloody allotment, you know.'

She smiled emolliently. 'Miss Armitage, please sit down. No one's accusing you of anything. But criminals don't always oblige by telling the truth. When we catch this man, we want to have all the facts clear, that's all.'

I rubbed my hand over my forehead. 'I'm sorry. But it's not surprising I'm jumpy. The point I'm trying to make is that I'm convinced that what he was doing on the Glebe is material to why he went for me like that. He didn't want me to see. In fact he was desperate that I didn't. That's the only explanation. If you find out what he was up to then, you'll know why he attacked me.'

'Of course. There are some of my colleagues at the site of the incident right now. Obviously they won't be able to conduct a thorough search until the morning.' She looked at her watch. 'Are you sure you'll be all right? You're sure you don't want to go to the hospital for a check-up?'

'No, I want to get some sleep.'

I did sleep, but woke early. I had made Mother's breakfast and helped her eat it, and was sitting in the kitchen drinking strong black coffee, when the expected knock came at the door.

DCI Green was standing on the doorstep with another plain-clothes policeman. He didn't smile. 'Good morning, Miss Armitage. How are you feeling?'

'Terrible.'

I let them in and poured us all coffee.

'Well?'

'So far, the only trace of your assailant is some splashes of what is probably blood. There's no sign of the tools you said he had been using. He probably had a van. There are fresh tyre tracks on the lane at the back of the church. That's probably the way he got into the field.'

'What about what he was looking for?'

'Yes, I was coming to that. It's a pity that your brother wasn't around. There appears to be some kind of stone structure at the bottom of the hole he'd dug. Old, apparently. I've arranged for it to be opened up. I thought you might like to talk us through what happened on the site at the same time. So your version is absolutely clear.'

I bit my lip over the remark about 'my version'. Nor did it seem the sort of invitation I could refuse. I was also, of course, consumed with curiosity.

I stood by the wall looking out over the field. PC Enstone stood in the middle with his hands in his pockets, kicking morosely at a tussock of grass.

I turned back to Green and his sergeant. 'I parked here. Look.' I indicated the two deep ruts gouged into the soft mud of the verge. 'I drove off in a hurry when I got away from him.'

'And what time was this?'

'Half past midnight. I looked at my watch.'

'And you'd just driven Mrs Norton home?'

'Yes. She'd been sitting with my mother. I don't like leaving her for more than a short time.'

'So you'd been out for the evening? May I ask where?'

'I don't think that is really relevant, do you, Chief Inspector?'

He made no reply. There was the sound of a vehicle behind us. We all turned to see a police Transit van pulling up on the verge. Four young uniformed constables climbed out and began to unload picks, spades, shovels and, I shuddered to see, a couple of long crow-bars.

Green motioned to them. 'This way. Let's get on with it.'

We climbed over the wall as I had done.

The four coppers took off their tunics and got to work, widening the hole that my attacker had begun. I thought how Jack would have raged and sworn at their crude spadework. I could see at the bottom that there was indeed some masonry work, a couple of stone walls about two feet apart covered over with a slab of flat flagstone. A drain or a culvert perhaps, but whether it was Roman I had no idea.

Green looked at their handiwork as they paused for breath. 'See that paving stone there?' He pointed at it. 'There's scratches and chips around the edge of it. Our friend must have been trying to lever it up. Let's see what's underneath.'

The most muscular of the young men seized the crow-bar and inserted the point beneath the stone where it rested on the wall. For a few moments, he heaved and grew red in the face and around the neck to no result. Then there was a crunching sound from the bottom of the hole. 'Here she comes, sir.'

A crack opened up at each side of the flag. A second constable jumped down and jammed the point of his pick-axe into one of the gaps and heaved. The heavy stone slab was pulled back and upright like the lid of a box. Then the two men jumped smartly out of the way as they allowed it to fall back against the wall of the trench with a thud.

Green sprang down quickly into the trench, peering into the dark space created. A gaggingly fetid smell of damp and mould arose. One of the officers handed him a rubber-handled torch. He bent down and poked carefully with a spade amongst the mud, dead leaves and other rotting vegetation down there. Suddenly, I heard his sharp intake of breath. With the other policemen, I leaned over the culvert.

He was brushing slimy debris off something at the bottom. There was the white gleam beneath the greenish muck, then, in blue, the unmistakable logo of ICI, the chemicals corporation. It was a plastic sack for agricultural fertiliser.

He stood upright, legs straddling the culvert. 'Looks like this is what he was after.'

'Anything in it, sir?' blurted out one of the young constables.

Green bent down again, searching for the neck of the sack. I saw him pull aside the plastic, and quickly replace it. He jumped out of the culvert, and with his arms outspread, motioned us away. His face was pale and for the first time, he had lost the bland official look of detachment.

'Jesus Christ!' he burst out. 'No wonder he was so keen to stop you seeing what's in there.'

'Why, what ever is it?'

'Only another fucking skeleton.'

VI

Oxford. The colleges emptied for the long vac. A hot August day. I strolled in the sunlight past Balliol into St Giles. A pretty young woman, in shorts, a miniature rucksack wobbling on her back, bare thighs flashing, whizzed past me on a bike. I gazed after her as she headed in the direction of the Banbury Road.

Oxford had been the one true love of my youth. I had tired of her, as young men do, and had suffered ever since. Even now she could still reproach me, reminding me of what I learned too late, that to abandon her had been an act, not of independence but of immaturity. I had had my chance to stay, but the ache of wanting to be somewhere else more exciting, where I would be too preoccupied to feel my hot youth draining ineluctably into the sands of time had led me away.

I waited by the crossing for the lights to change. In front, the façade of the Randolph Hotel rose up, schizophrenic in its desire to be impressive, half chateau and half railway station.

I was, remarkably, too early for my appointment. I must have caught the bug of punctuality from my sister. I headed for the bar and sat with a gin and tonic in the window staring out at the columned front of the Ashmolean Museum opposite.

I'd spent hours in the place as an undergraduate. There I had learned to reconcile my schoolboy seduction by the glamour side of archaeology, the Schliemann factor: the lure of the foreign, the exotic, the excitement of the discovery, the spell cast by buried treasure, with the study of bits of broken pot. If only I had stuck with that. If only the allure of fame had not blinded me. I could have been a minor academic, a Fellow with comfortable rooms in his college. If I'd not been seduced in more ways than one by that woman at the BBC, then I could have stayed in the arms of my lady Oxford. If only . . .

I got myself another gin from the bar. How ironical it was that I had made that Faustian wish to be offered part of my life over again, and then, only a couple of days ago, it had been granted, by the unlikely Mephistopheles of Clarissa Hetherington-Browne. She hadn't asked for my soul in return, but she might as well have done. Even I wasn't so far gone or so reckless as to want to undertake something attended with such extraordinary risk.

I'd got back reeling from that extraordinary meeting at Kensington Gardens to find a message to call Liz on my answering machine. When I heard what had happened to her, I packed up and went back to The Hollies straight away.

Forensic scientists and policemen were now crawling all over the Glebe, searching for evidence to unravel the identity of the skeleton my sister had been instrumental in discovering. I almost wept with frustration at the good excavating weather we were losing. At this rate, I wouldn't have a hope in hell of finding any substantial sign of the structure I believed lay under the site this season, which in turn meant that the chances of establishing my scholarly reputation were effectively nil.

On top of everything else, my long-buried American marriage had popped out of its grave, in the form of my ex-wife. I was getting pissed in the Randolph as a necessary preliminary to having lunch with her.

She'd called me the day after I'd returned to The Hollies.

'How did you get this number, Louise, and why are you calling me?'

'Why Jack, honey, you're not hard to find. I called your house, called the number on your machine, and your real estate agent gave me this one. He sounded an old-fashioned English gentleman.'

I cursed Geoff Lamplighter's susceptibility to feminine wiles.

'What about the why?'

'Why? What better reason than that I'm in London.'

'What are you doing over here?'

'Jack, this is more of an interrogation than a conversation. I'm here on business. I finally worked my way high enough up Hiram & Hartstein's greasy pole to get trips to Europe. Last year it was Bologna and Frankfurt. This year it's London. I called to see if we could get together.'

'I'm not sure it's a good idea, Louise.'

'I thought you British were supposed to be the civilised nation. Here am I extending the hand of peace, and all you can do is snap at it. Be magnanimous. Come on, Jack. Let's for once in our lives behave like grown-ups.'

I sighed. 'I'm not in London any longer, Louise. The number you called is in Oxfordshire. I'm at The Hollies.'

'The big old country house you were raised in? Jack, how romantic! And Oxford! You talked so much about it. Listen. I have an almost free day tomorrow, Jack. Only the breakfast and the ten a.m. are vital. I can cancel the lunch. I was going to do some shopping, but I have a better idea. How about we have lunch in Oxford? And The Hollies. How I'd love to see The Hollies. Please, Jack.'

Louise in this mood was a force of nature. I sighed. Blessed were the peacemakers. 'OK, Louise. OK.'

I'd put the phone down wondering what it was I had got myself into. I had already as many women in my life as I could cope with. What did I need another for? Particularly one like Louise.

I'd met Louise – always Louise, never Lou – Homewood at a party in a loft in SoHo. The loft was owned by a college

191

acquaintance. I'd gone to America after Fiona's death. The BBC had refused to renew my contract. I was estranged from my sister. I thought that England was finished for me.

My ex-tutor at Christ Church had given me the name of a contact of his in the States. That was how I ended up as assistant professor of Classical History and Culture at Van Rensslaer College, a little up the Hudson from New York City. VRC was a private university funded by an old money foundation. It specialised in the kind of liberal arts curriculum which it fondly imagined reproduced the style and the purpose of Oxbridge. It didn't have the kudos of a true Ivy League School, but was still a relatively pleasant place in which to be exiled. Amongst the mellow brick, manicured lawns and massive plane trees of the campus, one could pretend one was not in America at all.

The meeting with Louise was a reminder that the world outside still existed. New York, which I loathed, was in its bankrupt, potholed, capital of the third world state at that time. Louise worked for a publisher – the world's biggest, according to her, but I'd never heard of them. She was smart, glossy, and seemed to know everybody. I was slightly amazed that her demeanour showed she was very keen to add me to her address book. I kept telling myself she wasn't my usual type at all. Although she was around ten years younger than I, she was recognisably a member of what passed in America for the upper class and the product of the most expensive and thorough private education.

Nevertheless, lunch the following day turned inexorably into breakfast the day after that in her apartment off Lexington Avenue.

I was drunk the day I proposed to her. That's what I tell myself, anyway. Why she accepted, God knows. It was obvious to everyone that, except in bed, we were temperamentally unsuited. Unwisely, she moved into my small rented house near the VRC campus, and commuted. She soon tired of this, and began to badger me to return to Manhattan. I was quite happy where I was, so this became an issue, as did just about everything else.

Eventually, she went back to New York, and we divorced. I had affairs, drank heavily and didn't conceal my contempt for the American way of life, none of which endeared me to the puritanical college authorities. The chairman of my department, the chum of Giles Mortimer, my old tutor, became chronically sick, and retired early. His successor and I did not get on. He did not approve of me in general and was particularly critical of my research record, which was, admittedly, fairly lacking. I had a row with him and foolishly offered my resignation, which he promptly accepted.

My defeat by the Colonists nearly finished me. Back in London, I boozed and spent all my savings. I was whiling away my sober hours doing some desultory research in the London Library, when Sir Edmund Scarsdale, the then Director of the Farebrother Museum, overheard me give my name to one of the librarians. He asked me whether I was by any chance related to Celia Armitage, whom he'd known at the V & A. We had a pleasant chat, in which I happened to mention how I was fixed and he asked me to send his regards to my charming mother.

I thought no more of it, until, a week or so later, I had a note via the Library asking me to contact him at the Museum, which I duly did. He told me that he'd spoken to the Chairman of the Trustees, Lord Greville, and they'd decided to offer me the newly created post of Deputy Keeper of Roman and Dark Ages Antiquities. I was stunned by this quite unlooked-for good fortune, the first piece of luck I'd had for years. Moreover, I had only been there a few months when the Keeper had a coronary, and Eddie promptly promoted me.

I shuddered as I reflected for the umpteenth time how I'd blighted that good fortune as I'd blighted everything else in my life.

'Well hello, Jack.'

Her penetrating voice wrenched me from this bitter reverie. I scrambled to my feet.

'Hello, Louise.'

'Sorry I'm late. Blame your funny little British trains.'

She moved forward gracefully. She was wearing an eau-de-nil silk summer dress, and carrying a matching cashmere cardigan threaded through the strap of a cream leather Gucci shoulder bag. A pair of Ray-Bans reposed on her elegant blonde coiffure. Louise always had a certain style. I got a heady whiff of one of those modern perfumes. Opium was it?

'Kiss me and say you're pleased to see me.'

'I'm pleased to see you,' I said, bending down to give her a friendly peck on the cheek. She gave me a look which seemed to indicate that this didn't rate highly as a greeting.

Always the gentleman, I observed the hint, took her in my arms and kissed her warmly on her full soft lips. Slightly to my surprise, I felt her stir against me, as she returned the embrace. Aware of the eyes of others upon us, we separated a little reluctantly.

My pulse rate was up quite a few notches as we settled at our table in the restaurant with a bottle of Graves.

We chatted a little self-consciously about the trivia of travel and English life until the food arrived. Then she launched into the questions she must have been dying to ask from the beginning.

'Now, Jack. Tell.'

'You mean, did I remarry? No. I've never found another woman to put up with me. You know how hard that is.'

'I appreciate the problem. You weren't hard to live with, Jack. Just impossible. I thought, though, you might have mellowed.'

'No, if anything I'm more selfish and disreputable than ever. Ask my sister. I told you I'd gone back to the ancestral home. I'm sharing it with her.'

'So you've made it up? Jack, that's good news. Whatever

you say, you must have changed. And you've gone back to the place where you grew up? How wonderful.'

I shrugged. 'What about you, Louise? I can't imagine you're still on your own.'

She bent her eyes suddenly to her plate. Then she snatched at her glass and gulped at the wine. 'Can't you, Jack? There have been a couple of men in my life since you, but neither of them stayed. I guess I'm that kind of woman. Now I'm married to my company. Much more stable and less heart-breaking.'

She put down the glass, rummaged in her purse for a tissue and blew her delicate nose. She closed the bag with a snap, her expression determinedly bright. 'So why exactly did you leave London, Jack?'

'I used to work at a Museum. The Farebrother. I retired recently.'

I should have remembered that Louise was far too smart to be satisfied with this waffle. 'Retired? You didn't use to be so much older, Jack. Is it the climate over here, or did you lie to me about your age as well?'

'It was early retirement on health grounds.'

Louise gave the weary sigh I remembered so well. 'I wasn't born yesterday, Jack. You look dissipated but you're not sick. What really happened?'

I told her.

Louise sighed even more wearily. 'I always thought you had a death wish. So that's why you moved to the country. As pants the hart for cooling streams, when heated in the chase. Rural tranquillity, am I right?'

'This time, dear Louise, you couldn't be more wrong.'

'What do you mean?'

'I mean that that may have been my intention. But it hasn't turned out that way. The whole thing is a bloody nightmare.'

'Tell, Jack,' she commanded.

Again, I told.

A short way into my account, I felt like the Ancient

195

Mariner. Louise, a dead ringer for the Wedding Guest, was staring at me, her big blue eyes wide. She would have missed any number of nuptials and a few funerals into the bargain rather than the end of my tale.

Finally, I concluded, poured out the rest of the bottle of wine and looked hopefully round for more. Louise flapped a hand at the waiter, who came running. Louise had that effect on waiters.

'Jack, that is the most amazingly awful thing I've ever heard. Why it's almost kind of biblical. Your digging up your own father's body. You and your sister coping with the aftermath.'

'The sins of the fathers? But it's I who's the sinner. I blamed him for years, but my father was still a hero when he died. I know that now. His death was a random mindless act. Something the twentieth century specialises in.' I drank up the wine in my glass. 'Enough of this gloomy talk.' I waved at the windows through which the afternoon sun streamed. 'But westward, look, the land is bright. Oxford awaits you, my lady.'

We started the tour at the Martyrs' Memorial. I doubted that many undergraduates gave the monument a second glance, or understood its significance if they did. Burning for your beliefs was, like death before dishonour, quite unfashionable these days, as dead as Cranmer and Ridley and Latimer. Who even remembered Jan Pallach and the Prague Spring? A gaggle of Japanese tourists, togged up in their designer casuals and brandishing nothing more lethal than their camcorders, looked hardly willing, despite their nation's history, to sacrifice lifestyle to the demands of *seppuku*.

Then along the Broad past Balliol and Trinity. I pointed out to her the sculptured Roman emperors outside the Sheldonian. They reminded me of Beerbohm's Zuleika Dobson – she for love of whom the undergraduates of the university had to a man drowned themselves. I said it was fortunate that it was the vac, given that Louise, a vision in green and gold, would have had a similar effect on impressionable youth.

I showed her the Divinity School, rightly described as the most beautiful room in Europe, and above it, 'Duke Humphrey', the earliest part of the Bodleian Library. We strolled the High, and I pointed out the college of All Souls, who were too intellectually superior to deign to teach under-graduates.

We stood on Magdalen Bridge and leaned on the parapet, admiring the green water meadows and watching the swans glide on the Cherwell. We admired the perfection of the Radcliffe Camera, symbol of the English Enlightenment, arising from amidst the medieval streets of Oxford.

Finally, I took her to Christ Church, and showed her the staircase where the youthful Armitage had had rooms. Then we stood in Tom Quad, looking up at Wren's tower while I spouted yet more potted history.

'This is called Tom Tower, after its bell, Great Tom. The college was founded by Cardinal Wolsey – he dissolved a few monasteries to get the cash. He was going to pull down the Abbey church as well, but never got round to it. His boss Henry VIII took it over after he gave the old villain the chop. The church not only serves the college as its chapel, it's also Oxford's cathedral. The affairs of both are combined. Worldly clerics are an Oxonian speciality. Christ Church men call it the House, after its Latin name, Aedes Christi, the House of Christ.'

Louise turned to me, her eyes bright. 'Jack, this is all so magnificent. How did you ever manage to leave it?'

I smiled down on her. 'I was asking myself that question earlier.'

'And how did you reply to yourself?'

'I decided, like Candide, that all was for the best in the best of all possible worlds.' I took her arm and set off deter-minedly for the gateway. 'Time now for the ancestral home, where its chatelaine will provide us with a sumptuous English repast.'

Twenty-five minutes later, I swung the Morgan into the tree-hung driveway of The Hollies. The car springs thumped in the potholes and ruts, and then we rounded the bend and stopped on the sweep of weed-covered shingle.

I went round to Louise's side and helped her out of the low-slung bucket seat.

'Here we are. The venerable pile from which young Jack Armitage escaped to find his fame and fortune in the New World. Or rather didn't.'

She gazed around her. 'Jack, it's amazing. Like something out of a storybook. *The Secret Garden* or *The Children of Green Knowe*. Imagine growing up here. You were so lucky. Trees and woods and would you look at that lawn! Why, it seems to stretch for miles.'

'My thoughts exactly when I'm mowing it. I can't afford a ride-on.'

'Come on, Jack. Admit you love the place. How can you not?'

'I think at one time I did. Then so many things happened to make me want to get away from it.'

'And now?'

I shrugged. 'It's where I happen to be. In a few months I could be anywhere. Let's go inside and meet my sister.'

I took Louise into the drawing room and left her admiring the portraits of my forebears that covered the walls and went in search of Liz.

The kitchen was empty. There was no sign of her there or of any meal in preparation. Irritated, I called for her up the stairs. No answer. Then Mrs Hargreaves suddenly materialised at the door to the old morning room where my mother was now ensconced.

'Sorry, Mr Armitage. I heard you and your . . . lady-friend come in but I couldn't come out straight away. I was giving your mother her bath, and I couldn't, so to speak, just drop her.'

'No, quite. Do you know where my sister is?'

'Miss Armitage said as I was to tell you that she had had to go to one of them educational conferences. She had to go urgent like because the person who was going was ill and couldn't.'

'A conference? For how long?'

'A few days, I think, but she didn't say exactly. Now I'll be off in five minutes. Do you want to see your mother before she goes down?'

I shook my head and went back to the drawing room. It wasn't like Liz to disappear like that without even leaving a note. I was puzzled and a little concerned. There was something unconvincing about the story Mrs Hargreaves had been given.

I explained the situation to Louise. 'It looks like the meal I promised you is off.'

She didn't, though, seem at all concerned. In fact she was laughing. 'Don't look so mournful, Jack. If there's no dinner, we can make it. I'll rustle something up and then I want you to show me every bit of this wonderful old house, from roof to cellar. OK?'

A remarkably short time later, I was sitting in front of a steaming plate of spaghetti carbonara. I poured us each a large glass of Valpolicella. 'Bon appetit and my amazed compliments to the chef.'

She raised hers thoughtfully. 'Here's to you, Jack. And thank you for a beautiful afternoon.'

We dug into our food, which was extremely good, and for a moment or two there was a companionable silence.

Then Louise said, 'Well, Jack. This is just like old times, supper at the kitchen table.'

'Except this time, Louise, you cooked it. The first time ever I've had that privilege.'

'Why, Jack, how can you say such things? Are you implying I never looked after you when we were married?'

'Come off it, Louise, in the kitchen department you were a no-no. Take-outs, cold cuts and coffee. That's what we lived on when we ate in.'

'You're forgetting the booze. And what about other departments?'

'You know the answer to that.'

'Well maybe then that was enough. It was after all your main interest. I don't remember your complaining about deli pizza afterwards.'

'So now you're into cuisine?'

'I edit a lot of cook books. Some of it has kind of rubbed off.'

'Indeed it has. More wine?'

She reached out, removed the bottle from my hand and set it down out of reach. 'Jack, I want to see the house, and I want to see it with you in a sober state. That's the second. You've had enough. Plus you have to drive me back to Oxford.'

'Still telling me what to do, Louise?'

'Sometimes, Jack, everybody needs to listen, even you. Now before it gets dark, I want to see more of the garden.'

The first hints of autumnal chill came as the sun dipped down in Technicolor splendour behind the spinney, the tall beeches black cardboard cut-outs against the red sky. We made our way back to the house over the lawn on which the dew was already beginning to settle. Louise had slipped on her cardigan over her skimpy dress, and clutched her arms about her.

'"And summer's lease hath all too short a date." At my age you begin to count the summers,' I remarked as we went into the drawing room, the great west mullion bay window gilded by the sunset. I poured glasses of Cognac and handed one to her.

'Philosophical in your old age, Jack? Is this the man who

200

said he didn't care whether he lived past forty? That he felt as if he'd lived several lives already?'

'As you said earlier, we have to adapt. I guess coming back here, finding the truth about where my father went has made me more conscious of my own mortality. Those early years, I felt I was trying to prove something. That I was the great archaeologist, the great media star, the man who knew more than anyone about everything. I was so bloody arrogant. Looking back, I think my father's disappearance made me determined to succeed, to make him feel, in some way that he had done wrong in leaving me. As if in some way, he would know and feel sorry. I didn't care about what came after. Even when I came back here, it was still partly with the intention of making the greatest Roman discovery of the century. Still trying to prove myself. Perhaps I really should have stayed in Oxford. But then I would never have met you, Louise.'

'Maybe that would have been a good thing?'

'Is that what you think?'

She turned away and stared through the window at the now darkening sky where the evening star shone clearly. 'I don't know, Jack. There were good times, but a lot of bad ones. You were always searching for something, Jack. Many men would have been content. You had a tenured post at a good school. You had a wife who loved you – and I did, you know. You could have had a great future. Instead you went out of your way to blow it all. If you hadn't . . .'

'I know. Let's not go through it all again.'

'Maybe it would have been different if we'd had a child. That was when it went truly sour for you, wasn't it? When . . .'

I interrupted hastily. 'I said I didn't want to go through it all again.'

Her blue eyes were moist. She hadn't lost her talent for turning on the waterworks when it suited her. 'Jack, I was as disappointed as you when I found out the news from the gynaecologist. But you blamed me. As if the way I was made was my fault. You even said I'd concealed it from you. That you'd never have married me if you'd known that. That was so goddamned unfair. How did you think I felt, knowing I could never bear my own child?'

Louise's tears had turned to anguished sobs. I've always found women in hysterics difficult to deal with. In the past, my first reaction would have been to slap her, in the same way my mother would slap me when I showed weakness of that kind. My experiences over the years have, however, showed this to be no more productive with women than it was with the child. Some experiences I have learned from.

So I didn't slap Louise, or shout at her. I put my arms around her and gave her a handkerchief, the clean one Mother always told me to keep separately for unspecified emergencies.

'I never said so at the time but I'm sorry. It's number one on my list of Awful Things I've Said Which I Wish I Hadn't. It's a long list, believe me. I let people down. I let myself down. I was a shit, let's face it. I still am.'

She snuffled and wiped her eyes. 'No, you're not. I'm sorry too, Jack. I shouldn't have brought it up again.'

'It's OK, these things are always around for us,' I replied, still marvelling at how what would, in the old days, have become a no-holds-barred screaming contest ending in brain-seared exhaustion had so painlessly resolved itself.

We drank up our brandies.

Louise gave a rueful smile. 'We were nearly falling into our bad old ways. I came here to see your family home, not to fight with you. Let's get on with it.'

'All right then. Come on. Let's start with the library.'

Louise proved to be as indefatigable touring the house as Oxford. We covered it from stem to stern, finding rooms I hadn't ventured into since I was a child. The only room we didn't view was Liz's because Louise felt that that was private, and the morning room, because the sight of my mother, her

202

face so vacant and her body so fragile under her bedclothes was more than I could bear.

We sat exhausted together on the stop step of the staircase. I was very aware of being alone with this still very desirable woman. Her short dress had ridden up interestingly. She had always had wonderful legs, not over-slim, but well shaped and strong. As she moved to clasp her arms around her thighs, and rest her chin on her knees, I had a glimpse of frothy white lace at her crotch.

'Jack, this must have been a marvellous house for games. Did you ever play hide and seek here with other children? What great parties you must have had.'

'I don't recall we ever went in for children's parties. Mother never encouraged us to have friends round after my father left. I suppose she was depressed, as if she'd been jilted of her future. It became rather gloomy actually. Like Miss Havisham's.'

'I see. What a shame. I imagined great troupes of children whooping through the house, hiding in those enormous wardrobes, just like the one in the C. S. Lewis books, or in the attics. I bet there are attics, I used to dream of finding a real old dusty English attic.'

How could I have forgotten the attics? 'Yes, there are, and they are very dusty. We weren't allowed in them as children. They're crowded with junk. It might be fun to have a look up there.' I had a sudden vision of Louise going ahead of me on the winding staircase, Louise close to me in the slightly spooky gloom.

The door was concealed within the wainscot of the upper landing.

I unlocked it with the key kept on one of the hooks of the old board in the kitchen, still meticulously labelled in the faded copperplate of some long dead housekeeper. A warm wood smell drifted through the opening. I groped in the darkness, found the old-fashioned round metal switch and flipped the central toggle. From overhead a dim yellow light shone on the coarse wooden treads of the narrow winding staircase.

I turned to Louise. 'You go first. I'm behind you if you slip.'

The dust rose, tickling my nostrils, and the boards creaked as she mounted the stairs, positively bubbling over with childish delight. Her tight dress stretched over her bottom, the outline of her pants clearly revealed. She waited at the top of the steps. I came up close behind her, then reached in front for another switch. My arm brushed against her breasts and I was delighted to feel her quiver of response.

'Voilà.'

'Wow, Jack. How terrific.'

It was, I had to admit, in its own way quite impressive. A long tunnel of space under heavy beams, a smaller lower version of a medieval tithe barn. Every few yards, a massive A-shaped truss, studded with the heads of enormous coach-bolts supported the longitudinal purlins, crudely squared trunks of substantial trees, straight from the saw-mill, shreds of the original bark still adhering. The rafters were hidden by the rough planks which lined the whole roof, streaked and stained in places by the water which had leaked through loose slates.

Crammed along each side of a central aisle was a crazy, higgledy-piggledy mass of things, shrouded in the gloom and covered in thick dust and cobwebs.

There were chairs with missing legs, broken tables, a tall-boy with no drawers, an ancient treadle sewing machine, a phonograph with a His Master's Voice type trumpet, old wirelesses, in curved plywood and Bakelite, on one of which I remembered hearing the sepulchral announcement of the death of King George VI in 1952, boxes filled to overflowing with old newspapers and magazines, trunks and suitcases stacked up to the ceiling, a hip bath, a wheelchair, a pram so huge it would merit the term baby carriage. There were picture frames stacked three or four deep, a dressmaker's dummy, a collection of pots and pans, piles of crockery, rusty bicycles with pancake flat, perished tyres. There were boxes filled with toys that had been worn out when Liz and I had played with them as children. A poignant relic of the past was a pile of tennis rackets in wing-nut frames, the ones with which Liz had scaled the heights of junior tennis all those years ago.

God knew what other memories lurked in the dark places under the eaves behind the front rank of rubbish. The Astons had been squirrelling it away for nearly a hundred and fifty years.

Louise was in her element, uncovering at every turn some new curiosity. 'Why, this place is like that stately home I read about. Where the family lived for centuries, and never threw anything away.'

'Ah, yes. Calke Abbey. Well the Astons weren't aristos like the Harpur-Crewes, though they may have put on airs when they moved to the country, but they had similar habits. Anything that was broken or they tired of, they shoved up here.'

'Some of this stuff must be worth a fortune. Not to mention the things you have downstairs.'

'I hardly think so.'

'Yes, Jack, believe me. People collect anything and everything these days. Get a New York dealer in. He'd buy the lot, no messing.'

'Money's no good for me. I only spend it, as you know. Besides, Liz and I don't own any of it. It's in trust for Mother. She may live for many years yet. I mentioned selling the house to Liz, but she was dead against it. She says a move would kill Mother.'

'I think that's often said. But how often does it happen?'

'In Mother's case, it need be only once.'

She pointed at a much worn and scuffed trunk. Stamped into the leather were the initials RJA. 'What's in that? It might be clothes. I adore those classic dresses from way back.'

'I don't think you'll have any luck there. It was my father's.'

'Really? Aren't you curious, Jack? Can we open it, Jack? Would you mind?'

I hesitated. Coming up here with Louise had seemed as if it might be rather jolly. Now, suddenly, I was back with the familiar demons, torn between distaste and curiosity.

'Come on, Jack. You live in this great heap of history. I'd be in here delving every day. How can you resist?'

I relented. 'All right, go ahead. It's probably empty.'

She slid the catches and heaved up the lid. There was a smell of naphtha and a crackle of tissue paper. 'Wow, Jack. Look at this. Like Horatio Nelson's sea-chest.'

I stared with amazement at what she was holding up. A dark jacket, the gold braid at the cuffs gleaming in the dim light.

'There's more too. Look!'

She picked up the cap and set it on her head at a jaunty angle. 'Is this stuff for real, or is it some amateur operatic gear?'

'Oh no. It's for real. It's the uniform of a Lieutenant Commander in the Royal Navy. My father's. I suppose he must have put it up here when he left the service at the end of the war. Look, there's his ribbons. That one there is the DSO, the Distinguished Service Order. One of the highest there is. I remember his showing me the medal once – though only with the greatest reluctance. I wonder what became of it?'

Louise held the jacket to her and whirled around with it. 'It's so heavy and solid, like the cloth's an inch thick. Feel.'

I felt. 'No half measures for the Senior Service. If you rule the world, you have to dress the part.'

'There's nothing like a uniform to make a man look good. Put the coat on, Jack. Let's see how it is on you.'

'No, don't be silly, Louise. I can't. It won't fit.'

'Yes, it will. I know about these things.'

'Louise, please!'

She handed it to me. 'Admiral Nelson, Lady Hamilton commands you to dress like an officer and a gentleman in her presence.'

'OK. If you insist, my lady.'

It did fit, perfectly. So did the cap.

Louise clapped her hands. 'It could be made for you. Now you can't wear it with those. Take them off and put on the pants.'

I undid the belt buckle, unzipped and took off my jeans. The uniform trousers felt as heavy and solid as a suit of armour. She glanced around. 'I saw a mirror somewhere. Over there.' She dashed to a mahogany-framed cheval glass with a crack across the middle, swivelled it upright and rubbed it clear of dust with the end of a brocaded curtain. 'There you are. Straight out of a war movie. Aye, aye sir!' She gave me a mock salute.

I felt slightly queasy as I stared at the image in the spotted silvering of the mirror. No matter how perfect a fit, my father's clothes were not mine. I was not the man he was. I had not stood calm on the bridge of a destroyer during the hell of the Normandy invasion.

'No, Louise. I'm no war hero. Not even Noël Coward. I'm Tony Curtis dressing up in *Some Like It Hot*.'

She came slowly over to me, a different expression in her eyes. 'You look fine to me. You always did.' Her naturally husky voice was even huskier. She raised her hand to touch my face, her lips were full and slightly apart and her eyes were bright.

I kissed her and she moulded herself against me. I slipped my hand between her shoulder blades, found the tag of the zip and pulled it all the way down. The green dress rustled down her legs. I felt her fingers fumbling urgently at the waistband of my trousers, and they too fell to the floor.

'Jack, quickly. Before I . . .'

She pushed down impatiently the band of silk and lace at her waist, put her arms around my neck, leapt lightly into the air like a dancer, and gripped my loins between her thighs, thrusting me deep inside her.

* * *

I buried my face in the loosened tresses of Louise's abundant genuinely blonde hair, seeking her earlobe with my tongue. After our somewhat dusty and strenuous passion in the attic, we had moved down to my room.

She lay on her back, completely naked. Her breasts were still firm and shapely, though fuller than they had been once. Her areolae were as pink and rosy as ever. I moved my head down and very gently teased her right nipple with the tip of my tongue. It grew stiff immediately.

She moaned softly. 'That's nice. Don't stop.'

She stretched a little and the old brass bedstead creaked comfortably as I gave both breasts my full attention.

'Turn over now,' I whispered.

Her back was still as perfect as ever. I slid my hand slowly down her back until it rested in the hollow at the top of her buttocks. 'I'm just remembering my way around.'

I felt her move with renewed excitement, and her hot breath in my ear. 'You used to use your finger in, you know, and it drove me wild,' she whispered.

'Oh yes,' I whispered back, 'like this, wasn't it?' In response, her mouth pressed on mine, open in a transport of arousal.

'Do you know what the time is, Jack? Jack?'

I felt her hand on my naked shoulder. How often in my life hadn't I awoken to a woman shaking me and asking rhetorically if I knew the time?

'It's eleven o'clock, Jack. What time's the last train?'

In addition, I was expected to be a railway almanac. 'About now, I should think.'

'Jack,' she wailed in irritation. 'I have an appointment first thing tomorrow.'

'Relax, I'll get you to the first train out in the morning. How about I fix us a snack? I'm OK on snacks.'

As I went downstairs, I remembered that I should have been checking on my mother. Whilst I'd been with Louise,

I'd forgotten all about her. Anxiously, I opened the door of the morning room.

The night-light cast a dim glow over the bed. She was sleeping peacefully. To my relief, there was no sign that she had woken up or tried to get out of bed.

I bent down and kissed the withered lips.

There was some cheese in the fridge and the nice bread Liz got from the Italian baker in Waterbury. I opened a bottle of Burgundy and took it up on a tray.

Louise had rather fetchingly attired herself in one of my shirts.

We lay back on the pillows and ate and drank.

'I love midnight feasts, don't you? What was the name of the deli that did that wonderful pastrami? Is it still there? You know that was the best thing about New York, the food. Apart from you, that is.'

Louise brushed crumbs from her shirt-front. 'I can't believe I'm here like this, Jack. I keep thinking of you here as a boy, then your father's disappearance. And your finding him. Do you believe in ghosts?'

'What, no, of course not. Do you?'

'I don't know. There are some things you can't explain. We did a book . . .' She saw my mocking expression. 'No, a real book. By a respectable scientist. About premonitions, amongst other things. Perhaps in some way your excavating the Glebe was a result of your father's being buried there. As if at some level you knew or were led to know.'

I stared at her. 'What are you talking about? I'm not Hamlet. My father's spirit didn't come calling on me one night to demand vengeance.'

She didn't look at me, but continued to gaze at the opposite wall.

Then she said, abruptly, 'What happened on the official side, Jack? From what you said, your father went overnight from being a war hero to a traitor.'

'I think it was all part of the hysterical Cold War

209

atmosphere. Burgess and Maclean. Remember them? They were two Foreign Office types who defected to the Russians. That was in 1951, but there were still repercussions five years later. Another senior civil servant went missing and they jumped to conclusions.'

'And who were "they", Jack?'

'The newspapers, I think, to begin with. Then an MP asked a question of the Prime Minister in the House of Commons.'

'Which was no doubt given a dusty answer?'

'Not exactly. I think there was some phrase used about not answering on matters concerning national security. Which increased the speculation.'

'But would the Government manage the affair so carelessly as to let that happen?'

'I don't know. I suppose they were less adept at spin-doctoring in those days.'

'And what about the Soviets?'

'They denied it. But no one believed them. Certainly not the boys at school. They made my life hell. Even when I went to public school, the rumours followed me. I used to find my books daubed with hammers and sickles in red paint. My nickname was Ivan. It took years before it was forgotten. The sins of the fathers, again. That's what I couldn't stomach. I blamed him for what I had to go through. Years later, it became clear to me that there could never have been any truth in the story. I got my visa to the States and my green card without any problem. That wouldn't have happened if my father were on some kind of blacklist.'

'Jack, you never told me any of this before. Every American knows the CIA spies on its allies as well as its supposed enemies. We've done book after book on such things at H & H. The Company would have known if your father were a defector. If he wasn't, then the rumours that he was, rumours which would convince your Prime Minister, had to emanate from high up in the administration, not from the press. If it were the States, I'd say that story had the feel of an official plant about it. Disinformation. Except that one didn't normally use it against one's own side. Now why would the British Government set out to blacken the name of one of its own senior civil servants?'

'You sound as if you're trying to tell me something, Louise.'

'It's just a thought. But you remember that guy Clive Ponting?'

'Of course. He blew the whistle on something to do with the Falklands, didn't he?'

'Yes. He allegedly broke your Official Secrets Act, the most all-embracing catch-all this side of the old Iron Curtain. The Government threw the book at him.'

'And he was acquitted, wasn't he?'

'Yes. Your father, however, didn't have the advantage of due process.'

'What are you saying? That his character was deliberately blackened by his own Government?' I shook my head. 'But that would mean that my father must have been some kind of traitor. No better than if he had defected.'

'Not necessarily. We don't call Woodward and Bernstein traitors for revealing the Watergate conspiracy. Treason is only committed by the losers.'

'So you think that my father may have known something embarrassing to the Government? But what on earth could it possibly be?'

'I don't know, Jack. The chances are that we won't ever know. We know now why he was never able to reveal it. In his case, maybe they didn't stop at just labelling him as a defector. Maybe they decided to silence him once and for all.'

'The Government had him killed? That's preposterous.'

'Is it? Is it really, given what we know of the covert operations that went on in the Cold War? In a war, there are casualties. I think your father's ghost might well not be resting easy, Jack.'

* * *

I stopped the Morgan outside Oxford station, and helped her out. A cold wind whipped along the forecourt from the river, bringing with it a whirling kaleidoscope of litter.

On the platform were a few groups of City commuter types. There was a rumble as the Paddington train drew in, its lights greyish and obscured behind the dirty windows.

She was shivering as I held her. 'Goodbye, Jack. It is goodbye, isn't it?'

I said nothing, but bent and kissed her forehead.

'It's best that way. We have our own different lives now. The moving finger has writ. Yesterday was a time out of time. But I'll remember it always.'

'So will I. Goodbye, Louise.'

I gunned the engine through the traffic lights of the deserted city and headed home fast up the Banbury Road, pleased to have got cleanly away.

God, how relieved I was she hadn't made a scene, said that our getting divorced had been a mistake, or some such rot.

My father's uniform still lay on the chair on which I had flung it the previous night. I smoothed it over my arm, to get some of the wrinkles out. I was suddenly rather reluctant to consign it to the trunk in the attic. I opened the wardrobe, took out a hanger and threaded it through the shoulders of the jacket.

Before putting it away, I held it up to admire it. Having done that, I couldn't resist putting it on again. As Louise had said it did fit so snugly. I admired myself in the wardrobe mirror. I squared my shoulders and saluted myself, a little awkwardly and foolishly. I hadn't dressed up like this since I was a child.

Rather reluctantly, I started to unfasten the brass buttons. As I fumbled with one over my midriff, I heard a crackling in the material of the coat, as if some paper had been left in an inner pocket. I pulled it back to investigate. There was no inner pocket. There was, though, something stiff like card behind the silk of the lining. I examined it more closely. The stitching at that point seemed clumsier, as if someone unused to such work had sewed it up. It appeared that my father had unpicked the threads, placed something within, then sewn it up again himself. It must have been him. My mother was an expert needlewoman and would never have produced anything so careless.

Intrigued, I grabbed a pair of nail scissors off my bedside table, cut through the threads and pulled apart the two pieces of cloth. Eagerly, I slipped a couple of fingers into the aperture and felt about. Yes, it was a thin packet wrapped in green oilcloth. Within was a small pocket wallet of imitation parchment. I opened it to find a sepia photograph mounted inside.

It was little out of the ordinary. There were albums full of this kind of thing in the library. Family groups carefully posed by the photographer. Liz and I had gigglingly endured this ritual at the studio in Waterbury countless times.

A woman in a long dark coloured dress sat demurely on one end of a bench, a man in an equally dark suit of Edwardian cut gazed with fixed attention at the camera at the other. In between sat two children, their legs dangling in mid-air, dressed in sailor suits.

I realised with a start that this must be my father's own family. Why else would he have carried it around with him, having taken care that it would not be easily lost, and protected it against damage by the elements. I had never seen my paternal grandparents before, never known that a portrait of them existed. Why had my father never shown it to us?

I peered more closely at the two children. One of them was presumably my father. But which? They were wearing the same suits, they had identical haircuts of the same dark wavy hair my father had had in such abundance. And most remarkably of all, in features they were astonishingly alike. In fact they were identical. Was this some trick played by

213

the photographer, to produce two images of the same boy, much as I had on school photographs contrived to appear twice by running fast enough to beat the slowly panning camera? Ridiculous thought, but almost reasonable in the circumstances. For my father had never spoken of the existence of even a brother, never mind what on this evidence could only be an identical twin.

Why not? Why had neither I nor, I presumed, anyone else in our family ever seen this picture, given that my father regarded it as so precious? And why had he never retrieved it from this hiding-place at the end of the war to give it a place of honour? It seemed that he was determined to keep it out of view as if he was in some way ashamed of it. But if he were ashamed, why had he kept it? Why? And had I been presumptuous to pry into these matters?

The faces of the parents and their two enigmatic children stared at me. What secret were they keeping?

Louise had talked, crazily I had thought, of my father's spirit leading me to discover his remains. The Romans, however, would not have dismissed such a suggestion. That the dead influenced the living was axiomatic to them. And here was something else which I had uncovered. The idea was ludicrous, wasn't it, that I had not simply happened upon this photograph by chance? How could anyone of the late twentieth century imagine that my father, dead forty years, could still influence his son? Yet it was true that on the Glebe I had felt a presence.

And here also in this room. I believed that the identical faces of the children, innocently smiling for a photograph, held some message for me. Why had we never been told of our father's twin? Had he died as a child? Or thereafter? Or was he still alive? Might it be possible to track him down? In finding him, might I find some essence of the father I thought had been forever lost to me. Was that why I had been led to this point?

I felt dreadfully moved as I gazed at this small fragment

from the massive mosaic of the past. At once the casual manner I had affected with Liz, and which I had sustained for myself ever since, dissolved. I did so want to be close again to the father whom I had loved so much, and whom I loved still. I might never know the secret of his death, but I could at least make it my business to rediscover his life.

As I put the portrait back into its envelope, and then into the top drawer of my tallboy, I felt the hairs on the back of my neck bristle as if my thoughts and longings had indeed caused a turbulence in the current of the past.

I must show the picture to Liz. We would work together. If only she were here now. Not for the first time, I felt how much I had grown to rely on her presence. Where on earth had she gone and what was she doing?

I swung the Morgan on to the dirt track and bounced along a little way until I was sure it was out of sight of the road. When I turned off the engine, the only sound was of the wind in the trees. Baker's Quarry was as secluded a spot as I had been able to think of reasonably close to the village, and accessible by car from the main road.

I sat on a heap of stone under the stand of beech trees and smoked. The rain had stopped, and the sun was trying to break through the cloud. I checked my watch. Despite Ellen insisting I met her here, she was late.

She'd called me while I was having breakfast, banging on about how her mother had said I'd had another woman up at The Hollies, a rich American, while my sister was away. She'd insisted on seeing me. 'I want an explanation from you, Jack Armitage, and it'd better be a good one.'

Usually when a woman spoke to me like that, I told her to piss off and not come back. Perhaps I was getting old and soft, or perhaps Ellen was different.

I lit another cigarette and thought about what I was going to say. As I ran over it I realised with a bit of a shock that I was going to tell her the truth, more or less.

215

I heard a mechanical puttering and Ellen's little Honda bounced into the clearing and stopped alongside the Morgan. I've always hated bikes, but the sight of Ellen astride this one almost reconciled me to the awful things. She slid off lightly and removed the helmet, her streaked brown hair cascading around her shoulders. I had finally persuaded her to stop using the peroxide, and the original shade was gradually reappearing, so that, as I put it, her top and bottom would match.

I made her sit down with me on the stones.

'Well?' Her eyes narrowed and her mouth was hard.

I held up my hand. 'Listen, it's not what you think. It was like this.'

She listened in silence until I had finished. Then she said, 'Is that all true? She's going back to America? You did it with her on the spur of the moment? It wasn't as good as with me?'

'Cross my heart.'

'And hope to die?'

'And hope to die.'

She wrinkled up her face in thought for several moments. Finally she turned back to me. 'Jack Armitage, you're a bit of an old devil, aren't you? You can't help it, can you? You being so old as well. You're worse than some of those kids I used to go with when I was at school. But I can understand how it was. She was your ex-wife and all. I mean it's only like me and Barry when you think about it. We still do, you know, every now and again. I can't have a headache every time, he'd get suspicious. We did it last night as a matter of fact. Only he passed out just before I . . . and I had to, you know . . .'

'All right, spare me the details. So you're not still upset?'

'Come here, you sod, and I'll show you whether I am.'

She applied her velvety lips to mine, and it was then that I realised how I would have felt if she had rejected me. The kiss lasted a long time.

'You're not rushing off anywhere?' I asked when we separated for air.

She grinned and shook her head. 'No, I'm not due with Mrs Fothergill till four.' She stood up. 'I'll be back. I just have to go behind a bush for a minute.'

I watched her bottom in the tight jeans as it moved interestingly over the uneven floor of the wood, then she disappeared out of sight in the direction of the quarry.

I was getting the rug out of the car, when I saw her running back, tucking her flapping shirt into her waistband as she went. Her face was pale. 'Jack, quick, we've got to get out. There's somebody here. I was just squatting down when I saw an old van down by the front of the quarry. I think there's somebody in it.'

'You think? But you didn't see anyone? I'll take a look. It might have been dumped. Or they're miles away. Calm down and stay here till I get back.'

I approached the van cautiously. It was an old Ford, once white, covered in dents and scrapes, and the sills and wheel arches red with rust. I was right. Somebody had got rid of it here. That's why it was parked so far away from the road.

I was turning back to reassure Ellen when the sun emerged from a cloud and shone directly on to the windscreen of the van. Through the side window, I could see illuminated a huddled shape.

Was it someone sleeping? A tramp, perhaps, who'd got in to have a kip in the dry? He was quite still. I moved stealthily closer, then some instinct made me abandon caution and I ran.

I peered inside, my heart pounding. There was a man in the driver's seat, but he was not asleep, he was dead.

I owed this insight not to any subtle clinical judgement, but to the fact that the top half of his head was missing, the constituent parts of it being liberally spread over the interior. Resting between his knees, pointing at the shattered skull was the cause: a double barrelled shotgun, the dead man's finger still looped in the trigger guard. Crawling over the body and the roof lining was a buzzing mass of flies.

VII

SECOND BODY FOUND IN CROWCESTER

Police called to the scene of a bizarre night attack
on Elizabeth Armitage, the comprehensive
school teacher whose murdered father's 40 year
old remains were found last month during an
archaeological excavation conducted by her
brother, Dr Jack Armitage (50) in a field in the
Oxfordshire village of Crowcester, have made
another gruesome discovery at the site.

Further human remains, believed to have been
buried twenty years ago, have been unearthed
from another stretch of the same ancient culvert
in which was found the skeleton of high ranking
civil servant and former wartime naval officer
Robert Armitage. Detective Chief Inspector
David Green, in charge of the earlier investigation, admitted to reporters at a hastily con-
vened press conference in nearby Waterbury that
he was baffled by the latest turn of events. He
said that it was too early to tell whether the two
discoveries were linked in any way. Forensic
examination of Mr Armitage's bones had not yet
been completed and it might be several weeks
before the identity of the new victim and the
cause of death could be established.

Forty-eight years old Miss Armitage is

recuperating at the family home in Crowcester and has so far refused to talk to reporters, but it is understood that she disturbed an intruder on the site late last night, and that in the ensuing struggle, both were injured. DCI Green confirmed that they are searching for a man of medium height and heavy build with lacerations to his right arm. Local doctors and hospitals have been alerted.

Community leaders in Crowcester spoke today of their fear that a maniac who might strike again was on the loose in their picturesque village.

I threw *The Times* on to the floor, my annoyance at the prospect of being pestered by more reporters increasing the throbbing pain in my head, and poured myself another cup of coffee.

Jack's initial, heart-warming concern for my welfare, which had made him drop his business in London and come rushing back when I phoned him, had lasted, as was his way, for a few hours.

He had seemed even more preoccupied with his own concerns than usual. The latest discovery was, to him, only a reason why he couldn't re-start the excavation. After a bad-tempered telephone conversation with Green about the likely length of the delay, he had swanned off to Oxford, to have lunch with his ex-wife. Even women whom Jack had by all accounts treated with abominable selfishness seemed willing to go to considerable lengths for the pleasure of seeing him again. She was welcome to him.

I had called in sick. Linda had seemed relaxed about the situation when I'd spoken to her. She positively cajoled me into taking a few days off until the whole thing blew over once more. Such human sympathy was alien to our relationship, and it made me suspicious, perhaps uncharitably. Had she finally persuaded a majority of the Governors to get rid of me?

I put such thoughts aside for the moment. Nearly getting killed certainly put the petty concerns of Waterbury Comp into perspective. I gingerly touched the now scabbed lump on the side of my head as I thought over what had happened.

Despite what was implied in the newspaper article – no doubt with the intention of building up as much interest as possible – I didn't see how the two crimes could possibly be related.

I had thought, for an anguished moment, that it might be Teresa's body in the culvert. But as I had seen for myself, the remains had been concealed in a polythene fertiliser sack. I was sure such things were not in use in the fifties. That alone proved that this murder could not be contemporary with my father's, even without other forensic evidence which would no doubt be forthcoming.

The man who had attacked me had the answer to the mystery. He must have been desperately trying to remove the body in the culvert, before it was discovered in the course of the excavation. The only conceivable explanation for his doing that was that he must have been responsible for the death and the burial.

Presumably, as was often the case, he must have had some relationship with the victim, the classic English murder being a domestic crime, and he was terrified that the discovery of the body would inexorably lead back to him. That was, after all, why Green had inevitably decided that my mother was his chief suspect. It was therefore highly probable that even if I had not given the man in the Glebe the mark of Cain, he would eventually have been tracked down.

Therefore, I was the only connection between the two crimes, and that connection was purely the result of my own reckless interference.

That was the logical explanation, but it seemed to me still an uncanny coincidence that two separate murderers had

221

buried two separate victims a matter of yards apart in the same field at quite separate times.

I was carrying my breakfast things over to the sink, still puzzling over the matter, when the bell rang in the hall.

I bent down and shouted through the letter-box, 'If you're the press, go away and leave me alone!'

By way of reply, a hand bearing an identity card appeared in the aperture. I opened the door immediately.

'Good morning, Chief Inspector. Got through the welcoming committee, have you?'

'I doubt they'll hang around here when the latest news gets out.'

'You mean you've got some answers?'

'Perhaps. There's something I want to check with you.'

I showed him through into the kitchen.

'Now, what is it you want to know?'

'You said that you wouldn't recognise the man again, because it was dark and he appeared to be wearing a dark-coloured balaclava helmet. You're certain that's still the case? No distinguishing feature of any kind? You can't remember anything which would identify him? You didn't recognise his voice or accent?'

'No. He didn't speak at all. I've racked my brains but there's nothing significant. He was medium height, heavy build, that's all. He could have been almost anyone, given the conditions.'

'OK. When you struck him with the spade, what part of his body was that?'

'As I said. On the right arm.'

'Are you absolutely sure about that?'

'Yes. I aimed at the arm that was holding the crow-bar. I held the spade in both hands and swept it across him. But why are you asking me these questions, Chief Inspector? Have you arrested someone?'

'Not exactly.' He took a couple of gulps of coffee.

'Come on, Chief Inspector. You can tell something about

222

what's going on. You implied when you came in that the press will get hold of it sooner or later.'

'I suppose so. But this is still confidential, OK? We had a report yesterday evening from the charge nurse at the Accident and Emergency unit of Warwick Hospital. He said a man calling himself Bernard Richards was treated there at around two thirty a.m. yesterday morning. Within an hour or so of the attack, in other words. The patient had a severe laceration to his lower right arm, needing a local anaesthetic and considerable stitching. He claimed he'd had an accident earlier that day with a hedge cutter and hadn't got round to doing anything about it. The nurse was suspicious, and decided to call the local police. But our friend must have got wind of something, because when they looked in his cubicle, he'd pushed off. The address he'd given was false. When the alert came through later from Thames Valley, they put two and two together and called us.'

'So you think this was the man in the Glebe?'

'It's certainly possible.'

'So did the hospital give you a description?'

'Better than that, there was a video camera in the A & E reception. Have them everywhere these days, don't they?'

'So have you seen it?'

'They're rushing a copy over to us. It should be here soon.'

'What about the body?'

'No identification as yet. We're rather hoping the man with the arm injury may be able to help us there.'

'He'll deny it ever happened, won't he?'

'To begin with. But he'll have a bit of explaining to do as to how he got the wound. The gardening story won't hold up long, I'd guess. Eventually, he'll tell us, they usually do.'

'And do you think there's any connection with my father's murder?'

He shook his head. 'None. We've already had a report on the sack. That particular pattern wasn't in use until the mid-seventies, twenty years later. But that brings us to the second reason I came round.' He felt in his pocket. 'This.' He held out the little gold case with its thin gold chain.

I took it from him with trembling fingers. 'You've finished with it, then?'

'Yes. I had an unofficial report from the lab this morning. The, er, material I provided them with was adequate. It's as we had assumed. The body in the Glebe was your father's. The DNA matches that in the bones exactly. There is no possibility of error. I'm sorry.'

I shrugged and put the locket down on the table in front of me. 'I'd become resigned to it. After all, who else could it have been?'

'Now we have the statement from your mother's doctor about her condition, it's clear that nothing is to be gained from even attempting to conduct an interview with her. I'm in a position to draw up my report. Following that the Coroner will be informed that there are no pending criminal investigations to make necessary the continued adjournment of the inquest. That will, of course, involve evidence of the circumstances of the discovery of the body, and a forensic report. The verdict will be a mere formality.'

'Homicide by person or persons unknown?'

'Exactly. The matter will lie on the file, in case there is any more evidence. But to all intents and purposes, the matter will be closed.'

I sat at my desk in the drawing room with the household accounts. But I couldn't concentrate. The matter of my father's death might lie quite peacefully on the police file, but it didn't rest quietly in my mind.

I went out into the warm garden, and strolled along what my mother always referred to as the Long Walk, a paved pathway which led from the back of the house to the kitchen garden. In the days when we had had a full-time gardener, it had been edged by a herbaceous border, planned by my mother in accordance with the colour theories of Gertrude

Jekyll. Now a rampant white and yellow honeysuckle had covered almost the entire wall which ran alongside, the remaining ground colonised by nettles.

The bright sun gleamed on the flowers of the shrub and glinted on the fragments of crystal in the flagstones of the path. In the distance was the rumble of traffic on the Oxford road, and overhead the drone of a jet plane.

These contemporary sounds were the only things which prompted me to remember that I had moved in time. Without them, I could still be the little girl who had on countless summer days wandered the same garden.

I had day-dreamed, fantasising other lives. I knew that the children at the village school would often speak in frank envy of the life they imagined I led. But, on the rare occasions when my mother agreed that a friend whose family and antecedents had been thoroughly enquired into might come to tea, the girl or boy would be silent and ill at ease, dwarfed by the house and troubled by its air of Victorian gloom. When the jolly mother came to collect her child, they would spring at and clutch each other with a pleasure that I had never experienced.

The truth was that I envied them far more. Their houses were smaller, but they had the feel of real homes, where there were families who lived together, where their fathers were not away in London, where their brothers were not sent away to school.

When Daddy came back at the weekend, everything seemed different. There were treats he had picked up in the London shops that were not available in the austere grocers of rural Oxfordshire. Jack would come home on exeat and there would be hilarious games of football and cricket on the lawn, and I would show off my developing prowess on the tennis court. I longed for those weekends to last for ever and I dreaded the Monday mornings when Daddy would be gone to catch the early morning train to town from Waterbury before I was awake.

225

Then there was that terrible Monday morning when I had got up to find the house in turmoil. Mother was in her room, I was told by Mrs Pritchard, our housekeeper, and not to be disturbed. Later in the morning, she emerged strained and pale. She told me that she and Daddy had had a terrible row. He had decided to go away.

The only redeeming feature of that awful week was that Jack was brought back from school to keep me company. We were not allowed out of the grounds.

Then, a few days later, my mother had received the airmail letter from Paris. She told us that Daddy was with Teresa. He would never come home again. She had betrayed our trust and our hospitality. We were not to speak of him again. In her presence, we never had.

Children have an ability to hold in their minds conflicting versions of reality. Thus, at the age of eight, I had been told by my mother that she and my father had had a terrible row, and that he had left her, on the night that my father had bade me goodnight as usual, and had displayed no signs of the emotional disturbance which would surely have resulted. I'd never resolved this contradiction, fearful that I would have to choose either Mother's or Daddy's truth.

But now I felt compelled to go over it, whatever the consequences might be.

The night he had disappeared, he had come to say goodnight, as he always did. But Sunday was a special night, and with the anxiety of the child, I always asked him the same questions and like a catechism, he always gave the same answers.

'Will I see you in the morning, Daddy?'

'No, darling. In the morning, I have to go to London, to my work, just as I always do.'

'When will you come back, Daddy?'

'Next Friday, darling. You'll come with your mother to the station as you always do.'

'Where are you going now, Daddy?'

226

'Out for a little walk to the village, my sweet.'

And I would ask drowsily, as I did on every occasion, 'Will you go walled garden way or front drive way?'

'Tonight? Tonight, I shall go walled garden way.'

Then I would give the same secret smile and ask him, 'What will you do in the village, Daddy?'

And he would pretend to cough a little, as if confessing something a little shameful. 'I may just call in at the Trout to check the ale is not sour, my darling.'

'When will you come back, Daddy?'

'After you're asleep, my love.'

'Come in and kiss me when you come back, Daddy.'

'I always do.'

'Promise me specially you will, Daddy. That you'll come back and kiss me.'

'I will.'

'Cross your heart and hope to die.'

'Cross my heart and hope to die.'

But he never had come back. He had betrayed my mother, but more important to my childish mind, he had broken a promise to me.

The child had therefore readily constructed the fantasy that he had not merely gone away, but was dead. If he had died, he had not broken his promise. He could not have returned. Death had granted him remission of his obligation.

My mother's insistence on the destruction of his memory had provoked in me an opposite response. Dead people should have memorials. That was what Jack in that often strangely intuitive way had grasped when I had shown him the album.

As I grew up, the fantasy of my father's death had gradually lost its grip. I knew more about the relations of men and women. I could accept reluctantly that he might out of emotional cowardice have been unwilling that night to admit to his daughter what was his intention. Somewhere in the world he was living his own life. Occasionally, but not very often, I wondered whether he ever thought of me.

Now, of course, it was clear that the child's intuition, had, however bizarrely, been correct. The adult might have hoped, flying not only against intuition, but logic, that the bones in the Glebe belonged to some other man, but that hope was finally dashed. I had to accept that he never would return. But in that acceptance, there was a certain exultation. Those bones thrown into a ditch in the Glebe carried a message more powerful than a living man could convey. They said: this was a man who kept his faith as far as he was allowed. Death, not bad faith had prevented him. My father was the hero the little girl of eight had always believed him to be.

Nevertheless, no matter how emotionally satisfying that might be at one level, the conflicting truths of my childhood had not been resolved.

It was a conflict that even now, my mind shied away from. If Daddy had told the truth, my mother had lied. If my father had been attacked walking on the Glebe, then he could not have been fleeing to a rendezvous with Teresa. It was inconceivable that he would have wandered there in the dark on such an occasion.

Then I recalled something else. He had told me he was going on his usual route through the walled garden. That way avoided the Glebe completely, and went straight down into the village the most direct route, the way I still went myself when I didn't wish to drive. But I knew that on that night he had not gone that way, because I had watched him.

On Sunday nights, I always disobeyed my mother's strict instructions not to get out of bed. I would crouch by the window, cupping my hands over the glass so that the night light in my room would not spoil my vision. I would see him set off down the Long Walk to the walled garden, striding purposefully, his footsteps echoing in the quiet night.

That night as on other nights, I had watched and listened, waiting to hear in the silence of the evening the sharp click of the lock on the door that led from the kitchen garden out into the lane, my signal to go back to bed. The key which opened this door hung on the board in the kitchen. Daddy would pick it up on his way out and replace it on his way back.

I waited a long time that night, and the tiredness had gathered in my mind like the mist which hung over the water meadows of the Crow on autumn evenings, but still I heard no click. Perhaps I was so tired I had missed it. I was upset that this little part of the ritual had not followed the correct pattern. I had got reluctantly back into bed, when I heard the sound of footsteps, this time growing louder. I jumped out of bed, and hurried back to the window. I slid up the sash quietly, shivering in my thin night-dress in the sudden chill of the night air.

I could hear that the footsteps were passing the front of the house from the crunching of the shingle, but no matter how far I leaned out I could not see round the corner. As I listened I heard them die away into the distance. I thought it strange that my father had decided to go down the front drive, when he had told me he was going through the walled garden, particularly as he had set out in that direction. The incident being out of the normal pattern, had disturbed me.

I lay awake listening. My mother was in the drawing room, talking to Mrs Phillips, the doctor's wife. They had been to evensong together and it was their habit to discuss the service over a sherry. Eventually, I heard the front door open and my mother's clear voice saying goodbye, then the crunch of footsteps on the shingle, and the rattle of the engine of Mrs Phillips's Morris Minor.

I fell asleep wondering why Daddy had gone a different way. He must have forgotten the key. How strange that was, because Daddy never forgot anything.

In the turmoil of the morning that followed, the matter of the key refused to leave me alone. At the first opportunity, I ran to the kitchen to be smothered with kisses by Mrs

Pritchard. There I saw that the key was in fact missing. Daddy had taken it with him, so why had he not used it?

There had been a sequel to the matter of the key. Mr Pritchard the gardener found it a few days later in the potting shed in the walled garden. It had fallen into a flower pot. None of the grown-ups was at all interested, but to me it was of great importance. Daddy must have dropped it there. Without the key, he could not have opened the door into the back lane. That was why he had retraced his steps and gone down the drive. But why had he dropped the key in the shed? What had he been doing there? Over the years until it ceased to interest me, I had asked myself that question many times, but never thought of a convincing answer.

I couldn't think of one now, except that it seemed even more oddly significant. The only thing I could think, with the hindsight of Jack's discovery, was that if Daddy had gone the way he had set out to go, he would never have met whatever horror awaited him on the Glebe. That surely ruled out any premeditation. Anyone planning to attack him on his evening walk would have awaited him in the dark lane, the way he usually went. No murderer could have planned to meet him on the Glebe, if it was only by chance that he had taken that path.

I recalled again that enigmatic meeting with the late Gervase Tuddenham. I had been convinced he knew something, but what on earth could it have been? If my father had met Tuddenham or someone with him on the Glebe by chance, for what possible reason could they have killed him? But if that was what had happened, and if Tuddenham's death was no accident, then the man who killed my father was still alive and determined that neither he nor his reason for doing it would ever be discovered.

I was walking back to the house when I heard a car screech to a halt on the shingle. Who the hell was it this time?

I hurried round to the front to see Martin Rice climbing out of his red Jaguar.

'Liz. How are you? I heard what happened. I'm so sorry.' He came up to embrace me, his lady-killer smile on his face, but I held back.

'What are you doing, coming here today of all days, with half of Fleet Street snooping around the village, Martin? You must be mad.'

'Liz. Please, let's go inside.'

I poured him a mug of coffee, then sat down opposite him at the kitchen table. 'You don't have to bother to pretend you care about what happened to me, by the way.'

He reached out his hand to mine. 'Liz, darling. I was up in Birmingham yesterday. I was going to call when I heard about it on the car radio, but I was running so late with my meetings that . . .'

'Let's be grown-up, shall we, Martin? Only children feel obliged to lie. I've worked it all out, you see. I'd got used to being just a fantasy fuck, but I hadn't realised the fantasy you were having was about real estate values in North Oxfordshire.'

'For God's sake, what are you talking about, Liz?'

'I'm talking about you and me and The Hollies. Our *ménage à trois*.'

For a moment his lip curled with irritation, then the smile reasserted itself. 'Is that what you think? It was never like that, Liz, darling. Believe me.'

'Really? Well, whatever, I don't care any more. It's over, Martin. You can concentrate your energies on Dawn. Now I think you'd better go.'

'You're completely wrong, Liz. You're the sexiest woman I know. It's a misunderstanding. If it was something I said, I'm sorry.'

I stood up. 'Goodbye, Martin. I have things to do.'

'Sit down, Liz. Please. It's very important you and I have a talk. There's something I need to discuss with you. About the other night.' He reached out, caught hold of my arm and pulled me none too gently back down into the kitchen chair. He relaxed the pressure of his grip, but didn't let go. Now, he wasn't even pretending to smile. There was a hard look in his eyes and for the second time since I'd known him, I felt within him the potential for violence. The boy who'd grown up on the tough streets of London wasn't far below the surface.

'Let go of my arm, Martin.' I struggled in his grasp, but he retained his hold. 'For God's sake. I've nothing further to discuss with you. You're not welcome in my house. Please get out.'

'In a moment. Liz, listen to me carefully. This is important. Did you happen to see a fax which must have come in on the machine around the time you were making your call in the study? The sender is adamant it was correctly sent, but there's no trace of it.'

I looked at him closely. I observed with interest that not only was he angry, he was scared.

I gave a sudden hard twist of my arm – fortunately he'd grabbed my left – and wrenched it out of his grasp. I stood up so quickly I knocked the Windsor chair over backwards with a crash. I planted my hands on the table and leaned my face towards him, looking him straight in the eye. 'I resent the imputation in what you've just said. I saw no fax, Martin. And even if I had seen it, it would still be there in your study. I'm actually not in the habit of stealing other people's correspondence.'

The bland smile had returned. He said in his usual smooth tones, 'I'm relieved to hear it, Elizabeth, my darling. Believe me, I'd be very annoyed if it turned out that you were inter-fering with my business affairs.'

He stood up. 'I'm so glad you've set my mind at rest, Liz. It's not unknown for such things to go astray. I shall advise my colleague to be more careful in future. And if you ever want to change your mind . . .'

232

'Do you mean about the sex or The Hollies? The answer to both is no.'

I stood watching the big red car turning on the parking area, then heading off down the drive. I waited until it was out of sight.

I had been careful to disguise the alarm I had felt, but now the relief that he had gone flooded out, making me tremble. If I had been foolish to take the fax in the first place, I had been, arguably, even more foolish to lie about it just now. But I was damned if I was going to be threatened and man-handled in my own house by Martin Rice. What on earth was he so excited about, anyway? Maybe the item itself would explain matters?

I took the coat I had been wearing that evening off its hanger in the cupboard in the downstairs cloakroom. There was a blood stain on the collar. It would have to be dry-cleaned. I felt in the right hand pocket, took out the crumpled sheet of paper, and, in the brightness of the kitchen, smoothed it out on the table.

It was a handwritten scrawl on headed notepaper.

'Rice. The Gravesham Casket is ready for delivery. G.'

Casket? It sounded like something to do with funerals. That didn't seem at all the sort of thing for Martin to be so worked up about. Nevertheless, he had been concerned enough about its whereabouts to wish to retrieve it. It was not that he was uncertain about the contents, as the sender had obviously been in touch. It was the fact that the message itself was in my possession.

I read the enigmatic sentence a second time. Martin was presumably acting as some kind of agent for the man or woman who had signed G, whose address was printed in expensively discreet typeface at the top of the paper: Windsoredge House, Gloucestershire GL6 9DL.

The sun streaming in through the kitchen windows dimmed as if blinds had been drawn. I had to grip the solid deal table-top with both hands to stop myself collapsing on to the red-tiled floor.

I stared again at the signature and the address. It could not be him. Surely not involved with Martin Rice? But it had to be.

There was only one Windsoredge House in the whole of England, the beautiful seventeenth-century mansion he had bought as a virtual ruin after the US Army had used it for accommodating a troop of special forces during the war. He had restored it over the years, filling it with treasures amassed from a lifetime of collecting, and surrounding it with one of the country's most splendidly landscaped gardens. The finest private house in England, it had been called.

And I could have been its chatelaine. I could have been Lady Greville.

When I first met him, in 1969, he was still Christopher Greville, MP for Oxford Cowley. He was a member of the Conservative opposition party's Shadow Cabinet and a certainty for office should they return to government. I was the Secretary of the University College Political Society. I'd written to him, stressing my local connection, because I was on the lookout for potentially controversial speakers.

Contrary to his Establishment background, his distinguished war service and his post-war military and business career, he had extremely liberal political views. He was a rising star, rich, brilliant and according to the gossip columnists, very handsome.

Rather to my surprise, he answered my letter personally, saying he was delighted to accept the invitation. He gave a scintillating talk, scorning the necessity for the Cold War and coruscatingly critical of the increasingly baroque arsenals accumulated on either side. He was the only Tory speaker we'd had who, despite a few early heckles, was given by the end enthusiastic applause.

To me, he deployed a slightly old-fashioned courtesy. He complimented me on the conduct and organisation of the meeting. The following day there arrived at the flat I shared with a couple of other female students a huge bouquet of tastefully chosen flowers, together with a card addressed to Miss Elizabeth Armitage, 'a young woman with a great future. With kind regards, C.G.'

During the next few weeks, I found myself following his parliamentary and business career with interest. I read a profile which regarded him as a potential future leader of his party. My friends claimed, vulgarly, to have observed that he fancied me. I said this was ridiculous. Then in his mid-forties, he was old enough to have been my father. I knew, however, that he had never married, despite his name having been linked to various glamorous and intelligent women.

Towards the end of that term, I received in the post a plain white envelope. When I tore it open, I gasped out loud at its contents, a treasure that I had dreamed of but never had a hope of obtaining. A ticket for the Centre Court at Wimbledon for Ladies Final Day. He had scribbled on the back of his accompanying card: 'I do hope you will be able to be my guest.'

It was the beginning of a wonderful summer. In the weeks which followed, there were dinners at fashionable restaurants, theatres and even the Opera. He did not at any time put pressure on me to go to bed with him, or even suggest that he expected this as the return on his investment. I had, though, already made up my mind that I would.

Finally he suggested that I might like to see his country house: Windsoredge was so beautiful in the summer. He was able to go there so much less frequently than he would like. I could come to lunch on Saturday, perhaps? There was a gentle, unstated appeal in his manner as he spoke.

'Or for the weekend,' I suggested.

He smiled and took my hand. 'My dearest girl,' he replied.

The first time we made love was a revelation. I was not inexperienced, but his erotic skills were sophisticated beyond anything I had known. He had none of the traditional reticence or clumsiness in such matters of the upper-class Englishman.

When our mutual passion was at length satisfied, he bent over me and smoothed the hair from my forehead. 'My darling Elizabeth, you are beautiful, you are clever, you have youth. You make me so wonderfully happy.'

It was later, after dinner, as we strolled in the box-edged parterre he had recreated, copying it from a seventeenth-century painting of the house, that he asked me to marry him.

I was utterly astonished. Marriage to anyone, far less to someone like Greville, had never entered my head. A good marriage was my mother's obsession, not mine. There were books I was going to write, university chairs I was going to occupy. Such a future did not include marriage, even to one of the richest and potentially most powerful men in England.

Now, as I looked back on the life I had actually endured, it seemed that I should feel that I was crazily, wilfully perverse to have turned down such an offer. Certainly my mother would have thought so, which was one of the reasons I never told her of it. She might in her fury have dreadfully embarrassed him as well as myself, and I could not have borne that.

But at the time I had my reasons which were powerful to me then and still were. I hoped that even with the benefit of hindsight, I would have had the courage to have done the same.

Christopher was a wonderful man, but it would have been his house, his career. I would have existed on the fringes. I would have been another rare and beautiful possession amongst all the others he had amassed. I was then in my Henry James period, reading everything the Master had ever written. Although I had little enough in common with the heroine of *The Portrait of a Lady*, and although Christopher had given me no reason to suspect that he had a Madam Merle hidden away somewhere, I sensed there was enough of Gilbert Osmond in his character to make me wary.

He was equally astonished, uncomprehending, and even angry when I had turned him down. He asked me why and I told him as succinctly and as cogently as I could. He was unconvinced. 'I will respect your wish to have any career you like, my darling.' But I persisted in my refusal.

I should, of course, have broken off the affair there and then, but I didn't want to hurt him any more than I had already, and I was sufficiently ambivalent to wish it to continue. It dragged on, giving him false hopes, plunging me into disaster.

In my increasing unhappiness at my situation, I must have grown careless about taking my pill. I woke up one morning to find that the inevitable had happened or rather hadn't happened. I broke off the relationship immediately.

I didn't tell him I was pregnant. I knew that would make him even more determined to possess me, as I knew how much he wanted a child. I was afraid he would enlist my mother in his cause.

I hoped that afterwards, when my child had been born, I could tell him and maybe there would be some arrangement made for him to participate in the upbringing. I thought then that being pregnant meant that one invariably and straightforwardly went on to have a child. No one ever told me of the hazards.

He found out what had happened, of course. A man in his position could find out anything. He wrote to me in the Radcliffe, saying that he still wanted to marry me, that I could have another child. I read the letter as if it were a page from a novel in which I was not a character. How could he not at least try to understand how I was feeling? I saw too that even in that letter, he never said he loved me. He'd never said that, even when he asked me to marry him. Perhaps if he had said that and meant it, things might have been different.

Thus I sent him a hurtfully short reply, in which I told him that I could never have another child, and that my views on marriage had not changed. That was the last contact I had had with him. It never occurred to me to question just why he had so keenly wanted to marry me. I suppose I was so naive as to believe that my combination of qualities was unique. I would have dismissed as quite bizarre the idea that he might have had a quite different reason.

Over the intervening years, I had observed the public aspects of his career. The cabinet post had been shortlived, owing, apparently to 'policy differences'. Then in the first of the 1974 elections, he had lost his seat, gone to the Lords and returned to his business career. I was aware of his involvement with the Farebrother, natural, given his love of all things antique and beautiful. It was, I had thought at the time, an odd coincidence that Jack had ended up there. Or had Christopher, I speculated, a little wildly perhaps, taken pity on my brother and given him a job for my sake when he returned from America under a cloud? If so, that generosity of spirit had recently been exhausted. Given how Jack had behaved, I could not in all honesty blame him.

Christopher Greville was not only a might-have-been in my life, but in the life of England. In many ways, he had enshrined the English Enlightenment virtues of liberality and humane nobility of spirit. He was a lost leader, a reminder of how things could have been different.

Now our paths had apparently crossed again. As I re-read the enigmatic message on the shiny fax paper, I wondered once more what business it could possibly be which Christopher, Lord Greville of Windsoredge in the county of Gloucester, of Eton, Oxford and the Coldstream Guards could have in common with Martin Rice, street-wise, barely honest parvenu. It did him no credit at all.

Whatever it was, it was a connection which both of them were anxious to keep private. Otherwise, why had Martin scuttled over here, not only in anger but in fear?

I folded up the fax and put it safely into my handbag. It had profoundly shocked me to discover the link between them. Nor was it apparently a casual matter of estate agency. If not only Martin, but by extension, Christopher Greville was afraid of this paper becoming public, then it must mean that the matter in it was very important indeed.

I ate a desultory salad lunch while I brooded over the events of the morning. I felt my mind becoming over-burdened with the mounting ramifications. I desperately needed to talk to Jack.

I was washing up when the phone rang.

I was in half a mind not to answer it. It was probably the press. I let it ring, but the caller was persistent. I sighed, wiped my hands and picked up the receiver.

'Crowcester 332,' I announced in the deliberately cold tones I employed when I wasn't expecting a call.

The voice which answered seemed very faint. An old woman's voice.

'I'm sorry, I can't hear you.'

The reply was a little louder. 'Do I speak to Miss Elizabeth Armitage?'

'Yes. Who are you?'

'Dear Elizabeth. I could not expect that you would recognise my voice. Please prepare for a shock. It is Teresa. Teresa Korzeniowska.'

I checked my watch for the umpteenth time. 10.49. Had only a minute elapsed since the last look? I held it to my ear to check it was still ticking. It was, of course. The little Omega that my mother had given me for my twenty-first birthday still kept perfect time after nearly thirty years. Eleven minutes to go, then. A lifetime. I stood at the top of the flight of steps leading from the Place de la Concorde to the Jardin des Tuileries, gazing out over the roar of traffic in the great square, and its central obelisk, a totem looted from one fallen Empire by another. Paris, like London, was full of these relics, a vast museum of the futility of conquest.

It was more years than I cared to remember since I had been here. When I was small, we used to stop for a day or so in the city, on the way to the Aveyron, where, every summer, we rented a house in a fortified hill-village which perched on a rocky cliff above a serpentine bend of the river.

Daddy had loved France. Even as a toddler, he had encouraged me to learn the French words for the important objects in my little world. I had inherited his affection. My study year in Aix-en-Provence had made me fluent in the language. I had dreamed then of writing the definitive study of the links between French and English literature, dedicated to his memory.

In Paris we had stayed, I remembered, at a comfortable, even rather grand, hotel. In those immediately post-war days, England was still able to bask in its glory as the nation which had saved Europe, and every Englishman of the upper middle-class could easily afford the best of what the French had to offer.

Everything then had seemed to move with stately slowness, unlike the frantic pace yesterday.

After the tantalisingly brief telephone conversation with the woman who I thought had disappeared for ever into the past – 'Le Jardin des Tuileries, at eleven o'clock, please, Elizabeth. I have much to explain' – I had booked the last seat on the evening flight to Paris out of Heathrow and had driven like a madwoman down the M40.

I had left the cheap chain hotel near the Gare du Nord after a cup of coffee, too nervous to eat anything, and had been at the rendezvous two hours early. After pacing nervously along the shaded allées of the gardens, I had spent an hour in the nearby Orangerie, contemplating Monet's *Waterlilies*, attempting to immerse my troubled mind in their peaceful depths.

Five minutes past eleven. I surveyed without hope the crowds, mainly tourists, plodding up the steps. It was a brilliantly sunny day, heat already radiating from the blinding white of the gravel walks. She was late. Perhaps she would not come. Perhaps she had thought better of the meeting. Even if she did come, what would I learn of my father that could alter the bleak facts? What could take away the indelible vision of those brown-stained bones, his broken skull?

Then I saw, during a lull in the flow of pedestrians, a woman slowly and carefully negotiating the stairway. Although clearly elderly, she was tall and slim, with a helmet of fashionably short silver hair. She wore an expensively cut grey coat, silk stockings and black patent shoes, a stylish black leather Courrèges bag over her shoulder. She was the kind of Parisienne one saw on the boulevards or in fashionable cafés, conscious of their femininity and their chic even in their seventies and eighties. Could it really be her?

She paused at the top of the steps and looked around her. Her eyes met my questioning glance, and her face lit up in the sweetest and most welcoming of smiles. We ran towards each other and embraced. We were both trembling. I caught the faint emanation of her scent – something sophisticated but slightly old-fashioned, Worth perhaps. For a few moments, there was silence. Then she put her hands on my shoulders and stared at me.

'Elizabeth.' The tears started in her eyes. 'After so long.'

Although hollowed and lined by age, I now recognised, even after forty years, the high cheek-bones, the firm chin, the wide full-lipped mouth and the huge eyes, dark and lustrous still. Only her hair, cut short, and almost white, was unfamiliar, but in my memory I saw it spread upon the wide shoulders of her trench coat, glossy and jet black, like the tresses of a fairy-tale princess.

'Let's find somewhere to sit down, shall we?'

I put her arm in mine, and led the way over to an outdoor café shaded by trees which I had taken note of earlier.

We sat side by side at a small round table. She gazed straight ahead, lost in thought, perhaps uncertain how to begin. Then her lips, somewhat shrunken and pursed by the wrinkles around her mouth, and now pale pink, not the car-mine she had once affected, began to move.

'My dear Elizabeth. So much time has passed, but it seems no time at all since I saw you. Yet then you were a pretty little girl, and now you are a beautiful mature woman. I was young and vain enough to think myself good-looking and now I am old and ugly.'

I put my hand on hers. 'You are still beautiful, Teresa.'

She smiled the sweet smile at me. 'Teresa. It is so long since I was called that. But it is easier for you to call me Teresa, because that is who I am for you. And it reminds me so much of the past.'

I ordered coffee from the hovering waiter. 'The past has been very much present for me recently, Teresa.'

She reached out a hand and laid it on mine. 'And for me, my dear.'

I clutched at the frail, bird-like bones. 'Tell me, Teresa. Tell me what happened. I've lived so long between versions of reality. It's as if you're looking at a picture which is really two pictures joined together, and the parts don't match. Tell me about my father. I missed him so much. As the years went on, I couldn't believe that if he were alive he would not have found some way of telling me so. I wanted him to be dead, so I wouldn't have to live with the pain of his rejection and yet I desperately wanted him to be alive. Now I know that he is dead, was dead from the last moment I saw him, and I have looked upon his remains, I hunger to know how and why. Tell me the truth. Whatever it is, whatever your part in it was.'

I saw the tears gathering in the corners of her still remark-ably clear eyes. 'My dear, you shall know everything I know. It is a long story and it is as painful for me as it will be for you. But first, I must answer the question which I know hangs in the air between us, like the mist of one's breath on a winter's morning. I could not blame you for thinking such a thing. But I did not kill him, Elizabeth, nor play any part in his death. Please believe that. Please say you believe me.'

'I believe you, Teresa, with all my heart. I've never thought for a moment that you did.'

She wiped her eyes. 'I am so relieved to hear you say that. I loved him so much. It would be the most terrible irony if you had thought that I could ever . . . But you do not and I am so glad.'

'You were lovers? You did plan to go away together? But what happened, who killed him to prevent that?' The questions burst out of me. It was as if there was a kind of barrier in my mind which had held them back. Now their insistent force had swept that barrier away.

'Be patient, my child. I must tell it as it happened, from the beginning. Yes, we were lovers. But it is not how you think it was, Elizabeth. I did not descend upon your happy family that day when you and your brother surprised me in the woods and take your father away. You see, that had already happened.'

'What, you mean you knew him before that day?'

'Yes. Long before. During the war. I have to confess that little of what I told you, your brother and your mother that afternoon was true. You will I hope soon understand the reasons why I concealed the truth.

'I am not Polish, but French. My name is not Teresa, but Thérèse. I was no heroine of SOE. I remember I jumped even at the crack of your brother's toy cap pistol. I had met your father in London in 1943. I had got out of Paris in 1940, just before it was declared an open city and the Nazis, those unspeakable monsters, strutted in as conquerors. My father had a thriving business as a wine merchant, which he was unwilling to abandon and my mother refused to leave him. They preferred to take their chances, with the results that you must imagine. They perished in Auschwitz. For you must know, Elizabeth, we were not merely French, but Jews.'

'I'm so sorry. I didn't know. I should have realised.'

'Why should you? Thank God such distinctions have in the

civilised West at least become of far less account, particularly amongst the young. You are fortunate to have been born after the war, my child. You are free of the baggage of the past. But to continue. We had relatives in London. I had been trained as a secretary in Paris and I went to work for the Free French Government in exile. Because my English was, in those days, extremely good, I was employed as a translator of documents and interpreter. Naturally, I met through this work many British officers and officials, one of whom was your father. You have to remember the circumstances in which we found ourselves. He and I were both alone in London. Your mother was then in the WRAF at a station in Scotland. Such things happened. Neither of us thought, at the beginning, that our affair would be other than a passing matter. I had had others before. But it was different. I fell passionately in love with him, and he with me. But he was not free, and a scandal, in the climate of that time, would have ruined his career. We went our separate ways after the war. He returned to his home and his post in the British Civil Service. I returned to France, but it was not so easy to forget him.'

'You came back here, to Paris?'

'Yes. My wartime work enabled me to take up a post in the defence ministry. I threw myself into the job. All my family had perished in the Holocaust, and I had lost my only love. In time, I received promotions. My knowledge of English continued to help me. I became what you would call an Intelligence Officer, particularly concerned with the Middle East.

'At that time, France was a close ally of Israel. We equipped their Air Force with modern jets. When Nasser came to power in Egypt, we knew that he would not rest until he had persuaded the rest of the Arab world to move against the Israelis. It was only a matter of time. He had rebuilt his armed forces with modern Russian equipment. He wooed the West with his film-star good looks, and persuaded the Americans

244

to permit the loan for the Aswan Dam project, which was intended to make the economy of Egypt stronger than at any time since the Pharaohs. But all this you know. It is part of your history as well as mine.'

'I suppose so, though at the time, I was only a child. But what has all this to do with my father?'

'Be patient. You will see in a moment. When the Americans turned against Nasser and decided not to allow the loan for the dam project to go ahead, he defied the West by nationalising the Suez Canal Company. This was a deliberately provocative act. It directly threatened the vital interests of Britain, France and Israel.

'However, we in France knew that British foreign policy, because of its extensive interests in the Middle East, was generally pro-Arab, and the recovery of the Canal was not, in itself, a sufficient pretext for the full-scale invasion of Egypt and the removal of Nasser. If, though, the Israelis were to launch an attack on Egyptian positions in the Sinai desert, then there would be an opportunity for intervention by the British and French. There would be an ultimatum, followed by armed intervention, ostensibly to prevent the conflict from escalating and to separate the participants. In the course of this intervention, the Canal zone would be recaptured and Nasser toppled.

'The negotiations for an agreement to bring about such a piece of naked *realpolitik*, particularly as the British were concerned to conceal it from their American allies, who regarded the interest in Egypt of the British and French as neo-colonialist and therefore to be opposed, had to be conducted in great secrecy. It was in the course of those liaison meetings with the British, in which I was involved, that I returned to London and met your father once again.'

'He was on the British side of the negotiations?'

'Yes. One morning, I walked into the room where we were to meet our British counterparts, and there he was. It was electric. For me, although there had been other men since him, I knew when I saw him that the spark between us ignited still. At the close of business, I avoided my colleagues. I spent the night in his flat in Victoria, and it was as if we had never been apart. He told me of his miserable married life, with a wife who cared for nothing but the trivial concerns of her home village. He told me of the children he loved. I was in London frequently as the crisis dragged on, and the use of armed force became more and more inevitable. I saw your father as often as I could. It was then that I had the crazy idea of seeing for myself the home life which he hated and the two children he adored. I borrowed one of the French Embassy cars and drove to this village of Crowcester. It was while I was engaged on my espionage that I was surprised and captured.' She smiled at the memory.

'But why did you pretend to be Polish?'

'I could not be myself. If I admitted to being French, then my presence might somehow have come to the notice of the French Embassy and I might have been recognised. It would be a breach of government regulations. I thought of my cover on the spur of the moment. I knew of many such stories from friends and colleagues.'

'So that's why the police couldn't trace Teresa Korzeniowska. She never existed.'

'I'm afraid not. Your father was horrified by my little subterfuge. But it gave a certain frisson to our relationship. I see now it was a cruel deceit on your mother, but in those days, I thought only of him.'

'Please go on, Teresa. Were you going to run away together, that night?'

'Oh Elizabeth, I feel a kind of shudder in my soul when I think of that night. The brief answer to your question is No. Your father was far too dignified and careful a man to run anywhere. We had both come to the conclusion that the deceit could not go on. Once the business of Suez had been concluded, I would not be able to return so frequently to London. Your father would hardly ever be able to travel alone to Paris. Our love would once again be doomed, but neither of us wanted it to die. We decided that we must confront the matter head-on. We must see your mother that night, and tell her everything. We would attempt to negotiate a settlement with her. She and your father would remain technically married. There would be no scandal. I would quit my job in Paris and come to live in Crowcester as Teresa Korzeniowska. He would be free to see his children. It would be a reasonable and adult solution, such as would be regarded as normal in France.'

'My mother was not French. I can't imagine she would have seen it that way.'

'I also did not know how your mother would react. The fact is that the proposition was never put to her. I waited for your father that night in the village. We were to meet there to discuss the matter once more before returning to The Hollies together. He never arrived.'

I stared at her in surprise and disappointment. My hand jerked convulsively and coffee slopped over the table. I mopped it with paper napkins in a trembling hand.

'What do you mean he never arrived? Didn't you look for him?'

'Of course. I went up and down the streets of that squalid little village, its horrible houses all shut up and dark. I was mad, frantic with worry. I went as far as the gate of The Hollies into the lane and tried to open it but it was locked. He was nowhere to be seen. I looked everywhere but there was no trace. I did not know then that he had gone by the path across the Glebe. I did not know what had happened to him. But it was not long before I feared the answer.'

'What answer? For God's sake, Teresa, you know more than you're saying. Please tell me, whatever it is.'

'I feared the answer because of the nature of the world in which we both moved. And I feared it because of what your father had told me.

'You know of the matter with which we both had been

247

involved. The agreement reached was enshrined in a secret protocol signed on 24 October 1956 at a house in Sèvres, near Paris. It provided for collusive military action commencing at the end of that month by the Israelis, the French and the British, intended to lead to the recapture of the Suez Canal zone and the overthrow of President Nasser.

'Politically, in the context of the time, and particularly for the British, and their so-called special relationship with a virulently anti-colonial American administration, it was dynamite. Neither your Prime Minister, Sir Anthony Eden, nor your Foreign Secretary, Selwyn Lloyd ever admitted that the protocol existed. The original British copy was destroyed, either by Eden himself or on his orders. It was the highest of high State secrets at that particular moment in history. Your country was on the brink of war.

'Your father had chosen that Sunday for our showdown with your mother quite deliberately. He wanted to deal with the matter then because the deceit had always weighed heavily on his conscience, and because he did not know when next he might be able to attend to it. You see, he knew that his personal life would soon be submerged by the tide of world affairs. He had decided to resign from his post the following day in as public a manner as possible, and, in his resignation statement, disclose the existence of the Sèvres protocol.'

I shook my head in amazement.

'Why would he do such a thing?'

'Because, my dear, he was not only a patriot but an old-fashioned man of honour. He had fought bravely against the lawless tyranny of the Nazis. He could not bear to see the country he loved involved in such a conspiracy against a sovereign nation. He had consistently argued against it, as had his chief Lord Mountbatten. He thought it despicable. He hoped that international and public outrage at his disclosure would prevent the attack on Egypt from going ahead. I tried to dissuade him, but he would not listen. And of course, he has been vindicated. The bungled Suez operation destroyed Eden, destroyed Britain's credibility in the Middle East. The British Empire collapsed the day the troops landed in the Canal zone.'

Her eyes brightened as they stared piercingly into mine. 'Your father was a brave man. But he was confronting forces whose ruthlessness he did not anticipate. In the event, he neither met your mother, nor released his resignation statement. The answer that came to me as I shivered in the cold of that autumn night was that it was no accident that he had failed to appear.'

Her voice fell to a whisper and she gripped my arm fiercely, the long nails of her thin fingers stabbing into my flesh. 'He had been stopped.'

'Stopped? You mean he was killed by Government agents? But that's incredible.'

'Is it? Is it really? Such convenient disappearances arranged by governments are hardly unknown. And there were three governments determined to prevent such a catastrophic leak of a sensitive secret at that time. Desperate times require desperate measures. Ourselves the French, the Israelis, even the cricket-playing British had secret services which could do such things. I knew of them by repute, though I was never involved in such matters myself. The British Government had Hitler's favourite, Reinhard Heydrich, assassinated in Czechoslovakia and British agents kidnapped General Kreipe in Crete during the war. Israel's Mossad snatched Eichmann from Buenos Aires. The war in Algeria in the fifties revealed the ruthlessness of my own nation's covert operations. The bomb attack on the *Rainbow Warrior* showed that that mentality lives on. Even now, in Paris, in Tel Aviv and in London, there are men plotting similar adventures.

'That night, as I waited and waited, and he did not come, I feared the worst. Finally, I got into the car and returned to London. I cannot describe to you how I felt. I thought of calling The Hollies in the character of Teresa, but I realised

I did not have the strength to carry through the deception. By then, of course, the story was all over the newspapers, the false accusations of treason. I knew then that my worst fears had been realised. The officials who had had him killed were covering up their crime with a mass of lies.'

'So what did you do?'

'The only thing I could do. I came back to Paris. I did my work. I pretended to myself that none of it had happened. I was a coward, my dear. I was afraid that what had happened to Robert would happen to me if I started asking questions. Eventually, I met another man with whom I thought I could share my life. We married. He became well known as a diplomat. He knows nothing of all this. I have come here without his knowledge. Nothing can be done to put right the past, but I felt compelled to tell you, my child, what I knew.'

'My mother received a letter from Paris. She told us it had come from my father. That he told her that he had run away with you.'

Teresa shook her head vigorously. 'I know nothing of such a letter. I never wrote to her and your father never gave me a letter to send to her. I can only presume that the same people who lied about your father's defection, and who knew the truth, arranged for this further deception.'

'Why did you wait forty years to tell me this?'

'I had no proof of what I feared. Until his body was discovered, I knew nothing for certain. And then I was ashamed of my own part. I thought that you would not want to know me.'

I stared out at the crowds thronging the shaded walks of the Gardens, trying to conceal my bitter disappointment.

Not even Teresa, the nearest witness, could definitely explain what had happened that night. No one had witnessed his final walk across the dark, scrub-covered Glebe, no one had seen land the fatal blows, no one had seen him thrown into the rough grave.

Then suddenly, the thing burst upon me. No one had

seen him buried? But, yes, someone had! Fantastic though it seemed, he must have! That was the answer to the conundrum which had been puzzling me ever since the police had heaved up the stone slab that morning and found the fertiliser sack of bones beneath.

It was not a coincidence that the body had been laid in the same culvert in which my father had been laid. It was because the person who buried it had not only known of the existence of the culvert, they knew that it was a safe place to hide a body. The idea had been planted in them twenty years before.

Had the murderer been one of the village boys who had played about on the earlier excavation? Had he been hanging around the site the evening my father disappeared? Had he seen something that, out of childish fear or incomprehension, or an apprehension of threatened danger, he had decided to keep silent about, something which he only recalled when he in turn had stood over a corpse, killed perhaps in a fit of rage or jealousy, unpremeditated and unprepared? Had he then recalled that long ago night on which he had seen a body disposed of in a place so secret it had never been found again?

If that man could be persuaded to disgorge that knowledge, in conjunction with Teresa's evidence, then some way might be found to pursue those really responsible, in Government or the Secret Services, or at the very least to bring the matter to light, and restore something of my father's honour which they had tarnished.

I turned to her with the glow of these thoughts in my eyes. Quickly, almost incoherently I told her what was in my mind.

She seemed to shy away from me as if I were a madwoman. 'What you wish to do is not possible. I know of what I speak. We would achieve nothing. Even if your fantastic theory is true, who would accept the evidence of a vicious criminal, even if he had a clear recollection of that night? And if it were so clear, why did he not come forward at the time? No one would believe it. It would be dismissed as the nightmare of a child. No government would admit the things that we suspect them of having done. You must try to forget the past, Elizabeth. In war, terrible things are done. You alone cannot right those wrongs.'

'If you won't help me then I must think of another way. There will be archives, other people will remember. I will make them speak the truth. I will not give up on this, Teresa. Please, at least tell me your real name, and your address here. I promise I will not divulge them to anyone who would do anything to embarrass you.'

She shook her head. 'I am sorry, Elizabeth, that would only be to encourage you in a foolish scheme. For a brief moment, our lives tragically coincided. Now we must once more part. This time, for ever. I have another world in which I must play my part, and so do you. I must go, my dear. I have an appointment which I must not miss. It would cause my husband to ask me questions and I have already lied to him too much.' She picked up her handbag. 'You have come a long way and I think you are going home dissatisfied. I am sorry. But you must accept, Elizabeth, that the past is the past. Live and forget, as I have tried to do. And now, I must go. But I must leave enough to pay for the bill.'

She opened her bag and rummaged for her purse, produced a hundred franc note and thrust it into my hand.

I hurriedly got out my own wallet. 'Don't be silly, Teresa. Of course I will pay. Please. I insist.'

I leant over and grabbed at her elegant bag to thrust the note back. In doing so, I clumsily knocked it off the table. It fell upside down and some of its contents spilled out.

I knelt down to help her stuff them back, but she practically thrust me away. I was hurt to sense the real anger in the gesture. 'No, it is quite all right. I can manage. Thank you.'

She closed the bag, clutching it to her and stood up, her flash of temper gone. 'Goodbye, my dear child.'

We embraced and I felt her cheek wet with tears as it brushed against mine. I felt her thin bones trembling under the elegant coat. I had remembered her as magnificent and powerful, now like my mother she was diminished.

I watched her walk away in the direction of the Louvre, her dark figure moving over the white gravel of the allée like one of L. S. Lowry's matchstick people, until it seemed to shimmer and vanish into the billowing dust and the jostling crowds.

I summoned the waiter and paid the bill. Had I been weak to let her go? Or was I crazy even to think of taking on the task of bringing an entire system of secrecy to account for my father's death?

Only a day ago, the solution to the mystery of my father's death had seemed to be rooted in the domestic and cosy traditions of the English murder. What Teresa had told me had elevated it to the fantastic realms of some ghastly thriller. And then the bathetic conclusion to our momentous meeting, an argument over who should pay for a few cups of coffee. How many times hadn't I repeated that same charade with friends in England, even to the thrusting of the money back into their purses?

Suddenly, it was as if a laser seared through my skull.

I was on my feet, dashing out to look down the long vista. Where was she? How far could she have gone? Surely, I could catch her? I started to run down the white gravel path to the astonishment of the strollers on either side.

I had to catch her because I knew now that she had been lying to me.

Whatever else she had been, she was not now the French wife of a former French diplomat. Otherwise, why had I seen among the spilled contents of her handbag the dark blue leatherette folder of an old-fashioned British passport?

She had lied about one thing. Had she lied about everything else?

I gazed wildly down the tree-fringed avenue, where the

crowds gathered at the foot of the triumphal arch which stood in front of the courtyard of the Louvre.

As I ran, the incredulity with which I had struggled burst from its bonds. When I was with Teresa, I had been awed by her presence. I had wanted to believe her. Now I knew her story could not be true.

In my mind, I heard my father's ghostly footsteps coming back by the Long Walk and crunching through the shingle of the drive. No one had followed him. How could they have lain in wait, when he had decided at the last minute to go by a different route?

And Teresa had said, 'I did not know then that he had gone by the path across the Glebe.' She had not drawn that inference from where his body had been discovered. She had claimed to know it as fact. But how?

Why had she brought me here to tell me such elaborate falsehoods? Had she in fact killed him herself?

I had never been a sprinter, and in my half heels, encumbered with a skirt, my handbag clasped awkwardly under my arm, I would hardly have broken any records. My hair flopped heavily on my shoulders and flew into my eyes. The leather soles of my silly shoes skidded on the loose surface. How I longed for my Nikes. How absurd it had been to be infected by the air of this city and go in for chic and not practicality.

I could feel the curious glances of the passers-by upon me. I was getting hot and felt ridiculous. Surely an elderly woman could not have gone so far in so short a time?

Then, at last, I saw her. She had stopped at the end of the Gardens to cross the Place du Carrousel. I increased my pace, feeling the breath burning in my lungs and a stitch starting in my side. As I shoved through the crowd around the archway, I saw her on the opposite side of the road.

Without waiting for a break in the traffic, I ran across, being hooted and yelled at by drivers, and attracting the

254

censorious attention of the policeman who stood keeping an eye on the queues of tourists outside the great glass pyramid which covered the entrance to the museum.

I lost sight of her as I jostled through the archway leading to the Rue de Rivoli opposite the Palais Royal. I stopped as I emerged, glancing both ways.

There she was, across the street, only a little way ahead, in the direction of the Hôtel de Ville.

Now she was in plain sight, I slowed down to get my breath and to think. The best plan would be to follow her to her destination unseen. If I tried to confront her in the street she might deny all knowledge of me, say that I had been trying to attack her.

Ahead, I saw her turn into a side street. I quickened my pace. At the far end was a blue and white striped canvas awning over steps leading up to a pair of glass doors. Discreet gold lettering over the entrance proclaimed Hôtel d'Orléans. She mounted the steps and disappeared within.

I stopped in front of a shop selling antiques and wondered what I should do next. If I rang the hotel, she would probably refuse to speak to me. She might even decide to leave Paris and then I would never find her. I could hardly wait here for hours on the off-chance that she would re-appear.

The sound of laughter from the bar on the corner of the street suggested a solution. I responded to it before I had time to have second thoughts. I took my purse from my handbag, and dashed across the road into the lobby of the Hôtel d'Orléans.

The receptionist was a bored-looking young woman.

'*La vieille dame qui est entrée il y a une minute. Elle a oublié ceci au café.*'

'*Laissez-le ici, je le lui remettrai.*'

I smiled slyly. '*Ça serait préférable que je le lui remette en main propre.*'

I had relied on her helping a fellow worker to a tip and also being too idle to argue with someone who seemed harmless.

She shrugged again and nodded at the lift. '*D'accord. Chambre numéro trois cent vingt. Troisième étage.*'

I took a deep breath before knocking on the door of Room 320, then standing to one side away from the spyhole.

A voice came from within. '*Qui est-ce?*'

'*Un paquet pour Madame.*'

The door opened a few inches and Teresa gazed out warily. I came smartly forward and stuck my foot in the gap. 'Sorry, Teresa. Don't be alarmed but there's something I want to ask you.'

Her face contorted with anger. 'Why have you followed me here, Elizabeth?'

I was about to launch into a tirade of reproach, when an elderly male voice from within the room said, 'Who are you talking to, old girl?'

She half turned. 'No one, darling. Just the maid.'

I pushed my way in through the door, knocking Teresa to one side. 'Who is that with you? What on earth is going on?'

I came face to face with a tall white-haired old man in a Viyella shirt, blue blazer and cavalry twill trousers. I stared at his long lean sunburnt face, the aquiline nose, the bushy eyebrows, the thick, somewhat pendulous lower lip, now drawn back in anxious surprise at my intrusion.

Despite the changes wrought by the passing years, I knew him by the leaping of my heart.

It was my father.

VIII

The police arrived within twenty minutes of my call on the car-phone.

I was sitting in the front seat of the Morgan chain-smoking when Detective Chief Inspector Green strolled up, followed a few moments later by PC Enstone.

'It's over there at the entrance to the quarry. You'll forgive me if I don't accompany you.'

I was lighting up again when they came back, looking, I was pleased to see, fairly pale and shaken.

Enstone started to talk on his radio. Green came over and I got out of the car.

'Makes a nasty mess, a shotgun at close quarters, doesn't it, Mr Armitage?'

'Apparently. It was my first, and I hope the last. Any idea who it was?'

He didn't reply to the question but asked his own. 'What exactly were you doing here, sir?'

'I stopped for a piss. I saw the van and wondered why it was there.'

'So you were on your own?'

'Yes, of course. As you can see.'

He nodded. 'You didn't touch the van or any part of it? The door for instance?'

'No, of course I didn't. There was no need. It was obvious that he was beyond help. You didn't say whether you recognised . . . knew whose van it was.'

'You don't have any idea then?'

'No, why the hell should I?'

'How long would you say you were in the quarry before you called us?'

'Not more than a couple of minutes. But look here, why are you asking me all this? Are you trying to make out I've got something to do with this. That's absolutely ridiculous.'

'You have to understand that this is a suspicious death, sir. In the circumstances I have to satisfy myself as to all the facts. So far, you've told me one lie. I'm wondering how much of the rest of what you've told me is true.'

I didn't punch him on the nose, but that was only by a supreme effort.

'What the fuck do you mean by calling me a liar?'

He shook his head gently, as if dealing patiently with a simpleton. 'I didn't call you a liar, sir. I said that you had told me a lie. Can we please start again? You were not alone when you found the body. You had stopped here for a reason, not simply to relieve yourself. Now who was she?'

'All right, Chief Inspector. But how did you know?'

'There are recent tyre tracks. That's why we didn't drive in. I don't like to go barging in to the scene of an incident and possibly destroy vital evidence. There's a puddle at the entrance and some very clear impressions in the mud. The tyre-imprint of one vehicle, with very worn tread, the van, overlaid by another, your sports-car, and then a single tyre-track, a motorcycle or scooter. As for the gender of the third person, that, I must admit, was a guess. But not a very inspired one. What else would a man of your established reputation be up to in a secluded spot like this? You wouldn't come here to discuss archaeology.'

'I didn't want her involved. It's rather delicate.'

'We'll have to interview her. It's in your interests, sir.'

'You keep saying things like that. Do you really believe that I had anything to do with this? Besides isn't it obvious the man committed suicide? It looks to me as if he stuck the gun in his mouth and pulled the trigger.'

'That may be what happened. We won't know until there's been a proper forensic examination. Now perhaps you'll tell us the name of the lady. I'll also need an account of your movements for, say, the last twenty-four hours, and also the names and whereabouts of any witnesses who can corroborate it.'

I groaned. This was not happening. First Ellen, and now the long arm of the law was reaching out to Louise. I looked at him. His face had the look of someone who took pleasure in his work.

'Detective Chief Inspector,' I began in what I hoped was an emollient man-to-man tone. 'Let me be frank. I met Ellen Norton here an hour ago. If you talk to her – discreetly, please, as she is a married woman – she will confirm why we were here. Besides, if God forbid, I had had anything to do with the horror in that van, I would hardly have picked the same place for an assignation of that kind, now would I?'

He gave me a sardonic grin. 'We'll talk to Mrs Norton. I think that will satisfy the requirements of my report, for the time being at least. I wouldn't have thought even that necessary if it weren't that your relationship with the dead man leads me to make those further enquiries.'

'My relationship with the dead man?' I burst out in astonishment. 'What are you talking about? I don't even know who he is.'

'Didn't I mention it, sir? Well of course, formal identification has yet to be made, and I won't disturb the body for any papers till the socos get here, but PC Enstone thought he recognised the van and we've checked it on the PNC. It's registered in the name of Brian Rollright. PC Enstone told me there was a rumour in the village that you'd had words not long ago.'

'Christ Almighty.'

'That surprised you did it, sir?'

'Of course it bloody did.' Then I realised what he was saying. 'It didn't surprise you?'

259

'I have to say that the manner of it was more shocking than I might have imagined. But the late Mr Rollright had more reason than most to blow his brains out.'

'Because he was an utter shit? That didn't seem to have worried him up to now.'

'No, there was another more pressing matter. I got here so quickly today because I was already on my way to see your sister. I had some news for her. We had a videotape of a man hospitalised for an injury similar to the one suffered by her attacker on the Glebe. PC Enstone identified him. I wanted her to see the film as well.'

'And it was Brian Rollright?' I recalled what Ellen had told me of Fran's family. 'My God, the only reason that he could have been so desperate to stop the body being discovered must have been because he put it there. His wife was supposed to have cleared out suddenly, but in fact . . .'

'We believe that the body was that of Mrs Rollright. Obviously the forensic people are trying to track down records, but there seems little reason to doubt that it was her.'

'So she didn't walk out? Rollright murdered her and buried her on the Glebe.'

'It appears that is what happened.'

'Wait a minute,' I burst out. 'You bloody knew this before you started quizzing me on my movements. That was just a wind-up, wasn't it? You knew it was nothing to do with the shouting match I had with the bastard.'

His face was impassive, but in his blue eyes there was the hint of amusement.

'Oh very funny, Chief Inspector. Our whole relationship has been a bundle of laughs, hasn't it? But while you were jerking me around you should have been thinking about the poor kid who's got to be told all this.'

'Ah yes, the daughter.'

'The daughter! Does she know any of this?'

He shook his head. 'No. Nothing's confirmed. You might do better to wait.'

'What? Until the rumour machine goes into hyperdrive? I'll go round now, and you're not going to stop me.'

A smell of greasy cooking greeted me when she opened the door.

She didn't attempt to conceal her lack of enthusiasm when she saw it was me on the doorstep.

'Hello, Jack. What do you want?' She made it sound as if I were selling encyclopaedias or double glazing.

'I have to speak to you. Are you alone?'

'Yes, but . . . hey . . .'

I pushed past her into the scruffy room and slammed the door. On the gate leg table was a plate with smears of egg and a tomato skin. On the low table in front of the sofa, there was a half-drunk cup of grey coffee, precariously balanced on top of a tilting pile of papers and magazines, and an open paperback copy of *Culture and Imperialism*.

'Sit down, Fran.'

There must have been something in my tone because she sank down on to the vinyl cushion without a word, gazing up at me with a scared look on her face. In that moment the years dissolved, and it might have been me sitting there, at ten years old, brought back hastily from the rugger field at Summerfields, to be told my father had gone away.

I sat opposite her on a cheap dining chair with a plywood back which flexed under my weight as I leaned forward and down. 'It's about your father, Fran. I'm very sorry to tell you that he was found dead this morning. In his van. He'd . . . committed suicide. I was the one who found him. In Baker's Quarry.'

She stared at me, an expression I couldn't read on her face. Then she started to laugh.

I hastened to sit beside her, reaching out my arms to her. 'Fran, I know it's a shock.'

Still laughing, she pushed me away. 'Honestly, Jack, your expression. You can really put it on when you want, can't you? Your this-is-going-to-hurt-a-bit face, like a bloody dentist. You had me fooled for a minute. I thought you had something bad to tell me.'

'Fran, please, you're upset. You don't know what . . .' I said, conscious of the feeble conventionality of my words.

'Oh yes I bloody do. Come on, Jack. Let's go down the pub. You've always been on at me to have a drink with you. This is really something to celebrate. You're quite sure the bastard is dead?'

'Yes, he's dead all right. He did it with a shotgun. Half his head was missing.' The brutality of my words and tone seemed to sober her. Suddenly she sagged forward and collapsed into my arms, her head on my shoulder. I could feel her shake with deep dry sobs that seemed wrenched from the pit of her being.

Then she raised her face to mine. 'I hated him, you know. I used to pray when I was a child, when I still believed there was something there, for someone to bring me news like this. Every day of my life, I have wished that he was dead. Now, I can hardly believe it. I can't take it in. I'm devastated by the idea that I'm going to be happy.' She drew back to scrutinise my expression. 'Don't you want to know why? Can't you guess? Don't you know about one of the good old traditions of rural family life?'

Her words seared my heart. 'Oh God. You poor child. But I'm afraid there's more.'

'What do you mean?'

'About why he apparently committed suicide. You see there must have been some lingering conscience. He did it out of remorse.'

'Remorse, him? Remorse for what?' Then the glow in her features vanished as if a light had been extinguished. 'That other skeleton in the Glebe. It was her, wasn't it, my mother? That means he did kill her?'

I nodded. 'It hasn't been finally confirmed but . . .'

'I thought it might be. The night your sister was attacked,

he didn't come home. I wondered when I heard whether he was involved. Even still, I couldn't bring myself to go to the police. So it was Mum. I always knew she was dead. I never believed it when Dad said she had gone away. I used to ask him about it when I was little. About what happened. And even as a child I knew that he wasn't speaking the truth. You see, he could never get the story straight. You know, those details that children like. Was she wearing a coat when she left, what colour was it? What did she say about me and my brother? What day was it? Did she catch a bus or get a taxi? Where did she say she was going? I could tell he was making it up. One time he'd say she went off with another man, other times she went back to her family in Birmingham, then again that she'd gone after a job in London. None of it made sense. Derek used to get me to guess how he thought he'd killed her and where he had put the body. Sometimes when Dad was out, we'd go digging in the garden.'

'Oh, Christ. Didn't you ever tell anyone?'

'What, you mean the police? What notice would they take of a couple of kids? Particularly a little tearaway like Derek. He was in trouble for pinching when he was seven years old. My father used to knock him around for it. For getting caught, I mean, not for the stealing itself. Me he just fucked, but Derek he turned into a . . .'

'Into what?'

I saw the tears glistening in her eyes, and she shook her head. 'I tried to save him, I really did, Jack. When I went to Oxford, I still came back here in the vacations, so I could watch out for him. I knew that one day he'd . . .'

I held her hands tightly. She stared fixedly in front of her, trapped in her memories.

'We used to wonder what it would have been like if our mum had stayed and it had been Dad who went away. I don't remember her. I was only about eighteen months when it happened and Derek was just a baby. I used to have fantasies about what she was like. She wasn't from round here

263

you see. Nobody knew her. But she had a nice face, a beautiful face, really. Would you like to see a picture of her?'

I nodded, and then watched her slim figure as she disappeared up the winding stair. I could hear her feet thumping on the boards above. When she came down she was holding a cardboard folder of the type used by photographic studios.

'Dad never knew I had this. I found it one day when I was a kid. It had fallen down the back of the wardrobe in his bedroom.'

She sat down beside me and opened it.

I stared at the woman in the photograph, her natural unaffected beauty shining through despite the heavy make-up and the film-star smile. Something about her was deeply moving, as if her smile were meant for me alone, almost as if I could hear a soft caressing voice saying 'Oh, Jack'. Then my chest tightened in a spasm, my vision clouded, and I passed out.

'Jack!' I came to, to find Fran leaning over me. 'What's the matter? You've gone all pale. Is it your heart? Please, Jack!'

I clutched her, feeling as if my breath had to be dragged into my lungs with ten times the usual effort.

'Jack, what's happened?'

I dragged myself upright again, the dizziness finally receding. 'Don't worry, Fran. I'm all right. It was the photograph. Up to then, she'd just been your mother. Suddenly, I knew, by God, I knew.'

'Knew what?'

'She was called Mary Windrush. She was working in Boots in the Cornmarket in Oxford. In the spring of 1976 I used to do research at the Institute of Archaeology. It was when I was in television. She'd seen the programme and recognised me. We got talking. Then we did more than talk. I had a flat in Oxford in those days. We used to go there. Do you understand what I'm talking about.'

'Of course I do. So what happened?'

264

'I started seeing someone else. I ended the affair with . . . your mother. I was brutal. She was really keen on me. But Fiona was . . .'

'A bit posher than a girl who worked in a shop, I bet. So, you're having a belated guilt trip, Jack? It must happen all the time according to your sister's account of your sex life. Was I going to be like this Fiona, to poor little Ellen, who's completely besotted by you? Otherwise I might have been tempted. Then in a few years it would have been my turn. "I wonder what happened to that student I screwed in Crowcester."'

I took hold of her shoulders and almost shook her. 'You don't understand what I'm saying, do you, Fran? Don't you see? 1976. You're nearly twenty. You told me your birthday was on New Year's Eve, 1976. You must have been conceived that spring. Christ, Fran. Mary wasn't sleeping with that bastard Rollright, nor with anyone else, while I was with her. He can't possibly have been your father. Sweet Jesus, Fran! For the last few months, I've been wanting to go to bed with you. But I'm your father.'

She stared at me, as if she saw me for the first time. Then she turned away and began rooting in the mess of papers on the coffee table. She found a pack of Bensons, scrabbled one out, then tried to click her lighter, but her hand was shaking too much. I gently took it out of her hand, lit her cigarette, then took and lit one for myself.

She inhaled deeply, staring at the brown tiled fireplace opposite. Then she said, 'I can't take it in. It's like something out of an Elizabethan play or a Greek tragedy. I ought to be able to come up with some apt quotation. Your sister would, but I can't. All I really want to say is: Does it make any difference?'

'Of course it makes a difference. You're my daughter. I feel . . .'

'What do you feel? Ashamed of your incestuous feelings? You're not even a beginner where those are concerned.

Besides, how were you to know? Guilty about leaving my mother to her fate? You didn't force her to marry a man like Brian Rollright. That was her choice. Wanting to make it up to me in some way? Wanting to be a father to me? I don't see how you can be. All there is between us is biology. You may have contributed your half of my genes, but there's nothing else. DNA isn't the basis for a relationship. Anyway, I've had enough of fathers. I've finally got rid of one. What the hell do I want another for?'

'Fran, please. I do want to make it up to you. There's so much I can do for you.'

'Oh, there is, is there? I should have thought I've done pretty well for myself already, without your paternal hand to guide me. And what have you got to offer now? By all accounts, you're on the scrap heap. You've blown your life, Jack. Mine's just beginning. Leave me alone.'

I felt the tears pricking the corners of my eyes, so I got up and went over to the window. The sun's light was dimmed by the filthy net curtains. 'By all accounts? I don't have to ask who to thank for that do I? Crowcester's answer to Miss Jean Brodie, schoolmistress extraordinaire.'

'You're pathetic, Jack. Your sister is worth a million of you. Without her support and encouragement, I'd probably have killed myself. She gave me something to live for, some belief that I was worth something. I think it's time you buggered off. I want to be on my own.'

I blew my nose and wiped my eyes, then turned back into the room. She was still staring at the fireplace. I felt a heaviness in my heart such as I have never felt before, thinking of this intelligent, sensitive girl imprisoned and brutalised in this loveless hovel. The early chapters of her life had been written, and I could do nothing to amend them now. The arrow of time was irreversible.

'You're right. I am pathetic. But I want to change. I need a sign from you that there is a chance that we might start to build the relationship we never had. Please say you don't hate me entirely. Give me some hope. You may not believe this. But in some way I can't explain, what I felt for you the first time I saw you, what I've felt for you all along. Sex was only part of it. Dear God, please believe me, I know now it was love.'

She got up and stood by me. 'I don't know what I believe. But I don't hate you, Jack.' Then she turned and hugged me, and it was as if I had been buried alive and now saw light at the edges of the coffin lid as it was grasped and raised by rescuing hands.

We held each other, and I felt her slim body give way to great wrenching sobs drawn from the pit of her being. I lost any sense of time or place as we stood there.

Gradually her weeping quietened. She disengaged and looked up into my eyes.

'Are you really my father, Jack?'

'Yes, I believe I am, Fran.'

'Do you really love me?'

'Yes, Fran, I love you with all my heart.'

'You won't ever hurt me, will you, Jack? Promise?'

'I promise. I won't ever hurt you, dearest Fran.'

'You'll take me away from this place, won't you? There's nothing I can do for Derek now.'

I hesitated. 'Yes, I will take you away. Soon. But first, I have something I need to do. In London. Directly I get back, I'll call for you and tell you about it. Promise.'

I bent down and kissed her gently on the forehead.

When I opened the front door, the sunshine poured in, transfiguring the dingy interior, banishing the shadows. In the blaze of light, something flashed in the chimney alcove. The speck of radiance drew me to it.

Then I remembered the object I had seen on that first visit here. This time, when I reached out to take it, no one prevented me.

As my fingers gently brushed its chill surface, I felt that thrill of electricity I always feel when I touch a genuine piece of the ancient world, as if some energy connects me with the dead and the lost, and I can hear their distant voices.

It was the handle of a jug or bowl, its ends jagged where it had been broken away. The workmanship was exquisite. It was moulded with tiny naked figures amid sinuous vines, an item of real beauty in this ghastly den, amidst the dross and trash of poverty-stricken modernity.

It was as fine as anything I'd ever seen before. As fine as . . .

My hair rose on the back of my neck, and I shuddered, my eyes so fixed on the silver comma nestled in my palm that it seemed as though my vision burned through the flesh to my bones, and that the object glowed as if under radiation.

For suddenly I knew the very jug from which the handle had been torn. I had handled it often, and had often speculated as to where its missing part might lie, and whether the two might ever be reunited. Now I felt sure I held that part, but I was also sure that that was impossible. It could not be here of all places. Yet here it was. I did not believe in the supernatural, yet what other explanation could there be for this treasure to fall into my hands, as it were from the lap of the gods?

Fran was staring at me with alarm. 'Jack, what's the matter? You've gone all pale again.'

I pulled myself together. 'Nothing at all, my dear. You remember how intrigued I was by this little piece? It's yours now. I'd like to borrow it to examine it properly. I think it might be very important.'

She shrugged. 'OK.'

I slipped it into my pocket, and, after embracing her once more, stepped out into the bright day, reeling with the events of the last few hours, as if I were drunk on the headiest of champagne, yet also light at heart.

For now there was someone to love, someone whom I would not abandon again. Someone who deserved the best that I could offer. What I was about to do would restore me in her eyes as well as in my own. I would take any risk for love of her.

I paused in the courtyard, as did the other incoming tourists, to cast an eye over the imposing façade of the Farebrother Museum. Imposing is the right word. Not handsome, certainly not beautiful. Sir Camden Farebrother – always referred to as 'The Founder' in Museum parlance – the fabulously wealthy Victorian connoisseur who had donated the fruits of his eclectic taste to the nation, owed his pile to his family's railway interests, and the building which housed his collection had the look of one of the grander termini.

Having spent a convincing amount of time on my inspection, I tweaked the brim of my hat to a more jaunty angle and strode confidently up the entrance steps.

It was part of my so-called early retirement agreement with the Farebrother Trustees that I would not, except on their specific invitation or with their specific approval, enter the premises of the Museum. This was a banishment which I had at the time easily borne, but was now inconvenient. There were far too many people on the staff who were likely both to recognise me, and to know that I was not supposed to be there.

A drastic, not to say absurd solution, one matching the ingenuity of the great Holmes himself, was required. I accordingly went to a theatrical costume agency in Covent Garden and hired a brown wig and matching moustache and beard. These, together with a trilby hat from an Oxfam shop and a long navy blue mac which made me look much plumper and which I hadn't worn for years formed the basis of what I regarded as quite a creditable masquerade. It was a grey, rainy day with a hint of autumn, so fortunately the mac did not look out of place. It was a strange sensation to pass the doorway in this garb, not only as a mere visitor, but as an intruder.

There had been changes in my absence. Firstly, the charges

for admittance threatened by Clarissa were now in place, so I had to pay at a glass booth in which presided the forbidding female warder known in my time as Ida the Terrible. I had crossed swords with Ida on numerous occasions, but she barely gave me a glance as she handed over my ticket and a glossy leaflet inscribed How to Find Your Way Around, and featuring Ten Exhibits Not to Miss.

Then there was the fact that late on a weekday afternoon, the place was relatively full of people. There was even a queue at the bag search table. I followed the line as it shuffled along and clicked through the turnstile, passing nonchalantly under the eyes of several types who were well known to me. I received only the usual hostile stare reserved for visitors, which even Clarissa's Cultural Revolution had not yet succeeded in eliminating.

The most dramatic change was that the Museum shop, which had once been decently hidden away in a dark corridor, and sold only stodgy works of out of date scholarship written or commissioned by the hierarchy of the Museum, and poor quality postcards of a limited range of exhibits, now occupied the great open space under the central lantern of the vestibule. Indeed, you had to walk through it in order to get into the galleries. Now massively stocked with books and fancy goods of every description, it was planned on the lines of a souk or a maze, easy to get into, difficult to exit. I surmised that some of the less perceptive tourists would never penetrate beyond it.

I sauntered up the main staircase, feeling pleased at the success of my disguise, then turned into the Egyptian galleries. These, or rather the mummies they contained, had always been one of the most popular parts of the Museum, and that day they were thronged with a greater than usual crowd. Perhaps the ludicrous advertising campaign really had brought them in. There was safety in numbers, so I plonked myself down next to a group of German tourists on a bench opposite the group of animal-headed deities crudely hacked

270

out of basaltic rock which were supposedly one of the Museum's great treasures but which, like all Ancient Egyptian stuff, left me cold, and considered my next move.

I had gone straight back to The Hollies from Fran's. Liz had still not returned from her conference. I arranged with Mrs Hargreaves, by crossing the old battleaxe's palm with a considerable quantity of dosh which I could hardly spare, that she would stay and look after Mother until Liz's or my return, whereupon we would 'settle up' for what other scandalous amount was still owing to her.

I then phoned the Farebrother, assuming an American accent, and purporting to be the Director of the Hiram G. Schuster Museum of Denver, Colorado – 'Tell her this is a transatlantic call, honey' – got through to Clarissa. 'Miss Hetherington-Browne? Hi, there. This is Maurice Jackson, J A C K son. We had a meeting fixed for seven thirty p.m. this evening at the Barnsbury Hotel. I'm sorry I've been delayed in the States and can definitely *not* make it. Sorry, I'll call you to rearrange.' Clarissa was a bright girl and would twig, I was sure. I then threw a few things into the back of the Morgan and drove like the clappers back to town.

Clarissa rang the doorbell of my house on the dot of seven thirty. I was just in the process of refreshing myself after my exhausting day. She gave a disdainful glance at the bottle of Famous Grouse, now almost half-flown down my throat, and shook her head contemptuously when I offered her a dram.

'You need to have a clear head tomorrow, Jack.'

'I know. That's why I'm drinking tonight. Honestly, Clarissa, you sound just like my sister. You two ought to meet to compare notes about me.'

'For God's sake, Jack, try and be sensible for once. This isn't a joke. You may think it's all funny voices and play-acting, but it's deadly serious for me. My whole reputation is staked on this.'

'I suppose you think mine isn't?'

'Insofar as you have one, it is. All the more reason not to act the fool. Now listen. This is what I've arranged.'

I listened.

'Any questions?'

'No. All clear.'

She opened her briefcase. 'There's one other thing. This came in the other day. Tell me what you think.'

She handed me a photocopied sheet. 'I've marked the item.'

I peered at the tiny running head at the top of the page of the original. It was a periodical from an organisation I'd never heard of, The International Consortium for the Restitution of Jewish Property. The extract featured art objects. There was a small smudged photograph of a missing Renoir, a long description of a Meissen dinner service, and then an article ringed in red felt tip.

Antique nude statue of Hellenic God Apollo in standing pose. Late Greek or Roman copy. White marble. Approx. height 1 m. Property of Hirschbaum family of Vienna, Austria. Last seen late 1943 in possession of Waffen-SS officer. Surviving family member Melanie Hirschbaum Goldsmith of New York City remembers the following distinguishing characteristics which may subsequently have been restored: Damage to nose and to R. knee. Three fingers missing on L. hand. Substantial reward offered for news of whereabouts.

I stared at this paragraph for a long time. In its brief words was encapsulated a whole terrible period of human history, perhaps the very worst.

All empires had sacked and pillaged their victims, and modern nations still clung to their share of the vast diaspora of captured spoil. The great bronze horses which the Venetians had stolen during their thirteenth-century occupation of Constantinople still adorned the cathedral of San

Marco in Venice, and the marbles of the Parthenon, filched from the Greeks six hundred years later by Lord Elgin during the chaos of the struggle against Turkish rule, were still the glory of the so-called British Museum, which if truth be told was a treasure house of foreign loot, having in it few enough artefacts of purely domestic origin. The Founder had himself acquired his collection by methods which the touchy and fully independent nations of Europe and the Middle East would never allow today. In their time the Western imperial nations had carried off the culture of countless less aggressive civilisations. Anyone who knew anything about museums had to acknowledge the dubious morality of their stewardship.

But the Third Reich had been uniquely thorough in its destruction of a people and the theft of their possessions, to the very hair of their heads, the skins of their bodies and the gold of their teeth. It was to the shame not only of the nations who had turned a blind eye to the Holocaust, and enriched themselves with the Nazis' stolen gold, but also of the world of art and culture that the auction houses of Europe still dealt in items which were the pillage of the Hitler years.

I looked up at Clarissa. 'This is an exact description of the Harrington Apollo.'

'That was my reaction.'

'But it can't be.'

'Tell me about it, Jack.'

'As I recall, the Apollo came to the Farebrother from Grisedale Hall in Yorkshire on the death of the eccentric and reclusive tenth Marquess of Harrington. He was some distant connection of Eddie Scarsdale. There was a mass of stuff in the bequest. All picked up by an ancestor on the Grand Tour. We have the contemporary receipts. And, I seem to remember, there are some eighteenth-century sketches of the Apollo, and an accompanying statue of Diana, now apparently lost, in opposite niches of the vestibule of the Hall. The provenance is quite unshakeable.'

'Ah yes, provenance. The magic word.'

I stared at her, beginning to think the unthinkable.

Provenance. Often, the only difference between a fake and a priceless artefact was provenance. Clever fakes abounded. They were far more common than dealers and museum curators let on. The Egyptians had been making four-thousand-year-old relics for centuries, ever since they twigged that the crazy Westerners would pay fortunes for them. Sometimes such items could be easily spotted. Other times it was more dubious. You paid your expert and you made your choice. In recent years the urge to fake had been given an added impetus by the tightening of controls on the real thing. Governments hung on to their patrimony far more assiduously than they had in the past. The fakes filled the resulting hole in the market.

If, however, you had a history for the item, if you knew, in the case of an archaeological find, precisely from which hole in the ground your artefact had come, when it had been excavated and whether the soil level had been disturbed before excavation, you could be certain you had the real thing. In the case of items of art or sculpture, like the Apollo, the further back you could trace it to its period of creation, the more certain you could be that it was genuine.

I said slowly, 'What if it's not the artefact that's fake, but the provenance?'

She nodded. 'That's the way I've been thinking too.'

'Christ. How about that drink, now?'

I poured her a generous measure of whisky and she knocked it back in one go.

'In the case of the Harrington Apollo,' I said, 'we're talking about Scarsdale. The late Sir Edmund Scarsdale, Order of Merit, scholar and gentleman, for Christ's sake.'

'I know, Jack, I know.'

I poured her and myself another drink, and we sat in silence for several minutes, trying to digest the matter we had telegraphed cryptically to each other.

In the days when Scarsdale had been the relatively youthful

274

Director of the Farebrother, thought by even his colleagues to be dangerously energetic and go ahead, he had made some stunning acquisitions for the Museum.

He had had the gift of ferreting out collections of antiquities picked up by aristocratic travellers and thereafter consigned to the attics and glory holes of their country houses, usually with little idea of their real value. Some of this stuff had been shaken out during the twenties and thirties after the virtual disappearance of a cheap servant class following the end of the Great War had put paid to any number of comfortable lifestyles in palatial mansions.

The process had been accelerated by the end of the Second World War. Scarsdale had been quick to realise the potential of this for his own institution. As a member of a minor branch of one of the great families he had an automatic intro to a good many decaying gentlemen's country seats. Flattered by his attentions, and seduced by the idea of adding their family's names to the roll of the great museum benefactors such as Sloane, Duveen, Burrell or Tate, or indeed old Camden Farebrother himself, they had agreed, with the added inducement that such gifts to a national collection would ameliorate the pain of death duties, to donate some of their heirlooms to the Museum. They had also benefited from the advice which Scarsdale had been able to call upon to authenticate and value the items which would not be going to the Museum but to the sale-rooms.

Where he had not been able to persuade a gift or a bequest, he had bought, using the Museum's acquisition budget, or grants from national funds, or the money he had shaken from the pockets of those with cash but no culture.

Finally, I broke the silence. 'May I summarise the position as I see it? Scarsdale was responsible for acquiring many of the principal items in the Museum. They used to call him the Great Collector. We now strongly suspect that the statue of Apollo was Nazi loot. If so, Scarsdale successfully faked a series of documents, with the collusion of the heirs of the

275

Marquess of Harrington, to make it appear that it had been a family heirloom. It can only have been Scarsdale who did that. The Harringtons would never have been able to acquire the statue on the black market and fake its history. And as it was a bequest, there was no financial incentive to do so. The point is, if he did it once, did he do it again? Some of those other items he so miraculously acquired may not have been Nazi loot. They could have been stolen or illegally excavated from sites and locations all over the world, and then falsely entered in the Museum catalogue as bequests or gifts or purchases.'

I paused, puzzled. 'Of course, the strange thing is how that ties up with what Greville, on your account, has been up to. On my reading, it doesn't.'

'What do you mean?'

'Well, what we suspect Scarsdale of doing, while it's certainly intellectually fraudulent, and probably criminally fraudulent too, if it could be proved that he acquired objects which he knew or believed to be stolen, wasn't apparently done for his own gain, nor was it to the detriment of the Museum, rather the opposite. He enriched its collections considerably. Whereas Greville has, you believe, reversed the process. It's as if he'd taken over the fraudulent process started by Scarsdale and turned it to his own purposes.

'He's destroying the Museum. If it ever got out that even a small fraction of the collection is faked, then the Farebrother would be finished. That's to his advantage at present. Even if not all of the Keepers are in on the scam, he can rely on the natural tendency of the others not to allow themselves to cast doubt on their own exhibits. No one likes to believe they've been taken in by a fake. Remember how those faked Hitler Diaries convinced even major academic historians? People who know a great deal about a subject can sometimes be more credulous than those who don't. And museums are one of the last bastions of authority. If the Farebrother, with its reputation, sticks a label on an exhibit, it takes a brave man to question the authenticity of that exhibit, particularly if he is not given the facilities to examine it properly.'

'The thing is, I don't think old Scarsdale would have gone along with that willingly.'

'Perhaps he didn't know.'

'I think he did. It explains why he switched off so much as far as the running of the Museum was concerned. Greville had all the power, everyone knew that. Scarsdale was distancing himself from the business which was going on. He couldn't speak out, because Greville could make sure his own reputation was ruined. And in the end, reputation was what Scarsdale cared most about.

'The question I still have is how Greville found out in the first place. Obviously, once he knew, he had a hold over Scarsdale, and could do what he liked. But how did he find out? Scarsdale would hardly have told him. The other thing that strikes me is that Greville could have only started his own attack on the Museum after the mid-seventies. Up to then, he'd been a cabinet minister. He became Chairman of the Trustees only after the Tories were defeated in 1974.'

'Maybe he found out earlier about the scam, but didn't get the idea of using it for his own purposes until his political career was over? That's very interesting speculation, but the only way we're ever going to get anywhere near to the truth, Jack, is if you're successful tomorrow night.'

'Tomorrow and tomorrow and tomorrow, and all our yesterdays have lighted fools the way to dusty death,' I quoted inaccurately.

'Why did you change your mind, Jack?'

I hesitated, then said, 'Family reasons.'

She gave me a quizzical look, but I avoided her eyes. I gave myself a refill, then tipped the whisky bottle towards her glass. She covered it with her hand.

I protested. 'Oh, please. I do so hate drinking alone.'

She snorted sardonically. 'You must think I was born yesterday, Jack. If what I think you might be thinking is what

277

you're thinking, then I should stop thinking it right now.'

'Hopeless, eh?'

'Completely.'

At the door, she shook my hand gravely. 'Good luck, Jack.'

'*Ave, Caesar, morituri te salutant*,' I replied.

Back in the sitting room, I upended the whisky bottle over my tumbler. I watched the last amber drops slide out and plop down. I was not looking forward to tomorrow.

The Germans were on the march. I got up and tagged along with them, working out the details of my plan as we moved from gallery to gallery.

Finally, we arrived at my target, the gallery in which the vase was displayed.

This was one of the worst arranged from the point of view of the visitor. Nothing had yet been achieved under Clarissa to change its tatty appearance. The wonderful objects it contained were in old-fashioned glazed cabinets ranked along the walls, and the lighting was so subdued as to be sepulchral. We paused in the gloom in front of the case which held the Shoemaker vase. The Germans' guide held forth on the subject of Greek ceramics whilst his party strained their eyes to see what he was describing.

As he rolled out those lovely portmanteau words like *Weltanschauung* and *Kunsthistorische* which give such weight and sonority to the German language, I reflected how much easier this casual disregard for the visitor had made Greville's theft and substitution. Even a great world expert would be hard pushed to spot a fake in these conditions.

Having satisfied myself that the Harrington vase, or rather its simulacrum, was where it was supposed to be, and established the method which I would adopt when it came to stealing it, I had another matter to deal with, one which I had omitted to tell Clarissa about. I peeled off from the German party as they made their way down the staircase to the Far Eastern collections, and headed into my old fief.

I was so chuffed at the success of my infiltration that I carelessly omitted to check who was on duty.

At first, all was well. The Roman and Dark Ages galleries were peaceful. A few students with sketch pads and clipboards loitered and exchanged banter by the display of domestic pots and utensils. An old codger slept on the bench by the Dorchester Pavement. A couple of Third Age Americans in baseball caps and puffa jackets gazed at the illustrative model of a Roman villa and expressed their opinion that it weren't a patch on Nancy's place in Santa Monica. A gaggle of schoolchildren crowded and sniggered round the big display case which held the mortal remains of Sedgemoor Man, an unfortunate West Country traveller of the seventh century, who, having tumbled into a bog and drowned, had been preserved, in a leathery fashion, by the chemicals in the peat. I'd lobbied for years to have the poor sod, along with the Egyptian mummies, taken out and decently buried but had always been condemned for being unscholarly.

I wandered around, in a deliberately idle and unsystematic way, pleased that, in this part of the Museum at least, the display cases had always been brightly lit and informatively labelled. Clarissa had generously acknowledged, on the day she fired me, that she did not regard my department as being one of the ones in which what she called root and branch modernisation would be required.

I finally found myself, as intended, in front of the case containing the glory of the Roman exhibits, the Lothbury Treasure.

The Lothbury Treasure had been regarded as one of the most magnificent coups of Scarsdale's early years. The sixth Earl of Lothbury had been a nineteenth-century traveller in France and Italy, and letters written by him to his mother and sisters back home indicated that the Roman silver *ministerium* or table service which would bear his name for posterity had been purchased by him from a dealer in Burgundy, who had had it from a peasant who had unearthed it on his

279

land. He had brought it back to Lothbury Castle in the wilds of Northumberland. There it remained, apparently forgotten about for a hundred years. Scarsdale had heard about it through one of his relatives, seen it and secured it for the Farebrother under the nose of the British Museum.

Although I had admired it hundreds of times, and enjoyed the sensuous thrill of running my hands over the richly engraved and moulded surfaces of the beautiful serving dishes, the drinking bowls, the decorative statuettes, the plates, and the spoons, lifting as far as my lips the heavy silver drinking vessel with its bas-relief of a satyr holding a bunch of grapes, I gazed this time on one particular piece as intently as if I had never seen it before.

The jug. The beautiful, elegantly shaped, exquisitely crafted jug, its subtly curved belly chased with scenes of drinking and merry-making, perfect in every respect, save for the two jagged prongs of fractured metal at its top and bottom, where the handle had been broken off and lost.

This item had in retrospect been my downfall. If I had not, my mind full of visions of scholarly acclaim, cast doubt in the paper I had presented to the Trustees, on the unity of the hoard, a speculation prompted by the jug, the drinking vessel, and many of the other items, all of which I had dated around a hundred years later than some of their ostensible companion pieces, I might never have got into the row with Greville which had resulted in my dismissal.

And now, of course, I was certain that my reading of the Treasure, controversial though it was, was absolutely correct.

As I gazed on the collection which glittered with fiery radiance in the specially designed glass cube at the heart of the gallery, whose light in the partial darkness drew visitors like a magnet, I slid my hand through the trench coat slit of the mac and touched like a talisman the old-fashioned hard spectacle case in my jacket pocket in which was hidden, wrapped in tissue paper, the twist of metal I had taken from Fran's house.

I itched to examine it there and then in the bright neon light of the display cabinet. That would have been foolhardy in the extreme, and besides there was no need. I had scrutinised it closely under my microscope in my study the previous night. There was no margin of doubt. It matched the jug in every iota. The handle of a jug unearthed in Burgundy in the first quarter of the nineteenth century had been found six hundred miles away and a hundred and fifty years later.

When I had stood in Rollright's squalid sitting room the previous day, it had been even then evident that the handle belonged to the jug, but quite eerily inconceivable as to how that could be so.

Now, I was astonished to find, I had the solution to that mystery.

I stood there, stunned by the implications, when someone immediately behind me said, 'Wonderful things aren't they, sir?'

I almost shuddered as I recognised the voice.

Farrow's. Farrow was by a long chalk the most obnoxious of the warders, and my own special *bête noire*. He was personally repulsive, being gross and pale, with lank, dirty-looking hair, and, despite an overtly servile manner, a permanent supercilious grin. He resented his menial job, and believed that his talents and intellect deserved far better. It appeared that he saw in me the embodiment of this inequity.

Consequently, it was his special pleasure in life to try to put one over on me. He would ask awkward questions about the exhibits – the answers to which he had clearly mugged up in advance, no doubt in the public library of the vile south London suburb he called home – with the intention of tripping me up, or he would make obviously false statements in the hope that I would incautiously agree with them.

Farrow was, therefore, the last person I wanted to run into, and I cursed my negligence.

It was all I could do to stop myself saying, 'Back to your post, Farrow.' Instead, I muttered, lamely and I hoped unrecognisably into the fake beard, 'Yes, they are,' and started to move away.

But the bastard followed me, at a discreet distance, not only through my old department, but out into the corridor which led to Arms and Armour. When I cut down the staircase, I heard the thick rubber soles of his shoes squeaking in step with mine. This was strictly against the rules – warders on duty had to stay on their own patches – so it was obvious he had smelt a rat of some kind.

I was tempted at that moment to get the hell out of there, but the idea of being frightened off by Farrow of all people stuck in my craw, so I slipped into the gents' in the lobby outside Gallery 12 of Far Eastern.

I nipped smartly inside a free cubicle and waited. After a few moments of silence, I heard the sound of Farrow's boots on the tiled floor, and the wheezing of his breath. The question to be resolved was whether he was sure enough that I was me to mount a direct challenge. I was determined however that he wasn't going to psych me out, so I kept still. And so did he.

Thankfully, this test of nerves was not prolonged beyond a minute or so. His radio – another of Clarissa's innovations – started beeping. I heard him say, presumably in reply to 'Where the hell are you, Farrow?' 'Just answering a call of nature, Chief.' The door of the loo creaked open and banged closed.

I peered out into the corridor. He'd gone. I ran down the staircase to the ground floor again, then at a more dignified but still urgent pace, across the big gallery given over to the Greek bas-reliefs and architectural items that the Founder had, following the example of Lord Elgin on the mainland, purloined from a sanctuary on Aegina.

On the far side, another staircase led back to Far Eastern, and branching off that was a smaller flight barred by a red velvet rope on brass stanchions, and a discreet gilt sign which read STAFF ONLY.

I glanced around quickly. I had decided if challenged, to pretend to be an uncomprehending foreigner, a German, probably, as I was fairly fluent and there were plenty of them around today. Multilingual warders were unknown at the Farebrother, where the only form of life lower than the visitor was the non-English speaking visitor, so that they were believed to be capable of any manner of stupidity.

The coast was clear. I vaulted over the rope and took the steps two at a time. On the landing there were double glass-panelled fire-doors. I slipped through. As I did so I heard voices round the corner of the corridor ahead. I pushed down the handle of the door on the left-hand side. To my relief it swung open. Clarissa had remembered to unlock it.

I was in the darkness of the small room beyond just in time to avoid a couple of women from admin, as they chattered and giggled their way past outside.

I turned the key left in the lock and threw the light switch. It was no more than a glorified storage cupboard, high and windowless, with old wooden shelves from floor to ceiling, stacked with endless box files, of what seemed from the labels to be warders' time sheets going back to the year dot and beyond.

Thankfully, I pulled off the wig, carefully unstuck the fake whiskers, and massaged the itchiness out of my cheeks and chin. I leaned against the back of the door, feeling my pounding heart gradually slow to its normal rate. I would be cooped up in this cubby-hole for hours. Then, at dead of night, I would sneak out, avoiding the night security patrol, which consisted of the oldest and the deafest of the male warders as only they were prepared to work the graveyard shift, remove the vase from its cabinet, and return here to await Clarissa's return in the morning with her expert on Greek ceramics. Recited like this it sounded a piece of cake. I tried not to think of the appalling consequences which would ensue if anything went wrong.

It was a good omen that I found safely hidden in the third

file from the left on the fourth shelf from the floor, as we had arranged, a manila A4 envelope containing Clarissa's duplicate key to the display cabinet in which the vase was kept, together with an official museum display card with the legend REMOVED FOR CONSERVATION. This would keep the theft undiscovered for a few hours at least.

I was dying for a cigarette as I paced my cell, but I dared not light up in case the smoke drifted out into the corridor and was smelt, or set off an alarm. My mind was unquiet, but it was not only nicotine deprivation and confinement which made it so.

I felt in my pocket and dug out the spectacle case, opened it and extracted the silver handle from its tissue paper. The handle of the Lothbury jug. The jug which formed part of the hoard whose provenance was somewhere near Mâcon.

Scarsdale had faked that provenance, of course, as he had faked others. Presumably the scions of Lord Lothbury had been more than happy to keep quiet and accept the Museum's cash, and the kudos of attaching their name to posterity. Why had he done it? Presumably, he had been afraid that it would have been declared treasure trove and gone to the British Museum, who would have had first call on a find of such importance. As it was, the Treasure had been a major factor in enhancing the reputation of the Fare-brother.

I slumped down on the hard stone floor, my back against the far wall. Only in this position could I stretch out my legs. I leaned back, staring at the little piece of silver, listening to the distant voices it enshrined.

The majority of the Lothbury Treasure, including all its finest items, had never been anywhere near Mâcon, at least not since its fourth-century journey across Gaul. It had been buried in what was now rural Oxfordshire, in the grounds of a palatial villa, during the insecurity of the last years of direct Roman rule. It had been found during the 1956 excavation of the Glebe.

Why was I so certain? The answer was obvious, once you ignored the smokescreen of the false provenance created by Scarsdale. If the handle had come from Crowcester, therefore, so had the jug to which it had once been attached, together with the rest of the contemporary items in the hoard.

It was manifestly absurd to think that the late unlamented Brian Rollright had in his life of petty crime burgled the handle from Lothbury Castle or from anywhere else. He had found it when, as a small boy, he'd poked about on the Glebe during the 1956 excavation.

The schoolboy had kept his find. I still trembled with guilt when I remembered how I had pocketed the piece of red Samian ware I had found. I had it yet. Young Brian Rollright had done no more than I had, but his find was the more valuable and spectacular.

But how the hell had Scarsdale made the discovery in Crowcester and spirited it away to a new life as the Lothbury Treasure?

Suddenly there was the sound of the door knob being rattled furiously.

I froze, holding my breath in panic, as if my shallow breathing might be detected through the solid fireproof door. The knob rattled again, and a demotic voice on the other side said, 'Cheryl! Someone's gone and locked this storeroom.'

There was a groan from a second person, presumably Cheryl. 'We'll have to take all these files back again, bog it. Are you sure? Let me try.'

There was a more furious jangling from the knob, followed by a series of dull thuds, as Cheryl, clearly a big girl, applied her foot or her shoulder to the door.

I willed it to withstand the assault.

Finally, with more grumbles, they gave up, and I heard them vowing to search for the key tomorrow.

I glanced at my watch. Five minutes to five. If it hadn't been nearly going home time the girls might have persisted. Saved by the bell.

I felt in my pocket for the flask of whisky. Dare I allow myself a nip? Just a small one? I unscrewed the cap and took a deep draught, the liquor burning my throat and stretching a finger of fire through my empty stomach and into my loins. I fished in my other pocket and came up with a cling film-wrapped ham sandwich I had bought on the way to the Museum. I chomped it up and wished there had been another. I took another swig of whisky, then stuffed the flask firmly back into my pocket.

Beyond the door, there was the sound of footsteps and women's voices. The admin staff were leaving. In the far distance, I heard the harsh sound of an electric buzzer, the warning for the public to rouse themselves from whatever state of contemplation they were in, and take themselves off. In ten minutes, there would be another, even louder and more prolonged. The day staff would end their shift by checking the galleries and the loos.

Then the great bronze doors of the main entrance, which the Founder had had made from a plaster cast of those of Ghiberti, at the Baptistery of the Duomo in Florence, would be locked and barred. All the primary lights would be extinguished, leaving only the emergency circuits faintly to illuminate the staircase, corridors and fire exits. The day staff would be checked out of the staff entrance by the head warder, who would then hand over to the night staff, two in number. The alarms on the windows and the external doors would be activated.

The hatches battened down, the great ship of the Museum would sail undisturbed through another night, as it had already for nearly a hundred and fifty years.

Except, of course, for crafty Jack, the stowaway.

It was fortunate that the Museum's security system had been designed, like that of Troy, to withstand a siege, but not an inside job. Though it had been talked of, no money had been made available to alarm individual display cases. Nor had there been any investment in more reliable internal movement detection devices, such as almost every suburban family now relied on to protect their collections of Elvis Presley records or their video cameras. The Farebrother's system, as it had since the Founder's day, relied on night-watchmen.

The two security guards took it in turns, I recalled, to do a complete circuit of the museum every hour, checking in by phone to the police station at King's Cross twice during the shift. I would have to wait for the man on patrol to pass through the gallery where the vase was kept.

The illuminated hands of my watch read five minutes to two as I quietly unlocked the storeroom door and let myself out into the corridor. The only light was the faint green glow from the emergency exit lights. I padded softly to the fire-doors and pushed through to emerge cautiously on the landing.

I listened intently at the top of the marble staircase which gleamed golden in the amber glow from the Gothic arched window. I realised that the frontage of the building was now floodlit at night. In the circumstances, one of the happier of Clarissa's innovations. I crept down the first flight to the mezzanine and paused for a moment in the shadowy recess beneath the window occupied by a huge iron-bound Renaissance vestment chest. The next flight of steps descended into darkness. I made my way stealthily down to the next level. There was a small vestibule graced by a Canova nude Aphrodite of more than usual lasciviousness.

I gave the callipygous haunches of this lady a propitiatory pat as I headed into the dark entrance to Arms and Armour.

This had always been my least favourite part of the Museum, endless glass cases full of ancient swords and musketry, rows of dummies clad in armour, and the *pièce de résistance*, a realistically recreated torture chamber, crammed with all the devices for the infliction of pain which the last seven hundred or so years had produced. Needless to say

287

this was one of the most popular parts of the Museum for small boys and the retarded.

On that night, I shuddered as I passed by. Someone had forgotten to switch off the red light which simulated the brazier. It cast eerie shadows over the rack on which a wax-work victim was stretched, and over the hooded figure wielding his branding iron.

Now I paused, listening and looking carefully into the dark-ness. By my calculations I was at the halfway point of the tour of inspection. When I saw the flash of the torch or heard the sound of boots, I would get out of sight. I checked my watch. Two thirty. Any moment now. Sure enough, I heard a tuneless whistling, the thud of footsteps and the squeak of leather. Relieved that the patrol routine remained unchanged, I slipped underneath the generous caparison covering the mock-up of the medieval great-horse and its mounted armoured lancer. I had noted this as a likely hideout on my afternoon tour what seemed like centuries ago.

The footsteps halted. A gleam of light shone in the gap below the hem of the dusty smelling material. I could again hear the squeak of his boots as he turned to flash the torch around the gallery. He must only be a matter of a foot or so away. I breathed as slowly as I could. Now I knew what Menelaus and Odysseus and the rest of the little band felt like, crammed into that effigy on the plain of windy Troy, waiting and hoping their desperate plan would work.

The footsteps began again, the sound of them receding. I waited for a minute or so for him to get well clear, then scrambled out from my hiding-place.

At the end of the Arms and Armour galleries, there was another vestibule, with another staircase brightly lit by another Gothic window. On my right was the first of the Hellenic galleries, in which was the cabinet containing the vase I had come for. I took a deep breath, feeling in my jacket pocket for the little key. All that remained to do was to open up, grab the pot and skedaddle back to admin the way I had come. As the warder I had just encountered had come from behind me, the next tour would start in the opposite direction – again according to the book written years ago – so that I would be in no danger of running into the second man on the way back.

I scuttled across the brightness of the vestibule and then back into the obscurity of the gallery. On the side wall on the right-hand side was the glass-fronted cabinet. I fished out the key and from the other pocket took the little pen torch I had bought that morning. I would risk the use of it once, to make sure I didn't, after all this trouble, pinch the wrong item.

I shone the thin beam along the shelves. There it was. I slipped the key in the lock, and after a slight heart-wrenching resistance to being turned, I heard the tiny click as the dead bolt slid back.

I gently opened the door, then put down the torch on the ledge below, and with both hands, reached up to embrace the prize. My fingers had done no more than brush its surface, when from behind there came a blaze of light. I felt hands gripping my shoulders, and a voice in my ear hissed sneeringly, 'All right, Armitage. Let go of it and turn round.'

Stunned, I complied and came face to face with the grinning turnip head of Warder Farrow.

Behind him, holding a torch, was Lord Greville.

IX

Mrs Hargreaves popped out of the front door of The Hollies like the weather woman when I drove up. She rushed over to greet me as I climbed wearily out of the car.

'Liz. Thank goodness.'

I stared at her in alarm. 'Why? Is Mother . . . ?'

'No, Mother's absolutely fine. I'm just so pleased you're here to relieve me. I'm worn out, been at it morning, noon and night for days, not even Ellen to help me.'

'What about Jack?'

She followed me round to the boot and helped me haul out my luggage. 'Mr Armitage hasn't been here since the day after you went. He upped and offed to London.'

'London? I didn't know he was going to London.'

'Oh yes. And there's been ever such goings on since you left.'

Half an hour and two cups of coffee later, I was up to date on the happenings in Crowcester: the discovery of Rollright's body, the departure of Jack, the interviewing of Ellen by the police, the subsequent furious row between her and Barry, the departure of Ellen to stay with a friend in Waterbury, the hours of extra work that this had caused Mrs Hargreaves.

I swallowed up the remains of my mug. 'You'd better go home, Sue. You look all in. I'm sorry. I didn't know all this was going to happen. Take tomorrow off.'

'You look pretty tired yourself, dear, if you don't mind my saying so.'

Her broad plain face was touched with concern. I patted

her hand, then, suddenly, to the surprise of both of us, I hugged her tightly. 'Thanks for everything.'

She paused at the door. 'Mr Armitage said as how he would settle up with me when he got back. He left me some on account but . . . I made a note of my hours.'

I reached for my handbag.

I looked pretty tired, according to Sue Hargreaves. Tired? Was I tired? Tired beyond exhaustion. I had eaten nothing since breakfast of the previous day, and drunk only cups of black coffee.

I remembered scarcely anything of my return from Paris, having carried out the functions of travel as if I were an automaton.

Back in the familiarity of The Hollies kitchen, the vital functions reasserted themselves. I ate bread and cheese and drank wine. My frozen faculties returned.

So what did I feel? What could I feel? I felt as if my life no longer belonged to me. It seemed to be the lurid property of another. It was as I imagined a schizophrenic might feel. The events of the previous days might have happened to someone else and been programmed into my brain by malevolent agents.

But much as I might have craved it as a way of escape from hideous reality, I was not mad. I really had been to Paris. I really had seen and talked to a man who had been dead for forty years. And what he had told me was not the paranoid fantasy of a lunatic, but the dreadful truth.

That night, though I burned with longing for unconsciousness, I lay awake, tossing and turning, the scene in that Paris hotel running through my mind like a continuous loop of film.

I had pushed my way into the room. My father and Teresa clung to each other like children caught in a minor piece of childish mischief.

My father was the first to speak. His voice had changed.

It quavered and hesitated over the words. He was so old. I kept telling myself that. He is forty years older than the night he kissed me and walked out of my life.

'We had hoped to save you this, Elizabeth.'

'By telling me a pack of lies?'

'Sometimes lies are less hurtful than the truth.'

'"Human-kind cannot bear very much reality?" Do you think the lies have been comfortable for me?'

'They were necessary.'

'Are you really my father? Is that one truth I can hold on to? That you are who you appear to be?'

'Yes, I am. I am the man who used to be Robert Armitage.'

'Then if Robert Armitage is still alive, who is the man who was buried in the Glebe? The police carried out a forensic test on a sample of your DNA. They said there was no possibility of error. It was identical with that of the body. They must have been mistaken.'

'No, there was no mistake. If you will listen to me, I will tell you everything. But it will be very painful.'

My head swam, and a bitter taste of bile rose in my mouth. Teresa rushed over to me and helped me on to the sofa. She sat beside me and pressed a glass of water to my lips. I drank and then pushed her brutally away. I could see the pain reflected in her huge eyes.

'Who is this woman, then? She pretended to be a Polish refugee, then claimed to be a French Jew, a diplomat's wife. She lied. I saw her British passport.'

She spoke for the first time since I had entered the room. 'I'm as British as you are. I'm sorry, but you'll see soon enough why I had to tell you those stories.' She shot a glance at my father. 'I told you it wouldn't work.'

'My God.' I covered my eyes with my hands, feeling like Alice, tumbling in free-fall down the rabbit hole. Except of course, it was not reality I had left behind but Wonderland.

I struggled to control myself, forcing my eyes to open again. My father had drawn up a chair opposite me.

'There are no words, Elizabeth, to express what I am feeling as I look at you. All I can say is that what I tried to do was because I loved you and your brother so much. That is the irony of what happened. It was so that I wouldn't lose you, but I lost you just the same.'

'I don't know what you mean.'

'Of course you don't. You were a child then, and you have carried your child's understanding intact. You had no idea of the way things stood between your mother and myself.'

I burst out angrily, 'How do you know what I knew? I knew about the shouting and the arguments, the slamming of doors, the way my mother sobbed her heart out in her bedroom at night when you were in London. I know you hit her on at least one occasion. And now I know that she . . .' I hesitated, even now reluctant to inflict that pain on him.

'You know then more than I expected and I'm sorry. Yes, your mother and I had severe differences from the earliest days. The war had changed both of us. It had made me ambitious to be involved in the affairs of the world. It had driven her into herself, more and more obsessed with the minute affairs of her tiny corner of England. I hated The Hollies and the suffocating narrowness of Crowcester. I would have made the most of it – a country house like that could have been an advantage to me in my career – but she refused to allow me to invite my friends and colleagues for weekends. She said as it was her house, she would invite only those whom she liked. She did not want the current of world affairs flowing through her drawing room. Political talk and politicians bored her, she said. She had had enough of that when her father had dreams of government office. So, I spent more and more time in London, where I had kindred spirits. And there I met my darling Gwen.' He turned to her and gave her hand a squeeze.

'Gwen? Is that your real name?'

'Yes. I was born in London, although my father came from Wales. My mother's family were supposed to have had some kind of Continental connections somewhere along the line. That and the Welsh strain probably accounted for my slightly exotic appearance as a young woman – which of course was an advantage in my profession.'

'Your profession?'

'Can't you guess? I was an actress. Actually quite a good one. I did a season at the Old Vic. I was Juliet, Desdemona, Portia. I think I could have been outstanding. I might now be Dame Gwendolen Meredith.' She smiled fondly at my father. 'Look how much I gave up for you, Robert. All for Love. I never played Cleopatra on the stage, only in real life.'

He passed a hand over his face. 'We both lost everything except each other. We played for high stakes, and we lost.'

'What did you play? Who is the man who was buried in the Glebe?' I demanded, impatient as a child for the story to continue. Already the emotional turmoil provoked in me by this bizarre occasion was being replaced by a consuming curiosity.

'All in good time. I met Gwen at a party in Hampstead in 1955. She was bright and clever and beautiful. Such a contrast to my life in Oxfordshire. Your mother may have been satisfied by choral evensong, but I wasn't. Gwen was part of another world. We fell in love.'

'Did you tell my mother?'

'No. There was no point. There was nothing to be done. Your mother would not complaisantly tolerate the situation in the Continental manner, notwithstanding her attitude to divorce. She would be enraged by what she saw as my breach of faith. You know her character. She would insist on an all-too-public separation, in which I would have to confess my adultery. Such a scandal would have done my career in the Service no good. Attitudes are so different now. No one turns a hair. But in the fifties, middle-class society hadn't changed much in that respect since the thirties. But even more than that, I was afraid that after a divorce, I would

294

never be allowed to see my children again. The situation was hopeless.' The tears shone in his eyes.

Tears were in my eyes also as I heard this recital, suffused still after forty years with bitterness and recrimination. How much both my mother and my father had concealed from each other, how little they had explained their true needs and feelings, locking them away under conventional attitudes and conventional assumptions. Why couldn't they have talked it out, confessed their mutual transgressions?

With a dry mouth, I said softly, 'Please go on.'

He took out his handkerchief and blew his nose. 'So Gwen and I parted. I didn't see her for several months. Then one afternoon, I came home early from the office and found her having tea with my family.'

Gwen touched him on the arm, and smiled. 'I think that was my finest performance, darling. Talk about improvisation. Fortunately, I'd been rehearsing a play in which I had the part of a Polish countess, so I sort of fell into the accent when the children jumped out at me. Protective colouring. Once an actor, always an actor. I suppose I could have refused when Jack insisted I came home to tea, but I was intrigued to see what Celia was like. So I brazened it out.'

'But why were you in Crowcester?'

'It was as the fictional Teresa told you. I was desperate. Robert had refused to see me in London. He'd started commuting back to Oxfordshire instead of staying at his flat. So, I decided to tackle him on his home ground. I had a little car and I drove down to Crowcester. I was going to hang around and see if I could ambush him. I went on a little reconnaissance, and of course it was me that was ambushed.'

My father put his arms around her and held her tightly. 'I knew when I saw her again that I could not ever be apart from her. There had to be some way that I could free myself from my situation and not destroy my career in the process. And by chance the means came to hand. My brother Michael returned from Canada.'

'Your brother? You never told us you had a brother. You told us you were an only child.' I glared at him, accusingly. Was there no end to the reversals of everything I had thought I had known and believed?

'I never wanted to talk of him. It was too painful. He was a part of the golden past, the past which had been lost to me when my father and my dear mother died within months of one another. My grandmother could not afford to bring up both of us orphans, so she took me, and Michael was sent to live with her brother in Carlisle. We hardly saw one another after that. The families were not close. Michael was adopted and took my great-uncle's name. It is a situation that was not unknown in those days, but nevertheless was brutal in the extreme. I felt his loss as if he had died too, as if he too had been taken away from me. It left a wound which never healed. I felt my childhood ended that day. I had only one photograph of us together as small children, which I carried through the war as a kind of talisman.'

He paused, overcome, and I felt a stirring of pity for the grief of that small boy.

He recovered himself and continued, a bitter twist to his lips. 'Of course the result would have greatly interested the psychologists who were particularly interested in such separations.'

Vague memories of courses on educational psychology surfaced. Separations. My heart leapt as I grasped his meaning. Professor Burt, the one who turned out to have faked his research data, had particularly studied the separation of . . .

'Twins? He was your twin brother?'

'Yes. We were identical twins.'

I was back in the lecture room at the London University Institute of Education, seeing the notes I had made on the pad in front of me. 'The technical term is monozygotic. Created by the separation of a single fertilised egg. Genetically identical. My God, so he is . . .'

He held up a restraining hand. 'You're commendably

quick, Elizabeth. I must say the future I had planned for you did not perhaps take sufficient account of your undoubted intellect. But let us keep to the sequence of events. My brother accosted me one day as I came out of the Admiralty. I was overjoyed when I realised who it was, but even I could scarcely recognise him. He was shabby and had grown a beard. He was almost destitute. He had gone to Canada after the war, in which he had not distinguished himself, to make his fortune. He had tried various things, gold prospecting, oil-exploration, lumberjacking, without success and the little money he had had was gone. He had come in search of me as his only living relative. I put him up in my flat. In a matter of a few days, with a shave, decent meals and new clothes, I saw that our remarkable similarity of appearance had survived the vicissitudes of our different upbringings. But alas, nothing else. I found him coarse and uneducated. Worse than that was his attitude to me. He was jealous of my success. He claimed I had had the better deal from our childhood. He demanded that I should compensate him for his misfortunes. He wanted me to advance him a sum which would enable him to start a new life in a new country. After my dream of the pleasures of our being reunited had faded, the idea exploded upon me that he might provide the means by which I could both escape from my dismal marriage and preserve my future.'

It was as if I were watching a bonfire catch alight, like the ones of prunings and dead branches we had had at The Hollies in the autumn and at Guy Fawkes. At first there was the crackling of small flames unseen in the heart of it, then, suddenly, a great billowing cloud of acrid smoke. Thus the horror of what my father was about to tell me grew in my mind from scarcely acknowledged apprehensions to choking certainties in a matter of seconds.

'The means of escape from your marriage?' The words seemed to stick in my dry throat. I gulped more of the water from the glass at my side. 'That sounds like the plot of one of those detective yarns you read so avidly. The use of a double. To create an alibi, to get away with . . .'

I saw him turn aside his face, and I knew that I was right.

I said in flat tones, devoid of emotion, for what emotion was adequate for this disclosure? 'You were going to murder her, to murder my mother.'

He did not meet my eyes as he replied. 'Yes. That was my intention. I was desperate, perhaps a little out of my mind. It seemed the only way. I was trapped, damned, condemned for ever to be separated from the woman I loved. I don't expect you to understand. I scarcely understand it myself, now. I must seem like a monster. I was never that. But perhaps the war, which brought so much death, had corrupted me. I'd seen so many men die, what was one more death? Even the death of someone I thought I had loved.'

'What were you going to do?' Despite the horror which possessed me, I felt a tearing hunger to know everything.

'I planned everything meticulously. It ought to have worked. I don't know to this day why it failed. I convinced Michael to help me on the understanding that he would have no direct role in the business, and that he would have ample funds to start a new life in New Zealand. Early on Sunday evening, he would conceal himself in the potting shed at The Hollies. When I went out for my evening stroll, we would exchange clothes, then he would continue on the walk to the pub. I would quietly let myself back into the house, and wait for your mother's friend to leave, as she always did, with the dull-minded precision of the Crowcester matron, at the same time every week. She would be the witness that I had left the house and that your mother was alone. Meanwhile, my brother, as myself, would enter the pub, order my usual order, and in a discreet way make his presence evident to the company. Gwen was waiting in the phone box outside. She would watch him arrive and go inside, wait a few minutes, then telephone The Hollies, using an assumed accent to the operator. The telephone was in the hall. Celia

298

would come out to answer it, and discover that it was someone who wanted to volunteer for charity work or some such
thing. When she replaced the receiver, I would . . . attack
her. Gwen would drive to the house and enter by the stable
yard. At The Hollies, she would make an emergency call to
the police, in a hysterical voice, saying she was being attacked,
ending in a realistic imitation of a woman being strangled.
Thus the operator would have a record of the precise moment
of Celia's death. No suspicion could attach to me, as I would
in the eyes of the world, have been finishing an excellent pint
of Old Crow. My brother would return to The Hollies by
the back way, and we would again change clothes. He and
Gwen would drive back to London. I would wait in the
garden until the police came and, as if I had just arrived, we
would discover the body together. My wife would have been
killed by a burglar. I had previously removed some of her
jewellery to add authenticity. It would have been the perfect
crime.'

I shuddered. This was the man who had kissed me fondly
that night, promising to return. How could he have done that
with death in his heart?

I choked back my disgust, despite everything, fascinated
to find the solution to the puzzle which had bothered me as
a child. ' "The best laid schemes o' mice an' men gang aft
a-gley." Life isn't like those detective stories. You dropped
the key, didn't you? The key to the door in the walled garden.'

He stared at me, astounded. 'How did you know that?'

I told him.

'I knew that was a bad omen. I had the key in my trouser
pocket. It fell out as we changed. I heard it fall, but in the
dark, I couldn't find it. I had to send Michael back down the
drive and over the Glebe. After that the whole thing went
wrong. I know now, of course, why he never arrived at the
Trout. But at the time, I thought that he had lost his nerve
and walked out on the business. You waited, didn't you,
Gwen?'

'Yes. I thought he'd lost his way at first. I stayed in the car by the pub. Then I went looking for him in the High Street. I went all the way back to The Hollies, but there was no sign of him. It seemed obvious that he'd done a bunk. I'd always thought he was an unreliable type. Now he proved it. I drove back to The Hollies. I thought something might be saved.'

'You mean you wanted to go through with it?' I stared at her, and saw how even at this distance of years, her eyes flashed as she recalled it.

'Yes. I wanted to go through with it. Robert could have gone to the pub afterwards. I could still have made the call pretending to be Celia. But you couldn't do it, could you, my sweet?'

He shook his head slowly, his body seeming to crumple inside the carapace of the smart English clothes. 'No, I couldn't. At the crucial moment, I couldn't do it. Gwen arrived in the stable yard, went through the kitchen and opened the green baize door. Celia heard the noise, left the drawing room and appeared in the hall. At the same time, I emerged from my hiding place under the stairwell. It was like a grisly parody of an Aldwych farce. I knew by then of course that something was wrong. I had been waiting for the telephone to ring. For a moment, we all stood there, and then Gwen said . . .'

'I said, "Go on, Robert, get it over with. There's still time."'

'My God,' I exclaimed, 'did you ever play Lady Macbeth?'

My father frowned but ignored my outburst. 'Celia turned to me, and for a moment she looked as lovely and as vulnerable as she did when we had first met at a party in Bina Gardens before the war. She said, in the tone she used when speaking to servants or shopkeepers, "What on earth are you doing here at this time, Teresa?" Then she looked into my eyes, and she seemed to read there the whole story. She walked up close to me, almost flauntingly, and said, "I see, that's how it is. How blind and stupid I have been. Well, go on, then, Robert. As your floozie said. Get it over with."'

Gwen got up from the sofa and took a long cigarette from a box on the bedside table. 'I could have killed her myself for that word alone. Floozie, indeed, the stuck-up bitch. But I looked at Robert and I saw that it was all over. I could see that Celia knew it too. She positively radiated triumph. Then she set out her terms.'

'I remember that moment as if it were yesterday. She said in a voice that trembled not a whit: "You will leave this house tonight for ever, Robert. You have dishonoured yourself and disgraced the Queen's service. You will not return to your post at the Admiralty, but leave England like a thief in the night. You will suffer whatever ignominy is heaped upon you as a deserter. Furthermore, as you planned to carry out this dreadful crime as our daughter slept upstairs, showing yourself to be utterly unconcerned as to her well-being – what, pray, would have been the consequences for her if she had awoken whilst the thing was being done? – you must never attempt to see either Elizabeth or Jack as long as you live. If you breach any of these conditions, I shall expose you for what you are and what you attempted to do. I know precisely those to whom I should address myself and I shall be believed."'

Gwen stubbed out her cigarette and lit another. 'Like an excommunication, wasn't it, darling? Talk about bell, book and candle. You should have called her bluff. She would never have spoken out.'

The old man turned round as she lounged against the mantelpiece. His face quivered with anger. 'How many times haven't we been through this. You didn't know her. She could be implacable. And she knew everyone in authority in that county. Chief constable, magistrates, judges. I couldn't take the risk. I would have been ruined by the scandal. We had to salvage what we could. And we did, didn't we? We've had a good life, in many ways.'

301

She shrugged, dragging heavily on her cigarette. 'The truth is we've lived as exiles. We've spent forty years in New Zealand, raising sheep. We had to thank our lucky stars that you'd put money in Michael's name in a bank account to pay him off and that I had some money saved for a rainy day. You left with only the clothes you stood up in – and they weren't even yours, but Michael's.'

'But I had Michael's passport and identity papers as well. I saved myself the humiliation of having to keep my own identity.'

'So did you write to my mother from Paris?'

'Yes. I begged her to reconsider. But she didn't reply. I knew she wouldn't.'

'Then when he was branded as a traitor, he couldn't even think of returning. It wasn't only Celia he had to deal with then. The bitch made sure he could never return.'

'So you think she was the source of those rumours?'

'If she weren't, she did nothing to quash them. Who else would have had any reason to do it?'

'What does it matter now? In a year or two, maybe less, I'll be dead. Then they can say what they like.' He turned to Gwen with a fond look. 'But at least you would have been out of it, my love.'

Gwen reached out and grasped his hand.

I stared at the ancient lovers, still apparently as obsessed by one another as they had been forty years ago. The emotions churned within me. Some of them had adult names: despair, disgust, pity, hatred, fear. But beyond those was the nameless amorphous whirling pain at the centre of my being, which I had felt as a child, and since then only when I knew that the child I had carried was dead.

I tried to give this pain a shape when I said, 'You dragged me over here and concocted that elaborate pantomime so you could go on escaping the consequences of what you did?'

My father looked at me with cold incomprehension. 'It

302

was necessary. We read in the newspaper of the discovery of Michael's body. Even in the South Island, *The Times* can be obtained. One of the many reports stated that Celia was suffering from senile dementia. It meant that she could no longer injure us, but nor could she save us with the truth. We thought it likely that the police would suspect the woman who called herself Teresa. They would look for her. They might unearth someone who remembered my affair with Gwen and put two and two together. They might look for Gwen and find her, which meant they would find me. How could I prove that I was Robert Armitage, having lived as Michael Heaton for forty years? The reality of my identity was effaced by time. It had worked in my favour, it would work against me. We could both have been accused of murdering Robert Armitage. If, however, Teresa were to resurface with a story that could neither be proved nor disproved, then we thought that they would be less likely to connect Teresa with Gwen. We reckoned without the ill-luck which had dogged us throughout this whole matter. That and your swift intelligence, my dear. Now of course, we have managed to achieve the exact reverse of what we wanted.'

I drank more water, my head aching with unshed tears. 'You were still treating life as if it obeyed the rules of a detective novel. There's no super intelligent, sophisticated detective in the Thames Valley force who regards a forty-year-old murder mystery as a test of his prowess. There's only a bright but busy copper who thought from the beginning there was no kudos in the Armitage case. He wants only a convincing report to allow him to close his file. The police do detection by computer these days, you see. Like everyone else in modern society, they're not trained to think for themselves. The computer profile says that if someone's murdered, without any blindingly apparent external motive, then you first suspect the spouse. After all, in your case, they would have been right. You worried for nothing. They weren't very interested in Teresa. She left so few traces, they think that

Jack and I invented her to protect Mother. They'd never even heard of Gwen. They were quite happy to blame the spouse. They'd closed the file. All you've achieved is to get it reopened.'

They exchanged glances, and a tremor of fear rippled up my spine. Who knew what was going on in their minds? But I was strong, and they were old and frail, so old, so frail, like the branches of a tree long dead.

'So what are you going to do?' My father's voice was hardly more than a whisper from his shrunken frame. Gwen coughed heavily, bronchitically into her handkerchief. They watched me, trembling together.

'Do? About the two of you? Nothing, of course. What would it profit to destroy what little good remains? You're the reverse of Shakespeare's Caesar, aren't you, Father? Your evil, if that's what it was, has been truly buried with your brother's bones. So let it be. Let the dead speak more clearly than the living. But there is something else which remains to be done. Someone killed your brother Michael quite callously and randomly while he was walking across the Glebe. Do you not want to know why? Did you not feel anything when you read of the discovery of the body and realised that it was his?'

'No. I already believed that he was dead. When or how he had died, I didn't know and I didn't care. I blamed him for betraying me. For years, we had grown apart. Then that final act had shown he was no longer my brother. Clearly, I now acknowledge that I had misjudged him. What does it matter, though? You're wrong, my dear. Nothing can be done. It happened too long ago.'

'I think that something can and that something should be done. Any man's death diminishes me. I told Gwen when she was pretending to be Teresa. I think there is one man still alive in Crowcester who knows part of the answer. He's the man who tried to kill me on the Glebe. If the police find him, we may have a clue to the mystery.'

Again I saw the complicit, anxious glance pass between them.

'But don't worry,' I added, 'no one will search for you. Robert Armitage is dead. He died for me the night he kissed me and promised he would always come back to me.'

In the end sleep overwhelmed my defences.

It was late when I awoke to a bright day. Since my arrival, I knew that the confidence with which I had spoken to my father about his brother's murder had been misplaced. Brian Rollright's secret, if he had had one, had died with him. I should never know whether the two bodies on the Glebe had shared their resting place by accident or by design.

The mystery of the death of Michael Heaton, which in truth concerned no one but me, would never be solved. It was, as my father had said, too long ago.

And what of my father? Was it possible that for the few years which were left him he could again be part of my life? He had plotted to murder my mother. How could I ever forgive that? Yet, at the critical moment, he had stayed his hand. How did that act of clemency which showed that his conscience was not dead weigh in the balance against that?

And what of my brother? How would it appear to him? The boy had worshipped his father as boys do, then he had hated him. The discovery of the body on the Glebe had once more restored the paternal image in Jack's mind. His father was the hero he had always believed him to be. How would Jack react now to the knowledge that his father was, in all but the final act, a murderer? Could he cope with that knowledge? Or would he feel compelled to make public his father's crime, in order to save my mother's reputation?

Despite everything he had done, I could not bear the idea that my father should be hounded by the press or the authorities. He was an old man and that would kill him.

Did I have the right to withhold the facts from Jack? I was a keeper of secrets, but to keep this one meant that I would be playing God. Would there ever be a time when it would seem right to tell him? And when that time came, would I recognise it?

It was almost ten thirty by the time I'd dressed Mother, given her breakfast, washed her and settled her down in her chair in front of the gas fire, where she would eventually doze until lunch time. I made coffee and called Jack's house in London. He was out and I left a message on his machine.

I'd just replaced the receiver when I heard a car bouncing fast up the drive, then stop with a clatter of shingle in front of the house.

I went through into the hall, but no one had rung the doorbell. It must be Jack, turning out his pockets as usual, to find his key. I hurried to open the door.

A man was standing in the porch. He had his back to me, but it wasn't Jack. I was about to ask him his business, when, without warning, he whirled round and flung out a hand, giving me a violent push backwards over the threshold. He sprang after me into the house and slammed the door shut with his foot.

I collided with the hall table, slipped on the tiles and fell awkwardly against it to the floor, landing heavily on my backside and ending up in a half sitting position, my skirt rucked up my thighs.

He stood over me, legs apart, arms akimbo. I was too stunned and surprised even to cry out. I stared up at the thin, pale face of my assailant. It was strangely familiar. Then I recognised him.

It was Derek Rollright.

With a one-handed, theatrical flourish, he snatched open one side of his dark blue zipper jacket. Tucked into the leather belt of his jeans was a black hand-gun.

'Hello, Iceberg,' he said. 'I used to think you must have nice legs under them long skirts. I was dead right.'

I pulled my skirt down to my knees and climbed painfully to my feet, clutching the side of the table.

He stepped forward, took the gun out of his waistband and brandished it in my face.

'Get away from the phone!'

I backed away from him to the opposite wall, feeling the dado rail of the wainscot pressing into the base of my spine. I said to myself: think of him as a dangerous dog. Be calm, don't show you're afraid. As I was almost out of my mind with shock and terror, this was easier said than done.

His head still upright to keep his eyes on me, he bent down, felt for the telephone cable and yanked it out of the socket. Then for good measure, he tugged the instrument off the table on to the floor and crashed his heel down on it.

Apparently satisfied with this minor piece of destruction, he came up close to me. He jabbed the pistol into my midriff, making me wince. This caused a delighted grin to appear on his dry, chapped lips. Then he moved the barrel up my body, sliding it over my right breast, then across to the left, holding it pressed there. My nipples tingled and I shuddered, trying to keep my breathing shallow and under control.

'You're not bad, you know, Iceberg. Me and the other lads always wondered what you had in your knickers.' The pistol barrel dropped down sharply and thrust agonisingly at the junction of my thighs. Again, he grinned at my grimace of pain, and opened his mouth. Out slipped a coated tongue, like a snake emerging from between two stones of a wall. 'Something very nice, I think.'

I gazed steadily at him, trying to read the expression in his narrow eyes, the whites of which were tarnished yellow, the colour of newsprint exposed too long to the sun. His pupils seemed slightly shrunken in the brown irises. Was he on something? What did it matter? He was hardly here for a friendly counselling session from his old teacher. I remembered that Jimmy Philpott had used the word evil to describe him. At the time, I'd thought it extravagantly theological. Now I wasn't so sure.

'What can I do for you, Derek?' I asked in as carefully neutral a tone as I could manage.

He smiled. 'You mean, what can I do for you? Well, you'll see. Let's go and find somewhere more comfortable.'

Walking backwards, the gun still pointed at me, he edged along the wall until he came to the doorway of the drawing room.

He kicked open the door, then gestured with the pistol. 'In here.'

He followed me and slammed the door. 'Sit down there.' He pointed at the Knole sofa.

I sat on the edge of the cushion, but he shoved me back. 'You sit there and don't move, or do anything silly, or I'll be forced to blow your fucking head off. That would spoil what I've got in mind to pass the time.'

He gazed around. I looked with him. It was as if I were seeing the room for the first time.

Dust motes hung in the thick slabs of sunlight bursting through the dark mullions of the window, as if through the bars of a prison. The heavy brocade curtains, hardly ever drawn these days, were thick with dust. Dust had gathered on the bronze figurines clustered on the mantelpiece, and on the gilt frames of the pictures which crowded the walls. Dust lay on the parquet beyond the faded blue and reds of the Persian carpet. High above me, in the shadowed plasterwork of the ceiling, dusty cobwebs hung motionless. On the table behind the sofa, the dust clung to the pile of newspapers and magazines, stacked there for me to cut out features useful in school.

I thought of Miss Havisham's parlour in *Great Expectations*, where the jilted woman's wedding breakfast had lain rotting and cobwebbed for years. I too had lived imprisoned in my past, in a parody of family life, where I, the childless spinster, reluctantly mothered my helpless parent to the benefit of neither of us, awaiting death.

Now, unlooked for, Death had come, in one of his many guises. But first, I knew, we would have to dance together.

For a few moments, there was silence as he paced around the room, stopping occasionally in front of a picture, or to examine a piece of furniture. He came to the table with the silver salver loaded with bottles and glasses.

He gave a childish chortle of glee, poking around this hoard, until he found a bottle of very expensive malt whisky. In a quite creditable imitation of an upper class drawl, he said, 'I think it's time for a tincture, what? Care to indulge, old girl?'

Oddly enough, this gave me heart and roused me from my petrified lethargy. Certain rape and probable murder would, in common with life's other encumbrances, be better drunk than sober.

'I'd like a gin, thank you, Derek. The tonic's in the fridge in the kitchen.'

He gave a sharp, amused look. 'Do you think I'm stupid, Iceberg? Shall I just pop off and get it then, while you scarper? Or perhaps I should let you go? What, with all those knives you find in kitchens? No fear, Iceberg. You'll have to have it straight.'

'All right.'

He thought for a moment, then smiled to himself. Selecting one of the big Waterford tumblers, he filled it to the brim from the square green bottle and handed it to me.

I raised the glass to my lips and drank down half of it in several deep swallows. 'Thanks. Aren't you having one?'

He stared at me, then poured himself an equally large measure and quaffed down the whole tumbler. He smacked his lips and gave me a look of bravado.

I gulped down the rest of mine, then held out the glass. 'And again, please, Derek.'

Without a word, he tilted the green bottle, then handed back the refill. This time, I took a more judicious slug.

He filled up his own tumbler to the brim, raised the glass

to his lips and drank the whole off in a few deep swallows. He set down the glass on the tray, and swaggered over to me.

It was like some kind of ghastly courtship ritual. I drank more of the gin. My throat and guts were burning, but I wasn't drunk, unfortunately. I used to be proud of the way I could drink most men under the table, but now I wished I could have passed out.

As if reading my thoughts, Derek removed the glass from my hands, and put it back on the tray with a flourish.

'That's enough of that, Iceberg. Don't want you pissed out of your brain, do I?'

I watched him carefully as he came back to the sofa. He didn't seem to be unsteady, and his speech wasn't slurred. Surely, though, the booze must have affected him?

He shot back the cuff of his jacket and checked his fancy digital watch. As if satisfied, he sat down beside me.

He'd talked about having time. Was he waiting for something? If so, what could it be?

Then the answer leapt into my mind. Not something, but somebody. Jack. Somehow he knew that Jack would be returning here from London. That's why he seemed in no hurry. But how did he know that? And why was he lying in wait for him? Jack didn't even know him.

He lay back on the sofa, his hands clasped behind his head, his knees held wide apart, the gun butt protruding from his trousers like the top of a massive erection.

'This is very comfortable, Iceberg. Our Fran used to tell me about this house of yours. I never thought that I'd find myself here, with such a treat in store.'

I thought back to the lessons I'd taught Derek. Should I have realised at that time that he was a psychopath in the making? He had written some atrociously spelt and ungrammatical compositions on the subject of violence and murder, the imagery taken from videos and the television, but all the boys in his class were fixated on those subjects.

I moved closer to him. 'You're right. It is comfortable,

310

Derek. Why do you keep calling me Iceberg? You're not at school any longer. You're a man, not a boy. Call me Liz.'

He looked at me, surprise showing on his face. Then he snorted. 'Iceberg or not, you're pretty cool. We used to talk about you, you know. Whether you were really frigid. What you got up to and who with. Whether you were a les. You didn't pretend to be anything other than a posh bitch. You weren't always trying to be matey, like that poncey head-master, the one that snuffed it. "Morning, boys," he used to go, then scuttle off to his office. Stupid pillock. You weren't scared of us. I remember one of the books you made us read. It was all about an island and kids hunting and killing, first pigs, then one another. "Kill the pig," they used to go. I liked it. I remember the bit where they got a pig's head, stuck it on a pole and sort of worshipped it.'

'*Lord of the Flies*,' I said automatically.

'That's the one. I really remember that.'

I suddenly had an image of another dead totem, one that Jack had so graphically described to me.

'It was you who killed the sheep on the Glebe, wasn't it, Derek?'

He smiled, as if at a pleasant memory. 'Yeah. That was me. I had a bit of a struggle to get the pole right through. I don't think the bugger was quite dead at first.'

'I'd thought, up to now, in view of what happened to me, that your father must have done it.'

This amused him. 'Dad? That wasn't his style. He couldn't have thought that up. He was useless. If it had been me, you wouldn't have managed to whang me one like you did him. No way. I'd have smashed your fucking head in.'

Despite the circumstances which meant the information would never be any use to me, I was puzzled by the strange implications of Derek's admission. He seemed no less willing to talk about his particular area of expertise than any other man. And if this put off my fate by a few precious minutes, so much the better.

'I'm glad it wasn't you, then.'

What I'd thought was an innocuous observation had an explosive effect. He grabbed me savagely by the shoulders and shook me furiously.

'What do you fucking mean? I wasn't saying that it could have been. It never could have been me. Do you think I'd help that old bastard dig up my mum's body, so he could get away with murder? What do you think I am?'

To my astonishment, tears shone in his eyes.

'I'm sorry, Derek, I don't know what was going on. You said . . .'

He threw me against the back of the sofa and crouched forward with his elbows on his knees.

'I know what I fucking said. And I know what I fucking did. What I should have done, fucking years ago. I wasn't ever sure, you see.' He was sobbing now, and he turned his tear-streaked face towards me. 'But when I heard what the filth had found on the Glebe, I knew. Then he came snivelling to me, saying I had to help him, that he had to disappear while his arm was bad. He told me that it had been an accident with Mum, that he'd only given her a bit of a push. Well, that was like all the other fucking lies he used to tell us. So I fucking helped him to disappear, all right.'

I nodded, as if in sympathy, forcing back the horror which rose in my throat, saying calmly, 'I can understand how you felt, Derek.'

'Yeah? That was the best one so far. You should have seen his head go. Blam! Like a fucking bomb had hit it. Wiped the surprise right off his face.'

My lips were dry. 'The best one? Have there been others, then?'

'What do you want to know for? To tell the judge? You won't get no chance of that.'

'I'm interested. In everything to do with you, Derek.'

'Yeah? There've been a few. The one before Dad wasn't no good. Old bloke on a zebra in some fucking church place

312

I hadn't never heard of. Just thump and crunch, and drive off like shit. Where's the fun in that? Not much better than doing a fucking hedgehog.'

My whole body seemed to freeze and I could hardly get the words out. 'I can tell it wasn't much fun for you. Why did you do it then, Derek?'

'I don't fucking pick them, do I? They give me this.' He felt in his pocket, and produced an object in black plastic. A mobile phone. 'Same as with this job.'

'What job is this, Derek?'

'I thought you'd never ask. Well, it isn't all you. You're just an extra, the icing on the cake, like. Can't you guess? It's your fucking ponce of a brother. Mr Jack Lord God Almighty Armitage.'

'Why do you want to kill Jack?' I asked conversationally, as if I were engaging in party small talk.

'I told you. I don't pick 'em. Though in his case, it'll be a pleasure. Teach him to go messing around with our Fran. Though this time, they'll hardly go after Barry for it. That prat couldn't swat a fly unless he were liquored up for it. Now it seems like Jackie boy was shagging his missus after all. So what does Barry do but run off home to his mum?'

His eyes had widened as he had warmed to his theme. He had become animated, as if he were discussing the perform- ance of a football team in the pub with his mates. Looking at him in that moment, it was hard to believe what I had just heard. But the illusion soon passed.

This slim, pale young man was seriously disturbed. He was going to murder my brother, then rape and kill me. Unless . . .

In moving towards him, I had sat more upright and my head was level with the table behind the sofa. From that position, I caught a glimpse of a familiar object poking from beneath the pile of newsprint.

'Were you going to rape me now or afterwards, Derek?' This time I used a more throaty, caressing excited tone.

'Because the way I feel at the moment, I don't want to wait. I'm really turned on by what you've told me.' I reached out and very gently took hold of his hand, then slowly guided it to rest on my thigh. I pulled up my skirt, wriggling my bottom forward. 'Let me get these off.'

Then I reached up, pulled at my pants and rolled them with my tights down to my knees. I sat with my thighs wide apart.

He stared down, his eyes were bulging wide with excitement.

I reached my arm around his shoulders, drawing him towards my crotch. 'Kiss me down there, Derek. Oh yes, that's good.'

I steeled myself as I felt his tongue and his cold hands on my buttocks. I moaned a couple of times.

At the same time, I reached my right hand behind me to the table where I had seen the pair of scissors I used for the newspaper cuttings.

My fingertips brushed their plastic handles, and painstakingly I edged them nearer so I could grasp them.

At that moment, there was the sound of tyres on gravel.

Derek swore furiously, and withdrew his head from between my thighs. He scrambled to his feet, pulling the pistol from his belt. He ran softly to the drawing room window and looked out.

I took hold of the scissors and thrust them behind my back. I hastily pulled up my knickers and tights.

From the window, I heard Derek cursing to himself. Was it someone other than Jack?

There was the sound of a key in the lock of the front door. Jack's deep voice boomed, 'Liz, I'm home!'

Derek raced back from the window, pointing the gun in my face. 'Say you're in here.'

Shuddering with nervous tension, I screamed out, 'Run, Jack! He's got a gun!'

I thought he would stop to kill me on the spot. But he

didn't hesitate, and tore into the hall. I heard him yelling, 'Hold it, Armitage!' Then, 'Get out of the fucking way!'

I gripped the scissors like a dagger and dashed to the door.

Derek was halfway down the hall, his gun held at arm's length pointing at the two figures by the front door. One of them was Jack. The other, her arms flung wide, covering his body, was Fran Rollright.

'I said get out of the fucking way!' He was moving the weapon wildly and indecisively.

Fran said, 'Derek, please put the gun down. Please don't shoot him. Please, Derry.'

My heart leapt as I heard her. Oh Fran. Darling, darling Fran.

I saw his body flinch in surprise, his shoulders sagged and for a second his right arm dropped. Then it was raised again. 'You said you loved me best, Fran. What happened to Dad. That was for us, Fran. For us. We could be together. Now you don't love me best. You want this bastard Armitage.'

'No, Derry, please, you don't understand. No!' She clung more closely to Jack, her body spreadeagled against his.

His arm trembled but he took a step forward, aiming the gun. I had been inching towards him alongside the wall, the scissors held ready, willing him not to turn.

I was almost at arm's length, my eyes fixed on the greasy curl of hair on the back of his neck. As I slid my foot forward, my toe hit one of the loose floor tiles, and for a second, I stumbled.

It was enough. He heard me, swivelled on his heel, saw the scissors and screamed. 'You fucking, fucking bitch!'

I stared into the black circle at the end of the gun barrel, as I backed away in terror down the hall.

Behind Derek, the door of the morning room opened and a figure stood on the threshold, a tall upright figure in a navy blue dress and matching cardigan. It was Mother.

He whirled round again at this fresh interruption.

She addressed him in a voice which still carried some of

its former peremptory vigour. 'I am waiting for my lunch. Where is Hargreaves, young man? Go and find her this instant! Well, go on! What are you waiting for?'

Derek said, 'Fuck off, you old cow,' stuck the pistol in her ribs and fired.

Jack and I both moved at the same moment.

He got there first. He leapt on Derek like a tiger, and they both crashed to the floor, Jack's greater bulk completely covering Derek. I screamed at Jack, 'The gun, get the gun!'

From the tangle of wildly struggling limbs came the muffled explosion of another shot. Jack stopped moving.

Derek struggled to extricate himself, his gun hand trapped beneath Jack's body, foaming at the mouth and howling obscenities. I drew back my arm and with all my force rammed the scissors into his neck. He screamed in agony, his free hand tugging at the steel blades, his blood spraying out, adding its own arabesques to the already intricate patterns of the encaustic tiles.

I rolled Jack over. His white shirt front was flooded with scarlet, a ragged hole with black burned edges just above his waistband. Through it his blood poured like a river. I stared up at Fran's chalk white face, my arms and shoulders stiff and unbending with a numbing cold.

The doorbell clanged.

Fran turned like an automaton, twisted the lever of the Yale lock and let in Ellen Norton.

'How are you, Miss Armitage? I've brought you these.' Detective Chief Inspector Green produced a brown paper bag, from the top of which poked the woody stem of a bunch of grapes, and set it clumsily on the top of the white melamine bedside table.

'Thanks. As to how I am, I don't quite know how to answer that. I'm alive, at least. And Ellen has made me very comfortable here.'

'Is there any more news on your brother?'

'He's still in intensive care. Which actually means he's doing quite well. The hospital thought he wouldn't survive the night. It was only because Ellen knew how to deal with the bleeding that he made it at all. She kept her head when she saw what had happened. If she hadn't come along, he wouldn't have made it. Fran and I were in shock and useless at that moment.'

'You mustn't blame yourself. I've seen experienced police officers crumple up at far less serious incidents. I'm very sorry about your mother. That was terrible. To shoot dead a helpless old lady in cold blood. No wonder you were in shock.'

'She saved us. If she hadn't appeared like that and distracted him, he would have killed us all. I've read about those kinds of flashes into normality happening in dementia sufferers. How strange though that it should happen then.'

'As you say. You're lucky it did. By the way, I can set your mind at rest on one thing. There won't be any charges relating to the death of Derek Rollright. It's clear that in the circumstances you used reasonable force to prevent a greater loss of life.'

'It's not something I feel good about.'

'No, I can understand that. I don't suppose you've thought any more about why Rollright should have behaved like that?'

I held his gaze unwaveringly. 'No, he didn't say much to give me a clue. I taught him at school, and that often causes strong emotions, but there was nothing that I remember that would cause lasting resentment. Perhaps the death of his father finally made him blow up. Who knows what goes on in the minds of people like him? I don't know why he appeared to have a grudge against Jack. Perhaps he represented the whole ruling class. We've experienced antagonism on that score from otherwise normal people.'

He gave a ghost of a smile. 'I leave all that to the psychiatrists. They'll have their say at the inquest. Without Rollright to tell us, though, we'll never know.'

'No, we never will.'

He coughed nervously. 'There's another matter. I thought you should know about it in the circumstances. I believe you're acquainted with a Mr Martin Rice.'

'Yes, of course. He's married to the headmistress of Waterbury Comprehensive School. And his company sponsored my brother's excavation of the Glebe.'

He nodded. 'Of course. I'm aware of Mr Rice's connections and activities. But, how can I put this? You know him in a more personal capacity, I believe?'

'Why do you believe that?'

He sighed. 'You can rely on my discretion, Miss Armitage. I know that the matter is delicate. However, I have to tell you that Mr Rice's car, a red Jaguar XJ6, was observed entering the drive of Ewescombe Manor, his country house in Gloucestershire on 24 July this year. It was followed a short time later by a white Ford Escort registered in your name. A woman answering your description got out and was let into the house by Mr Rice. We understand that Mrs Rice was away visiting relatives that weekend. You remained inside with Mr Rice for some hours.'

I burst out with hardly simulated fury. 'This is quite incredible, Chief Inspector. What business is it of the police where I went that night? The house was for sale and Mr Rice was giving me a view of it at the only time which was mutually convenient.'

'You told Mrs Norton you had gone to a meeting with colleagues.'

'I am no more in the habit of sharing my personal business with Mrs Norton than I am with you, Chief Inspector. Now would you please leave and take your unpleasant insinuations with you.'

'I wish you included telling the truth as one of your habits, Miss Armitage, not just the version of it which fits the circumstances. Frankly, I don't care what you and Mr Rice were up to that night, and if you say he was showing you round, then I'll pretend I'm just a stupid copper and believe it. There's plenty of my colleagues who always accept what a real lady tells them. What I am concerned about is whether the relationship with Mr Rice, personal or professional, is at present continuing, and whether you know where he might be, or if not, whether he is likely to make contact with you, particularly after the matter in which you have just been involved. If he does, then I should be grateful if you'd advise him to get in touch with me. It would be better for him if he were to co-operate with us.'

'Co-operate? What's he supposed to have done?'

'I can tell you that Mr Rice's various companies have, as of this morning, ceased trading, and that a warrant for the arrest of Mr Rice has been issued by Waterbury magistrates.'

'I see. Well, I certainly neither know nor care where he is, and I have absolutely no reason to think he would in the least wish to contact me.' Then another thought struck me. 'You must have been following him that night. Why were you doing that then if he's only now done a flit?'

I saw an evasive flicker in his eyes despite the professional poker face. Suddenly it struck me.

'Wait a minute. You can't have been following us. I would have noticed another car behind us on that lane. You must have been watching the house. You had an undercover surveillance operation going. You wouldn't have done that if you'd wanted to get Rice for, say, creative accounting at his property companies, would you?'

He didn't reply, but I sensed his concentration.

'So what crimes are you after him for?'

He gave me a long hard look, then he said, 'The information hasn't been made public. But in the circumstances, I can tell you the alleged offences concern conspiracy to contravene various statutes relating to the control of dangerous drugs.'

'Drugs? What kinds of drugs?'

'The worst.' His voice was cold. 'We're not talking about recreational substances, Miss Armitage.'

My head swam and I snatched at the glass of water by the bedside. Rice, a drug peddler? Of course, he was just the type. The property businesses were a means to launder the proceeds. Then at the same moment, I recalled the fax I had intercepted. Could the business which he and Christopher Greville apparently had in common involve drugs? Surely not? But if it were that would explain why they were both so anxious for the connection to be kept secret. The thought sickened me.

Green was regarding me keenly. 'Are you all right, Miss Armitage?'

'I'm very shocked by what you've told me about Martin Rice. I don't approve of any drugs. I've seen the lives of some of my pupils ruined by them. I want you to know that I knew nothing whatever of these activities of his.'

He gave me a grim smile. 'If I had for a moment suspected otherwise, Miss Armitage, I'd have included your name on the arrest warrant. I'll leave you in peace now. Perhaps you would call me if Mr Rice makes contact – or if there's anything else you want to tell me.' He handed me a slip of paper. 'That number will enable you to reach me at any time.'

Peace was the last thing he'd left me in. What on earth should I do? There might possibly be some far less sinister reason for dealings between Greville and Rice, though what that could be I had not even an inkling. If I showed Green the fax, I might be implicating an innocent man.

As on countless occasions in the previous few days, I longed to consult with the only person who would understand. But Jack, my poor darling Jack, was, at present, in no fit state to be consulted. As I had when I was a girl, I clenched my hands into fists, trying to convey to him some of my strength of will. Don't give in, Jack, I urged through set teeth, don't give in. Please don't give in.

There was a knock at the door and Ellen appeared, bearing

a tray with tea things. Her expression was bright, although she had obviously been crying. She had been at the hospital.

'What news?'

'No change, Liz. But that's a good sign, apparently. It means he's holding on.'

I forced myself to support her optimism. 'Jack's tough, Ellen. He won't give up easily on something he values as highly as his life. I remember once he broke his right forearm falling out of a tree. He was determined that he was not going to miss the opening of the cricket season. So, the first match, he went in with the plaster on to bat left handed, and scored a fifty.'

But even as I spoke these cheering words, my heart was heavy. The match that Jack was now playing in was Life v. Death.

We drank tea. Ellen sat on the pink candlewick bedspread. I took her small hand in mine.

'You saved his life, Ellen. You were magnificent. If you hadn't come by then, he would have died on the spot.'

'Funny how things turn out, isn't it? When I saw Jack going off with Fran in his car, I was that mad. I finished serving and shut up the shop as quick as I could and went after them. I was going to tell him what I thought of him. Then Fran told us in the ambulance about how he was her real father, and that he'd been taking her to The Hollies to tell you about it. Wasn't it a good thing I didn't know that at the time?'

'Yes, and it was a good thing you kept calm and used your first aid, when Fran and I were useless with shock. I always regarded you as more capable than you thought you were at school.'

'I mucked about, mostly though, didn't I? I wish now I had my time over again. I'd study really hard.'

'It's never too late, Ellen. If you want, I'll help you.'

'Do you think, if I was more educated, it would make a difference, with . . .'

'With Jack? Who knows what makes a difference with him? If he had any sense, he'd appreciate what he had already. Whatever happens, do it anyway, Ellen. Do it for yourself.'

The following morning, I got out of bed for breakfast. I'd managed to persuade Ellen that I didn't need twenty-four-hour care and that she should go to work at the shop.

I hadn't seen the newspapers. According to Ellen, reporters had been hanging about the village once more, hoping to add human flesh to the bare bones of the official accounts. On this occasion, though, the community had closed in on itself. No one would talk about Derek Rollright. They had refused to reveal where I was staying, even when offered bribes. The landlord of the Trout refused to serve anyone with a camera or notebook computer. Fran had gone to stay with friends in Oxford.

I was surprised therefore when there was a rap at the door. I pulled aside the net curtain and looked out. A small, dark-haired, very smartly dressed woman stood on the doorstep. She had, I thought, media person written all over her.

I ignored the knock and went back to the woman's magazine I had been reading, one of a pile left me by Ellen. Not my usual fare, but I couldn't cope with anything more demanding.

She knocked again, this time louder and more prolonged. Then she was calling through the letter box. 'Miss Armitage, Miss Armitage, please let me speak to you.'

Furious at the intrusion, I went into the tiny hall and yelled, 'Go away!'

'Please, I have to speak to you about your brother. It's very important.'

I yanked open the door and thundered down at her, 'What do you know about my brother? You're not from the hospital?'

'No, but I'm not a reporter either. My name is Clarissa Hetherington-Browne.'

322

I made coffee and we sat at the new pine table in Ellen's small kitchen.

Her small face was pale and drawn, and despite the warm day, she was shivering.

'I was completely shattered when I heard the news on the radio. When it said that your mother had been killed and that Jack was fighting for his life, I felt so guilty, so cowardly.'

'But why, I don't understand . . .'

'No, of course, you don't. You don't know that it was all my fault. If Jack dies, then I'll have as good as killed him myself.' She put down her mug, and collapsed into anguished crying.

I hastened to put my arm around her thin shoulders. She clung to me like a child. Eventually, the paroxysm died away. She took a handkerchief from her bag and wiped her eyes.

'I'm sorry, barging in like this. But I made up my mind I had to see you, whatever the consequences. I couldn't get any answer on the phone at your house. So I called in sick and drove down here. The first place I went was the shop and asked the girl there for The Hollies. She wouldn't tell me at first, but then I explained who I was, and eventually, she told me where to find you. I want to tell you everything.'

She talked for an hour about her discovery of the fraud at the Museum and how she'd persuaded Jack to help her unmask it. As she spoke, her pale face gradually recovered a more healthy colour. I sat listening, spellbound.

'When I left Jack at his house in Barnsbury, the night before he was to go to the Museum, he said, as a kind of joke, in Latin, "Caesar, those who are about to die salute you." You know, the Roman gladiators' address to the Emperor. I didn't suspect then how true that might prove. I swear I never thought he would be in physical danger, that he might d . . .'

I took her hand. 'Jack isn't dead. He's holding on. But even if he did . . . It couldn't be your fault. I don't understand why you think what happened here was because of what he was doing at the Museum.'

'I haven't finished the story. I'd arranged with Jack that I would go very early to the Museum the following morning and let him out of the storeroom where he would have returned after taking the vase. When I opened the door of the room, he wasn't there. Puzzled and desperately worried, I went to my own office to phone him. There, I found Lord Greville waiting for me, sitting in my chair behind my desk.

'He smiled his charming smile, and, getting up, said, "Good morning, my dear Clarissa. How impressive to see you so bright and early. How impressed my fellow trustees would be if they could see you. You're not the only one who's been early at his post. Though in his particular case, it seems to have slipped his mind that he is no longer employed by this august institution. I have the oddest feeling you know that Armitage was roaming around here in the small hours. Perhaps you'd like to tell me about it."

'I didn't see any point in pretending any longer. If Jack had been caught, then the whole business was blown. So I told him that I would be going to Scotland Yard that morning to disclose everything I knew about his theft of artefacts from the Museum. He was completely unmoved. He said, "I doubt very much that you are going to do that, my dear Clarissa. The fact is that you, who thought you were so clever and resourceful, were completely out of your depth. I'd had my eye on you. There was the business with the archives, the statue of the Virgin, the impromptu visit you paid me a few weeks ago. I decided that I'd somewhat underestimated you. Fortunately, you chose as your instrument a man who is as degenerate intellectually as he is morally. Do you not know that in life as in art, the clown does not play Hamlet? His ineptitude has nipped your scheme in the bud."

'I was absolutely stunned by his cool effrontery. But at the same time, I was wondering what on earth had been going on. What had Jack been saying? So I persisted. "You can't stop me from going to the authorities."

'He merely stared at me disdainfully. "And what precisely would you tell them? So you know about the Virgin. That was bad luck. But it has been fully restored. No expert is going to risk his reputation to go breaking it again. Here in the Farebrother are gathered some of the world experts in their fields. They will say that all the objects under their care in the Museum are totally, indisputably, genuine. The records will back them up. Which scholars will dare to contradict them? What is the difference between the genuine and the fake after all, when the two are, by any non-destructive test, truly indistinguishable? They might as well be twins, conceived in the same womb, genetically identical. Even their own begetters couldn't tell them apart. The world of art is full of people who are forever claiming that this item or that artefact is a fake. Hardly anyone listens. They're renegades, eccentrics, men of no reputation, like Armitage, for instance."

'And then he said . . .' She started to cry again, not with the same intensity as before, but with a broken, dispirited weeping that moved me deeply.

'What is it, Clarissa? What did he say?'

She recovered herself a little, clutching her handkerchief in her small hand. 'He said, "If you still feel tempted to risk the loss of a comfortable livelihood, and to invite the ridicule of your colleagues, you should be aware that there are a great many things which I have made it my business to know about you, my dear Clarissa. Some of them you have made no secret of: your birth in a council house in the squalid neo-Stalinist city of Hull, your comprehensive school education, your admission to Cambridge, your successful transition to Civil Service high flyer. But there are other matters about which you are more reticent."'

She hesitated, looking up at me imploringly. 'Please, you won't . . .'

I smiled at her, a warmth towards her such as I had rarely known spreading through me. 'I shan't breathe a word.'

'He said, "The way you swing, as I believe the modern

jargon has it. Clearly, in some parts of society, there are those to whom your sexual orientation would seem quite banally unexceptionable. However, the Board of Trustees of the Farebrother is not one of those. Nor are, I happen to know, your ex-husband and his family. I know the Hetherington-Brownes well. They were not at all pleased when you and Simon married. An only son is not a property to be bestowed lightly. They were more gratified when it ended quickly, although they were disappointed that you retained custody of their only grandchild. If, however, they were to learn of some of the things you get up to, then there might well be a challenge to that custody. It could become very acrimonious and messy, and you might lose the son, upon whom, I gather, you dote.'''

I was utterly appalled. Was this the man who, despite everything which had happened between us, I had never ceased to regard as having a kind of nobility?

'What a foul threat. But a court wouldn't do that, would it? Not in these days?'

She wrung the handkerchief in her hands. 'I couldn't risk it. I couldn't bear to lose James. Once Simon's parents got their hands on him, they'd turn him against me. Even if they lost, there would be the dreadful publicity. I don't want him to find out about his mother like that. The fact is,' she hesitated, glancing at me. 'I have been indiscreet. In a way in which the tabloids could make hay with. Don't you see the position I was in? I was faced with losing the only thing I really valued. Against that, the Farebrother was nothing. And when it came to it, I had no proper proof. Without the vase, without Jack, without access to the archives, I was blocked. So, I gave in. I agreed with Greville that I would continue in my post, under his specific direction. He said he would recommend to the trustees that my salary was increased in recognition of the outstanding contribution I had made in my first year at the Museum. To complete my humiliation.'

I put my hand on hers. 'I understand. It was a terrible

326

position to be put into. I don't think, in the circumstances, you could have done anything else. But what I still don't understand is why you think what happened with Greville has anything to do with what happened here. What had happened to Jack?'

'That was Greville's *coup de grâce*. After I caved in, he buzzed the intercom, the door opened and Jack was frog-marched in by the most hideous of the warders, a man called Farrow. He was very pale, and seemed utterly depressed. We looked at each other, and we knew the game was up. Greville said to me, "Why don't you shake hands with your new colleague, Clarissa? Dr Armitage is being appointed to the new post of Special Exhibitions Co-ordinator. It will involve him in a great deal of foreign travel." Jack said, "I'm sorry, Clarissa, but I took the thirty pieces of silver." "So did I," I replied. After that we parted and I didn't see him again.'

She paused, her eyes again bright with tears. She rubbed them with her handkerchief before resuming.

'I don't think Greville stuck to that bargain. I think he sent Rollright to kill him.'

The horrible truth which I had been striving not to allow myself to acknowledge was now out in the open.

I burst out, as if mere vehemence could drive it back into the shadows, 'No, no! That's impossible! He wouldn't do something like that! Not Chris . . .'

I stopped myself in time, but she was looking at me curiously. I hastened to say, 'What I mean is that if Chr . . . Greville had thought he had bought off Jack, why do you think he would have arranged to have him killed? It doesn't make sense.'

'Perhaps he suspected Jack wouldn't be content to remain bought off. That he would continue to work against him. Whatever the reason, I'm convinced that Greville was involved. You see, one of the newspaper reports stated that Rollright had been employed, since his release from youth

327

custody, as a driver by a firm called Westwood Security. I knew from my research into Greville that it's one of his companies. I think that's a very large coincidence.'

'Maybe, but it's hardly proof, is it? The police wouldn't investigate Greville on that basis.'

'No, of course. If only I could find proof. If there were only something, something on paper . . .'

'On paper?' I saw again the scrawled fax on the Windsoredge notepaper. The phrase which had seemed so impenetrably dark to me now blazed forth in letters of fire. Why hadn't I realised? If only I had spoken to Jack! The Lothbury Treasure, the Harrington Apollo, the Melwood Virgin. Of course!

Hoarse with tension, I asked her, 'Is there an exhibit at the Farebrother called the Gravesham Casket?'

She stared at me in amazement. 'As a matter of fact there is. An exquisitely carved cedarwood, gold and ivory box. Italian, fourteenth century. Why do you ask? What's the matter, Liz? You've suddenly gone pale.'

'What would you do if you could get proof against Greville? Something you could take to the authorities. Something they couldn't dismiss. Something that would put him under the spotlight, stop him dead in his tracks. Would you go with it, take a risk?'

She sighed deeply. 'Since what happened to your mother and to Jack, the thing has changed. Greville's not just a thief, he's a murderer. Yes. I'd go for it. I'd take the risk. But why . . . ?'

I held up my hand. 'Wait and I'll show you.'

I dashed upstairs to fetch my handbag.

I laid the flimsy sheet of fax paper carefully on the table in front of her. I heard her quick intake of breath as she read it. 'Where did you get this?'

'Never mind that for the moment. What do you think?'

'It's definitely something. But how did you come by this? And who is Rice?'

I felt a cold shudder as I recalled what we had done together. Perhaps, I urged upon myself, Greville had not been consulted. Perhaps it was Martin Rice who sent Derek Rollright to The Hollies. Perhaps that was why he couldn't risk a loose cannon like Jack being in possession of incriminating information.

I saw suddenly how Greville's faking and theft of artefacts might be linked to Rice's drug-trafficking.

'What's the matter, Liz?'

I replied slowly and with emphasis. 'We need to think very, very carefully about our next move. We are both in great danger.'

'What do you mean?'

I told her.

At last, he opened his eyes. 'Liz?'

His voice was dreadfully weak. Some slight colour had come back to his cheeks, which a matter of a day ago had been fish belly white.

I sat on the chair by the bed and clasped his hand.

'I knew you were on the mend, Jack,' I said, blowing my nose vigorously into a large handkerchief, 'when the nurse told me you'd asked her if she would get you a large gin and tonic.'

I had to stop myself from wincing at the effort he had to make to smile. 'This is a private ward, after all. Been here long?'

'An hour or so. I was watching you sleep. You looked just as you did as a little boy. Peaceful.'

'Surprising, isn't it? I've slept better in here than I have for years. I must get shot more often. And I was having a lovely dream.'

'"In dreams begin responsibilities" as Mr Yeats said.'

'Don't remind me.'

'Mother's dead, Jack. She was killed instantly, according to the post mortem.'

329

'Yes, Liz. I knew she couldn't have survived. I don't suppose she could understand what was going on at all.'

'Nor did I, then. Jack, I've been talking to Clarissa. She came to see me. She was very upset. She told me everything. She blames herself that you're in here.'

'That's ridiculous.'

'She thinks that Greville sent Derek Rollright to ensure your silence.'

'But why? Greville had me over a barrel. He said he would turn me in to the police. That Farrow would swear he'd caught me red-handed stealing a Greek vase. He told me that I couldn't rely on Clarissa. He'd bought her off. Without her support, I had no evidence. I would have no credibility. I'd be only an embittered drunken ex-employee. So he made me an offer. A sinecure job that would keep me out of the country and away from the Museum for a large part of the year. I agreed. It was humiliating but I had no choice. You see, it wasn't only for me. It was for Fran. That was why I went along with Clarissa's crazy idea in the first place, and that was in the end why I caved in. I wanted to do something for my daughter. I could hardly do that in jail could I? I was no threat to him. He had no need to kill me.'

I told him about Rice and Greville's partnership, of Derek Rollright's job with Greville's company. 'I think Rice might have been the moving force.'

'No, it can't have been Rice either. The job thing must be just a weird coincidence.' To my alarm, he was struggling to sit upright, despite the drips and tubes which criss-crossed him. 'It couldn't have been because of the business at the Museum or the drugs. Derek Rollright was after me long before Greville or Rice knew about Clarissa and me. It couldn't have been Greville or Rice.'

'What are you talking about?' But at his words, a kind of hope arose in my heart. Maybe the man I had admired had about him yet some tattered remnants of integrity.

I gaped at him as he told me about the attack in the brewery

330

office. 'Why on earth didn't you tell me about that, Jack?'

He tried to shrug, then hissed with the pain the gesture caused him. 'I thought at first it was Barry Norton, following up after he took a swing at me in the pub. I didn't know then he was all piss and wind. I didn't want to make trouble for Ellen. Afterwards, that copper Enstone mentioned that Derek Rollright was in the pub that night. He gave me to understand he was a nasty bit of work. He wasn't wrong. He even suggested he'd done the vandalism at the dig. I couldn't see what he had against me. Enstone said I should ask you about Derek Rollright, but I never did.'

I said quietly, 'Jack, Derek Rollright admitted to me that he had vandalised the office at the brewery and that he did that terrible thing to the sheep.'

'Christ. But why?'

'He didn't get round to telling me that.'

'Have you told the police?'

'No.'

'Why not?'

'Because.'

'Jesus, Liz. You're like you were as a child. All tight-mouthed and secretive.'

'OK, Jack, never mind the compliments. The police must assume, as I did, that Brian Rollright was responsible for the vandalism, that he'd been trying to get the site closed to give him time to remove his wife's body. Then Derek told me he trashed the site – in fact he was extremely pleased by the literary flourish represented by the sheep. But he was adamant he wasn't helping his father, but working to his own agenda. Why would he lie about that to me? I didn't of course know about the earlier attack on you. If I had, and if we'd talked about it, we might have seen that those events had a pattern.'

'What pattern?'

'Well, Derek couldn't have had a personal grudge against you. All right, you'd been hanging around his sister, but she'd given you the cold shoulder and he knew that. You weren't a threat. It was what you were doing that was the threat.'

'What? The excavation on the Glebe?'

'Precisely. Someone already knew that Father's body was buried there. That must mean that they put it there themselves or knew who did, and therefore were implicated in his murder. They tried to stop the excavation to prevent the discovery of their crime. Derek Rollright attacked and tried to kill you.'

'But if that was the motive, then they didn't succeed.'

'No. You proved more determined than they had perhaps imagined.'

'Liz, this theory of yours assumes that the finding of Father's body would inevitably result in the mystery of his death being unravelled, with consequences for someone who is still alive. That hasn't happened. There was a major police investigation which got nowhere. They closed the file. If there was a murderer still extant, they were in the clear. And if that was the case, then why did Derek Rollright vandalise the site after the discovery? And then go on to mount another attack on us? That smacks of desperation – but there was nothing to be desperate about.'

'That's true, Jack. I don't understand it myself. But I think they really were desperate. Otherwise, why would they have had Derek Rollright murder Gervase Tuddenham only a day or so after I went to see him at his home in Wells?'

'What?' I thought he had looked astonished before, but it was nothing to how he looked now. 'It must be the drugs they've been giving me in here. I think I'm hallucinating. I thought I heard you say . . .'

'You didn't mishear, Jack. I went to see Tuddenham because I discovered his letters to Mother. I'm sorry you have to hear of this now, Jack, like this. They had been having an affair which ended abruptly immediately after Daddy disappeared.'

I saw the flicker of pain cross his face and he closed his eyes for a moment.

'It's OK, go on,' he whispered.

'Are you sure? You're not too tired?'

'Go on.'

I resumed, watching his face carefully. 'That the affair had ended just then seemed a suspicious coincidence. Tuddenham was scared, and he only relaxed when he realised I was talking about the relationship. He denied it, of course. When he realised that I had thought it was a reason why Mother could have been implicated in Father's murder, he defended her vigorously. It seemed to me he could only have done that if he had known the truth. I was on the point of going to see him again when I read his obituary in *The Times*. Derek Rollright described killing an old man in a place which sounded like Wells in a hit and run, the way that Tuddenham died.'

Jack was shaking his head. 'You've enjoyed playing the amateur sleuth, haven't you? Why not tell the police? Let them sort it out?'

'Amateur sleuth? Why is that worse than amateur burglar?' I retorted angrily. 'Can't you understand why I didn't go to the police? For one thing, they wouldn't believe me, for another, it might cause whoever is behind all this to have another go at us. I think we're still in danger, Jack. I don't know why they wanted to prevent you excavating the Glebe even after you found Father's body, but they did, and they still do. Jack, what's the matter?'

His eyes were burning in his pallor. He was flailing his arms desperately, trying to turn over in bed, and reach over to his bedside cabinet, almost tearing aside the tubes and bottles in his haste.

'Jack, should I call the nurse? Do you need some pills from there?'

He fell back exhausted on the pillows, pale and shaking with the effort. 'No, not pills. The little blue thing. Please give it to me.'

I found the old-fashioned hard spectacle case on the shelf

333

and handed it to him. Finally, still partly out of breath, he croaked, 'Liz. We've both had half the answer, like a photograph that's been torn apart and only makes sense when it's put together. I've only now seen the connection.

'Here, my dear sister, is the key to the mystery.' He tapped the object he was holding. With trembling fingers, he prised it open, and lifted the wad of cotton wool within.

'There, Liz.'

I bent over to look at the twisted skein of silver, than raised my eyes to his in enquiry.

'This unlocks a veritable Pandora's box. It proves that the late Sir Edmund Scarsdale, OM was a liar, a forger, and a disgrace to scholarship. It suggests that the attribution and provenance of a goodly proportion of the Farebrother's more recently collected items are questionable. It also explains why someone was very anxious that I should not start my excavation of the Glebe, or that having started, should not continue.'

'What do you mean, Jack?'

In a quiet voice, which plainly cost him an effort, he told me.

I touched the silver gently with my little finger, cautiously, as if it were alive.

'We could never prove that's what happened. And even if we could, we still wouldn't know who actually did it. I suspect Tuddenham knew. He's dead. Scarsdale's dead. Anyway, he would have known how the Treasure was transferred to the Farebrother, but maybe that was all he knew. After forty years, how can we find this man?'

'I don't know. But, as you said yourself, he's still out there and he thinks we can.'

I went back to The Hollies the following day to get some clothes and other things. I went the back way, parking the car outside the kitchen entrance by the old stables. The front gates had been closed for the first time in years.

A gloom had settled over the old house. There was a

334

particular quality to the silence, as if a heart had stopped beating. I went up the back stairs to my bedroom to pack a suitcase. But when the job was finished, I couldn't resist coming down the main staircase, under the eyes of generations of Astons.

The tiled floor of the hall gleamed brighter than it had in years. A faint smell of pine disinfectant hung in the air. When the police forensic people had finished with their photographs and their samples, Ellen had come with mop and bucket to remove the encrusted blood. Yet one more thing to be grateful to her for. Suddenly I felt weak and old. I knew I could never live in The Hollies again.

The door of what Jack had called my prison was open. I was free, if only I had the courage to step outside.

I sat on the bottom step, staring at the front door, forty feet away. I had read that people who believed in the supernatural claimed that ghosts particularly manifested themselves on stairs and in corridors, uncertain places of passage and transition, natural interfaces between one world and another. If that were so, then the hallway of The Hollies would have a full complement of wandering souls. Would my father return here to lurk beneath the turn of the staircase, forever nervously twisting his strangler's hands? Would a phantom Derek Rollright be condemned eternally to mime a silent rictus of agony, as he strove to pull the deadly blades from his neck? And would my mother, a tall grey figure, haunt the threshold of the morning room, where she had for years hovered between life and death?

The tall mahogany door to her quarters was still half open. I went to close it, but when my hand touched the brass knob, I felt a tingle as of static electricity, and I knew I should have to see the room for the last time.

The curtains were still drawn and I tugged them open. Sunlight fell in great slabs on the oatmeal fitted carpet and across the double bed, its covers undisturbed, awaiting a sleeper who would never return.

My mother had, for ten years, spent most of her waking

hours, if that was what they were, in the plum velvet wing chair in front of the plain grey marble fireplace, gazing into the hissing flames of the gas fire. Her expression conveyed nothing of her inner world. What I had learnt in the last months made me realise the pain that must lie beyond her bland indifference.

Had she ever looked with recognition through the photograph albums, one for each year of her life, the last one only partly filled labelled 1986, the year her world had effectively come to an end, which I had arranged in date order on the shelves in the chimney alcove? Mother had made these herself, and they formed an extraordinarily complete record: mother as a child, as a girl, as a young woman, as a bride, then her greatest role: as chatelaine of The Hollies, the uncrowned queen of Crowcester. Here were all the fetes, the garden parties, the receptions, the fundraising dinners. Under her stewardship, the church had been restored from tower to crypt, the village hall, once a ramshackle corrugated iron shed, was splendid in Hornton stone, Crowcester had won cup after cup for tidiness and floweriness, the old folks had parties and treats galore, the children had a well-equipped playground, and there were tennis courts and a football field for the youth of the district.

I stood leafing through the pages of a volume picked at random. My eyes blurred as I saw her bright and animated features in picture after picture. She seemed so beautiful. So alive. So young. I glanced at the date of the volume in my hand. 1956. What had led me to select the record of that fateful year? I shuddered as if a cold draught had passed by me, but the room was stuffily warm.

I stared at the black and white snapshot before me. She smiled graciously for the camera, next to the slight figure of Gervase Tuddenham, the other man who had betrayed her. When was it taken? 'Church Tower Restoration Fund Garden Party August 1st 1956' read the label in Mother's meticulous script.

As I looked closer I saw that behind them was a man, taller than either, his face half turned away from the camera. But, to my amazement and horror, I knew him. I would have known him anywhere. Suddenly, the events not only of the last few months, but of my entire adult life, like the coloured stones of a kaleidoscope, revolved into a new pattern.

I dropped the album and fainted. When I came to, I was lying prostrate on the oatmeal carpet, the dusty smell of it in my nostrils. How long I remained there, weeping, I do not know.

When I arose, I felt strangely light. I slipped the snapshot from its passepartout corner fixings, and replaced the album in its place on the shelf. Jack had been right of course, but in a way he would never have guessed at. There was a great deal to be done.

As I closed the great oak front door behind me, the sigh of the hinges seemed to be the voice of the presences within the house. Dear God, I prayed, let it be a long time before my brother joins them.

In my hand, I bore away the photograph on which was the face of a murderer.

I could hear Ellen sobbing upstairs in her bedroom as I opened her front door. Poor Ellen, she had taken the news the worst of all. I felt so sorry for her, but there was nothing I could do or say.

I had been back to The Hollies for the first time in days to collect the post. I sat at the kitchen table reading the letters and cards which had arrived that morning. The news had been released only the previous day. I was amazed and deeply touched by how many people had already responded.

Colleagues and acquaintances, former girl-friends by the dozen, distant relatives I hadn't heard from for ages. In hundreds of different ways and hundreds of scripts, people did their best to express their grief, their shock, their outrage.

Such charm, such wit, such generosity was the collective burden of their tributes.

As I had passed through the village that morning, people whom I hadn't spoken to for ages came up to me and said how sorry they were.

I drank coffee with a trembling hand and read the front page story in that morning's *Times*.

THIRD VICTIM OF CROWCESTER SHOOTING DIES

Dr Jack Armitage, seriously wounded in the mystery shooting incident at Crowcester in Oxfordshire, died last night in the Radcliffe Hospital, Oxford. A hospital spokesman said that Dr Armitage, who was fifty, had been responding to treatment but had suddenly relapsed into unconsciousness. His sister Elizabeth was at his bedside. She is understood to be staying with friends in London.

Colleagues spoke warmly of the dead man's kindness, his intellectual brilliance and his scholarly accomplishments. Lord Greville, the Chairman of the Trustees of the Farebrother Museum, where Dr Armitage was for many years Keeper of Roman and Dark Ages Antiquities paid tribute to his professionalism and imaginative flair . . .

I couldn't bear to read any more of such hypocritical cant, and flung the newspaper aside. The following day, I would be paying my own tribute to Jack.

The tall grey-haired man walked slowly along the gravel path.

He wore the Sunday casual dress of an elderly member of the English upper middle class: old tweed hacking jacket and cavalry twill slacks. Occasionally, he bent down to twitch out a shred of couch grass which had intruded its ill-mannered self on the otherwise immaculate tan-coloured surface.

I waited on a wrought-iron seat in a charming arbour formed by a curve of dense yew hedge. Before me rose the honey-coloured front of the mansion, pierced by massive mullion windows. Like the more famous Hardwick Hall, the great house was 'more window than wall'. A fine double staircase curved up to the piano nobile. A fountain with a sculptured group of water nymphs holding conches played on the box-hedged parterre, rainbows reflected in the glittering spray.

In the stable yard behind, I could hear the clatter of tea cups and loud matronly English voices discussing whether they preferred the gardens of Windsoredge to those of Hidcote.

I stood up as the old man drew level. 'Hello, Christopher.'

He stopped dead as he recognised me, and for a moment, I thought he had suffered some kind of seizure, so pale and waxy were his features.

'Let's take a stroll, shall we?'

I slipped my arm into his and guided him unresisting along a wide path flanked by stone imitations of famous antique statues, towards the picturesquely rocky, tree-covered hill which overhung the gardens. Halfway up, on a kind of platform hollowed out of the cliff, there was a folly in the style of a Greek temple, its sculptured portico supported by Ionic columns. A wide, steep, balustraded staircase, in the same honey stone as the house, climbed the mount to this eye-catcher.

The temple was in shadow, but in front of us, the gardens of Windsoredge House were still bathed in golden sunlight. It was almost closing time. Processions of visitors, moving slowly, with the languid reluctance of the departing, pausing now and then to admire yet again the herbaceous borders, still ablaze with late summer flowers, or the roses climbing over the pergolas, could be seen making their way along the gravel walks to the gate in the enclosing wall of the estate, where, across the lane, a field had been turned into a temporary car park. The drowsy hum of voices, the more distant sounds of engines starting and metal doors banging drifted up to us, borne on the slight breeze which eddied in the still warm air.

But on the stone bench on the shaded podium of the temple, there was no one except the two of us.

At last he broke the silence. His face had recovered something of its usual high colour and his voice was as firm, precise and melodious as it had been nearly thirty years before.

'I thought I was prepared for you to make contact. Clarissa admitted to me that she had confided in you. But to see you after all these years in such circumstances was nevertheless a shock. My dear Elizabeth, please believe me when I say that I never meant that you or your mother should be involved. When I heard what had happened at The Hollies, I was sickened. I warned Rice that the Rollright youth was an uncontrollable psychopath.'

'What about Jack? You can't pretend you never intended to kill him?'

He grasped my arm with a thin, liver-spotted hand, sparsely glinting with silver hairs. 'I wanted him to be hurt, but not seriously. A warning only. I could not rely on him to maintain his silence about the Museum in the way I could with Clarissa. Your brother was quixotic, reckless. You know that. But believe me I never did intend that he should die. It was none of my doing. I am sorry that it happened, sorrier than you can ever imagine. But nothing that either of us can do or say will change the fact of his death. Moreover, now that your brother is dead, you can corroborate nothing, prove nothing. Clarissa is no longer willing to help you.'

'So, you expect me to do nothing? You have my brother murdered to save your filthy business. You can't expect me to remain silent.'

The grip on my arm tightened. 'I understand your feelings, my dear Elizabeth. How could I not? But greater things are at stake than paltry revenge. The enterprise on which I am embarked includes others far less scrupulous than I.'

'Enterprise? You mean making money, don't you, Christopher? Was that why you sold your soul?'

'My soul? What strange antique language you use. But then you were always more at home in the nineteenth century. It wasn't money, as you call it. My dear, money is what you use to pay the electricity bill, or the man who repairs the drains. Any fool can make money, and many fools do. What I have is power. Far more interesting and worth a lifetime of pursuit. The craven electorate of Oxford Cowley did me a handsome favour when they rejected me, although at the time I hardly appreciated it. Even after my party regained power, I would have remained an impotent back-bencher for the rest of my career. That ghastly ill-bred woman Margaret Thatcher disliked me even more than she did most of the rest of my colleagues.'

'You might none the less have done the State some service.'

'Really? As chairman of some piddling parliamentary committee? When I've actually become one of the great social reformers of the age. Remember J. S. Mill's *On Liberty*, Elizabeth? The State should not be suffered to dictate the way we amuse ourselves. I always regarded the arbitrary laws which permitted some drugs and not others as ludicrous and repressive. My views made me none too popular with my party. Soon they will be changed, through the force of public opinion. And I have brought about that change. As Oscar Wilde ought to have said, the best way to get rid of a law is to break it.'

'And what of your partner Rice? He's not interested in social reform. He's nothing but a vicious crook, laundering his cut of the proceeds through dubious property deals. Would J. S. Mill approve of peddling stuff to destroy children?'

He answered with no appreciable variation in his level, well-modulated tones. 'Narcotics give colour and intensity to otherwise miserable lives, allowing them to blaze in the firmament for glorious months, rather than flicker in the mud for tedious years. I give people what they want at a price they can afford. I am able to get the best deals because of what I could offer in return. A good trader knows not only his customer, but his supplier. Beyond a reasonable competence, money does not satisfy. A man who is both wealthy and powerful yet desires something more. Something that will assuage their vanity, something which by possessing it will add to their self-image. Beauty. But not only beauty. A pebble fresh from the sea is beautiful. It's the uniqueness of beauty that is most craved by the powerful, the magic of the original. That's what the men want who can easily buy anything else in the world. Only that will truly satisfy their lust to possess.'

His voice had taken fire as he spoke. I knew that he described this passion so well because he shared it.

'That's where the original artefacts you stole from the Farebrother went? To the controllers of those drugs cartels you dealt with?'

'Yes, the man who can offer what no one else can captures the market. How quick you are, Elizabeth! And how magnificent you look today apparelled in your righteous anger like an avenging deity. Nothing in your life has ever achieved this intensity, has it? You've attained the level of ecstasy which Pater described: burning with a pure, gemlike flame. The irony of it, Elizabeth. Thirty years ago, I offered you the world and you rejected it. You could have been great and you chose to be little.'

I stared at him, but said nothing.

'Instead of marrying me, you subsided into provincial life, like a character in one of your Victorian novels. All your

342

intellect and passion wasted on ignoble ends. But think! It's not too late. I'm an old man, but not so old. After my death, for the rest of your life, you would be rich beyond your imagining.'

I shuddered and unclamped his hand from my arm as if it were a species of loathsome, clinging insect. 'Don't touch me, Christopher. The very idea disgusts me. Not only because of the wickedness you commit now. But because of the evil of the past, the evil I learnt of only yesterday, the evil you committed forty years ago. You see, I know now why you pursued me, from our first meeting at University College, why you took me to a great height and tempted me with the world. Because of guilt.'

I could see the colour once more leaking from his face, the confident manner crumbling. 'Guilt?' His voice was scarcely more than a whisper. 'What do you mean?'

'I mean that when you offered me marriage, it wasn't because you loved me. You love nothing except this house and your collections. You're incapable of human love. No, it was to atone for the way you had robbed me of my child-hood. You pitied me for what you yourself had done to me. You thought you could replace what I had lost by being father and husband combined. You thought that would make it up to me. And in so doing, restore to yourself your own self-image of enlightenment and magnanimity, which you had lost through your coward's act.'

He stared at me, his eyes wide with fear. 'You know, don't you? Somehow you know.'

'Yes, I know. I know that forty years ago, on a dark autumn evening, on the Glebe in Crowcester, you clubbed my father to death in cold blood.'

He covered his face with his hands. 'It's not possible. Tuddenham swore to me that he hadn't told you a thing. How in God's name did you find out? How?'

'Jack told me before he died about the Lothbury Treasure. He found irrefutable evidence that it had come from

343

Crowcester. It had been illegally removed from the Glebe excavation. Its true provenance was concealed when it was acquired for the Farebrother. You thought he was getting too near to the truth in the research paper he wrote. That was why you provoked him into that scuffle which led to his being sacked from the Museum, wasn't it?'

He raised his head from his hands. 'Yes. Yes, why should I pretend otherwise. It's history. You can prove nothing. Your brother himself set off the chain of events which led to his death. The irony was that he had joined the Museum only as a result of my influence. Scarsdale happened to mention he had come across him in the London Library. I asked him to appoint your brother to the staff. I wanted to help him, just as I'd wanted to help you. As with you, that act of making amends eventually went awry. Armitage had some idea of himself as a scholar. Unfortunately, he chose Roman silver as his specialism. He formed the opinion, from the internal evidence of the Lothbury Treasure, that there must have been two hoards, which was in fact the case. Scarsdale and I had put together the pieces genuinely acquired by the Earl of Lothbury with the best silver items from the hoard in Crowcester. The rest, the gold coins, the ingots, we disposed of through our contacts.'

'It was Tuddenham who told you about the Treasure. I saw you and him photographed together at a village fete in one of my mother's albums. When I saw that, I realised that you must have known about the original excavation, and that you must have been the conduit by which the Treasure reached the Farebrother. Once that was clear, it was evident that there was a motive: to silence a solitary pedestrian who happened on your removal of the silver.'

'A photograph in an album! What slim filaments of chance connect us to our pasts! Gervase Tuddenham was my cousin. It was he who discovered the Crowcester hoard. Or rather his dog did. He had a fox terrier. He was walking it on the Glebe one evening in the autumn of '56 just after the dig

344

had been completed. The dog scrabbled at the ground near what had been the last trench of the excavation and disappeared into a hole. He stuck in his arm to drag it out, and emerged clutching a handful of Roman gold coins. Instead of reporting the find, he told me. Even in those days I had a reputation as a collector. Gervase was a worldly and ambitious young man. He wanted to rise in the Church, but chafed at its restraints, particularly financial. He kept the matter secret from the Archaeological Society and sought my advice as to how he might profit from his find. And I in turn approached my old wartime colleague Edmund Scarsdale.'

'You'd helped him acquire things for the Museum before?'

'Yes. In the turmoil of post-war Europe, there were many items which could be obtained. There were many men trained by governments in the arts of forgery and deception. It was no more difficult to concoct what the Intelligence services called a legend for a precious art object than it was for an agent. If your father had not blundered on to the Glebe, then all would have been well.'

I waited in silence, my every heartbeat painful to me, for what would surely follow. At last, the fog of years was clearing away. Finally, the last pieces were to be set in the great and terrible mosaic of the truth.

He was staring out across the perfection of his gardens. 'Please believe me, Elizabeth. I never intended to kill him. It was an instinctive act, born of anger and fear of discovery. He loomed up out of the darkness and accosted us. The spade was in my hands. Before I knew what I was doing, I had lashed out with it, once, twice, I don't know how many times. The next thing I was aware of was Gervase bending over the body, shining his torch on the face. He cried out, "God have mercy! It's Robert Armitage, Christopher! He's dead. You've killed him." Then he turned his back on me, knelt by the body and spoke the office for the dead. It was the most appalling moment of my life, one that I have never ceased to dream of with horror, and to regret in every waking moment. I vowed then to do what I could to expiate that moment of recklessness, which of course, I was left free to do. By some miracle the act remained undiscovered.'

I restrained my burning anger at the use of the word 'miracle' in such a context, keeping my voice cool and neutral. 'You hurriedly concealed the body in the Roman culvert. Tuddenham told you that it was believed that my father had deserted my mother for another woman. There was no police search for a missing person. You must have used your position in Government to spread the rumours that my father had defected, destroying his reputation and moving the spotlight away from Crowcester. So much for your act of contrition. I marvel at the way you seem to believe your version of what you've told me. When was it exactly that you decided to kill Jack?'

'I read that he was about to excavate the Glebe in the *Waterbury Advertiser*. It's one of my own newspapers. I have copies delivered to me. The name of Armitage leapt out at me. I saw with horror that, in a manner unspeakably ironic, the thing I had feared for forty years was about to happen as a result of something I had brought about. If I had not connived at your brother's dismissal, he would have remained at the Farebrother, his wretched paper would have been ignored and he would never have started the dig on the Glebe. Not only that, but Rice, of all people, had agreed to fund it. I dared not try to put pressure on him to withdraw, for fear of compromising myself. I could think of only one means by which the thing could be stopped.'

He had seemed to shrink within his clothes as he spoke. His head was sunk down upon his knees. I had to bow my own to hear him.

'You lied to me, Christopher, when you said at the beginning that you had never intended that Jack should be killed, didn't you? It wasn't Rice's idea to use Derek Rollright. It was yours. Jack knew nothing of the fraud at the Museum, when Rollright first tried to kill him at the excavation.'

He raised his head, his eyes gazing into the hazy distance. 'Rollright had been taken on by one of my transport companies. He was reported to me as having certain talents which might prove useful. What's more, he had the appropriate local knowledge. But he proved unreliable. Your brother evaded the first attempt, and Rollright vanished for several days. In the interim, the remains had been discovered and the police were involved. It was a very difficult time for me. Then, to add to my desperation, I received a telephone call from Gervase. He told me you had visited him. He was almost hysterical, saying he wanted to confess the whole thing before he died. He always blamed himself. He considered his greed had led me into mortal sin.'

'So you had him killed as well.'

'It was swift and merciful. Gervase was weak and venal, but he had a conscience. I didn't, however, see why I should suffer for the dubious benefit of his soul.'

'But, after that, why did you persist in having Jack killed? Why did you turn Rollright loose on him like a mad dog? Why? After he'd found the body, there was nothing else to find . . .' I stopped abruptly. The look in his eyes, at once terrified and evasive told me everything. 'There was something else, wasn't there, something you must have left behind in 1956, something that would, if discovered, connect you with the Glebe?'

I took his thin, old man's shoulders and shook them. 'Admit it. Admit it. By God, I'm going to search every inch of the Glebe with my bare hands if necessary until I find it.'

He remained quite still staring out over the prospect of his estate, like an eighteenth-century squire, master of all he surveyed. Then I saw there was a faint smile on his papery features. 'You're so very clever, Elizabeth. So very clever. It wasn't only guilt, my dear. And what is expiation for a crime and pity for its victim if not a kind of love? It was you. I wanted you. You would have been mistress of Windsoredge. Now there's nothing I can do to help you.'

I followed the direction of his gaze. Racing up the steps to the folly was a man in the uniform of a security guard. Tall, solidly built, his face tanned under the peaked cap.

It was Martin Rice.

I sprang to my feet and ran over the slippery paving stones into the darkness between the columns. But at the back of the mock temple was only a sheer wall of rock. There was no way out.

He thumped me hard in the stomach, then as I leaned forward retching, he grabbed me round the throat with his forearm, crushing my windpipe so hard I almost passed out. He dragged me, struggling furiously, back to the open air.

There he threw me to the ground, kicked me in the ribs, twisted my arms behind my back and snapped on a pair of handcuffs.

Greville had risen to his feet, a little unsteadily. 'Rice, please, that's enough. There's no need to . . .'

'Don't you tell me what there's no need to do, you stupid old fool. This fucking shambles is your fault! To worry about forty years ago, when we're pulling off the sweetest deal in history! On top of that, to send me that open fax. Without that, she'd never have connected us. Now see what the bitch has been up to!'

He snatched up my white handbag, tore open the flap and tipped it upside down. There was a thud as the oblong lump of black plastic tumbled on to the paving stones amidst the scattering of other more usual female paraphernalia. Rice raised his heavy-soled shoe and brought it crashing down, smashing the object to pieces.

'See that? A fucking police radio. While you've been having your chat, the Regional Crime Squad have been listening in, taping every word. I only just got word from my contact at Thames Valley that my old friend Dave Green had set up a sting. I tuned in on my CB as I drove here.'

Greville's face was contorted with fury. 'Is this true, Elizabeth?'

'Yes, it is.'

He gesticulated wildly at Rice with an old man's impotent rage. 'No, you are the fool! You should have maintained respectability, as we agreed, not engaged in extramarital affairs – and with Elizabeth Armitage, of all possible women.'

Rice took a couple of paces forward, and crashed his fist into the old man's chest. Greville collapsed on to the bench, clasping his breast-bone, fighting horribly for breath, his face ashen.

Unobserved for a moment, I kicked off my encumbering high heels and ran to the low wall of the temple platform. I stared down at the gardens below, relieved and exhilarated by what I could see.

'Look!' I cried out. 'They're coming for both of you bastards.'

There was the sound of screaming and shouting as the horticultural enthusiasts of middle England ceased to file peacefully out of the gate. They scattered in all directions, as down the gravel path leading to the steps to the folly ran several black-fatigue clad figures carrying guns.

Behind them was the figure of DCI Green, his electric blue suit unmistakable even at a distance. The two leading marksmen took up positions at the bottom of the stairway, behind the cover of the balustrade, pointing their carbines in our direction.

Green stopped by a plinth bearing a marble copy of the Venus de Milo.

He shouted through a loud-hailer. 'Armed police! Throw down your weapons and lie flat on the ground! Now!'

Rice viciously grabbed my right arm, and I screamed with pain from the old injury. My anticipation of rescue had been foolishly premature. He was pointing a pistol in my face. For the second time in my life, I stared into the black oblivion at the end of the barrel.

'Over there, move!'

With savage blows to the kidneys, he pushed me to the

349

top of the stairway, so that we were in clear view of the policemen below.

'I'm coming down! Try to stop me and I'll kill her!'

I struggled in his grasp, feeling the cold metal pressing into my neck. There was silence for a moment, then Green's voice boomed out through the megaphone, 'Stay where you are, Rice!'

'No! Tell your plods to get back!'

I sensed uncertainty in my rescuers. Rice was seizing his moment. He knew that if a siege developed he would have no chance.

I gazed down the long steep line of steps. At the top, we were already in shadow, but halfway down the declining sun splashed the stone slabs with gold.

With all my strength, I barged sideways, knocking Rice off-balance, then leapt into the air, launching myself like a long-jumper towards the light.

As I'd hoped, my precipitate, reckless movement took Rice by surprise. If he held on to me, he would fall himself. He let go.

I landed upright on the fourth or fifth step down, jarring my heels, but remembering to bend my knees, and not to fall forwards. My feet slipped from under me, and, my arms pinioned and helpless, I toppled back against the rounded edge of the step behind me, my head thudding against the surface of the stone tread.

I didn't black out, despite the pain. Above me, I could see Martin Rice alone at the top of the stairs, diminished by perspective. He seemed to be reaching forward, stretching his hand out to me, as one would to one who had taken a tumble.

But in his hand was the pistol, and his face was a mask of hatred.

Shots rang out from below. He staggered, his arm dropped, and he fell to his knees. I heard a clatter as the gun hit the top step with the tinny sound of a toy discarded by a heedless child.

X

The autumn had been exceptionally kind, but now the weather had turned. A chill east wind blew as we walked arm-in-arm through the cobbled yard. We stopped on the edge of the great pit where the brew-house had stood.

I went first down the makeshift wooden steps to the level surface about the size of a tennis court which had been uncovered. A bright green tarpaulin stretched from the edge to the centre.

'I wanted you to be the first outsider to see this. As I always did, little sister.'

She smiled. 'Except when you didn't.'

I bent down, ignoring the pain which shot up from the patchwork of surgery on my guts.

She saw my wince, and exclaimed, 'Jack, for goodness' sake be careful. You know the doctor told you . . .'

'Not to drink, smoke, eat rich food, go with strange women. If I were to follow his advice, then I might as well have died in reality, not just in fiction, life would hold so little spice.'

'Don't be ridiculous, Jack. All he said was to ease up on things to begin with and not to over-exert yourself.'

I pulled aside the plastic sheeting.

'Look.'

'Oh Jack! The colours. It looks as if it were finished only yesterday.'

'Indeed it was. What is seventeen hundred years in geological time? A fraction of a blink of an eye.'

' "History is now and England".'

As we both stared down at it, I still felt as if I had to pinch myself that it was real, after what had gone before. But it was real. The largest tessellated pavement yet found north of the Alps. The reception hall of no mere villa but a palace. I had been right. The excavation would go on here for years. English Heritage had scheduled it. The Farebrother, as part of its new publicity drive, would sponsor it. Archaeologists far more technically qualified than I would soon be crawling over it. But from my post at the Museum, I would watch over it. It would remain my baby.

'Do you recognise the figure?'

'Of course I do, Jack. He's Orpheus, holding his lyre.'

'He was a popular motif with the workshops of Corinium. You know the myth, of course, a scholar like yourself,' I added teasingly.

'Oh, a challenge! I know it quite as well as you do, brother mine. Shall I prove it? Here goes.'

She paused for a moment, as if collecting her thoughts, then her voice, as sweet and clear as it had been as a girl filled the great space in which we stood as if she had been a story-teller of the ancient times.

'Now, Orpheus was the greatest musician who ever lived among gods or men. He could charm all birds and animals with the sweet sounds of his lyre. Even the fish leapt from the seas to hear him. Even the rocks and trees moved according to his bidding. He was also a hero among men. He travelled with Jason and the Argonauts to far Colchis to bring back the Golden Fleece. On his return he met and fell in love with the beautiful Eurydice. Theirs was a blissful union. Until one day, Eurydice, while sporting with Orpheus in the Vale of Tempe, was bitten by a snake, and died. Orpheus was grief stricken. His whole world had collapsed around him. Even his music brought him no pleasure, his lyre seemed to him a mere empty shell. At length, he could bear it no longer, and journeyed down to the underworld to request Hades, the god of the dead, to allow his beloved to return to the world of men. On the way his music charmed even the frightful three-headed dog Cerberus who guards the gates of death. Hades agreed to release Eurydice on one condition: that he did not gaze upon her face until they were once again in the light. But on the return journey, Orpheus, compelled by some self-destructive force which three thousand years of human commentary has never explained and never will, looked back, and his darling was lost to him.'

I was very moved by the familiar story. 'Full marks, Miss Armitage. Is that how you tell it to them in school, Liz? You're wasted there, I've always said so.'

She smiled ruefully. 'Not any more, Jack. I'm taking early retirement at Christmas. Linda finally got her way with the Governors. English is from now on not the language of Shakespeare and Milton and the Authorised Version, but merely a global linguistic interface.'

I stretched out my hand to hers. 'I'm sorry, Liz. You've spent half your life in that place. I know how terrible it is to be chucked out like that. What are you going to do?'

'I shan't be short of activities. There's The Hollies to sort out. I doubt you'll want to have much to do with that. We've had lots of interest. Martin Rice always said it would be worth a fortune.'

'Well, don't give any of it to me. Get Williamson to set up a trust. For Fran, and . . .' I stopped, feeling somehow silly at the surge of excitement that shot through me.

She laughed, laughed in the way she used to laugh, and hugged me. 'Jack, you know something I don't!'

'Ellen told me not to tell anyone, until it's definite, but . . .'

'I'm not anyone, Jack. You always wanted to tell me first, remember, except . . .'

'When I didn't. I know. Well, she is. And Ellen and I are getting married as soon as her divorce comes through. You can be best woman.'

'I'd love to, Jack.'

'Ellen wants to start studying again, as much as she can while the baby is small. She needs A-levels for nurse training.

I thought, I mean I was hoping you would come to stay with us in London and . . .'

Again, she laughed. 'Of course. It'll be a pleasure. But I won't need to come and stay, Jack. We're going to be nearly neighbours. When The Hollies is sold, I'm going to live in London too. Clarissa has a house in Highbury and I'm going to lodge there. I'm going back to London University to do a Ph.D. Clarissa has a friend at Birkbeck who she thinks will be interested in my ideas.'

'That's wonderful, Liz.' At the mention of Clarissa, a question had half risen to my lips, but I suppressed it. I was learning to be tactful in my old age. When Liz wanted to tell me, she would tell me. Trust had to be earned.

I laid the sheeting carefully back over the mosaic figure.

'After Orpheus lost Eurydice, he continued singing, but he was changed. He sang songs against human sacrifice. In consequence, he angered the bloodthirsty followers of the god Dionysius. They attacked him and he was torn limb from limb. But as they threw it into a river, his head was still singing. It sang on as it was carried by the current down to the wine-dark sea. Tossed by the waves, it sang across the ocean, until it came to rest on a far distant shore, where some say it's singing still.'

'I believe it is, dear Jack.'

We walked hand in hand across the Glebe, as the sun started to dip behind the beech wood on the far side of the river, through the wicket gate into the churchyard. We stood for a long time, ankle deep in the long, damp grass gazing at the new white marble headstone:

In Loving Memory of
Robert John Armitage, DSO,
born 20th July 1915, died 28th October 1956
and of Celia Margaret Aston Armitage, his wife,
born 10th January 1916, died 3rd August 1996.
May They Rest in Peace

Liz's voice was small in the gusty twilight. 'I'm glad it's all over, Jack. More than anything, I'm glad we're together again.'

'So am I, Liz. I realise now I've never thanked you. When we were children, you had every reason to hate me. I must have been insufferable. But time after time, you saved me. And now you've brought me back from the dead.'

'You don't have to thank me, Jack. You don't have to thank me for loving you.'

'I love you, Liz. And I can say what I've always thought, but never told you. I admire you so much, for your kindness, your intelligence and your courage. If it hadn't been for you, I really would have died. So would Fran, and probably Ellen too. Greville and Rice would have gone on with their vile trade. Clarissa wouldn't have had the strength to face up to Greville alone. You thought up the plan of making Greville confess. You made the police and the hospital go along with your plan. You were so brave, walking into the lion's den that day. You couldn't have known how things would turn out.'

'I must say it became rather too much of a cliff-hanger at the end. Fortunately, they had a weapons squad on stand-by, just in case. But they hadn't expected Rice to appear quite like that. There's a big hunt going on for the informer.'

'I think I rather underestimated the Chief Inspector.'

'Now Superintendent, actually. So did I, at first. He's a bright chap. He'd been on Rice's track for quite a while. He has quick reactions too. It will come out at the inquiry that it was he who shot Rice. He grabbed a rifle when he saw what was about to happen.'

'He needed you to help him, though. You're a very bright girl. You always were.'

'You're no slouch either, Jack. You worked out the whole business of the Treasure and how it could have led to Daddy's death even when you were in intensive care.'

'And you saw why Greville was still so anxious to prevent

the excavation. I should have seen it too. It was logical. Archaeology and forensic science have the same premise. Nothing can be done on this earth without leaving a trace. Greville must have discovered too late that he had lost his engraved gold propelling pencil that night on the Glebe, either where the treasure was discovered or where they buried Father. Incriminating in either location, and he could hardly go digging for it, could he? I was more pleased to find that than any other artefact I've ever discovered, not excluding the Orpheus pavement. I think it would have pleased Father too.'

In the gathering dusk, her hand clutched mine, and I gave an answering squeeze.

'Poor Father. Oh Liz,' I exclaimed, 'how much there still is that we don't know for certain! Was he really having an affair with Teresa? Who sent the letter from Paris? In fact, was there ever such a letter or did Mother invent it for some reason? What is clear, though, is that the fact of Father's death means that he never meant to abandon us for ever. That's right, isn't it?'

She clutched my hand even more tightly. 'Yes, Jack, he never meant to abandon us.'

'How I so long to see him again! If only for an hour. One always says that of the dead. But we don't have the Orpheus touch do we?'

'What would you ask him, Jack?'

'I'd ask him about himself. All those details of his life I never knew. I've never got around to telling you, Liz, amidst everything that's happened. But I found an old photograph in Father's naval uniform. It showed Father and his parents and a boy who could only have been his twin brother. Wasn't that strange?'

Her voice seemed very faint and far away as she replied, 'Very strange, Jack, darling.'

'Yes, an identical twin. He must have kept that photograph all through the war. I wonder what could have happened?

Perhaps the brother died in childhood, or perhaps they were separated in some way? That used to happen in poor families. Do you think it would even now be possible to find out what became of him? He might by some miracle be still alive. It would be like bringing a part of Father back to life. With your new friends in the police, perhaps we could try? It might not be too late.'

To my amazement, she threw herself weeping on my shoulder.

'Oh dear, darling Jack! How much he meant to you! No, it's not too late. It's never too late to forgive.'

Then before I could ask her what on earth she meant by that, she pulled away from me. 'I've got a secret, Jack. But I shan't tell it to you here. Not in this place. It's cold and I'm hungry. Let's go back to the fire and have crumpets for tea, and I'll tell you. Race you there!'

Then, like the children we still were, we chased each other down the path, through the lych-gate and out into the High Street, laughing as we ran.